A Village Scandal

Dilly Court is a *Sunday Times* bestselling author of over thirty-five novels. She grew up in North-East London and began her career in television, writing scripts for commercials. She is married with two grown-up children, four grandchildren and a beautiful great-granddaughter. Dilly now lives in Dorset on the Jurassic Coast with her husband.

To find out more about Dilly, please visit her website and her Facebook page:

www.dillycourt.com
/DillyCourtAuthor

Dilly Court

A Village Scandal

HarperCollins*Publishers*

HarperCollins*Publishers* Ltd
1 London Bridge Street,
London SE1 9GF

www.harpercollins.co.uk

First published by HarperCollins*Publishers* 2020
1

A catalogue record for this book is available from the British Library

ISBN: 978-0-00-828778-8 (HB)
ISBN: 978-0-00-828779-5 (B)

This novel is entirely a work of fiction.
The names, characters and incidents portrayed in it are
the work of the author's imagination. Any resemblance to
actual persons, living or dead, events or localities is
entirely coincidental.

Set in Sabon Lt Std by Palimpsest Book Production Limited,
Falkirk, Stirlingshire

Printed and bound in the UK by CPI Group (UK) Ltd, Croydon CR0 4YY

MIX
Paper from
responsible sources
FSC™ C007454

FSC
www.fsc.org

This book is produced from independently certified FSC™ paper to ensure
responsible forest management.

For more information visit: www.harpercollins.co.uk/green

For Nicky and Sarah, and the hardworking and devoted staff of Jelly Babies Day Nursery

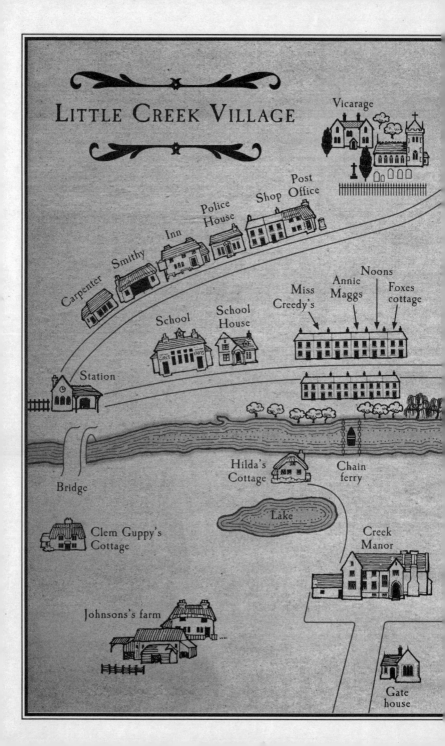

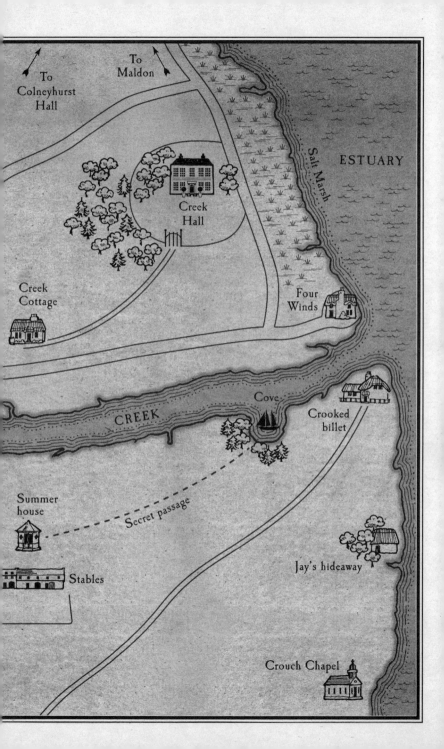

Chapter One

Little Creek, Essex, April 1869

Daisy stood at the top of the grand staircase, clutching her bridal bouquet. The old manor house was eerily silent, all the servants having left for the village church, with the exception of James, the footman, who was waiting to assist her into the carriage.

'You look beautiful, Daisy.' Sidney Marshall gazed up at his niece with misty eyes. 'Jay's a lucky fellow.'

Slowly, mindful of her long train, Daisy made her way downstairs. Was it her imagination, or were the portraits of stern-faced dignitaries actually smiling down at her? She was blissfully happy, and yet at the back of her mind there was a niggling worry that she could not explain.

'This is all so different from our rushed ceremony on Christmas Eve, Uncle.'

'It's nothing less than you deserve, my dear.'

Daisy was still not convinced. 'I hope people won't think it's too much.'

Sidney proffered his arm. 'Of course not. They'll all be thrilled to share your happiness.'

'I hope so.' Daisy laid her hand on his arm. 'We'd better leave now. I don't want to keep Jay waiting.'

The Saxon church was bathed in spring sunshine, and the dark shapes of the yew trees contrasted dramatically with the daffodils swaying gently in the breeze, their yellow trumpets creating bands of gold amongst the neatly kept graves. It was several degrees cooler inside the building, and the smell of musty hymnals contrasted sharply with the scent from the floral arrangements, and just a hint of mothballs emanating from the congregation. The whole village had turned out to celebrate the wedding, and everyone had dressed in their Sunday best. There was a low buzz of conversation, as if people were afraid to raise their voices in such a holy place.

'I know that Daisy is your niece, Eleanora, but this isn't what I'd call a proper wedding.' Grace Peabody, the vicar's wife, pursed her lips and turned her head to stare at the guests, who were rapidly filling the pews. 'It should simply be a blessing of the marriage that took place at Christmas. Heaven alone knows why my husband has gone to all this trouble, but it's typical of John – he would have been too soft-hearted to refuse. Personally, I don't see the need for all this fuss and bother. It's not as if Daisy and Jay are real gentry.'

Eleanora Marshall gazed at Grace in dismay. 'Jay insisted that Daisy should have her big day with all the family present. I think he felt that she had been cheated out of a proper wedding.'

'That's nonsense, Eleanora. Of course the ceremony on Christmas Eve was the real thing. Do you think my husband would have agreed to anything less?' Grace gave her a quelling look. 'It's just a pity you weren't there.'

'It was the weather,' Eleanora said apologetically. Somehow she always felt at a disadvantage when she was in Grace's company, and compelled to explain the reason for their absence from Daisy's wedding ceremony for the umpteenth time. 'We couldn't get back from London because of the snow. The roads were blocked and the trains had stopped running.'

'You don't have to remind me.'

'I would have liked them to wait, but I wouldn't wish the young couple to live together in . . .' Eleanora lowered her voice to a whisper, '. . . you know what I mean, Grace. At least they were married in the eyes of God.'

'Well, I suppose Daisy wanted a big reception and all that it entails.'

'Oh, no. Daisy isn't like that. It's Jay who always wants to be the centre of attention.'

'That doesn't surprise me. He was always in the public eye as a young boy, and invariably for the wrong reasons.' Grace turned her head yet again, squinting as a beam of sunlight danced through the stained-glass window, momentarily dazzling her. 'I see that Daisy's brother has arrived with his fiancée. How did he feel about his sister's rushed nuptials to someone like Jay Fox? I suppose I should try to call him Jay Tattersall now, but it doesn't trip easily off my tongue.'

'Jay is entitled to use his real father's name, Grace. As for Toby, he takes everything in his stride.' Eleanora tossed her head, forgetting the precarious angle at which she had pinned her new straw hat. The ostrich feathers, which had looked so charming in the shop window, tickled her nose and threatened to make her sneeze.

Ignoring Eleanora's struggle with her fashionable headwear, Grace turned her attention to Jay and his best man, Dr Nick Neville, who were waiting patiently at the altar. She shook her head, oozing disapproval from every pore. 'I see that Jay's sister is seated in the front row, flaunting herself as if she was already married to the doctor.'

'I believe they're almost engaged,' Eleanora said nervously.

Grace rolled her eyes. 'Not so long ago Dove Fox was keen on the schoolmaster, and her sister, Linnet, was making eyes at the doctor. Now they seem to have swapped partners, as if life was like some sort of country dance. Those girls are flighty, if you ask me.'

'Young people today aren't bound by the strict rules that you and I had to abide by, Grace.'

'It's not that I disapprove of someone like Dr Neville courting one of his servants, but Dove ought to be more circumspect. That's all I'm saying.'

'She's Daisy's sister-in-law now, and that makes her part of our family,' Eleanora protested, stung by this further attack on those close to her. 'It's perfectly proper for her to sit there with her mother and young Jack.' Eleanora shifted uncomfortably in her seat. Hard wooden pews were no doubt designed to make sure that the congregation did not fall asleep during long sermons, but she wished she had a cushion. She shot a sideways glance at Grace, who, as the vicar's wife, had set herself up as unofficial arbiter of manners and morals in Little Creek. Although it was not in Eleanora's nature to be humble, she was a relative newcomer to the village and had been careful not to offend Grace, but she was a fair woman and she felt the need to stand up for Dove. 'I'm sure she will make him a good wife,' she added.

'I disagree, Eleanora. Dr Neville could do better for himself. The Fox girls should know their place in society, that's all I'm saying.'

'I think you're forgetting that their brother is now lord of the manor,' Eleanora said mildly. 'I'm sure that Jay will try to live up to the responsibilities that he's inherited.'

Grace raised her gloved hand to shield her mouth. 'I remember when Mary Fox was married to that bully of a first husband, she wore rags and had to send her children out to work when they were barely out of petticoats.'

'That's all in the past,' Eleanora protested.

'Mary might have risen from being a skivvy by marrying the squire, even if it was on his deathbed, but you can't make a silk purse out of a sow's ear. A real lady would keep her servants in their place, and yet she's brought the entire staff of the manor house with her. It simply isn't the done thing.'

Eleanora had finally had enough of Grace's uncalled-for malice, and she rose to her feet. 'I can hear a commotion outside. The bridesmaids must have arrived, so I'd better go and see if I can do anything to help.' She hurried down the aisle, nodding and smiling at friends and acquaintances.

Toby Marshall reached out to catch Eleanora by the hand as she was about to walk past him. 'Is anything wrong, Aunt?'

'No, dear. I was just going to make sure that the little ones were behaving. Daisy should be here at any moment.'

Toby glanced at Jay, who was standing before the altar with his best man. 'The bridegroom looks nervous. I'd have thought this would be easier the second time around, although why he would want to put himself through this again is a mystery to me.'

'Hush, Toby.' Minnie clutched his arm, stifling a giggle. 'Someone will hear you.'

He turned to his fiancée with a broad grin.

'Everyone knows they were married in a rush at Christmas, Minnie. It's not as if Daisy's in the family way.'

'Really, Toby, I don't appreciate your sense of humour,' Eleanora said crossly. 'This is the house of God; you should be more respectful, and that sort of idle chatter gives the gossips something to talk about.'

'Sorry, Aunt.' Toby sank back onto the pew. 'I think you'd better go and see to the bridesmaids. It sounds as if they are getting impatient.'

'Yes, I'd better help Hilda, but you must mind your manners, Toby. You're not in London now.' Eleanora hurried out of the church into the warm spring sunshine.

Minnie nudged Toby in the ribs. 'That wasn't fair, Toby. You shouldn't say things like that to your aunt.'

'Well, all this palaver is a bit silly, considering that my sister and Jay have been happily married for months. Anyway, it will be our turn next. I'll make certain that our wedding is twice as grand as this one.'

Minnie smiled. 'I think my parents will have something to say about that, darling. Papa will want to marry us in his church, and Mama will have the last word when it comes to the wedding breakfast.'

Toby leaned over to brush Minnie's cheek with a kiss. 'Let's run away to Gretna Green. I don't think I could go through all this again.'

She chuckled and squeezed his hand. 'But you

will, and I rather fancy being a summer bride rather than waiting until the autumn.'

'As soon as I've found us somewhere to live we'll get your father to post the banns.'

Outside the church Hilda was rearranging her younger daughter's tumbled curls after the carriage ride from the manor house.

'You girls look splendid.' Eleanora said, smiling at ten-year-old Judy, who was wearing a white muslin dress made for her by the village dressmaker, which exactly matched the one worn by seven-year-old Molly. 'Did you leave the boys with Mrs Fuller, as I suggested, Hilda?'

'Yes, Mrs Marshall. I wasn't going to bring them anyway. They're too young to know how to behave on such an occasion.' Hilda clutched her daughters' hands. 'We have to wait here until Daisy and her uncle arrive, and then you walk very slowly up the aisle, scattering the contents of your baskets. You know what to do, Judy.'

'So do I,' Molly lisped. 'We practised yesterday, didn't we, Judy?'

'Yes, Ma. Stop worrying.' Judy tossed her head. 'We're very important because we scatter the herbs that will keep away evil spirits.'

Eleanora stared at her aghast. 'Who's filling your head with that nonsense?'

Judy eyed her warily. 'Cook said so. She knows a lot of things.'

'Well, dear, I don't think you'll find any evil spirits in the church. It's a holy place, and you and Molly are going to make a pretty carpet of flowers and leaves for the bride to walk on.'

Hilda nodded. 'Yes, indeed. Listen to Mrs Marshall, girls.' She turned her head at the sound of an approaching carriage. 'Here comes Daisy now.'

The Tattersalls' landau had been taken out of the coach house, dusted off, cleaned and polished and decorated with swags of greenery and white ribbons. Daisy sat beside her uncle, who was beaming with pride as the carriage drew to a halt, and the footman leaped off the box to open the door and put down the steps.

'Do be careful, Sidney,' Eleanora said anxiously. 'We don't want any accidents on Daisy's special day.'

'Don't fuss, my dear. I'm as agile as a man half my age.' Sidney clambered to the ground, groaning as his arthritic knees took his weight, but he managed a weak grin. 'You see.'

'I see an old man pretending to be younger than his years.' Eleanora took the children from their mother. 'You can go and sit with Mrs Ralston, Hilda. I'll keep an eye on the girls. Come along, my dears. We'll wait in the porch.'

Hilda frowned and opened her mouth as if to argue, but a stern look from Eleanora made her change her mind and she went to sit at the end of the pew where the Creek Manor servants were waiting expectantly.

'Are you ready, Daisy?' Eleanora asked as she was about to shepherd the bridesmaids into the church.

Daisy alighted from the landau with the help of her uncle and the footman. She shook out the voluminous skirts of the ivory silk gown that Jay had insisted she had made for the occasion, although if she were honest she would have preferred to wear something less formal. Her veil was held in place by a simple wreath of white camellias, and she carried a matching bouquet.

'You look beautiful, my love,' Sidney said, wiping tears from his eyes. 'You are so like your mother. I remember how lovely she was. It was no wonder that my poor brother fell hopelessly in love with her.'

'Thank you, Uncle.'

Daisy was suddenly nervous. Until now she had taken everything in her stride, but she could hear the buzz of conversation emanating from the church, and as she approached the porch on the arm of her uncle, she could see that every seat was taken. There were people standing at the back of the nave and a few late-comers were outside, hoping to squeeze in after the wedding party. This was simply a blessing on her marriage to Jay, she had told herself during the drive from the manor house to the church, only this time there were many well-wishers. It was all so different from the actual ceremony last Christmas Eve, when she and Jay had tramped through the snow on their way to the church. The only guests then had been Guppy and Ramsden, two of the crew from Jay's ship, the *Lazy Jane*, with Mrs Peabody and her maid to act as witnesses.

'Are you ready, Daisy?'

She glanced at her uncle and smiled. 'Yes, I am.'

'We're coming, Eleanora.'

'All right, Sidney. No need to shout.' Eleanora shooed the young bridesmaids into the nave and stood aside. She watched anxiously as they processed slowly up the aisle, concentrating on their important task with set expressions, while Miss Creedy, the regular church organist, hammered out the 'Bridal Chorus' from Wagner's *Lohengrin*, occasionally hitting the right note.

With her hand resting on her uncle's arm, Daisy followed them, fixing her gaze on Jay. He turned to look at her and his smile still had the power to make her heart beat faster. She could hear the music and the soft shuffling of the congregation as they rose to their feet and stood in respectful silence, but for Daisy it might have been Christmas Eve all over again. The only person she could see was the man she had married in the depths of winter. The last four months had been the happiest she had ever known, and now she could look forward to a lifetime together, with the added blessing of any children that might come from their blissful union. It had not happened yet, but she lived in hope.

Nick Neville turned his head to give her an encouraging smile. It was odd, she thought dreamily, at one time she had been certain that Nick was the man for her, but then Jay had quite literally swept her off her feet and she knew now that he was the love of her life. They were already legally married, and this ceremony – merely the affirmation of the bond that they shared – was mainly for the benefit of others. Daisy herself would have been quite happy to continue as they had been since Christmas, making every effort to right the wrongs that Squire Tattersall had committed in his selfish lifetime, but the title of lord of the manor carried with it heavy responsibilities. The old squire had been neglectful and greedy, and now Jay was intent of making reparation for his father's wrongdoings.

Daisy smiled tenderly as Jay took her hand and John Peabody began the ceremony, speaking in a deep, rich voice that echoed off the vaulted ceiling of the old church.

It was over and the bride and groom left the church to cheers, clapping, and people tossing handfuls of rice. Hand in hand Daisy and Jay walked the short distance to the latest innovation in the village, designed and financed by Jay himself. The manually operated chain ferry was ready to take the guests across the water to a landing stage on the far side, and transport had been laid on to take the bridal party to the manor house for the wedding breakfast. Jay handed Daisy into the boat, followed by his mother, Eleanora and Sidney, Hilda and the two bridesmaids, and lastly eleven-year-old Jack, who jumped aboard at the last minute and went to sit beside Judy. There were more cheers as the ferry was winched across the water, and when they disembarked it was winched back to collect the rest of the family and the guests in relays.

'That's a wonderful contraption, my boy,' Sidney said appreciatively. 'I just hope it doesn't affect the fishing grounds.'

Jay smiled and shook his head. 'It won't, sir, I promise, and you are welcome to fish in the lake, if that appeals to you.'

'My husband is obsessed with the sport,' Eleanora sighed. 'I must admit I'm getting a little tired of eating trout and I dislike pike; it tastes muddy.'

'Cook can do wonders with that particular fish,' Hilda said eagerly. 'She stuffs it with breadcrumbs and herbs and I don't know what, but it's very good to eat.'

'Lemon juice, Ma.' Judy met her mother's surprised gaze with a grin. 'I learn a lot from watching Cook at work.'

Sidney patted Judy on the back. 'I can see we have a budding chef in our midst, Hilda.'

'Maybe Hilda doesn't want her daughter to work in a kitchen.' Eleanora shifted from one foot to the other as her high heels sank into the muddy track. 'Are we getting in the carriage with you, Daisy? Or do we have to wait for another to come and pick us up? I have to say, I don't want to travel on a farm cart. It would ruin my new gown.'

Jay handed Daisy into the waiting landau. 'There's room for two more and the little ones, because they don't take up much room. There's another carriage on the way, but it's not too far to walk.'

'I hope you're not suggesting that we ladies trudge up the hill on the muddy track,' Mary said crossly. 'I agree with Mrs Marshall. We should travel in the carriage with you.'

'I'll walk,' Sidney said firmly. 'But Mrs Begg ought to ride.'

'I'll come with you, Mr Marshall,' Jack said eagerly. 'I feel like a walk after sitting through all that hymn singing and praying.'

Sidney ruffled Jack's curly brown hair. 'I couldn't agree more, son. Perhaps Judy and Molly would like to come too, and we'll have a look at the lake. We might see a few carp.'

Hilda was about to protest, but Judy had already skipped on ahead. 'You ride, Ma,' she called over her shoulder. 'I want to see the fish.'

'Me, too.' Molly ran after her.

'See what you've started, Sidney.' Eleanora wagged her finger at him, but her husband merely smiled as he handed her into the carriage. 'The children need to wear off some of their youthful high spirits, my dear, and I enjoy a bit of exercise.' He held his hand out to Hilda.

'Thank you, sir. But you will make sure the girls don't fall in, won't you? Their dresses are new and they cost a pretty penny. Daisy paid for them herself.'

'Let the girls enjoy themselves,' Daisy said, chuckling. 'They've played their part today and behaved perfectly in church.' She moved closer to Jay, slipping her hand through the crook of his arm. 'Let's go home.'

He brushed her lips with a kiss. 'Drive on, Fuller. We have guests to entertain.'

'Who would have thought that Creek Manor would one day play host to the whole village?' Mary Tattersall edged into the corner of the seat to make room for Hilda and Eleanora. 'If you'd told me that when I was a girl, I'd never have believed it.'

Eleanora turned her head away. 'We were in London then. Sometimes I wish we'd stayed in Whitechapel.'

'Surely not, Aunt,' Daisy said anxiously. 'Would you really prefer to live above the shop than here in Little Creek? You have a comfortable cottage, and it's all yours.'

'I suppose so.' Eleanora uttered a loud sigh. 'But I miss the hustle and bustle of the city, and the shops.'

'Some people are never satisfied,' Mary said darkly. 'If you'd suffered the hardships I've had to endure you'd be grateful for what you've got, Mrs Marshall.'

'I'm sure we count ourselves very fortunate to have come to such a delightful part of the country.' Daisy spoke before her aunt had a chance to argue. 'I love Little Creek and I'm more than happy to live in Creek Manor.' She held Jay's arm a little tighter.

'I am the luckiest woman in the world to have such a wonderful husband and family. I couldn't ask for more.'

'My sentiments exactly,' Jay said, smiling. 'I'm married to the most beautiful woman I've ever known, and we have everything we could possibly want, so let's not spoil the day with petty arguments.'

'I'm sure I wouldn't want to be a wet blanket.' Eleanora shot a wary glance in Mary's direction.

Mary nodded and managed a tight little smile. 'I didn't mean to offend you, Mrs Marshall. It's just that I've been the subject of unkind gossip for so many years that I sometimes speak out of turn.'

'Quite so, and as we're related by marriage I think it only proper that you call me Eleanora. We must support each other, Mary.'

Daisy leaned against Jay, inhaling the masculine scent that was his alone. She felt at this moment as though her heart would burst with happiness, and the sun was shining. It was a perfect spring day.

After greeting the guests Daisy and Jay led them into the dining hall, where more tables and chairs had been brought in to seat everyone, and a feast had been laid out in readiness. Wine, ale and cider flowed and, although subdued at first, the guests began to relax and enjoy themselves. Their voices rose in a crescendo, adding to the clatter of knives and forks on china plates and the clink of glasses.

When at last everyone was satiated with food and

drink, there was the traditional cutting of the wedding cake, and then Sidney rose to his feet and raised a toast. Jay made a brief speech in response and announced that there would be dancing in the great hall to the tuneful accompaniment of Mr Keyes, the village shopkeeper, on the concertina and Constable Fowler on the pianoforte. The instrument had been found tucked away beneath a tarpaulin in the coach house, and Mary vaguely remembered the first Mrs Tattersall having the piano in the morning parlour where she spent many an hour playing soulful music. A piano tuner had been summoned from Maldon and now it was as good as new, or almost. Daisy was no expert, but when she had been governess to the Carringtons' youngest child, she had sat beside Master Timothy in the drawing room of the London mansion while he did his five-finger exercises. The Steinway, which had been imported from Germany at enormous expense, had made the most wonderful sound, even though the young musician was there under sufferance, bribed by the promise of a poke of humbugs if he completed a half-hour practice. The manor house pianoforte could not compete with such a superb instrument, but if the notes were tinny no one seemed to notice, and George Keyes played his concertina with more enthusiasm than expertise.

Jay and Daisy took the floor and led the dancers in a waltz, followed by a lively polka and then a gavotte. Breathless and smiling, they stopped to take a rest while the guests formed a circle for the country dance, Gathering Peascods.

'This really is a day to remember, Jay,' Daisy said softly. 'You were right, it's good to share our happiness with everyone.'

He smiled and leaned over to kiss her on the lips. 'Here's to a lifetime together, Daisy mine. I'll never leave you.'

It was her turn to smile. 'Not even to refurbish the *Lazy Jane* – I know she's the second love of your life.'

'No, sweetheart. My days at sea are over. I'll pay another master to take care of the old girl, but this time they'll trade in legitimate goods. No more smuggling for me.'

'I'm glad. It might have ended so badly.' Daisy looked up at the sound of someone calling Jay's name and a young man pushed his way through the dancers.

'Captain, I need to have a word.'

Jay rose to his feet. 'What is it, Lewis? I didn't see you at the wedding breakfast.'

'I was called down to the creek, sir. There's been a spot of bother.'

'What's happened?'

The note of anxiety in her husband's voice made Daisy reach out to clutch his hand. 'What's wrong?'

'I don't know, but the boy seems to be in a state.' Jay turned back to Lewis, who was sweating profusely and panting as if he had run a considerable distance. 'Calm down and tell me what's happened.'

Lewis shook his head. 'You need to come with me, Captain. You're the only one who can save the *Lazy Jane* from them Dornings.'

Daisy leaped to her feet. 'No, Jay. You can't leave in the middle of the reception. Whatever it is can surely wait for a few hours.'

Jay shook his head. 'It's not like Lewis to panic. I'll go and sort it out and be back before you know it. Save the next waltz for me, my darling.' Jay blew her a kiss and hurried after Lewis, who was already halfway towards the door.

'What's going on, Daisy?' Mary was at her side, staring anxiously after her son. 'Why has Jay rushed off after that boy? I sense trouble.'

Daisy frowned. 'I don't know, Mary. But he promised to come back soon. Jay always keeps his word.' She watched the man she adored leave the great hall and she felt the cold draught as the door closed behind him. She shivered suddenly as cold fingers of fear ran down her spine.

Chapter Two

Toby slipped his arm around Daisy's shoulders. 'I'm sure he'll be back soon.'

'Yes, of course,' Daisy said without much conviction.

'I'd stay, but I have to report for duty at the hospital tomorrow morning.' Toby gave her a searching look. 'And I need to get Minnie back to Mrs Wood's lodging house before she is locked out. I've bribed the maid to let her in, but she might fall asleep.'

'Will you be all right, Daisy?' Minnie asked anxiously. 'It seems wrong to leave you like this.'

Daisy managed a smile. 'Jay would never miss his own party. But of course you must go now. Fuller will take you to the railway station.'

Toby gave her a hug. 'He'd better treat you well, or he'll have me to deal with.'

'Jay is the best of husbands. He'll be back soon.

I know he will.' Daisy watched her brother and his fiancée as they took their leave of their aunt and uncle, and she waved to them as they left the great hall. She forced herself to smile, but she had a bad feeling in the pit of her stomach. Something was wrong, but Jay would make it right, of that she was certain.

The dancing grew more energetic and the company more raucous with every glass of fruit punch, ale or cider that was drunk, ceasing briefly when the musicians demanded a break. Daisy tried hard to put her worries to the back of her mind. She told herself that the emergency had been exaggerated and that Jay would return soon. They would laugh about this later, when all the guests had gone home and the house was relatively quiet, but after two hours and no sign of her husband, she was beginning to be restive. She had to fend off questions from her aunt and Mary, both of whom had seen Jay leave with Lewis, and Daisy tried to sound confident when she said that Jay would return within the hour. It was becoming apparent that whatever had called him away must be far more serious than she had thought, and by the time the last guests had left for home Mary was frantic and Daisy had stopped pretending that all was well.

'Should we stay with you tonight?' Eleanora asked anxiously. 'Your uncle and I will gladly keep you company until Jay returns home. He's very thoughtless to leave you like this.'

Mary bristled visibly. 'There must be a good reason for Jay's continued absence. He was always a considerate child and he hasn't changed.'

'Well, it appears that something very urgent must have kept him away,' Sidney said mildly. 'The poor fellow has missed a good party.'

Eleanora turned on him angrily. 'Trust you to say something silly like that, Sidney Marshall. Can't you see that Daisy is distraught? Who knows what might have befallen him?'

'Come, come, my love. I don't think he'll have been attacked by wild animals or savage natives in Little Creek.'

'Don't be ridiculous, Sidney. Of course neither of those things will have happened to him, but he might have had an accident of some sort, or fallen into the sea.' Eleanora turned to Daisy. 'Can he swim?'

Daisy glanced out of the window. It was dark outside and the grandfather clock in the great hall had just struck the hour. 'I don't know, Aunt,' Daisy said vaguely. 'The subject never came up.'

'Then you should find out . . . And you ought to learn to swim, Sidney. You're always wading into the river with that fishing rod of yours. What would happen if you slipped and fell? I'd be a widow and how would I manage then?'

Sidney slipped his arm around her shoulders. 'Ellie, my love, you're getting worked up about nothing. I think we ought to go home and leave Daisy in peace. Jay is a sensible fellow and I've no doubt he'll return soon.'

'But he might have drowned!' Mary's face paled to ashen. 'You're right, Eleanora. An accident must have occurred to keep Jay from his own wedding reception.' She covered her face with her hands and her shoulders shook.

'There, Aunt. See what you've done,' Daisy said crossly. 'Of course he hasn't drowned. We don't even know why Jay was called away, but there must be a good reason for his continued absence.'

Sidney gave Daisy a sympathetic pat on the shoulder. 'I'll take her home, if your man will send for the carriage.'

Daisy beckoned to Molesworth, who was standing at a respectful distance. 'Please send for the carriage to take my aunt and uncle home.'

'I'm not crossing the river in the dark,' Eleonora protested.

'The ferryman only works in daylight hours, Aunt,' Daisy said patiently. 'You'll have to go the long way round, but it's a fine evening. You should get home within the hour.'

Mary paced the floor, wringing her hands. 'Anything could have happened. If he didn't go to the ship, he might have gone to one of the farms. He might have been trampled by cows or gored by a bull.'

Daisy slipped away. She had had enough of such unhelpful speculation and she was growing more and more concerned with each passing minute. Ignoring the fact that she was still wearing her bridal gown and satin slippers, she hurried through the house to the servants' quarters and snatched a rough woollen cloak from a peg near the rear entrance. A lantern was always left near the door and she unhooked it, struck a match and lit the wick. She left the house unnoticed by the servants, who, judging by the sounds of jollity coming from their quarters, were continuing the celebrations. Daisy smiled in spite of her anxiety. Tomorrow would be a very different story and those who were drinking too much wine and beer would suffer accordingly. But this was a special day, or rather it had been before Jay's mysterious disappearance.

Holding the lantern high enough to illuminate the pathway, Daisy quickened her pace as she made her way to the summerhouse. It was the first time she had ventured alone into the underground passage that had not so long ago been used to bring smuggled goods ashore, but she was too worried to think about anything other than finding Jay. If he had stayed aboard *Lazy Jane* just to help plug a leak or mend a broken mast she would be very angry.

It was cold below ground level, and damp rose from the mud beneath her feet as she trod carefully on the slippery stones. The thin beam of light from the lantern bobbed with every step she took, and sinister shadows seemed to close in on her. There was no turning back now and she was determined to find

Jay, whatever the cost. The sound of her footsteps echoed off the walls, and for a terrifying moment she thought she could hear someone panting so close to her that she could touch them, until she realised it was her own erratic breathing that she could hear.

After what seemed like an eternity she saw the entrance to the tunnel illuminated by a shaft of moonlight, and she broke into a run. Once outside she took deep breaths of the fresh sea air, and she could hear the sound of the waves breaking on the shingle. Emerging through the undergrowth, she scanned the horizon for any sign of the *Lazy Jane*, but there was just the reflection of moonlight on the water. Stunned and barely able to believe her eyes, Daisy realised that the ship had sailed, apparently taking Jay on some mysterious and unexpected voyage. Months ago he had promised her that he would never set sail again, and he had promoted his first mate, Clem Guppy, to handle the ship while trading on the right side of the law. She could not believe that he would have willingly broken that solemn promise.

She stood for some minutes, wrapping the coarse cloak around her as a chilly east wind rustled the branches of the trees that overhung the beach. She scanned the water again and again in the vain hope of catching a glimpse of the vessel, but apart from a few white-tipped waves, the creek was calm and glassy. Then the thought struck her that perhaps Aunt Eleanora had been right. Lewis had seemed agitated when he came for Jay: maybe there had been a crisis at his father's farm. She had not seen Mr and Mrs Johnson, Lewis's parents, at the church or at the reception, so maybe there was something seriously wrong. Daisy retreated into the tunnel and this time the horrors had gone – after all, it was just a short cut back to the summerhouse at the end of the rose garden.

She entered the house, once again without being seen, and the sounds of merriment were even louder than before. She smiled to think that at least some of the household were enjoying what should have been the happiest day of their mistress's life, only now it was turning into a nightmare. Daisy had intended to walk to the Johnsons' farm, but it was a mile away at least and her dancing slippers were already ruined. Besides which, if she turned up at the farm wearing her wedding gown and in an obvious state of distress it would make Jay appear foolish, if he was there – and if he was not, she could hardly bear to imagine what else might have befallen him. She decided to go to their room, although she knew that sleep would evade her until Jay returned. Flashes of lightning lit the room, followed by cracks of thunder that were so close together it sounded like a fusillade of bullets being fired at the house. Daisy jumped into bed, closed her eyes and pulled the covers over her head.

* * *

Next morning, after a restless night when she had barely slept, Daisy reached out as she had done every day since they were married, but Jay's side of the bed was cold to the touch. She snapped into a sitting position, running her hand through her tousled hair. So it was not simply a bad dream. Jay was still missing, and the worries she had attempted to dismiss came flooding back with a physical force that made her gasp.

She leaped out of bed and stripped off her night-gown, allowing it to fall to the floor. The maid had not appeared to light the fire but Daisy was oblivious to the early morning chill. She threw on her riding habit and dragged a comb through her long, dark hair, securing it in a chignon at the nape of her neck. This was not the time to worry about her looks or the latest fashion; her greatest need was to discover Jay's whereabouts and it was just possible that Lewis's father, Farmer Johnson, might have the answer.

Daisy left the house, startling the bleary-eyed footman who rushed to open the door for her. 'If Mrs Tattersall asks where I am, James, you may tell her that I've gone for a walk.'

He nodded mutely and stood to attention as she walked past him. She caught a whiff of stale alcohol on his breath, and it was obvious from his bloodshot eyes and hangdog demeanour that he had been cele-brating into the early hours. However, that was the least of her worries. She set off towards the stables, but as she entered the cobbled yard she saw Faulkner, the head groom, with his head held under the pump. He straightened up abruptly at the sound of her voice and made a grab for a grimy towel, which he wrapped around his bare torso.

'Mrs Tattersall, ma'am. I'm sorry, I wasn't expecting to see you here.'

'It's all right, Faulkner. I apologise for disturbing your ablutions, but I need my horse saddled immediately.'

He glanced over her shoulder. 'Will the squire be riding with you, ma'am?'

'Not this morning.'

'Shall I accompany you, ma'am?'

'No, thank you. I'll go alone.'

Faulkner opened his mouth as if to argue, but he closed it again, nodded and backed away. 'I'll have your mount ready in a few minutes, Mrs Tattersall.'

Daisy had had plenty of time to practise her equestrian skills since her marriage, and Jay had taken pleasure in showing her parts of the county that she had not previously seen, but now she was going out alone in the hope of discovering her husband's whereabouts. Since last evening she had gone through a range of emotions from puzzlement to anger, and from anger to desperation. She waited impatiently and at last the stable boy brought her bay mare to the mounting block and held her head while Daisy settled herself in the saddle.

He eyed her warily. 'Mr Faulkner said I could go with you, ma'am. If you so wished.'

Daisy was about to refuse, but she had second thoughts. 'You grew up in Little Creek, didn't you, Barney?'

'Yes, Mrs Tattersall.'

'Then you'll know Lewis Johnson.'

'Yes, ma'am. We was at school together.'

'Saddle up then, Barney. I want you to find out anything you can about Lewis's whereabouts yesterday. If he's at home all the better, but if not then it's vital that I know anything that would give me a clue as to why he came to the manor house in such a state last evening.'

'I'll be like one of them detectives then, ma'am.' He gave her a wide grin and raced back into the stable, returning so quickly that Daisy was certain Faulkner had assumed that she would allow the boy to accompany her, and had the pony saddled and ready. She dug her heels into the mare's sides and clicked her tongue against her teeth. 'Walk on, Cinders.' They rode sedately until they were out of sight of the main house and then Daisy encouraged Cinders to a trot, then a canter and finally a gallop over the fields to the Johnsons' farm. She dismounted in the farmyard, tossing the reins to Barney.

'I won't be long.' She strode across the yard, causing the hens pecking for food to scatter with loud squawks of protest and the sheep dog rushed at her, wagging his tail. She patted his head absently as she made her way to the back door and knocked.

It was opened by Mrs Johnson, who was red-eyed as if she had been crying. 'Oh, Mrs Tattersall, ma'am. I weren't expecting you.' She wiped her hands on her apron and stood aside. 'Won't you come in?'

'Thank you.' Daisy stepped inside and was immediately assailed by the delicious aroma of baking bread. Two large hams were hung in the chimney breast, curing in the smoke from the blazing fire, and a kettle hummed merrily on the hob. A girl of about fourteen, whom Daisy recognised as being Lewis's younger sister, Janet, was kneading dough at the vast pine table in the centre of the beamed kitchen. The flagstone floor was white with flour dust in a large circle around her.

'You'll have to excuse the mess, ma'am,' Mrs Johnson said apologetically. 'We wasn't expecting visitors this early.'

'I think you know why I've come.' Daisy decided that the direct approach was best. 'Your son Lewis came to our house last evening with a message for my husband.'

Mrs Johnson looked away, twisting the folds of her apron in her work-worn hands. 'Yes, I believe he did.'

'Might I see Lewis? I need to speak to him urgently.'

'He didn't come home, missis.' Janet continued to pummel the dough as if it were her worst enemy.

'Mind your tongue, Janet,' Mrs Johnson said crossly. 'Who asked you, anyway?'

'Well, it's true.' Janet flipped the dough over and punched it with both fists.

'Lewis is a good boy.' Mrs Johnson met Daisy's anxious glance with a sidelong look.

'Yes, I know that,' Daisy said earnestly. 'I got to know him quite well when I was on board the *Lazy Jane*. But I'm here to ask for your help because my husband hasn't returned home either. Do you know what it was that Lewis had to tell him?'

Mrs Johnson shook her head. 'No, ma'am. Except that it was to do with the ship.'

'Lewis wants to go to sea again,' Janet volunteered. 'He don't want to work the farm like our brothers.'

'Hush, Janet. No one asked you.' Mrs Johnson's eyes filled with tears and she blinked them away. 'Lewis can't settle to life on shore.'

'Was the *Lazy Jane* anchored in the creek yesterday?' Daisy asked anxiously.

'If it was, our Lewis would know.' Janet shot her mother a rebellious glance. 'He watches out day and night for its return.'

'I'm afraid he'll get into bad company,' Mrs Johnson said desperately. 'Lewis is a good boy but he hangs around with some of those in Burnham that are out-and-out rogues.'

'I'm sorry.' Daisy looked from one to the other. 'But that doesn't explain why he came to fetch my husband or why neither of them has returned home.'

'I can't help you, ma'am. I wish to God that I could.' Mrs Johnson covered her head with her apron and sank down on the nearest chair, sobbing.

Janet abandoned the bread dough and rushed to her mother's side. 'Look what you done now, missis. Go away and leave us be.'

Outside in the relatively cool air of a late April morning, Daisy beckoned to Barney, who was holding the reins of both animals while he chatted to one of the farm workers. He broke away and led the horses towards her.

'Did you discover anything useful?' Daisy asked when he drew near.

'I dunno, missis. It might or it might not be what you want to hear.'

'Just tell me, Barney. Let me be the judge.'

'Well, I was chatting to Lewis's older brother, Wilf, and he said that Lewis had been hanging around with the Dorning brothers.'

Daisy stared at him, frowning. 'I don't know them.'

'You wouldn't want to, missis. They're not the sort of people you'd wish to know.'

'So what are you saying, Barney?'

'I'm saying nothing, missis. It's just that the Dorning boys is, or I should say was, also Benny Sykes's cousins.'

'And you think that Benny's death has something to do with Lewis's disappearance?'

'Like I said, missis, I dunno nothing. I'm just telling you what Wilf said.'

Daisy thought for a moment. 'Where does Mrs Sykes live? I seem to remember it's somewhere close by – it was the pig man's cottage, but I've lost my bearings.'

'It's not far. Down the lane, about a quarter of a mile. Shall we go there next?'

'Help me up onto the saddle. We'll call on Mrs Sykes. I should pay my respects.'

Mrs Sykes was up to her ankles in dung as she cleaned the pigsty. Her hair was tied up in a ragged scarf and she was enveloped in a large none-too-clean apron, her feet encased in boots several sizes too large so that she was in danger of stepping out of them each time she moved. She leaned on the shovel, staring at Daisy with a suspicious frown.

'Mrs Sykes, I'm sorry to interrupt when I can see how busy you are,' Daisy said hastily.

Mrs Sykes stared at Daisy, the lines on her face deepened by a frown. 'Can I help you?'

'I don't suppose you remember me, Mrs Sykes.'

'Yes, I do. You and Captain Jay came to see me after my Benny's terrible accident in the galley. He were always a clumsy boy, but he didn't deserve to die in such a painful manner and without his ma to hold his hand.'

'As I said then, I'm very sorry for your loss.'

'But that ain't why you've come all the way here today, is it?'

'No, it isn't. I do need your help, as it happens,

Mrs Sykes. You must know that Lewis didn't return home last evening.'

'Yes, so I heard.'

'Lewis came to the manor house with an urgent message for my husband. They left together and no one has seen them since.'

'I don't see how I can help.'

'I've heard that Lewis is close to his cousins, the Dorning brothers. I was wondering if they might know something.'

'I don't have nothing to do with my brother's boys. They turned out bad, and I told Lewis not to have anything to do with them.'

'I understand,' Daisy said gently. 'But I'd like a word with them.'

'I don't advise it, ma'am.'

'Where would I be likely to find them, Mrs Sykes?'

'The Anchor Inn or the White Hart. Everyone in the area knows the Dorning brothers, to my shame. Thank the Lord my brother died of a fever some years back. He never lived to see the family name dragged through the estuary mud.'

Daisy backed away. 'I'm sorry, Mrs Sykes. But thank you for your help.' She started back up the lane to where Barney was waiting with the horses.

'You might find out things best left forgotten,' Mrs Sykes called after her.

Daisy returned to the manor house, and she made an excuse to go out again after a quick luncheon with her mother-in-law. Mary, like herself, was growing more worried with every passing minute that there was no news, but Daisy had no intention of giving Jay's mother false hope and she did not mention her conversation with Mrs Sykes. The Dorning brothers might be exactly what their aunt said, a pair of good-for-nothings, but on the other hand they might know what had distressed Lewis and made him seek Jay's help. The message he had given Jay was the key to the whole mystery, and Daisy knew that something serious must have happened to keep Jay from her, particularly on their wedding night. She would discover the truth, no matter what it cost.

Daisy entered the smoke-filled taproom of the Anchor with Barney at her side. The old pub on the water's edge was crowded with fishermen and farm workers, and the air was heavy with the smell of ale and rum. A driftwood fire crackled in the hearth and straw covered the flagstones, absorbing the mud brought in on the men's boots. Conversation ceased abruptly as heads turned to stare at the well-dressed young woman who had suddenly entered their domain. The potman hurried up to Daisy.

'This ain't the place for a young lady like yourself, miss. Why not try the hotel in the main street?'

'I haven't come to stay,' Daisy said hastily. 'I'm looking for the Dorning brothers.'

The silence grew more intense and the atmosphere changed noticeably. Daisy could feel a buzz of unease in the room, as if a beehive had been disturbed by robbers after the honey.

'You'll not find them here.' The potman edged her towards the door. 'I'd go now, if I was you, miss.'

'At least tell me where I might find the Dornings,' Daisy said in desperation.

'Aye, boss. We know their cousins,' Barney added. 'Got a message from the family, so to speak.'

'Why didn't you say so afore?' The potman shooed them outside. 'I wouldn't say so in front of them in there, but I'll give you this bit of advice. Try the old chapel on the edge of the marsh, but don't say I said so.'

'Where is it exactly?' Daisy asked eagerly.

'The boy will take you there.' The potman turned to Barney. 'You know the one I mean, son?'

'I think I do.'

The potman chuckled. 'That's right, boy. Don't give a straight answer, or you might find yourself in hot water.'

'Tell me where this place is, if you please.' Daisy was growing impatient. It was late afternoon and in an hour or two it would be too dark to find their way. She had a sudden vision of Jay facing some unknown danger and she could do nothing to save him.

'. . . And then you keep on following the coastline until you come to the chapel. Did you get that, miss?'

Daisy stared at the old potman. Her thoughts had been miles away, but out of the corner of her eye she could see Barney nodding, and she managed a smile. 'Yes, thank you. You've been very helpful.' She took her purse from her reticule and gave the man a silver sixpence. He raised her hand to his lips and bowed his head.

'Ta, miss. You're a real lady.'

'We'd best go now, missis,' Barney said in a low voice. 'We've still got a long way to go.'

The haze of doubt and longing cleared from Daisy's brain and she took a deep breath. 'Fetch the horses, Barney. We'll be on our way.'

They rode for several miles and the sun, which had come out briefly, was now plummeting to rest behind a bank of purple clouds. A chill, salt-laden wind blew in from the sea and Daisy was glad of her thick riding habit and leather gloves. Barney was not so well wrapped up, but he did not seem to feel the cold and he was obviously enjoying his time away from his normal routine in the stables. They had left the village behind and were now in open countryside with a distant view of the sea. Daisy was beginning to think they were lost when Barney pointed excitedly and over the rise she saw the roof of the small Saxon chapel.

'Best let me go first,' Barney said in a low voice. 'If the boys are there and you ride up they'll either run or they might turn nasty.'

'Surely they wouldn't attack a woman?'

'I wouldn't count on it, ma'am.'

'All right, but don't take risks. If they seem

unfriendly just walk away. If they seem reasonable ask for a parley.'

'For a what, ma'am?'

'Tell them that Captain Fox's wife would like to speak to them. They might know my husband by his former name.'

With a nod and a wave of his hand, Barney urged his horse to a trot and headed for the chapel. Daisy could only wait and hope that if the Dorning boys were there they would be willing to cooperate. She leaned over to pat Cinders' neck, crooning softly to the horse, who showed her appreciation with a gentle whinny. But dusk was rapidly swallowing up the saltings, and in less than an hour it would be dark, with no lights to guide them on their way home. Daisy waited anxiously and was beginning to think that something dreadful might have befallen Barney when she heard the muffled sound of hoof beats on the tussocky grass and he rode into view.

'Well?' She could hardly wait for him to catch his breath.

He shook his head. 'No one there and no sign of anything untoward, missis. They're not stupid enough to leave anything for the law to find, and it didn't look as if anyone had been there for quite a while.'

Disappointed, but not surprised, Daisy nodded. 'Thank you for trying, Barney. I think we'd better head for home. It'll be nightfall soon and it looks like rain.'

The rain came down in sheets, not little dainty spots, but a torrential shower that soaked through Daisy's clothing in minutes, despite the thickness of the material. They rode on in silence as darkness enveloped them, blotting out the landscape. Daisy had to rely on Cinders' surefootedness to get them across the clifftops to the lane, which led eventually to the gates of Creek Manor. The gatekeeper rushed out to admit them, and if he was surprised to see the lady of the manor dishevelled and soaked to the skin, he was too well trained to show any emotion. Daisy rode on and dismounted outside the main entrance, leaving Barney to lead Cinders to the stables for a rub down and a well-earned feed and a rest.

James stood by the open door, staring straight ahead, for which Daisy was grateful. She caught sight of herself in one of the long mirrors as she headed for the staircase and she was shocked by her bedraggled state. It was one thing to feel wet and uncomfortable and quite another to see her wet hair hanging loose around her shoulders and her perky little riding hat totally ruined. She doubted if her habit could be saved, but that would not have mattered an iota had she come home with news of Jay's whereabouts. She reached the top of the stairs and was about to enter her bedroom when Mary came hurrying towards her.

'Oh, my goodness, just look at you, Daisy. Where have you been?'

Hilda was close behind her. 'Never mind that. You need to get out of those wet clothes or you'll catch your death.'

'I thought you were going for a ride around the estate,' Mary said, frowning.

Daisy opened her mouth to reply, but her knees buckled and she drifted into unconsciousness.

Chapter Three

Daisy suffered nothing worse than a mild chill and she recovered quickly, although Mary insisted that she must rest in bed for a few days. Keeping to her room was a way for Daisy to evade the inevitable questions about her attempt to find the elusive Dorning brothers. Their apparent disappearance was explained when she was glancing through the local newspaper, and their names were mentioned in a report on the assizes in Chelmsford. The Dornings had been convicted of some minor crime, and were languishing in prison – so much for seeking their help. Daisy was disappointed but even more determined to discover what had happened to her husband. She refused to believe that he had abandoned her and his family, but there was no word of the *Lazy Jane*, and the mystery deepened.

Although Jay's continued and unexplained absence

haunted her night and day, the estate had to be managed. Mary was too distraught about her son's disappearance to be any practical use when it came to running the house, even with the help of her old friend Ida Ralston. Daisy learned that the two women had started work at the manor house as young girls, and Ida knew all about the late squire's unwanted advances, which had left Mary pregnant with Jay, alone and unprotected. Even so, Mary seemed unable or unwilling to take on the responsibilities that had been thrust upon her since she had married Squire Tattersall on his deathbed.

After a visit from a frantic Mrs Ralston, who thrust a sheaf of unpaid bills and demands for payment at her, Daisy decided that lying about in bed or on the chaise longue in her boudoir was not going to help. She washed and dressed in one of her best morning gowns and sent for Hilda, who had shown a marked aptitude for hairdressing. She put up Daisy's hair in a very becoming style, and when Daisy looked in the mirror at her wan face, Hilda suggested the application of a little rouge to her cheeks and lips. The result was very effective and the reflection smiled back at Daisy, making her feel able to cope with almost anything. Daisy went downstairs to the study, taking with her the unpaid bills. She sat down at the large, leather-topped desk and opened the ledger containing the household accounts.

The amount outstanding was quite frightening to someone unused to handling such matters. Jay had managed the finances since he inherited the estate, but it did not take Daisy long to realise that he had let things slide. The debts were huge, and the servants had not been paid since the beginning of the last quarter. When she opened the safe there was very little cash in the strongbox, and she realised now that leaving financial matters to her husband had been a terrible mistake. She had believed him when he said he was capable of running a large estate, and she had been content to trust him, but now she regretted her complacency.

She had abetted him when it came to spending money on the refurbishment of the cottages they owned in Little Creek, which the late Squire Tattersall had allowed to fall into rack and ruin. Mary had raised her children in one of these dwellings, which were unfit for human habitation – even pigs would have turned up their snouts if they had been housed in any one of them – so Jay had first-hand knowledge of what it was like to live without even the most basic amenities. It was from the overflowing privies of these hovels that the cholera epidemic had stemmed last summer. Improving the cottages was a project that she and Jay had begun immediately after Christmas, and the tenants had been moved to Creek Hall, Dr Neville's family mansion, which he had turned into a cottage hospital. The very young and the elderly were all in need of medical care, and those who were reasonably fit were treated for minor ailments and either continued their outside occupations or helped with the cleaning or found work in the kitchen garden. Perusing the accounts book, Daisy was horrified to discover just how much money Jay had paid out, and there was still money owing. He might return today or tomorrow, but his continued silence did not bode well. Daisy realised that she must take control and the first step would be to visit the bank in Maldon. She reached for the bell pull to summon a servant and send for the carriage.

The bank manager was polite, but wary, and the reason for this as Daisy discovered, was that Jay had withdrawn a large sum of money the day before his sudden departure. Whether or not he had visited the bank in person was something that the manager could not confirm. He sat behind his large imposing desk, steepling his fingers as he rested his elbows on the tooled leather top.

'I'm sorry, Mrs Tattersall. I'm unable to give you any more information.'

'But I need to know my financial situation, sir.'

'The account is in your husband's name. I cannot divulge any details, even to you.'

'But I want to withdraw money. I need it to pay the servants and run the estate in my husband's absence.'

He shook his head. 'I'm afraid not, Mrs Tattersall. Your husband didn't make any such arrangement.' His expression softened. 'I'm sure he will return very soon and you will not need to worry.'

Daisy stared at him in dismay – if only she could

be so certain. Jay had once told her that he was a wanderer at heart, and maybe the chance of one last trip at sea had been too tempting to refuse. Whatever the reason for his disappearance, it was unforgivable to leave her and the estate virtually penniless. She rose to her feet.

'I can see that I'm wasting your time and mine,' she said stiffly. 'Thank you for being so frank with me.'

He stood up awkwardly. 'I'm so sorry I can't be of assistance, Mrs Tattersall. But rest assured . . .'

Daisy did not wait to hear the end of the sentence. She left the office and walked out of the bank to find Fuller waiting with the carriage. James leaped from the box to open the door and put down the steps. She climbed in and sat down, still feeling dazed and disorientated.

'Do you wish to go home, ma'am?' James asked anxiously.

She shook her head. How would she break the news to Mary, let alone the servants? Unless Jay returned within the next few days they would face bankruptcy. 'I want to go to Creek Hall first.'

'Yes, ma'am.' James closed the door and she heard him climb back onto the box and pass on her instructions to Fuller.

The carriage lurched forward and Daisy closed her eyes. She needed to speak to someone, and her first thought was her old friend Nick Neville.

* * *

Nick poured sherry into a glass and handed it to her. 'You look as though you need this, Daisy. It's purely medicinal, so drink up.'

Her hand trembled as she took the glass from him and she sipped it slowly. It would not do to be drunk in the early afternoon. 'Thank you, Nick.'

He pulled up a chair and sat beside her. 'This is about Jay's sudden departure on your wedding day, isn't it? From the state you're in I'd guess that he hasn't returned.'

'No, he hasn't. I haven't heard a word from him.'

Nick took her hand and gave it a comforting squeeze. 'I've known Jay all my life, and this wouldn't be the first time he's gone missing. I know it's different now you're married, but for a man who's spent almost half his life on board ship, it can't have been easy for him to give it up.'

She took another sip of the sherry. 'Are you saying he's run away to sea?'

'No, of course not, but he still owns the *Lazy Jane*, and don't take this the wrong way, Daisy, but that bundle of wood and canvas was his first love. If the master he put in charge was cheating him or running the vessel into danger, Jay would go to the rescue.'

'Yes, and that's the thought that I've been clinging to. But I paid a visit to the bank this morning and, apparently, the day before he left so suddenly, Jay withdrew a large sum of money. He must have gone to the bank, knowing that he was leaving me to run the estate, but he made no provision for me to draw funds.'

'I'm so sorry, Daisy. That does look bad, but I know that Jay loves you, if that's any comfort.'

'You always say the right things, Nick. I wish I could believe you, but I just don't know what to think.'

He released her hand and reached for his glass. 'You'll manage until he returns, and if there's anything I can do to help, you have only to ask. I haven't much money, but if you need a loan . . .'

'No, Nick. That's not the answer, although it's very generous of you to offer. You've helped enormously. I was panicking, but you're right – I can cope, and I will. I'll find a way to keep things going until Jay returns.'

'You're a very competent nurse. I'd employ you willingly, although I couldn't afford to pay you much.'

She smiled and placed her empty glass on the table. 'I think Dove might have something to say about that, Nick.'

'She's a wonderful woman, but I run the cottage hospital and I make all the decisions.'

Daisy pulled a face. 'That should change when you're married.'

'We have an understanding, it's true, but I haven't proposed marriage yet.'

'But you will.'

'Almost certainly, but I need to be very sure that I'm doing the right thing, for both our sakes.'

Daisy rose to her feet, gazing down at the man she had once thought she might marry. Nick had many good points, but she herself could never live with a man who wanted to dominate her so completely, and she felt almost sorry for Jay's sister. Dove was a nice young woman and she deserved a husband who would love her unreservedly and treat her as an equal.

'Thank you for the sherry and for listening to me so patiently, but I must go back to the manor house. I have a lot to think about and some important decisions to make.'

Nick stood up and grasped her hand, giving it a squeeze. 'If there's anything I can do, or if you simply want to talk, you know where to find me.'

When Daisy arrived home she went straight to the drawing room where she found Mary seated by the fire, mending a small garment.

'Well, what happened at the bank? Did they give you enough money to pay the servants?'

Daisy perched on the edge of a chair, clasping her hands tightly in her lap. 'It's not good news. Jay withdrew a large sum of money, but he made no provision for me to draw on the account.'

'The servants have to be paid and the tradesmen won't wait for ever. We can't exist on credit much longer.'

'I know, and then there's the renovations to the Little Creek cottages. They will have to cease for the time being. We will just have to economise and hope that Jay returns very soon.' Daisy tried to sound positive, but for the first time in her life she was at a loss as to what the next step should be.

'You'll think of something, Daisy. You're a bright girl and Jay was fortunate to marry someone like you. I know you'll make the best of things. I just wish I knew what had happened to my son.'

'I'm sure we'd have heard if there had been an accident of any kind, Mary. We just have to trust him and hope he comes home soon.' Daisy tried to sound positive, but with every passing hour her hopes were fading. She rose to her feet. 'I'm going to my room to take off my outdoor things. I'll see you at dinner.'

In the sanctity of the room she had shared so blissfully with her husband, Daisy sat on the dressing-table stool and took off her bonnet. She was a married woman but she owned nothing. Everything was in her husband's name and even if she had money of her own before their marriage, it would now belong to Jay. It was something she had never had to think about before now. It was a sorry state of affairs, and meant that she was unable to raise the money to settle their debts. She knew nothing about the process of bankruptcy, but unless she could work miracles, it was more than a possibility. Then there was the disgrace and scandal – the name of Tattersall, which had been tarnished by the old squire's actions, would be permanently dishonoured.

Suddenly she needed some air and time alone. Daisy hurried from the bedchamber and made her way unnoticed out of the house, using the door of the flower room, which led straight into the garden. The air was fresh and clean after a sudden shower, and sunlight sparkled on the raindrops that were left hanging from the branches of the cherry trees. She walked towards the summerhouse, admiring the daffodils as they nodded their golden trumpets, and the sweet scent of pink and blue hyacinths wafted around her like expensive French perfume. Birds were nesting and it seemed as though the world was beginning anew.

'That's what I must do,' Daisy said out loud. 'I must begin again.' Without thinking she mounted the steps and lifted the trapdoor.

It was dark and musty in the passageway that led to the cove, but Daisy managed to light the candle that was always left at the bottom of the steps together with a tin box containing matches. She made her way carefully at first, and when she saw a glimmer of light she quickened her pace. She felt an urgency and a quiver of excitement in her belly as she burst out into the fresh, salty air.

There, a hundred yards or so from the shore, was a sight that made her cry out with joy. The *Lazy Jane* was bobbing gently at anchor in the cove, and a jolly boat had been beached and apparently abandoned on the shingle.

She cupped her hands round her mouth and shouted. 'Ahoy there.'

When there was no response she called again, but there did not appear to be anyone on board. If Jay had returned he would have come straight home, of that she was certain, and the feeling of elation faded into one of concern. He would not have left the ship unmanned. For a moment she was tempted to row out to the vessel, but climbing the Jacob's ladder in a voluminous silk morning gown would be difficult, not to say impossible. She hesitated, torn between the desire to go on board and the practicalities of such a venture. Besides which, she might have missed Jay. Perhaps he had seen Lewis home, in which case their paths would not have crossed. She turned and made her way back to the tunnel, negotiating it in the dark and feeling her way along the walls. Next time, she would bring a lantern, but if Jay was at home she vowed she would never venture below the ground again.

Daisy searched the house, but there was no sign of Jay. She was tempted to ask the servants if he had been seen, but something held her back. Perhaps it was fear of what she might learn, or maybe she already knew the answer. Jay had not come home. Disappointment and depression threatened to overwhelm her but Daisy had little choice – to give way to despair was unthinkable. She changed out of her best gown and dressed in one of her oldest and plainest skirts and a simple white blouse. Wrapping a shawl around her shoulders she set off to walk to the Johnsons' farm, but a brief chat with one of the workers convinced her that Lewis had not returned, and she retraced her steps. Then she remembered that Jay's first mate, Clem Guppy, lived close by, and she made her way to the cottage where he lived with his mother when he was between voyages.

A small wizened woman in her sixties opened the door just a crack, peering suspiciously at Daisy. 'What d'you want?'

'I'm Mrs Tattersall and I'm looking for your son, Mrs Guppy.'

'He ain't here.'

'Do you know where I can find him? I need to speak to him urgently.'

'I don't know nothing.'

Mrs Guppy was about to shut the door when a voice Daisy recognised called out, 'Let her in, Ma.'

Reluctantly his mother stood aside. 'Don't come here causing trouble, missis. You might be lady of the manor, but I won't have my son put on by the likes of you.'

The door was wrenched unceremoniously from her hand and Guppy lifted his mother bodily aside. 'Good afternoon, Mrs Tattersall. What can I do for you?'

'The *Lazy Jane* is at anchor in the cove,' Daisy said boldly. 'Did you bring her back to Little Creek?'

'She's out to cause trouble, Clem. Send her on her way.' Mrs Guppy glared at Daisy, but Clem brushed her aside.

'Go and put the kettle on, Ma. Where are your manners? That's what you're always saying to me.'

'Cheeky devil!' Mrs Guppy retreated into the house, leaving her son standing in the doorway.

'Are you going to invite me in?' Daisy looked him in the eye. 'I'm not leaving until I have some answers, Clem.'

He stood aside. 'You'd best come in then, but Lewis is here, too.'

'His family are worried about him. He should go home.'

'He will, when the time is right.' Clem ushered her into the room that served as kitchen and living room with a staircase on the far side, leading to the first floor.

Lewis was seated at a table, but he leaped to his feet at the sight of Daisy and his face split into a wide grin.

'It's good to see you again, missis.'

'And you, Lewis.' Daisy sat down in the chair Clem pulled up for her. 'Where's my husband?' She looked from one to the other. 'Come on – you must know. Especially you, Lewis. You were the one who came for him on our wedding day.'

Lewis's fair skin flushed to a deep pink. 'I dunno, ma'am. I truly don't know where the captain is now.'

'Neither of us does,' Clem added hastily.

'So you were in on it, too.' Daisy met his gaze with a stubborn lift of her chin. 'I'm not leaving until you tell me everything you know.'

Mrs Guppy slammed a Brown Betty teapot down on the table. 'Never let it be said that Clara Guppy don't know how to treat a guest. Clem, get them cups and saucers down from the dresser and wipe them on your shirt-tail. The drying cloth got ate by the goat.'

Clem obeyed his mother without a murmur. At any other time Daisy might have smiled to see a big man so obviously under the maternal thumb, but at this moment she was more concerned as to Jay's fate. 'What happened to the captain, Lewis? Please tell me everything you know.'

Lewis shot a wary glance at Clem, who nodded and sat down, folding his arms across his chest.

'Well,' Lewis began tentatively, 'I found out that the Dorning brothers planned to board the *Lazy Jane* on the night of the wedding, when they knew that nearly everyone in the village would be enjoying the celebrations at Creek Manor.'

'But they're in prison. I found that out for myself.'

'Not all of 'em,' Clem said grimly. 'There are four Dornings and the father, and they're all bad lots, every one of them. They blame the captain for the accident that killed Benny Sykes. He was a relation of theirs, and they're a clannish lot. Of course, it wasn't Captain Jay's fault, but you try telling that to the Dornings.'

'But what's happened to my husband?' Daisy repeated anxiously. 'Where is he?'

'We don't rightly know, missis.' Clem filled a cup with strong tea and handed it to her.

'Stop shilly-shallying and tell the woman the truth,' Mrs Guppy said angrily.

Daisy shot her a sideways glance. 'Tell me, please.'

'Clem, do you speak or do I?' Mrs Guppy stood arms akimbo, glaring at her son.

He cleared his throat noisily. 'Well, Mrs Tattersall, ma'am, we managed to get on board, but they'd hired a gang of roughs from Burnham and we was overpowered.'

'They set sail,' Lewis continued eagerly. 'Because they knew if we was put ashore we'd have the law on them.'

Clem nodded. 'And when we was a good way out to sea they put us in a jolly boat and cast us adrift.'

Daisy's hands flew to cover her mouth as she gasped in horror. 'But you're both here. Where is Jay?'

'A storm blew up, missis,' Clem added reluctantly. 'We was caught broadsides by a huge wave and swept overboard. The boat broke in two and the captain was clinging to one half, and me, Lewis and Ramsden to the other. It were pitch-dark and we lost sight of him.'

'But you're here, safe and well,' Daisy said in desperation. 'How did you get ashore?'

'We was picked up by a fishing boat and landed a bit further up the coast. Lewis and I had to walk most of the way until we got a lift in a farm cart.'

'How could you save yourselves and leave my husband to drown?' Daisy leaped to her feet, struggling with the tears that threatened to overwhelm her. 'Where is Ramsden? I want to hear his side of the story.'

'He went home to his missis. But he'll tell you the same as us. There weren't nothing we could do.'

'Why didn't you alert the authorities?' Daisy demanded angrily. 'Why didn't you report this dreadful deed?'

'We got no proof, ma'am,' Guppy said humbly. 'It'd be our word against the Dornings, and they're as slippery as eels.'

'It weren't their fault.' Mrs Guppy put a skinny arm around Daisy's shoulders. 'Sit down and drink your tea, my duck. You'll feel better in a while.'

'The fishermen did what they could,' Clem said gently. 'But the storm was so bad we was lucky to get ashore in one piece.'

'Aye, that's true enough.' Lewis eyed her warily. 'We're real sorry to give you such bad news.'

'Are you saying there's no hope?' Daisy's throat constricted so that she could barely speak above a whisper.

Mrs Guppy frowned at her son and shook her head when Lewis opened his mouth to respond. 'We could tell you that there's always hope,' she said firmly. 'But we'd be setting you up for disappointment later. Best get used to the idea now, if you ask me.'

'But the *Lazy Jane* is at anchor in the creek.' Daisy looked from one to the other, in a mute plea for a glimmer of hope. 'Why would they bring the ship back if they'd stolen it? And why wasn't anyone on board, not even a man on watch?'

Clem shrugged and shook his head. 'I dunno, missis. Maybe they got no use for her right now, or maybe they don't want to get done for piracy and murder.'

A shudder ran down Daisy's spine and she shivered convulsively. 'I – I think I'd better go now.' She headed for the doorway, but Clem was on his feet in an instant and moved quickly to hold it open.

'What shall us do about the ship? You're the gaffer now, I suppose.'

'I suppose I am,' Daisy said dazedly. 'Well, I'm putting you in charge, Guppy. You must go on board and wait until I've decided what to do next.'

'That I'll do. Shall I see you home, missis?'

She shook her head. 'No, thank you. I'll be all right.'

'I'm going your way.' Lewis jumped to his feet and crossed the floor in a couple of strides. 'I got to go anyway. My folks don't know that I'm safe so I need to put their minds at rest.' He proffered his arm. 'I'm sorry about the captain, ma'am. He was a good sort – the best.'

Daisy was too upset to argue and she leaned on Lewis's arm as they walked slowly towards the manor house, parting at the gates of the Johnsons' farm.

'You will be all right, won't you?' Lewis asked anxiously. 'I could walk the rest of the way with you.'

She managed a weak smile. 'I'll be fine, thank you, Lewis. You go home and let your mother and father see that you're safe and well.'

He nodded and went to open the gate. A sheepdog raced towards him, barking hysterically and wagging his tail.

Daisy sighed. She felt cold as ice and numbed with shock, too heartbroken for tears as she put one foot in front of the other, trudging slowly towards Creek Manor. All the hopes and plans they had made for the future had been shattered by what she had just heard. How she would break the news of Jay's tragic end to his mother was something that Daisy could hardly bear to imagine. To put the dreadful news into words meant acknowledging that Jay was gone forever, and that was something she could not, would not believe.

The old manor house loomed closer, looking foreboding now as the clouds gathered, threatening yet another heavy shower. The first drops fell just as Daisy entered the grounds and the warm rain trickled down her face, mingling with her own tears. She could not face the family yet and she took shelter in the summerhouse where, just a few hours ago, she had emerged filled with joy because Jay's ship had returned. Now she knew the truth she would like to see the *Lazy Jane* sink to the bottom of the sea. It would be retribution for making her a widow when she had only recently become a wife. Now she would never bear Jay's children or grow to old age in his company. She held her head in her hands and wept.

Chapter Four

When the storm of crying ceased, Daisy drew a deep breath and wiped her eyes. Giving way to grief would not help Jay, and she refused to believe that he was dead. Surely, after being so close that they seemed to be of one mind she would know if anything terrible had happened to him? She sat for a while, composing her thoughts before venturing into the house to break the news that Jay was missing, which allowed the possibility that he might still be found alive.

She found Mary and Hilda in the morning parlour. Mary turned to her with a hearty sigh. 'Daisy, we've just been going through the store-rooms with Mrs Ralston, and we've only enough provisions to last another week or so. I've already spoken to the head gardener and we've almost gone through the winter store of root vegetables.

It will be some time before the kitchen garden is producing enough to feed us all.'

Hilda gave her a searching look. 'What's the matter, Daisy? You've been crying.'

'I'm afraid I've just had some bad news.'

Mary threw up her hands and collapsed onto the nearest chair. 'I knew it – something terrible has happened to my boy.'

'We don't know exactly,' Daisy said cautiously. 'Clem Guppy told me that the Dornings are related to the poor fellow who died after an accident on the *Lazy Jane* and they've been harbouring a grudge against Jay ever since. Anyway, they boarded the ship and took it out into the North Sea, where they set Jay and his crew adrift in a storm. The jolly boat was wrecked and Guppy, Ramsden and Lewis were picked up by local fishermen, but they don't know what happened to Jay.'

'What are you saying?' Mary demanded angrily. 'If you're trying to tell me that my son is drowned, then say so.'

'They lost contact with him, but it's possible he was rescued by another boat. I won't believe that he's dead. He's alive somewhere, I know he is.'

Mary stared at her, pale-faced but suddenly calm. 'It's my punishment for my past sins. I should never have agreed to marry the old squire. He was a dying man and he didn't know what he was doing. Now my son has been taken from me.'

'The squire might have been dying,' Hilda said

calmly, 'but that man knew exactly what he was about. He's got you trapped here for life, Mary. It was his twisted way of punishing you for making him face his wicked past.'

Mary shook her head and her eyes filled with tears. 'We're finished, Hilda. We can't afford to live here, but we haven't got the money to move elsewhere, and now this. It's all too much.'

'We'll manage somehow.' Daisy went to sit next to Mary on the sofa, and clasped her hands. 'I won't believe that Jay is gone for ever. I know he's out there somewhere and he needs our help.'

'How can we do anything? We can't manage without Jay and we'll soon be homeless.'

'I'm not giving up.' Daisy rose to her feet. 'There must be a way out of this.'

'You could sell the manor house,' Hilda said warily. 'There are the empty cottages that belong to you, too.'

Mary brushed tears from her cheeks. 'I lived in one of those for more than twenty years. I wouldn't house pigs in them as they are.'

'They're uninhabitable at the moment,' Daisy added, frowning. 'We were renovating them, but there's no more money to pay the workmen, so that's out of the question. There must be something I can do – I need to think.'

'I have a terrible headache.' Mary put her hand in her pocket and pulled out a crumpled handkerchief, but as she did so a slip of paper fluttered to the floor. 'I'll go to my room and lie down.' She bent down to retrieve the note and handed it to Daisy. 'This came for you earlier. I'd quite forgotten.'

'I'll get Cook to make a tisane for you,' Hilda said gently as she helped Mary to her feet. 'Do you want me to come with you?'

'I'm quite capable of getting to my room on my own, thank you.' Mary brushed off Hilda's restraining hand and swept out of the room without a backwards glance.

'Grief takes people in different ways,' Daisy said hastily. 'She's just upset, Hilda. Don't take it to heart.'

'I know, dear. I've been through it, too. My poor Stanley didn't deserve to die like that – run over by an omnibus in full view of the passers-by. I still have nightmares about the accident that cost me so dear, and I don't enjoy hopping about with my peg leg like one of them kangaroos they've found in Australia.'

Despite her sadness this made Daisy smile. 'You don't look like a kangaroo, Hilda. No one would guess that you received such a terrible injury. That's one advantage of wearing long skirts.'

'You and I are born to survive, Daisy. But never mind all that – what's in the note?'

Daisy unfolded the sheet of expensive writing paper and studied the contents. 'It's from Mrs Harker, the colonel's wife. She wants me to visit her at Four Winds tomorrow to discuss "a business matter".'

'We nursed her daughters back to health during the cholera outbreak,' Hilda said, thoughtfully. 'Maybe she wants to show her gratitude in some way.'

'There's only one way to find out.'

'They say that she's the one who holds the purse strings,' Hilda said thoughtfully. 'She inherited a huge fortune and the colonel only had his army pay until he married into money.'

'I could certainly do with some money myself – or a small miracle – but I won't be beaten, Hilda. Tomorrow morning I'm going to pay a call on Mrs Harker and find out what she wants.'

The drawing room at Four Winds was large, light and filled with spring sunshine. The chintz-covered chairs and sofas were made even more inviting by the addition of brightly coloured cushions, and bowls of hyacinths filled the air with their sweet scent. Elegant in a lavender silk afternoon gown trimmed with lace, Mrs Harker motioned Daisy to take a seat.

'I heard about your troubles, Daisy. I wanted to tell you how sorry I was to hear of your loss.'

Daisy stared at her, nonplussed. 'But it was only yesterday that I discovered what happened to my husband.'

'I'm sorry, but one of my maids is related to Eli Ramsden. She heard about the shipwreck last evening, and I'm afraid news like that gets round very quickly. You have my sincere condolences.'

'Thank you, but I haven't given up hope, Mrs Harker. I think I'd know if anything terrible had happened to Jay.'

'You were married for such a short time, and I'm afraid we missed your wedding. The girls and I would have loved to attend, but we went to Portsmouth to see my husband off. He's returned for another tour of duty in India.'

Relieved to have a change of subject, Daisy managed a smile. 'How are your daughters, Mrs Harker? I hope they are fully recovered from their bout of cholera last year.'

'They are very well now, thanks to you and Dr Neville, and I've made a point of raising funds to keep the hospital going. Little Creek might be a small village, but it serves quite a large area.'

'Dr Neville is as dedicated as his father was, and now he can carry on the late doctor's work, largely thanks to you.' Daisy eyed her warily. 'I don't wish to sound impertinent, but you said in your note that you had a business matter to discuss.'

'Yes, that is so.' Mrs Harker tugged at an embroidered bell pull. 'Would you prefer tea or coffee, Daisy?'

'Tea would be lovely, thank you, Mrs Harker.' Daisy sat back on the sofa, wondering what was coming next.

'I think we can dispense with formalities, Daisy. You must call me Marjorie, and I want you to think of me as your friend.' She sat down in a chair by the fire, which blazed up the chimney even though it was a mild spring day. The sincerity in Marjorie Harker's voice and the look of sympathy in her grey eyes was almost too much for Daisy, and she had to swallow back tears before she could respond.

'Thank you.'

'I realise you must be in a difficult situation, and if there is anything I can do to help, please say so.' Marjorie looked up at the sound of a tap on the door followed by the appearance of a neatly uniformed maid.

'You rang, ma'am?'

'Yes, we'll have tea and cake, Nora.' Marjorie shot a worried glance in Daisy's direction. 'On second thoughts, bring the brandy decanter, two glasses and some dry biscuits, too. I think we're in need of a little resuscitation.'

Nora curtsied and left the room.

'Are you all right, Daisy? I didn't mean to upset you.'

'I'd be lying if I said that all was well. There is money in the bank, but it's in my husband's name and I can't withdraw even the smallest amount. I can't pay the servants or the tradesmen's bills.'

'I understand, of course.'

'It's mortifying, and frustrating because there's so little I can do to alleviate the situation.'

'Yes, I can see that. In fact I might be able to help you.'

'I wasn't looking for a loan, Mrs Harker. I hope you don't think that.'

'Of course not, Daisy.' Marjorie hesitated at the sound of teacups rattling. 'Enter.'

Nora edged her way into the room, bearing a tea tray, a decanter, two glasses and a plate piled high with small savoury biscuits. 'Thank you, Nora. Put it on the table, please.'

'Shall I pour, ma'am?'

'No, you may go. I'll see to it myself.' Marjorie waited until the door closed. 'I'm sure she's disappointed because they'll be agog with curiosity below stairs.' She reached for the decanter and poured two tots. 'My husband is hoping for promotion, but it's by no means certain.'

'I'm sorry, but I don't see how that affects me.'

'I love Four Winds. It's my home and my daughters grew up here, although they were born in India. But if Roland is to succeed in his ambition I feel that he needs a little help. I have the money and the connections, but Four Winds isn't large enough to entertain in style or to throw the kind of parties I have in mind. I realised that you must be finding it difficult to run the manor house without your husband's financial support and that gave me an idea.'

Daisy accepted a glass of brandy and took a sip to calm her nerves. 'What are you suggesting, Mrs Harker?'

'We'll work it out in a business-like manner, but I would be prepared to rent the Manor House for up to one year, and I would pay handsomely for the privilege, including settling any debts that you have already accrued. Don't look so surprised, my dear. I know very well what it costs to run a large establishment, and I know it sounds vulgar, but money is no object as far as I'm concerned.'

'That sounds very interesting,' Daisy said cautiously.

'There is another reason, Daisy. To put it bluntly, my daughters are unlikely to find husbands in Little Creek.'

'But they must have opportunities to meet young, unattached army officers.'

'My husband is based somewhere on the North-West Frontier, not the sort of place for wives and daughters, and he's likely to be there for another year or more. My girls are in their prime now, but it won't be long before they are on the shelf. I want them to meet young men with ambition and resource – what I don't want are fortune-hunters who will take advantage of their youthful naivety. Do you understand what I'm saying?'

'But are there no eligible army officers?'

'I don't want my girls to become soldiers' wives. It's not the sort of life they ought to endure – I know because I've been married to the colonel since I was sixteen.'

'I'm sorry,' Daisy said, frowning, 'but how would moving to the manor house help? Wouldn't your daughters be moving in similar circles?'

'Not quite.' Marjorie's eyes sparkled with enthusiasm. 'I'll make sure that my guest lists are very comprehensive, and that is why I want the manor house. Just imagine the parties and assemblies we could have there.'

'We?' Daisy eyed her warily. She sensed that there was a sting in the tail of this seemingly heaven-sent offer.

'Yes, of course. I'm not throwing you out on the street, but I would expect you to work for your board and lodging. If there isn't enough room in the servants' quarters, bearing in mind that I'm taking my staff with me, then perhaps there's a dower house or a keeper's cottage that would suit you and your mother-in-law. And there's that rather strange woman who lost her leg, and I believe she has children – of course I couldn't have them living in the house. But I'm sure you've already thought of that, Daisy.'

'What exactly would my position in the household be? Am I to be a servant?'

Marjorie threw back her head and laughed. 'No, of course not. You'll be there more as a paid companion with a few other duties thrown in. I haven't thought that out yet, but you would be like one of the family. What do you say?'

Daisy opened her mouth to refuse. She could see herself being reduced to the status of an underling in her own house – and Mary would be back below stairs, where she had started – but the truth was pressing down on her like a lead weight. She had little choice: she must either accept Marjorie Harker's terms or face bankruptcy.

* * *

Daisy left Four Winds, having shaken hands on an agreement that would free her, at least temporarily, from the burden of running the manor house. She had a generous amount of cash with which to pay immediate bills, and an iron-clad determination to see that the changes went seamlessly. She set off for home, taking a detour to Guppy's cottage. There was another matter that simply could not be ignored: the *Lazy Jane* must be put to good use. Maybe in future Jay's ship would provide her with a decent living.

She found Clem alone in the cottage, his fearsome mother having gone to the village to buy some groceries. Clem ushered her into the kitchen.

'Take a seat, missis.' He pulled up a chair for her. 'What can I do for you?'

'I'm seriously thinking of going into business, Clem. The *Lazy Jane* is mine, to all intents and purposes, and I don't want the Dorning gang to get their hands on her again. Besides which, she's a stout vessel and should be put to good use.'

He stared at her as if she were speaking a foreign language. 'You want to take up free trading, missis?'

'No, I was thinking of a more legitimate business. There must be work out there for a ship that size.'

'Even if I got the crew together we've no captain.'

'I put you in charge yesterday, and now I'm making you captain.'

'I've no experience, missis. I take orders.'

'Then there's no finer way to gain the necessary

69

qualifications, Clem. I'm convinced that you could do it, and I'm putting my trust in you. If I find the cargoes, would you be prepared to take up the challenge?'

'Begging your pardon, but it's a man's trade. I don't know of any women involved.'

'There has to be a first. At one time I was desperate to become a doctor, but I settled for training as a nurse. This is different and I'm not prepared to step back simply because I was born female.' Daisy rose to her feet, leaning her hands on the table as she fixed Clem with a penetrating stare. 'Are you prepared to work with me?'

He grinned sheepishly. 'Don't seem like I have much choice, missis.'

'That's right.' She stifled a sigh of relief. 'I leave it to you to choose your crew and get the ship ready to sail.'

'I'll need money for provisions.'

'Of course.' Daisy took a leather pouch from her reticule and laid it on the table in front of him. 'That should be enough for a start.'

'What cargo will we be shipping, missis?'

'I'll let you know when it's settled.'

Guppy leaped to his feet and saluted. 'Aye, aye, Captain.'

She smiled. 'I'm merely the owner. You're the captain, Guppy.'

Daisy left the tiny cottage, mounted her horse and rode homeward, taking the longest route in the hope of finding an empty cottage on Creek Manor land that was large enough to take herself, Mary, Hilda and the children. There was no dower house, as Marjorie had suggested, and the tied cottages were all occupied, except for one on the edge of the estate.

Daisy dismounted and tethered the horse to a stunted tree. She approached tentatively just in case there were some itinerant workers who had come across the empty dwelling and decided to make it their own. The front door was badly damaged and hanging from one hinge. She peeped inside but the only occupants seemed to be the huge spiders hanging from ornate webs, although, judging by the scuffling behind the skirting boards there were also rodents in residence. The windows were broken and the range was rusty, its grate spilling over with ashes, birds' feathers and bits of moss. The accommodation appeared to be one reasonably large room downstairs, and Daisy had to pluck up courage to take the narrow staircase to find out what she could expect from the bedrooms. She fought her way through a mesh of cobwebs and cockroaches scuttled in all directions at the sound of her approach. The smell they left made her reach for her hanky and she held it to her nose, but once she reached the tiny landing she discovered two bedrooms, each containing an iron bedstead and piles of leaves blown in during the winter storms. The good news was that the roof seemed to be sound; there was no sign of a leak anyway. A quick look out of the window revealed a small back garden complete with a well and an overgrown vegetable bed. A wooden henhouse had seen better days, but could possibly be rebuilt, although there was no sign of a privy.

Daisy made her way downstairs and out into the bright sunshine. She dusted off her riding habit and untied her horse, mounting with the aid of a tree stump, and she set off for home.

She dismounted at the foot of the manor-house steps, and handed the reins to Jack, who had come running from the stables where he had chosen to train under the aegis of Faulkner, the head groom.

'Is it true, Daisy? Is Jay lost at sea?'

She gave him a hug. 'I'm sure I'd know if he was, Jack. The truth is we don't know what happened to him, but Guppy and the others were picked up by another vessel. We can only hope that Jay might have been as lucky.'

Jack wiped his eyes on his sleeve. 'They told me he was drowned.'

'We don't believe that, do we?'

He shook his head. 'No, we don't.'

'That's a good chap. Take Cinders to the stables for me, please. You'll be the first to know if I get any news.'

He nodded and walked off, leading the horse. Daisy stood for a moment, gazing up at the timbered building that had been her home for a few short months, although it felt like much longer. She had grown fond of the old house, with its narrow corridors and beamed ceilings, but Creek Manor was about to enter a new phase in its four-hundred-year history. A new, if temporary, lady of the manor would be greeting her guests and presiding over dinner parties in an attempt to further her husband's career, as well as finding husbands for her two daughters. Daisy suspected that she herself would be expected to carry out a great many more duties than Marjorie Harker had suggested, and her position in the household would be something akin to that when she was governess to the Carringtons' younger son. She would no longer be mistress of the household and that would be hard to take, but she braced her shoulders and mounted the steps to the front door. First of all she had to convince Mary and Hilda to go along with Marjorie Harker's wishes. It was not going to be easy.

Having spent an hour or two using all her powers of persuasion on those closest to her, Daisy was exhausted, and she knew that the hardest was yet to come. Mary had been adamant that they would have to move out of the manor house, which was self-evident, and Hilda had then been riddled with guilt for allowing Daisy to support her and her children after the accident. She talked about the workhouse as if it was the only way out and it took a supreme effort from Daisy to convince Hilda that she needed her support as well as her friendship. In an effort to convince both Hilda and Mary, Daisy took them to look at the cottage, but that only made matters worse. Mary was now talking about moving back into her old cottage in the village, because it was more familiar and in only a slightly worse condition. It was only when Daisy promised to have all the available ground staff working to renovate the little house that Mary and Hilda finally agreed to consider a move.

That night Daisy fell into bed exhausted and slept until dawn.

She awakened next morning ready to face the inevitable. She had been putting off a visit to her aunt and uncle, knowing that they would try to dissuade her from moving out of her home, but it was important to get to them before the gossips had broadcast the news.

Eleanora listened patiently enough, although judging by her prune-like pursed lips and raised eyebrows, Daisy had a feeling that her aunt had already got wind of her change of circumstances.

'Have you been listening to village gossip, Aunt?' Daisy tried not to sound impatient but she realised that she was getting nowhere. The atmosphere in the parlour was tense and Eleanora was clearly not going to be easily mollified.

'It's a sorry day when Mr Keyes in the village shop knows more about one's family than oneself.'

'It all happened very quickly,' Daisy said hastily. 'You don't understand, Aunt.'

Eleanora sniffed and turned away. 'I might have

understood had you deigned to tell me of your decision to move into a derelict cottage. Your uncle is very upset and so am I.'

Daisy reached out to clutch her aunt's hand. 'Listen to me, Auntie. I find myself in a very difficult situation. Jay has disappeared, although I refuse to believe he's dead, but he had made no financial provision for me to manage in such an emergency.'

'You could have come to us, Daisy. Your uncle and I are not wealthy, but we would have helped out.'

'I doubt if you could cover the sum needed to pay the servants' quarterly wages and the bills from the tradesmen for the wedding breakfast. Inheriting somewhere like the manor house comes at a price, Aunt.'

'But surely there must be money in the bank, my dear.'

'Possibly, but I cannot draw on it. The *Lazy Jane* is the only asset over which I have any control, and I'm hoping to go into business, even if it's in a small way at first.'

'And what about Jay? Have you forgotten him already?'

Daisy jumped to her feet. 'That's cruel. Of course I haven't forgotten him, but there's very little I can do, and I have people depending on me. I can't just curl up and die, even if I feel like it sometimes.'

Eleanora's eyes opened wide. 'Don't say things like that, Daisy.'

'I'm just trying to put your mind at rest, Auntie.

The agreement with Mrs Harker is only for a year, and during that time I hope to be able to build up a business with the ship.'

'What will your brother say? He won't approve of you moving into that dreadful cottage.'

'You haven't seen it, Aunt. It's a roof over our heads and there just isn't room for us in the servants' quarters.'

'Servants' quarters?' Eleanora's cheeks reddened and her eyes watered. 'What have you come to, Daisy?'

'It's no worse than being governess to Timothy Carrington. At least I have the respect of the servants and they'll understand that I'm doing this to save the manor house.'

'Well, if you put it like that I suppose I'll have to suffer the disgrace.' Eleanora wiped her eyes and stuffed her lace-trimmed hanky up her sleeve. 'Will you stay for luncheon, Daisy? Hattie will want to see you before you go.'

'I'll stay to eat with you, but then I have other errands to run, so I hope that Uncle Sidney decides to join us.'

'He loves you, dear, but unless you develop fins and a tail I doubt if he'll notice that you're missing.'

After an emotional time spent comforting Hattie, while attempting to impress upon her that leaving the manor house was only a temporary measure and not a total disaster, Daisy was relieved when Linnet returned from shopping in the village. Hattie was clearly put out to discover that Linnet had been told of the coming upheaval by her mother.

'Why am I the last to know about this?'

'Daisy and I are sisters-in-law, Hattie,' Linnet said cheerfully. 'Ma tells us everything.'

Hattie tossed her head. 'At least Creek Cottage is bought and paid for. No one is going to put us out on the street. You'd better be careful, young lady. Don't get ideas above your station just because Daisy married your brother.'

Linnet's pale skin flushed scarlet. 'You know I didn't mean it like that, Hattie.'

Daisy put her arm around Linnet's thin shoulders. 'I'm proud to have you and Dove as my in-laws, and young Jack, too, although we don't see so much of him now that he's working in the stables. He seems happy enough there and Mrs Harker is going to keep all the servants on.'

'Jack always loved animals,' Linnet said, smiling. 'He's a good boy, but he could have gone the other way if you and Mrs Marshall hadn't taken him in hand, Hattie.'

'Oh, well, we do what we have to do.' Hattie puffed out her chest and ladled soup into a tureen. 'Lay up the table in the dining room, if you please, Linnet. Daisy is staying for luncheon.'

'I'll give you a hand, Linnet.' Daisy followed her

to the dining room. 'I'm going to see Nick after luncheon.'

After a rather tense meal with her aunt, who kept reverting to the subject of Daisy being forced out of her home, Daisy was glad to escape and ride the short distance to Creek Hall. She went straight to the kitchen where she hoped she would find Mrs Boynton, Nick's housekeeper, and sure enough she was there, seated at the deal table, drinking a cup of tea. She put the cup down and rose to her feet.

'Mrs Tattersall, this is a lovely surprise.'

'I'm still Daisy to you, Mrs Bee. How are you?'

'I'm fine, dear.' Mrs Bee sank down again, eyeing Daisy warily. 'But how are you? I heard what happened.'

Daisy pulled up a chair and sat opposite her. 'I'm coping as best I can, Mrs Bee, but it's not easy.'

'I know it must be hard, but it's only temporary. You won't be living in the cottage for ever, and of course I was sorry to hear that Jay might have – well, you know what I'm saying, dear.'

Daisy smiled and shrugged. 'All I can do is to hope for the best, and we'll manage somehow. Anyway, is the doctor at home? I was hoping to catch him in between his rounds and surgery.'

'Yes, he is. We've only got two in-patients and he's seeing to their needs.'

'Is Dove here?'

'I used to hope that you and Master Nick would

get together. You seemed so well suited.' Mrs Bee sighed, shaking her head. 'Then those Fox girls came onto the scene and it seems that they can't decide which man they want. I can't keep up with them and their airy-fairy ways.'

'So Dove is staying on here?'

'Well, so it seems. I don't think Master Nick knows quite what's happening, although to be fair I think Dove is far more suited to be a country doctor's wife than her flighty sister.'

'I must speak to Nick.'

'I'm losing patience with them all. We didn't behave like that in my day.'

'I don't know what's got into young people nowadays,' Daisy said, chuckling.

'You may laugh, Daisy, but this will all end in tears – mark my words.'

Leaving Mrs Bee to finish her tea and brood over the failings of the younger generation, Daisy made her way through the familiar passageways of the old house where she had once thought she might become mistress. She went upstairs and met Nick as he left one of the rooms set aside for in-patients.

'Daisy, this is a pleasant surprise.'

'Nick, I have something to tell you.'

Chapter Five

'Are you sure this is the right thing for you?' Nick ushered Daisy into the small bedroom that had been turned into an office. 'You're still in a state of shock after losing your husband.'

'He has a name, Nick. I know you didn't approve of my marriage to Jay, but I love him and I refuse to believe that he's dead.'

Nick pulled up a chair for her and he went to sit behind his desk. 'It's all round the village that the Dorning gang were involved in his disappearance. Don't you think you'd have heard from him by now if he had been rescued?'

'Not necessarily. He might have been picked up by another vessel and taken to a foreign port. I'd know in my heart if anything dreadful had happened to him.'

Nick shook his head. 'But giving up your home for a year isn't going to solve anything.'

'What do you suggest? I can't touch the money in Jay's bank account and I can't run the estate on air. I've got tradesmen dunning me at the gates and the only asset I have is the *Lazy Jane*.'

'But you don't seriously think you can make your fortune as a ship owner, do you? You have no business experience, and no one to help and guide you.'

'By letting out the manor house I can pay off my creditors and keep the staff employed. If I don't take control of the *Lazy Jane* the Dornings will almost certainly use her for their own purposes. I can't afford to pay the crew to idle about doing nothing.'

'Yes, I see that, but do you have to move into that tumbledown cottage? I know the one you mean because the shepherd who once lived there was one of my father's patients.'

'There isn't room for us at the manor house and it would be difficult living there with Marjorie Harker as mistress instead of myself. I've given it a lot of thought and I'm sure this is the only way forward, Nick.'

'It seems that you're set on this, so you obviously don't need any advice from me.'

'I just didn't want you to hear about it second-hand. We're old friends, aren't we?'

'I thought we were more than that.'

'At one time, maybe, but you have someone else close to you now.'

'Yes, I'm very fond of Dove and she's a good nurse – untrained, of course, but I prefer that. I like to do things my way and not be dictated to by a domineering matron.'

'I hope you'll be good to her, Nick. Just remember she's my sister-in-law now. I have a wider family to consider.'

Nick gave her a searching look. 'You're not speaking for yourself, are you?'

'No. Sadly I'm not in the family way. It might have been easier had that been so, and at least I would have had something of Jay's to build my life around. As it is, I have to go on the best I can, and I'd like to think that my friends are with me.'

A reluctant smile creased his lean features. 'You can always rely on me, Daisy. If all else fails I'll take you on as matron here. You're a very good nurse.'

'Thank you,' she said, smiling. 'I might have to take you up on that one day.'

'There's just one thing, Daisy. Does Toby know about this move of yours?'

'He knows that Jay is missing, of course, but I haven't told him that Marjorie is taking over the manor house. I'll write to him tonight, but there's nothing he can do. There's nothing that anyone can do.'

'I wish I had enough money to pay your debts for you.' Nick took her hand in his. 'You know where I am if you need me, Daisy.'

Marjorie Harker and her daughters were due to move in at the end of the following week, leaving Daisy very little time to make the cottage habitable.

She left the packing to Mary and Hilda, and while she was still in charge she put the outdoor servants to work on renovations to the small dwelling that would be her home. The domestics were sent to sweep, scrub and clean every part of the building, and the handyman fixed the damaged woodwork and mended the broken windows. The gardeners were set to dig over the vegetable bed and plant seedlings grown in the greenhouses on the estate, and Mrs Ralston organised a search of the Manor attics to find oddments of furniture and rugs that were no longer required in the main house. Hilda altered discarded curtains to fit the windows and Cook raided the pantry, sorting out jars of jam, jellies and pickles to stock the small pantry.

Daisy wrote to her brother, explaining why she had taken such a drastic course of action, but knowing Toby's lackadaisical attitude to everything other than his profession, she did not expect to receive a reply.

Considering her duty done, she left Hilda to supervise the preparations at the cottage while she rode to Maldon in search of a legitimate cargo for the *Lazy Jane*. Guppy had kept her up to date with his efforts to find a crew and the ship was now ready to sail. Daisy was afraid that if she did not find a cargo quickly, Guppy and Ramsden might take it into their heads to follow their old illegal trade, and that was something she wanted to avoid at all costs.

*   *   *

Having left early in the morning, Daisy arrived in Maldon soon after midday, and the moment she started making enquiries at the various shipping offices she realised that it was not going to be easy to break into a business dominated entirely by men. The reception she received at her first encounter with an agent was one of polite disdain, and she was made to feel so uncomfortable that she left the premises minutes after entering. She received similar treatment from the next one and the next, and walking along the quay proved to be such hostile territory that she was beginning to wish that she had brought Guppy or Ramsden with her. It was a warm day and she was hot and thirsty. She had not eaten since breakfast, and then she had only nibbled a slice of toast. She decided to venture into a respectable-looking inn, but the landlord was not welcoming.

'We don't serve your sort in here.'

Daisy stared at him in dismay. Abel Perkins, the landlord of the local pub in Little Creek, was always polite to the extent of being obsequious, especially since she had become mistress of Creek Manor. 'I just want a glass of cider,' she protested. 'And a pie or anything you have to eat.'

'I don't serve women on their own. It's against the law and you ain't welcome here, missis.'

'This lady is with me.'

Daisy spun round to see who had spoken in such a confident manner. The man met her surprised gaze with a humorous smile.

'I believe you asked for a glass of cider, isn't that so, my dear?'

Daisy nodded mutely, too shocked to argue.

'And my lady requires sustenance, landlord. What have you to offer?'

The man behind the bar smiled and nodded. 'Why, Mr Walters, the lady only had to mention your name and she would have been shown into my private parlour.'

'I dare say, but you haven't answered my question. We are both hungry. What is on the menu?'

'My wife makes a very tasty beef stew, sir. With her freshly baked bread it's a great favourite, followed by her apple pie and cream.'

'Then that's what we'll have, and two glasses of cider. I take it that's acceptable to you, my dear?' His dark eyes twinkled with amusement as he met Daisy's stunned gaze.

'Er, yes, thank you,' she said vaguely.

'Of course, sir. Will you come this way?' The landlord lifted the hatch in the bar counter and led them through the taproom to a private parlour. 'Make yourselves comfortable. Your order will be brought to you.'

The door closed behind him and Daisy turned to face her champion. He was obviously a gentleman, judging by his expensively cut jacket, breeches and riding boots, and his voice was cultured with a hint of merriment, as if he were ready to laugh at any moment. She eyed him warily.

'Who are you?'

'You'll pardon the liberty, Mrs Tattersall, but I saw the way you were treated in the shipping agent's office, and the appalling rudeness of the landlord, so I had to step in.'

'You were in the agent's office?'

'My name is Marius Walters and I am a merchant.'

'A merchant?'

'I trade with foreign countries and I gather from what I overheard that you have a ship for charter.'

'Yes, I do.'

'Then we might be able to do business, but I suggest we eat first, and get to know each other a little better.'

'I'm not sure I ought to be here.' Daisy glanced round anxiously. They were alone in the private parlour, and even though this man seemed genuine, and instantly likeable, she was nervous. 'I know nothing about you, and you don't know me.'

He drew up a chair and held it for her. 'Then shall we start with your name, or must I continue to call you Mrs Tattersall?'

'I'm Daisy Tattersall from Creek Manor.' She paused, frowning. 'Or rather, I own Creek Manor, but I'm living temporarily in a cottage on the estate.'

He pulled up another chair and sat down beside her. 'How fascinating. I assume there must be a good reason for this?'

Daisy hesitated as a young barmaid entered the room bringing their drinks, which she laid on the table. 'Grub's coming in a minute,' she said brusquely as she retreated, leaving the door to close of its own accord.

'Appalling service, but excellent food,' Marius said, smiling. 'I always eat here when I'm in Maldon.'

'So where do you come from?' Daisy raised her glass to her lips and drank thirstily. The cider was refreshing, but on an empty stomach it proved quite potent and she hoped the food would arrive soon.

'Here and there, Daisy. I may call you Daisy?'

'I don't see why not, since we're breaking all the rules.'

'Rules are there to be broken.' He sat back, eyeing her curiously. 'Why did you come all the way to Maldon, on your own, knowing nothing about the shipping industry?'

She felt the blood rush to her cheeks. 'That's my business.'

Marius's smile faded. 'I am sorry. I seem to have upset you quite unintentionally.'

'I'm recently widowed,' Daisy said, looking away. 'It's not easy to talk about it.'

'Again, I apologise for my clumsy remark. Have you no one to handle business matters for you?'

She turned to give him a straight look. 'I'm perfectly capable of managing my own affairs, and quite frankly it has nothing to do with you, Mr Walters. I'm very grateful to you for trying to help, but perhaps I'd better go now. I think this is a mistake.' She was about to rise but he caught her by the sleeve.

'Don't go. It would be a shame to waste the stew, which I'm sure will prove to be delicious.'

The humorous gleam in his dark eyes was hard to resist and brought a reluctant smile to Daisy's lips. 'Well, I am hungry.'

'Then you'll stay?'

'I will.' She sat down again. 'But then I must try to find an agent. I can't allow the ship to lie idle.'

'Let's enjoy our meal,' he said as the door opened and the barmaid staggered in with two large bowls filled with savoury-smelling stew. She left and returned moments later with a basket of hot rolls and a large pat of butter. She took cutlery from the pocket in her apron and laid it on the table.

'Eat up,' she said cheerfully. 'There's folks who would kill for Mrs Tompkins' beef stew.'

Daisy and Marius exchanged amused glances.

'Thank you.' Marius slipped a coin into the girl's outstretched hand and she grinned appreciatively.

'Ta, mister.' She left the parlour, closing the door carefully this time.

The food was delicious and they ate largely in silence, pausing only to make favourable comments. They finished the meal with apple pie smothered with a generous helping of cream, followed by coffee.

'That really was delightful,' Daisy said earnestly. 'But I think you must be extremely interested in the *Lazy Jane*, or you wouldn't have gone to all this trouble for a complete stranger.'

He laughed. 'You're not a stranger now, Daisy. I

know your name and a little about you, but what I do know is that you're a very brave woman. It must have taken a lot of courage to come here on your own, let alone attempting to enter a business about which you obviously know nothing.'

'I have little choice. The ship is the only asset I have at present.'

'I won't press you for more details. I can see that it's difficult for you to talk about your situation, but might I make a suggestion?'

She met his serious gaze with a straight look. 'Please do.'

'Allow someone to help you.'

'By that I assume you mean yourself.'

'Precisely. I'm not making any promises, but I would like to see the *Lazy Jane*, and then I can judge whether or not she's suitable for my purposes.'

'Might I ask what type of goods you trade in?'

'Anything and everything, from coal and iron to corn. I've recently parted company from my shipping agent, and I was thinking about chartering a ship purely for my own use. Your vessel sounds promising.'

'When would you like to see her?'

'I'm free now. Are you planning on returning to Little Creek . . . did you say that's where she's at anchor?'

'I don't think I mentioned it, but yes, she's anchored in one of the creeks. Perhaps we could ride together. I didn't enjoy riding here on my own.'

He chuckled. 'I can imagine the locals' faces when

they saw a young lady travelling without a groom or a chaperone. It was a bold move, Daisy, but not without risks.'

'I thought the days of highwaymen were ended.'

'Maybe, but you would have been in difficulties if you were thrown from your horse. They can be temperamental creatures if something scares them.' He held up his hands in a gesture of surrender. 'All right, Mrs Tattersall, I know you're perfectly capable of handling even the friskiest of animals. Shall we go?'

It was late afternoon when they arrived at the creek where *Lazy Jane* lay peacefully at anchor.

'She's a fine vessel,' Marius said with a nod of approval. 'Just the right size for what I have in mind.'

Daisy glanced at the jolly boat, which had been hauled up onto the shingle so that it was above the high-water mark. 'There'll be someone on watch, but I'd have to contact Guppy to take you out to her.'

'Guppy?'

'Clem Guppy was Jay's first mate. I made him captain because he's a good man and he's reliable.'

'This looks like the ideal spot to land illicit cargoes.'

Daisy shot him a speculative glance. 'You're not a revenue officer in disguise, are you?'

'Would it matter if I were?'

The sparkle in his eyes gave him away and she

breathed a sigh of relief. 'Not now, but it might have done in the past. The old squire was involved in such dealings, but I want nothing to do with anything illegal.'

'Very wise, Daisy. My business depends on trading honestly and fairly. I'd be stupid to risk my reputation for a short-term gain, but I would like to see over the ship. Perhaps you could get your man to arrange it for tomorrow.'

'Yes, I'll call at Guppy's cottage on my way home, but what will you do? Will you return to Maldon now?'

'No, I think my horse deserves a rest. Does Little Creek boast an inn where I might stay the night?'

'It does, but I'm still mistress of the manor house until Friday. After what you did for me today the least I can do is to offer you accommodation and a meal. We can call in on Guppy on the way home.'

'That sounds perfect, if you're sure I'm not putting you out.'

'I wouldn't offer if I didn't mean it, and tomorrow you can take a good look at the *Lazy Jane,* and speak to Guppy. He'll tell you anything you want to know.' She wheeled her horse round and set off at a canter without waiting to see if Marius was following, but she knew without looking back that he was close behind. She had been in his company for a few hours only, but she felt as though she had known him all her life. After the maelstrom of emotions and traumas of the past weeks it was good to have someone she felt she could trust. She might be an independent woman, but if Marius were to charter her ship it would ease the burden of worry and raise some much-needed cash.

Guppy was at home and so, unfortunately, was his mother. Mrs Guppy was stirring a pot on the range, looking even more like the wicked witch from storybooks than before. Her grey hair hung in wispy strands around her face and when she closed her mouth, which was not often, her toothless gums met together, bringing her chin so close to her nose that she resembled Mr Punch.

'I dunno what you want by turning up at mealtimes,' she grumbled, continuing to stir the noxious-smelling mixture. 'My Clem don't get this sort of food on board ship. He's a boy what needs his mother's cooking, and regular mealtimes, which he don't get because you keep turning up uninvited, missis.'

'Ma, that's no way to speak to Mrs Tattersall,' Clem said mildly. 'She's the boss now that the captain's not around.' He sent an apologetic look in Daisy's direction.

'I'm sorry to interrupt your meal, Mrs Guppy.' Daisy managed to keep a straight face although Clem's mother referring to him as a boy had made her want to laugh. 'We won't take up more than a minute or two of your time.'

Guppy rose from his seat at the table. 'Where's

your manners, Ma? Ask the missis if she wants a cup of tea.'

'Ask her yourself. I'm busy. I got no time for toffs.' Mrs Guppy turned her back on Daisy and Marius, and continued to beat the contents of the saucepan to a pulp.

'I just came to introduce you to Mr Walters, who is interested in chartering the *Lazy Jane*. I said you would take him out to her tomorrow, Clem.'

Marius held out his hand. 'How do you do, Guppy?'

'How do, sir?' Guppy wiped his fingers on his trousers before shaking hands. 'What time would suit you?'

'Shall we say nine o'clock? I have to travel on afterwards and I have business in Colchester.'

'Where shall I meet you, sir?'

'Come to the manor house, Clem,' Daisy said hurriedly. 'Mr Walters is my guest tonight, since it's too far for him to ride home. I'll come with you.'

'You will?' Marius stared at her, eyebrows raised. 'Are you familiar with the vessel, Mrs Tattersall?'

'I travelled from London to Little Creek in her not so long ago, although it was not by choice.'

'You're all fine talk now,' Mrs Guppy said in a low voice. 'But we all knows you were in service afore you come here, and then you was wiping people's unmentionables in Dr Neville's house.'

'That's enough of that, Ma.' Guppy ushered Daisy and Marius outside into the fresh air. 'You'll have to excuse the old girl. She don't mean half of what she says.'

'That's quite all right, Clem.' Daisy laid her hand on his arm. 'We won't take up any more of your time. We'll see you tomorrow morning at nine o'clock.'

'Yes'm.' Clem stepped back into the cottage and closed the door.

Marius held Daisy's horse while she mounted. 'Are you sure it will be all right for me to stay at the manor house? I don't want to inconvenience you.'

Daisy smiled down at him. 'I am still the lady of the manor, despite what Mrs Guppy says.'

Marius mounted up. 'I look forward to a long talk after dinner. You've had a very interesting past, according to that lady.'

'And I want to know more about you, sir. You might be a felon, for all I know.'

'Would that be an end to our business dealings, ma'am?'

'Not necessarily. My husband had served time in prison before I met him, and he's the most honest man I've ever known.' She encouraged her horse to a brisk trot, leaving Marius to follow in her wake.

Mary was obviously impressed with Marius, who kissed her hand and gave her a smile that brought roses to her normally pale cheeks. But Hilda and Mrs Ralston stood back, lips pursed and brows furrowed as they looked him up and down. Daisy could see that they were sizing him up and suspicious of his motives, but she was happy to go ahead with a business deal regardless of what secrets were locked away in his past. All her instincts told her that she could put her trust in him to do his best for her and the *Lazy Jane*. Her brief attempt to enter the world of commerce had ended in humiliation, but with a little help from Marius she would prove them all wrong. The name of Tattersall would be well known again, only this time it would be for the right reasons.

'Mrs Ralston will see that a room is made ready for you, Mr Walters,' Mary said eagerly. 'And Hilda will inform Cook that there is one more for dinner.'

'You're lucky that Jack went rabbiting last evening.' Hilda folded her arms, glaring at Marius beneath a lowered brow. 'It's stew, unless that's not good enough for a gentleman like yourself.'

'Hilda!' Daisy frowned at her, shaking her head.

'I'm particularly partial to rabbit stew,' Marius said, smiling affably. 'Please don't go to any trouble on my behalf, I'm very grateful for a comfortable bed for the night and a home-cooked meal. I travel a great deal and it's nice to be in such a delightful home.'

Mrs Ralston managed a hint of a smile, but Hilda tossed her head and marched off in the direction of the kitchen.

'I'll give you a hand, Ida.' Mary and Mrs Ralston hurried after Hilda.

'It seems that I have a lot to prove,' Marius said with a wry smile. 'Your servants are quite right to be protective, but I assure you that my intentions are honourable.'

Daisy ushered him into the drawing room. 'I'm sure they are, Marius. Would you like a glass of sherry? Or would you prefer something stronger?'

'Sherry would be fine, thank you.'

Daisy tugged on the bell pull and waited, but no one came. She tried to make idle conversation, but she was secretly annoyed by both Hilda and Mrs Ralston: their attitude left a lot to be desired and Daisy's nerves were on edge anyway. This business deal was too important to be vetoed by servants who knew nothing about such matters. She rang again and when the summons went unanswered she made an excuse and left the room.

Hilda was in the kitchen and she was chattering away to Cook but she stopped the moment she saw Daisy. 'Is anything wrong, Daisy?'

'You know very well what you're doing, Hilda, and I won't have it. I've been ringing the bell and no one came, but worse than that, you were rude to my guest and that's unforgivable.'

Hilda pouted ominously. 'You only just met him today. You shouldn't put your trust in a man like that – he's too smooth talking, and he smiles a lot.'

'He's just being pleasant, and you can't make snap judgements about someone just because he smiles too much. Mr Walters helped me out of a very difficult and embarrassing situation today. He's a merchant, and if he charters the *Lazy Jane* we'll all benefit, and perhaps I won't have to rent out the manor house in the future.'

'You always speak first and think afterwards, Hilda,' Cook said severely. 'You want to watch your tongue.'

'You was interested enough while I was telling you about our guest. We might all be murdered in our sleep with a strange man in the house.'

Cook's eyebrows shot up to disappear under the frill of her mobcap. 'Don't say things like that. I'll have to put a chair under the doorknob tonight.'

'You're both being silly.' Daisy threw up her hands. 'Hilda, I want you to keep your opinion to yourself, and I want sherry and two glasses in the drawing room. Send the tweeny if you can't bring yourself to be civil to my guest.'

Daisy swept out of the kitchen and hurried back to the drawing room. Soon she would be reduced to the status of a servant in her own household, but tonight she was still Mrs Tattersall of Creek Manor, and tomorrow she hoped to make a trade agreement with Marius Walters that would secure the future of the *Lazy Jane*, the ship that Jay had loved with all his heart. Keeping the vessel safe and using her to make money that might provide enough income to keep the estate from bankruptcy had become the most important thing in her life. If Marius could provide the business she was prepared to overlook almost any transgression he might have made in the past. She took a deep breath, painted a smile on her lips and entered the drawing room. This would go well, she told herself, despite the surliness of the servants.

Next morning, at nine o'clock, Clem rowed Daisy and Marius out to the ship. Daisy had dressed for the occasion and had left off the steel crinoline cage that she normally wore beneath her petticoats. She was wearing a simple linsey-woolsey skirt, a cotton blouse and a light shawl, and her only nod to fashion was her straw bonnet trimmed with a single silk rose. She managed to climb the Jacob's ladder without any help from Clem, although Marius held out his hand to assist her when she boarded ship. It was an unconscious action and done without making her feel awkward or embarrassed, for which Daisy was extremely grateful. Her liking for Marius Walters had increased greatly, but this was a commercial venture, and personal feelings must be put aside. She left Clem to show him around the ship.

They met up again in the saloon where Ramsden had provided coffee.

'Well?' Daisy said casually. 'What do you think, Marius? Are we in business?'

Chapter Six

The *Lazy Jane* had been chartered by Marius Walters for a respectable sum, which would be enough to pay the crew and purchase provisions, and Daisy was to have a share in the profits. They toasted their new partnership in coffee on board the ship, and Marius promised to have his solicitor draw up the contract and send it to Daisy for her approval and signature. They walked back to the manor house, chatting like old friends, and Daisy sent James to the stables with a request for Marius's horse to be brought to the front entrance. As she stood in the warm spring sunshine Daisy felt that everything was beginning anew. The horrors of the past few weeks were behind them, although not forgotten, and she felt a sense of hope for the first time since she discovered the parlous state of their finances. One day, she was certain, Jay would come home, until then it was up to her to keep the estate from ruin and look after the people who depended upon her.

Minutes later Jack brought Marius's horse from the stables. 'He's a fine animal, sir.'

'This is Jack Fox,' Daisy said hastily in case Marius thought it unacceptable for a stable boy to speak up. 'He's my husband's younger brother.'

'You're very knowledgeable, Jack,' Marius said, smiling.

'I'll have a horse like this one day.' Jack held the animal while Marius mounted and then handed him the reins.

'I'm sure you will. Thanks for looking after him.'

Daisy slipped her arm around Jack's shoulders. 'Goodbye, Marius.'

'I prefer *au revoir*. We'll meet again soon, Daisy.' Marius urged his horse to a walk and then a sedate trot.

'Are you still happy working in the stables, Jack?' Daisy asked anxiously. 'You're a bright boy. I think you could do better.'

'I like it well enough, but I wish Jay would come home.'

'We all do, Jack.' Daisy ruffled his hair and watched him walk away with a swagger in his step. There were times when he reminded her of Jay, and this was one of them. She entered the house, coming to a sudden halt when she saw the floor piled high with boxes, trunks and tea chests. She turned to Molesworth for an explanation.

'Mrs Harker sent this luggage on in advance, ma'am. I was in two minds as to whether or not to accept it, but as she'll be arriving tomorrow there didn't seem much point in sending it back.'

Daisy gazed around in horror. 'It looks as though she's moving in for good, not just a year.'

'That's what I thought, ma'am. But it's not my place to say so.'

'Perhaps this is all she intends to bring from Four Winds.'

'One would hope so, ma'am.'

'Where is Mrs Ralston? I must speak to her.'

'I believe you'll find her in her parlour, ma'am.'

'Thank you, Molesworth.' Daisy crossed the entrance hall and headed for the back stairs.

She found Mrs Ralston seated at her desk, poring over an open accounts book, but she stood up when she saw Daisy, and her expression was grim.

'What's the matter, Mrs Ralston?'

'I don't know if I can continue here with that person acting as mistress.'

'Why? What's happened to upset you?' Daisy pulled up a chair and sat down.

'I had a visit from Mrs Jones, the housekeeper from Four Winds. She insists that she's going to be in charge while her mistress lives here, and she demanded to see my accounts for the past year. She made me feel as if I was cooking the books, as they say.'

'But that wasn't in our agreement, Mrs Ralston. I know that some of Mrs Harker's servants were to remain at Four Winds. I would have thought she'd leave her housekeeper in charge.'

'I'm not working under that woman, ma'am. There isn't room for two of us in this office, which I might point out has been mine for twenty years.'

'Of course not, and I won't allow anyone to oust you from your position.' Daisy rose to her feet. 'And I shall tell Mrs Harker so.'

Marjorie Harker, looking elegant as always, received Daisy in the drawing room at Four Winds. She regarded Daisy with a cold stare. 'If I am to be mistress of Creek Manor for a while, I do not expect to have my decisions questioned.'

Taken aback by the sudden change in Marjorie's attitude, Daisy took a deep breath, controlling her emotions with difficulty. 'But, it was my understanding that Mrs Jones would remain here to look after your home while you were staying at the manor.'

'That was my original intention, but on second thoughts I knew that I would need well-trained servants, given the scale of the entertaining I'm planning. Therefore I will put everything under holland covers and lock this house up until I decide to return.'

'Are you saying that you might wish to occupy my home for a longer period of time?'

'That depends, but you are already in the process of moving out, Daisy. It won't be your home after today, although I expect you to be on hand to see that everything runs smoothly.'

'I'm not sure I understand.'

'I know you were just a governess at the Carringtons' mansion in Queen Square, but you will have observed how things are done in that type of household, and I want you to advise and oversee matters so that nothing goes awry. There will be no remuneration for your work, but you will be living rent free on my land, and you'll have meals provided. I think it will be a mutually beneficial arrangement.'

It was on the tip of Daisy's tongue to inform Mrs Harker that she, Daisy Tattersall, had just entered a business agreement with Marius Walters, and expected to be financially independent quite soon, but the steely-eyed woman who sat opposite her was not the smiling, sweet-natured person that Daisy had first met. Marjorie Harker had suddenly changed into a calculating harpy, who would not be gainsaid, and Daisy began to pity the colonel. Maybe it was preferable to be posted on the North-West Frontier than to be a pawn in the game played by his wealthy, scheming wife.

'Well, thank you for your candour, Mrs Harker.'

'Everyone needs to know their place, don't you agree?' Marjorie said with an icy smile.

Daisy rose to her feet. 'I really must leave now. I have a lot to do.'

'See yourself out, Daisy. My servants are busy packing the last of my best china. All my silverware is counted and if anything goes missing I will hold you personally responsible.'

Daisy turned on her heel and left the room. If she stayed she knew she would say something that she would regret. Marjorie Harker was taking responsibility for the estate's outstanding debts as well as the servants' and groundsmen's wages. To put this in jeopardy would be foolish. She marched out of the house and made her way to the stables where a groom had taken her horse. A brisk ride would calm her down, but she would be very careful how she handled Marjorie Harker in future.

Daisy, Mary, Hilda and the children moved into the cottage on the estate early next morning, well before Marjorie and her daughters were due to arrive. It had been decided that Daisy and Mary would share the smaller bedroom, leaving the larger one for Hilda and her four children. It was not an ideal solution, but Hilda was philosophical.

'It's better than the rooms we rented in Whitechapel,' she said stoutly. 'And the nippers think it's fun, so I don't mind. At least we're together and we're not starving. What more can we want?' She carried a pile of bedding into her room. 'Come and help me, Judy, love. Molly can keep an eye on the little 'uns.'

Judy bounded up the stairs. 'I was hoping I could stay on and help Cook, but she says there won't be room for me in the kitchen, what with them stuck-up servants coming from Four Winds and all.'

'We don't know what the servants are like,' Daisy said firmly. 'We will have to learn to live together, but it's only for a year at most. It will soon pass.'

Mary came puffing up the narrow staircase and joined Daisy in the room they were to share. 'I'll make up the bed.' She placed the linen on the chest of drawers and selected a sheet. 'I can't help thinking that Jay would have a laugh if he could see us making up a bed for you and me, Daisy.'

Daisy tried to smile, but she was close to tears and she turned away. 'He laughed at everything,' she murmured. 'I miss him so much, Mary.'

'I know you do, dear.' Mary shook out a sheet and laid it on the uncomfortable-looking mattress, which was all they could find that was not going to be in use by the new occupants of Creek Manor. 'I regret every minute I didn't spend with my son. I should have stood up to Lemuel, but he had a fierce temper and a hard fist.'

'You did your best and I'm sure Jay knew that.' Daisy wiped her eyes on the back of her hand. 'What did Dove and Linnet say about you having to move out of the manor house?'

'They were horrified, of course, but there's nothing any of us can do, so we just have to get on with it. But I pity you having to go there every day and watch another woman take charge of your home.'

'It's only for a year.' Daisy repeated the words like a mantra.

'They're coming,' Judy called out excitedly. 'I can

see their carriage from the bedroom window, and there's a cart following them piled high with luggage and three or four horses being ridden by servants. It looks like the circus when it came to Little Creek.'

A circus it was. Daisy hurried back to the manor house in time to welcome the new occupants, arriving breathless after she had raced up the hill.

Mrs Jones marched in first and came face to face with Mrs Ralston.

'The servants' entrance is round the back of the building,' Mrs Ralston said icily.

'You don't have to tell me how to conduct myself, Ida Ralston. I was housekeeper at Four Winds when you were still a chambermaid here at the manor house. I'm in charge now and I'll thank you to remember it.'

'Don't get on your high horse with me, Mrs Jones. I could tell a tale or two about your past, if I was so minded.'

Daisy stepped in between them. 'That's quite enough, ladies. This isn't an ideal situation, but we have to make it work somehow.'

'I think you'll find that my mistress has something to say about that,' Mrs Jones said haughtily. 'I take my instructions from Mrs Harker.'

'Then I'll have a word with her when she arrives.'

'She's here now.' Mrs Jones jerked her head in the direction of the front entrance. 'We'll soon see who's in charge.' She marched across the hall to greet her mistress as she stepped over the threshold, and they exchanged a few words.

Daisy strained her ears in an attempt to overhear what they were saying, but she could tell by Mrs Harker's expression that she was not best pleased. Daisy sensed trouble brewing and she decided to take control of the situation before it became out of hand. She advanced on them, forcing her lips into a smile.

'Good morning, Mrs Harker. Welcome to Creek Manor.'

Marjorie looked her up and down with a supercilious frown. 'Not a good start, Daisy. I expect my servants to be treated with respect, and Mrs Jones will be in complete control of the household from now until we leave. Is that understood?'

'Yes,' Daisy said calmly. 'But that goes for my servants, too. If I find they are being bullied or mistreated in any way I will find them alternative accommodation. You need them, Mrs Harker. If you are to entertain in the grand manner you will need all the help you can get.' Daisy faced Marjorie Harker, not giving an inch, and it was Marjorie who looked away first.

'Get on with your work,' Marjorie said, turning to the servants, who were gaping at them wide-eyed.

Everyone scurried off in different directions, except Mrs Ralston and Mrs Jones, who continued to face each other like gladiators.

'I have a suggestion,' Daisy said firmly.

Marjorie beckoned to her daughters. 'Come in, girls. Don't loiter in the doorway. This is our new home.' She turned to Daisy, frowning. 'What is it?'

'As you said, this will be a large and busy household. Might I suggest that we divide the housekeeping between Mrs Ralston and Mrs Jones?'

'In what way?' Marjorie did not look convinced. 'Patience, stop scowling,' she added, pointing at her younger daughter, who looked as though she were about to cry.

'Mrs Ralston understands the working of the house below stairs. She knows the best suppliers of food and wine, and she is more than familiar with the way the kitchen operates. Don't forget that the old squire used to entertain royally at one time.'

Marjorie nodded reluctantly. 'Yes, I do remember that, although we were never invited.'

'On the other hand,' Daisy continued with growing confidence, 'I'm sure that Mrs Jones would be excellent at handling matters above stairs, including the housekeeping accounts, which would be very important to you. What do you say?'

'Do other large establishments work in this way?' Marjorie asked warily.

'Oh, yes, they most certainly do.' Daisy spoke with certainty, although she had no idea whether or not it was true, but it seemed to convince Marjorie.

'Then that's how it will be.' Marjorie waved her housekeeper away before spinning round and catching Patience a clout. 'Will you stop moaning? You're driving me mad. How will I ever find a husband for you if you carry on like a spoilt child?'

Daisy felt instantly sorry for Patience, who clutched the side of her face and genuine tears rolled down her pale cheeks. 'If you young ladies would like to follow me, I'll show you to your rooms.'

'I'd rather be at home,' Charity said crossly. 'This old house is probably haunted.'

'Don't say that,' Patience moaned. 'Now I shan't sleep a wink.'

Daisy chose to ignore them and she marched off in the direction of the staircase. If they chose not to follow her that was their problem, not hers. She ascended without looking round but she could hear the patter of their feet on the treads and she knew she had won this particular skirmish. They were spoilt and could be petulant, but she had nursed them through cholera during the epidemic and she knew their faults and also their redeeming features, although at this moment she did not like either of them very much.

Marjorie was to have the room that Daisy had shared with Jay, and sanctioning that had hurt more than Daisy could have imagined, but it was the largest bedchamber with a wonderful view of the grounds, and glimpses of the creek as it threaded its way between the trees like a molten silver ribbon. Charity, being the elder, had been allocated Mary's former room, but this brought another petulant outburst from Patience when she discovered that she had been given a much smaller bedchamber, with a view partially obscured by the shrubbery at the side of the house. Daisy stood in the doorway while the sisters argued.

'It's not fair,' Patience grumbled. 'I always have to have the smaller bedroom. Just because Charity is older than me it doesn't mean I am second best.'

'Shut up, Patty.' Charity glanced round the room. 'It's not too bad, and you only sleep here.'

'But you have a better view and a bigger clothes press. It's always the same wherever we are.'

Charity gave her sister a push towards the four-poster bed. 'Have a lie-down and sulk. I'm tired of listening to your constant moaning.'

'I hate you, Charity Harker.' Patience flopped down on the bed. 'At least I've got a feather mattress. I hope yours is filled with hay.'

'Don't take any notice of my baby sister, Daisy.' Charity tossed her head and stalked out onto the landing, pushing Daisy aside as she slammed the door. 'This whole move is madness, if you ask me.' She flounced back to her own room. 'I'm not going to be treated like a something in a cattle market for Mama to sell off to the highest bidder. When I marry it will be for love, and not for a title or a large estate.'

Daisy left Patience to get over her tantrum. She could hear her sobbing even through the closed door, but just now Charity seemed to be the one who needed comforting. Daisy followed her back to the larger bedchamber. 'Is there anything I can do for you, Charity?'

'You married for love, didn't you? Mama said your husband was a criminal, but you married him all the same.'

'Yes, Jay and I were very much in love, but your mama is wrong about one thing. My husband did get into trouble with the law when he was very young, but it was for a minor offence and he served his time in prison.'

'But you loved him anyway?'

'Yes, and I love him still.'

'But Mama said he was lost at sea.'

'I don't know what's happened to him, but I would feel it in my heart if he were dead.'

Charity's pale eyes filled with tears and she clasped her hands to her bosom. 'How truly romantic. If only I could find someone like that.'

'You will one day, I'm certain. In the meantime would you like me to send your maid to you? I expect you want to unpack.'

'I suppose so. It looks as if we've got to stay here, but I'd rather die an old maid than marry a man I didn't love.'

'I'll go and find your maid.' Daisy beat a hasty retreat. The Harker family had only been in the house for an hour or so and already her nerves were stretched to breaking point. Perhaps bankruptcy would have been easier to bear than the torment these women seemed intent on putting her through.

Somehow Daisy managed to struggle through the first morning without losing her temper, although at times she was tempted to tell Marjorie Harker a few home truths and walk out, but she knew that this would be futile. Marjorie had the upper hand and she obviously revelled in her new-found power, but the peak of Daisy's humiliation and frustration occurred when the family assembled in the dining hall for their midday meal. Daisy was about to take her place at table when Marjorie shook her head.

'No, Daisy. That won't do.'

'I beg your pardon?' Daisy stared at her nonplussed. She had been careful not to take her rightful position at the head of the table.

'You're forgetting your place. You will take your meals in the morning parlour, alone, while I am mistress of Creek Manor.'

Daisy rose to her feet. 'I am not employed by you, Mrs Harker. You don't pay me a wage.'

'Perhaps you would rather live with your aunt and uncle?' Marjorie said sweetly. 'But in that case I would have to evict your mother-in-law and your lame friend with all her brats. It's not my fault you find yourself in this position, so either abide by my rules or leave now.'

'What does it matter where she takes her meals, Mama?' Charity demanded.

'We'll have some very important guests arriving next week. We will act as if we were to the manor born, and that doesn't include dining with underlings.'

Charity looked as though she was about to start an argument, but Daisy held up her hand. 'You've made yourself perfectly clear, Mrs Harker.' She left the table and could only be thankful that none of the servants had been present to witness her embarrassment. Outside in the oak-panelled corridor, she stopped and took a deep breath. Whatever happened she would save Creek Manor for Jay when he returned and safeguard his legacy, but for now she must do whatever was necessary to survive. She made her way to the kitchen and entered to stony silence. Cook and the Creek Manor servants were ranged on one side of the long deal table, and Marjorie's cook and her underlings were on the opposite side. The atmosphere was as tense as Daisy imagined it must have been on the battlefield at Waterloo before the fighting commenced.

'What's going on?' Daisy demanded, forgetting her chagrin in the need to save the situation below stairs. There were sharp knives laid out on the table and by the look on the kitchen staff's faces they might at any moment seize a weapon.

When no one answered Daisy walked up to Cook. 'Mrs Harker and her daughters are waiting for their luncheon, Mrs Pearce.'

'Begging your pardon, ma'am, but them lot won't co-operate. They say that Mrs Harker wants things done her way.'

Daisy glanced across the table. Marjorie Harker's cook was tall and thin with a face like a dried-up prune. 'It's Mrs Salt, isn't it? You are Mrs Harker's head cook.'

'Yes, ma'am.' Phoebe Salt's hooded eyes narrowed to slits. 'Mrs Harker is very particular about the way her food is served. I've had nothing but criticism from Mrs Pearce, and your servants have gone out of their way to be difficult.'

Daisy could tell by the attitude of Cook and her staff that there was some truth in this and she stifled a sigh. There was no sign of Mrs Ralston, who should have been overseeing the workings of the kitchen, but Daisy suspected she might be locked in mortal combat with Mrs Jones. Daisy had a sudden vision of the two housekeepers wrestling for control of the huge iron ring containing the keys to the manor house and cellars.

'I realise this is a difficult situation,' she said in measured tones. 'It's not easy for any of us, and I'm sure you will understand my position. I am here to advise and assist Mrs Harker, so I can only suggest that Mrs Pearce and Mrs Salt take turns in running the kitchen. Mrs Salt knows her mistress's preferences, but Mrs Pearce is well versed in organising the kitchen and the various larders, the laundry and the still room. Do you think you can work like that?'

The opposing sides glanced at each other, whispering and nodding, although some shook their heads.

'It doesn't seem as if we have much choice, ma'am,' Mrs Pearce said reluctantly. 'I'll work with Mrs Salt if she'll promise to do similar.'

Mrs Salt shrugged. 'I agree, but only if everyone abides by the rules.'

'Then I suggest you get back to work and serve luncheon to Mrs Harker and the young ladies.'

Cook put her head on one side, giving Daisy a searching look. 'What about you, ma'am?'

'I'll have my meals on a tray in the morning parlour, Mrs Pearce.' Daisy could feel the ripple of whispers as she left the kitchen. Servants seemed to have a sixth sense when it came to discord above stairs, and now the rightful mistress of Creek Manor had been ousted so that she was neither a servant nor a member of the family. Daisy found herself in a similar position to that of a governess, suspended in limbo between above and below stairs. She made her way to the morning parlour and waited for someone to bring her meal.

After a solitary luncheon Daisy found herself with nothing to do. She could not imagine what her duties might include for the rest of the day, but in the middle of the afternoon she was summoned to Marjorie's presence in the drawing room.

'I realise that this is new to you, Daisy,' Marjorie said with a patronising smile, 'and so I've written a list of the tasks I wish you to perform each and every day, although that doesn't include the time when my guests arrive. I expect you to oversee the smooth running of the household, as well as attention to detail for the comfort of my important visitors.' She handed a sheet of expensive writing paper to Daisy. 'Study it at your leisure but I want you to begin right away, teaching my girls the social graces they will need when we entertain eminent guests.'

Daisy glanced down the list, shaking her head. 'I was only a governess at the Carrington mansion, Mrs Harker. They were a wealthy family, similar I imagine to your own, but they didn't mix with high society.'

'But you were once engaged to the son and heir, whom I believe went into the diplomatic service. That is the sort of husband I want for my girls, and mixing with such people will surely improve my husband's chances of promotion.'

Daisy felt almost sorry for the woman, who was trying so desperately to catch rich and influential husbands for her daughters, neither of whom appeared to be an eager bride. But perhaps her pity should be reserved for Charity and Patience, whose lives were being ruled by the actions of a domineering mother and neglectful father.

'I will study this, Mrs Harker, and because we have an agreement I will do my best for the girls, but I can't promise anything.'

'You could at least help them to look more fashionable. If Charity had her way she would spend her time reading foolish romances, and Patience would be out all day riding her horse. I want you to make them into attractive young ladies, who know how to make polite conversation without scowling or bursting into tears. And I want my dinner parties to be the talk of the county. I want my reputation as a hostess to reach the attention of society hostesses in London.'

'I can only do my best,' Daisy said slowly. 'But looking at this list, it doesn't seem as though I have any time to myself.'

'What would you wish to do? You have no husband, and no children. You are living in a cramped cottage with two other women and four children. I would have thought you might enjoy your time free from money worries.'

'Surely I will have Sunday free so that I may visit my relations as well as attending church?'

'You will be busy here, although you may attend church with us, and I'm sure your aunt and uncle will understand. Now please leave me. I have a headache coming on. You may start now with a lesson in deportment for my girls. I've noticed that you hold yourself very well. You can make them walk round with books balanced on their heads, or a backboard strapped to their shoulders. Patience stoops and that must be cured. Do you understand what I'm saying?'

'Yes, Mrs Harker.'

'Just remember at all times that you are a servant at Creek Manor. You take your orders from me. If you play your part we will get on well – if not . . .'

Chapter Seven

Daisy was kept busy from early morning until late at night. Despite the lengthening hours of daylight she often had to pick her way across the fields to the cottage in total darkness, and sometimes in pouring rain, but Marjorie was relentless in her desire to have everything ready for the important guests who were due to arrive the following week. When she was not supervising the girls in their attempts to improve their chances of catching the eye of an eligible bachelor, Daisy was given the tasks usually performed by a lady's maid. Miss Wendell took care of Marjorie and until now had looked after Charity and Patience, but she had been overwhelmed by the increased demands on her services and had taken to her bed with a sick headache, leaving Daisy no choice other than to take over her duties.

At the end of each long and trying day, with the constant friction between the warring servants and the argumentative sisters, Daisy was quite glad to be on her own in the laundry room, washing fine lace or ironing the girls' best gowns. She might have been at a loss as to how to handle a flat iron, had it not been for Hattie, who had taught her the art of heating the iron on the range and gauging the temperature by spitting on it, or holding it close to her cheek. When just a child, Daisy had wondered how Hattie had done so without burning herself, but in time she had acquired the skill, and she was fast becoming an expert. It was back-aching work, but it was quiet in the laundry room and a relief to be away from complaining voices. She had developed a fellow feeling with the servants, and she vowed that when the time came for her to take back responsibility for the household she would become a better employer and a more considerate mistress, although this was beginning to feel like an impossible dream.

On Sunday Daisy attended church with the family, although she did not sit in the same pew. Afterwards, when she stepped outside, she was able to have a brief conversation with her aunt and uncle. Eleanora was upset and angry to find her niece being treated like a menial, but Sidney managed to calm her down and dissuaded her from confronting Marjorie Harker.

'It's a business arrangement, my dear,' he said mildly. 'Daisy has agreed to it and if that's what it takes to save her home, then she was right to do so.'

'But she's being treated like a skivvy. Daisy was brought up to be a young lady, and we paid good money to have her educated. I thought she would do better for herself.'

Daisy exchanged wry smiles with her uncle. 'I'm quite all right, Aunt Eleanora. A little hard work never hurt anyone, and it's not for ever.'

'I blame that man you married. He was always unreliable and a rover.'

'Aunt! How can you say such things?'

'Yes, my dear. That's a bit strong, considering the poor fellow is . . .' Sidney glanced anxiously at Daisy. 'He's missing and may not return. I'm sorry, Daisy, but you'll have to face facts one day.'

'Until I know for certain I refuse to believe that Jay is dead.' Daisy turned to acknowledge Marjorie, who was calling her with a note of impatience in her voice. 'I have to go, but I'll try to come and see you when I get some free time.'

'It's slavery, that's what it is,' Eleanora said grimly. 'That woman is taking advantage of you, Daisy.' She looked round and waved to Nick, who had just emerged from the porch. 'Dr Neville will back me up on that, I'm sure.'

Nick approached them, smiling. 'What will I agree to, Mrs Marshall?'

'Daisy is being treated like a slavey. That woman is using her and she'll ruin Daisy's health. You must tell her so, Doctor.'

'I'm perfectly well,' Daisy said stoutly. 'And I

have to go now, or else I'll have to walk back to Creek Manor. You'll excuse me, Nick.' She hurried off without giving him a chance to respond, but her uncle's remark had touched a nerve and she knew that was what everyone was thinking. Everyone, that is, except herself – she was convinced that Jay would return one day. She could only hope it would be soon. She quickened her pace. 'I'm coming, Mrs Harker.'

The first guests were due to arrive and the servants were up extra early, as was Daisy. She had been put in charge of arrangements including the choice of the rooms for each individual, although as yet she had not been allowed to see the guest list. All she knew was that there were three single gentlemen and two married couples, all of whom were in government service of some sort. Marjorie had not thought it important to share any more details and Daisy had been too busy to enquire. She liaised with Mrs Jones in the preparation of menus, and she had acted as go-between with Mrs Ralston when it came to placing orders with the various tradesmen, excluding the wine merchant, which was a task she left to Molesworth. She suspected that his years of serving Squire Tattersall had given him plenty of experience in choosing fine wines, and she had no doubt that he helped himself to a bottle or two from the cellar.

There was a feeling of nervous anticipation in the house, and Daisy had the unenviable task of helping

Charity to dress first, and to put her hair up in the most becoming style. There were the usual arguments over which gown was the most suitable; Charity wanted to wear an afternoon gown with a fetchingly low décolletage, which Daisy said was unsuitable. Charity threatened to take the choice to her mother, but Marjorie was in the middle of her own toilette and not to be disturbed. In the end Charity settled for a compromise and agreed to wear a pale-blue silk taffeta gown lavishly trimmed with lace. It was not what Daisy would have recommended, as the neckline was still far too daring for a morning gown, but Marjorie's elder daughter was used to having her own way.

When Charity was reasonably satisfied with her appearance Daisy had to repeat the process all over again with Patience, who decided from the start that she wanted to put on her riding habit.

'I am not part of this,' she said sulkily. 'I don't want to be married, so there's no point in dressing me up like a doll.'

'Then you'd better tell your mama.' Daisy threw up her hands. 'I don't care if you find a husband or not, I'm just following instructions.'

'I'll tell Mama what you said.' Patience slumped down on her bed, pouting.

'In this instance I think she'll agree with me,' Daisy said calmly. 'Wear your riding habit if you like, but you're the one who'll have to deal with a very angry mother.'

Charity put her head round the door. 'Oh, for goodness' sake, put on a proper dress, Patty. You can go riding later, but do this for Mama.'

'Oh, all right.' Patience slid off the bed. 'I'll do it, but I won't be nice to the fat old bores that Mama has invited to stay.'

An hour later the family were lined up in the entrance hall waiting for the first guests to enter. Molesworth was poised ready to do the honours and James and Mrs Harker's footman, George, stood on either side of the front door. There had been an altercation between the two men, which had almost come to blows. George insisted that he was the head footman, a position jealously guarded by James, and Daisy had had to intervene before one of them bloodied the other's nose. There might be a reluctant truce, but the pair glared at each other across the marble-tiled floor.

Daisy herself was stationed behind Marjorie, although for preference she would rather have been below stairs, but her attendance had been an order and Daisy knew better than to question the colonel's wife.

'Mr and Mrs Harold Woodward,' Molesworth announced in a sombre tone.

Marjorie stepped forward. 'Welcome to Creek Manor. I hope you had a pleasant journey?'

'Tolerable, thank you.' Mr Woodward bowed over Marjorie's hand. 'My wife and I are delighted to be here, Mrs Harker.'

Mrs Woodward smiled and grasped her husband's arm as if for protection in a strange environment. 'How kind of you to invite us to your quaint home, Mrs Harker.'

Daisy was bristling at the insult to Creek Manor, and then she recognised Letitia Woodward. The overdressed, overfed woman might be putting on airs and graces, but she was a distant cousin of Agnes Carrington, from the poorer branch of the family. Mrs Carrington had let it slip on one occasion that Letty had married well, considering her father was only a butcher, and everyone assembled had laughed.

'And these charming young ladies must be your daughters, Mrs Harker.' Harold Woodward's eyes strayed from Charity's face to the swell of her firm young breasts.

'This is my daughter, Charity,' Marjorie said hastily. 'And my younger daughter, Patience.'

He gave Charity a vague smile and his gaze wandered to Daisy, who was doing her best to melt into the background. 'And who is the charming lady hovering just behind you, ma'am?'

There was no avoiding them now and she stepped forward. 'Good morning, Mr Woodward. I'm Daisy Tattersall, Mrs Harker's private secretary.' She promoted herself, but it was easier to give herself a title that they might understand.

Letitia Woodward eyed her curiously. 'Have we met before, Miss Tattersall?'

'Not formally, ma'am. I was governess to Master Timothy Carrington. You might have seen me when you visited your cousin in Queen Square.' Daisy had the satisfaction of seeing the smile fade from Letitia's face. It would not be so easy for Mrs Woodward to patronise her hostess, knowing that Daisy was aware of her humble beginnings.

'Thank you, Daisy,' Marjorie said icily. 'You may show Mr and Mrs Woodward to their room.'

Daisy bit back a sharp retort. Showing guests to their rooms would not normally have been done by someone in Daisy's position, but she realised that it was Marjorie's way of putting her in her place for introducing herself to the Woodwards, and now she was going to pay for her boldness.

'Will you come this way?' Daisy led them across the entrance hall to the wide staircase and she did not look back, although she could feel Marjorie's gaze following her. Daisy held her head high and continued to ascend the stairs with Mr and Mrs Woodward close on her heels.

Having settled them in the butterfly bedroom, so called because of the wallpaper hand-painted with butterflies and flowers, Daisy had no choice other than to return to the entrance hall. She could hear carriage wheels crunching on the gravel and the sound of footsteps, but as she rounded the curve in the staircase she came to a sudden halt. Three men had entered, one after the other, and the last of them was none other than her former fiancé, Julian

Carrington. If she had seen the guest list she would have had time to prepare herself, but their last encounter had ended in acrimony on both sides. He was as handsome as ever and although not much above medium height he carried himself well, with an air of confidence that he seemed to have developed during his time in the diplomatic service. His companions were older, one of them verging on middle-age and the other possibly in his thirties. Daisy clutched the banister rail for support. She was tempted to retreat to her room, but she could hardly remain there for the duration of Julian's stay. There was no alternative but to continue down the stairs and put a brave face on an embarrassing situation.

Julian looked up and their eyes met, but he showed no sign of recognition and that made it easier for Daisy. She took her position behind Marjorie and assumed the cloak of invisibility that was an essential for a well-trained servant. She did not look up when Marjorie introduced Mr Woodward's entourage to her daughters. The names of the two other men escaped her but the sound of Julian's voice brought back memories of a difficult time in her life. Their engagement had been secret and unofficial, although Julian had bought her a very pretty diamond ring, which she had kept hidden from view and even that had caused seemingly endless complications. They were to have announced their betrothal at Christmas, but the memory of the letter ending their relationship was still etched on Daisy's heart.

Julian's behaviour subsequently had left much to be desired, and now she would have to pretend that nothing had happened. It was awkward, but the situation was unavoidable and she would cope with it in one way or another.

It was a relief when Marjorie instructed James to show the three gentlemen to their respective rooms. Julian had still not acknowledged Daisy, but if that was the way he wished to continue it was perfectly all right. When it came to the midday meal, Marjorie's refusal to allow Daisy to eat with the family had turned out to be a boon, and Daisy was happy to take a tray to the deserted morning parlour. She carried out her duties for the rest of the day and managed to avoid him.

The last of Daisy's chores was to help both girls to get ready for bed, although she could not think why they still needed someone to act like a nanny. Patience was exhausted and Daisy tucked her up in bed with a certain degree of sympathy, but then Patience was only sixteen, and young for her age. She was still a child at heart and more interested in horses than she was in prospective suitors. If Daisy had had her way she would not have been involved in Marjorie's almost frantic search for suitable husbands for her daughters. All Daisy could do was to treat Patience with as much kindness and under-standing as she could muster, with the occasional lecture on manners and a sharp rebuke when Patience overstepped the mark, which happened all too often. Daisy smiled to herself as she closed the bedroom door: she had swapped her position as governess to a young boy to tend to the needs of an over-indulged and even more demanding young lady.

Satisfied that she had done all she could for the younger daughter, Daisy went to Charity's room, and found her seated at the dressing table, gazing dreamily into the mirror.

'Would you like me to brush your hair, Charity?'

'I don't mind you calling me Charity when we're alone, but I hope you'll remember to say "Miss Charity" when we're in company.' Charity met Daisy's gaze in the mirror with a stubborn set to her jaw. 'You aren't the lady of the manor now.'

'I think I know that,' Daisy said drily. 'And I suppose you mean you want me to be subservient especially when a certain gentleman is present?'

'I don't know what you're talking about.' Charity's cheek flushed scarlet and she looked away. 'Please take the pins out of my hair. They're sticking into my scalp.'

'Of course.' Daisy proceeded to take down the elaborate coiffure and brushed out the tangles. 'What did you think of your mother's choice in suitors?'

Charity looked up, frowning. 'I will pick the man I am going to marry.'

'So you didn't think much of any of them?'

'Mr Flanders is much too old. I don't care if he has a senior position in the Foreign Office and lots of money.'

'Then what about Mr Jenkins? He's a good few years your senior, but he's quite good-looking.'

'Don't be ridiculous. I'm eighteen, Daisy. He's twice my age.'

'Then that leaves Mr Carrington.'

Charity's colour deepened. 'He's very good-looking, and quite charming. I think I like him but I hardly know him.'

Daisy kept her thoughts to herself and changed the subject. She finished her task of preparing Charity for bed, said good night and left the room. It was late and she still had to walk the mile or so to the cottage with only the moonlight to guide her across the rough pastureland on the far side of the deer park. She took her cloak from a peg in the servants' quarters and let herself out through the back door, but as she rounded the building she caught a whiff of cigar smoke and she realised that she was not alone. It was obviously one of the guests enjoying a cigar after a long evening of dining, drinking and playing cards, and she hoped that she could escape into the shadows unseen. She pulled the hood of her cloak over her head and stepped out, tiptoeing across the stony terrace, but the sound of footsteps behind her made her stop and turn round to face him.

'Daisy, I need to talk to you.'

She knew that voice only too well. 'What do you want, Julian?'

'That's not a very nice way to greet the man you once promised to marry.'

'You might think it's all a joke, but I don't. The last time we met you demanded the return of the ring you gave me, and then I had a visit from your mother accusing me of stealing your property.'

He dropped the butt of his cigar on the gravel and ground it in with the heel of his shoe. 'Oh, that! Well, you know what Mama is like. She's very protective of her family.'

Daisy turned away. 'I'm tired and I'm going home.'

He fell into step beside her. 'Why aren't you living in the house? If you're Mrs Harker's private secretary, why are you tramping across the countryside late at night?'

'It's none of your business. Now please go away.'

He caught her left hand in his. 'You're wearing a wedding ring and you introduced yourself as Daisy Tattersall. Where is your husband? Or was it all a fabrication?'

Daisy wrenched her hand free from his grasp. 'Leave me alone, Julian. If you don't I'll tell Mrs Harker exactly what sort of man you are, and you won't stand a chance with either of her daughters.'

'What are you talking about?'

'That's why you're here, isn't it? You need to marry a wealthy woman, and Charity Harker will inherit a tidy sum from her mother, plus, I should imagine, a generous dowry.'

'Really?' He stared at her in the light of the flambeaux that were situated along the front of the house.

'You didn't know?'

'I did not.'

'Then why are you here, Julian? I wouldn't have thought a stay in the country would appeal to you.'

'I could say the same for you, Daisy.'

'This is getting us nowhere and I'm exhausted. I'll say good night.' She was about to sidestep him when he barred her way.

'Will you allow me to walk you home?'

'Why would you want to do that? We've nothing to say to each other, and you're a guest in this house.'

'So what are you doing here, Daisy? You still haven't answered my question. Are you married?'

'I am married, and for your information my husband is the lord of the manor, but circumstances have temporarily reduced me to acting as Mrs Harker's servant. Does that satisfy you?' She walked away without waiting for his response, but Julian fell into step beside her.

'No, it doesn't. Where is your husband now, and why is he allowing you to suffer such humiliation?'

'I can see that you won't give me any peace until you know. Jay is missing at sea, but he'll come home one day soon, of that I'm certain. Are you satisfied?'

He dropped back and allowed her to continue on her way, although she sensed that he was watching her until she was swallowed up by the darkness. Clouds obscured the moon, and she could hear movement beneath the trees, and even though she knew it would be the deer or other animals, it was still frightening to someone born and bred in the city.

It was with a feeling of intense relief that she opened the gate in the picket fence and walked up the path to the cottage. The homely aroma of baking bread, and the inevitable smell of furniture polish that seemed to follow Hilda wherever she went was a reminder that Mary and Hilda had done their best to make their new surroundings comfortable. They were cramped when it came to sleeping arrangements, but Daisy was so tired that she knew she would sleep well, despite her mother-in-law's loud snores.

She was up early next morning and relieved to see the sun shining from an azure sky. The walk to the manor house was pleasant enough and the air was fresh and sweet. Life here would have been wonderful if Jay had not answered the urgent summons to his ship on their wedding day. In her mind's eye Daisy could envisage the *Lazy Jane*, bobbing gently on the incoming tide as she lay at anchor in the creek, like a courtesan awaiting the arrival of her lover. She wondered if Marius Walters had done a deal that would prove profitable to her as well as to himself. She wished that she had a way of keeping in touch with him, purely in the interests of business, but it would be a relief to have some good news, and with it the hope that they would be self-sufficient sooner rather than later. She was tempted to make a detour to Guppy's cottage to find out what was happening to the ship, but that would make her late, and if Guppy was not at home she would have to deal with the fearsome Mrs Guppy. Perhaps she could find time to walk to the creek and see for herself, or maybe she could accompany Patience on a morning ride and just happen to guide her in that direction. It would provide an excuse for absenting herself from the house for an hour or two, and Marjorie Harker was unlikely to put a stop to anything that would make either of her daughters happy.

But when Daisy reached the house she went first to the kitchen, where she walked into a battleground. Mrs Pearce was bristling with anger and her subordinates were clustered around her, while Phoebe Salt paced the floor wringing her hands.

'What's the matter now, Mrs Pearce?' Daisy made an effort to sound calm, but she could see from the expressions on the faces of the two cooks that this was going to be difficult to resolve.

'It's my turn to do all the meals today,' Mrs Pearce said with a break in her voice. 'But she says I'm only doing breakfasts for the guests and she's going to make a special luncheon for them.'

'Mrs Harker is mistress of Creek Manor now,' Mrs Salt snapped angrily. 'She requested her favourite dish and that's what she'll get. We must all compromise, Mrs Pearce.'

'Compromise?' Mrs Pearce's eyes bulged as if

133

they were about to pop out of her head. 'It's a compromise when you want your own way, but it's a different kettle of fish when it comes to what I want.'

'The mistress asked me to make a special luncheon for the gentlemen. I'm used to cooking high-class meals for gentlemen.'

'I don't doubt it,' Mrs Pearce snarled. 'No decent woman would be seen dead in one of them places.'

'How dare you? I've never been so insulted in all my life.'

'Oh, come now, Phoebe. That's hard to believe.'

'Did you hear what she just said, Mrs Tattersall?' Mrs Salt's lips quivered ominously. 'I'm going to tell, madam.'

'Tell-tale tit,' Mrs Pearce said childishly. 'You know the rest, Phoebe Salt – your tongue will be split, and I've got a sharp knife so don't tempt me.'

'That's done it. When I tell my mistress that you've threatened me with violence you'll be sacked on the spot.' Mrs Salt headed for the door but Daisy forestalled her.

'Now, now, ladies. This really isn't the way to behave.' Daisy glanced over her shoulder at the kitchen maids, who were watching and hanging on every word. 'I won't have threats of violence in my kitchen, and Mrs Salt, this still is my kitchen. I am the owner of Creek Manor and the house is rented to Mrs Harker for a temporary period. She wanted to bring her own servants, but that means you all have to get along. I won't allow my staff to be bullied.'

Mrs Salt tossed her head. 'We'll see about that. I'm going to speak to madam now.'

'No, you will not,' Daisy said firmly. 'You are the under-cook today, and tomorrow you will be head cook. Is that understood?'

'It will be reported to madam,' Mrs Salt muttered as she made her way back to the table.

'Do what you like,' Mrs Pearce said crossly, but then she caught Daisy's eye and she managed a weak smile. 'If you assist me today, Phoebe, I'll do the same for you tomorrow. I can't say fairer than that.'

'Huh!' Mrs Salt picked up a sharp-looking knife and attacked a side of bacon. 'If my mistress complains it will be you who'll get into trouble.'

Daisy took the opportunity to slip away unnoticed as the preparations for the meal recommenced, with Mrs Pearce issuing instructions and the kitchen maids scurrying about in their efforts to please her. Daisy had intended to go upstairs to supervise the setting of the table in the dining hall, but she had a sudden desire for fresh air after the fierce battle of wills between the cooks. She let herself out through the scullery door and headed for the garden, where the spring flowers were fading but the crab apple trees were in full bloom and purple wisteria clambered over a rustic pergola. Daisy walked slowly between the rose beds where the buds were just beginning to open, but as she approached the summerhouse she came to a sudden halt when the trapdoor opened and a man emerged from the dark depths. She held her breath, her lips moving soundlessly as she tried to say his name . . .

Chapter Eight

'Dash it all, you gave me a fright, Daisy. I wasn't expecting to see anyone this early in the morning.'

'I gave you a fright! I thought you were . . .' Daisy's voice trailed off and she took a deep breath. For a heart-stopping moment she had thought Jay had returned, and she struggled to control her emotions. 'Why are you here, Marius?'

'I'm sorry if I startled you, but I went to the creek to give Guppy the good news.'

'Good news?'

'I've a large cargo waiting in a warehouse on the docks at Maldon, and the *Lazy Jane* will sail on the tide. I came to tell you, but I can see I've chosen a bad time.'

'No, it's not a bad time. I just thought when I saw the trapdoor open that it was someone else.

You must come into the house and have some refreshment before you go.'

'You thought it might be your husband. I'm sorry, Daisy.'

'I live in hope,' she said simply.

'I'll be staying at the Blue Boar in Maldon until the cargo is loaded, and as this is the first time I've chartered the *Lazy Jane* I've decided to sail with them.'

Daisy eyed him curiously. 'Don't you trust Guppy?'

'I do, but I'm protecting my investment, and yours, too.' He met her gaze with a frown. 'You look pale, Daisy. Is all this proving too much for you? I mean, it can't be easy living as a virtual servant in your own home.'

'Thank you, but I'm managing quite well.'

'That doesn't sound very convincing.'

'It is hard, Marius. I don't mind admitting it, and there's a further complication.'

'A complication?'

'I was engaged once, at least unofficially, but my fiancé broke it off at the last minute.'

'Don't tell me that he's one of Mrs Harker's house guests?'

'Yes. It's just a coincidence but it makes my position even more difficult.'

'Is there anything I can do?'

She managed a smile. 'No, nothing more than you're doing now. My family were sceptical when I told them that we had gone into business together, but I knew it would work out well.'

He grasped her hand and for once there was a serious look in his dark eyes. 'I am your friend, Daisy. You don't deserve the indignity of being a servant in your own home, or having to deal with a man who treated you so badly. He must be a bounder as well as a fool.'

'It's all in the past, as far as I'm concerned.'

'But he doesn't agree with you?'

'I'm not sure, but one thing I've learned is that Julian is a fortune-hunter, and at the moment I imagine he's torn between wanting to get his hands on Creek Manor or courting Charity Harker, who will inherit a fortune when she comes of age.'

'A nice fellow, but at least you see him for what he is. I wish I could do more for you, Daisy.'

'It's not for ever. I keep telling myself that, but everything depends on whether I can make enough money from the *Lazy Jane* to remain in Creek Manor, or if I will have to sell up. I'm putting my trust in you, Marius.'

'I won't let you down. My business ventures have gone well so far, and with a fast vessel like *Lazy Jane* we should make good speed and an excellent profit. But I must go now. I left my horse tethered on the edge of the foreshore, and it's a long ride to Maldon.' Marius reached out to clasp Daisy's hand again. 'I'll call on you as soon as we put ashore on the return journey, although I imagine we'll be gone for a week or so.'

She withdrew her hand swiftly. It was disconcerting

and tantalising to feel the warmth and strength of a man's fingers curled around her own. His nearness resurrected some of the feelings that Jay had aroused in her, and it was not comfortable. She took a step backwards. 'Thank you for keeping me up to date, Marius. I hope all goes well.'

'And I hope your situation here improves, Daisy. I really wish I could do more for you.' He turned away reluctantly and climbed the steps to the summerhouse.

The last she saw of him was a cheery wave as he lifted the trap door and descended into the darkness. She felt a sudden sense of loss – it was like saying goodbye to an old friend, even though they were barely acquainted. She was walking back towards the house when she heard someone calling her name and she stopped and turned her head to see Julian hurrying towards her.

'Is anything wrong,' she asked anxiously.

'No, not as far as I know. I saw you from my window and I fancied an early morning stroll.'

She met his gaze with a straight look. 'What is this all about, Julian? Why are you bothering to single me out? You know that I'm a married woman.'

His pained expression seemed genuine enough, but Daisy knew that he was used to putting on an act for his mother, and there was no reason to assume that he was behaving any differently now.

'Oh, Daisy. Must we be at loggerheads all the time? We were close once.'

'You were the one who broke off our engagement.'

'You don't have to remind me of my youthful foolishness.'

'It was a little over year ago, Julian. I doubt if you've changed very much since then.'

'But I have, Daisy. A year working as an underling in Paris has made me think long and hard about what I want out of life.'

'I'm not very interested in your soul-searching. I have work to do.' She was about to walk away when he caught her by the wrist. She stared down at his elegantly manicured hand, which was as soft and white as that of any lady. 'Let me go. I have things to do.'

'I hate to see you like this, my dear.'

'I was a servant in your parents' home. This is nothing new.'

'But you've risen in society since then, Daisy. You own this estate and you're a widow. You need someone to protect you from fortune-hunters.'

'Isn't that exactly what you are? I didn't believe you last night when you said that your reason for being here had nothing to do with Charity Harker, and the fortune she will inherit from her maternal grandfather.'

'And it was true. I've never stopped loving you, Daisy.'

She put her head on one side, eyeing him speculatively. 'If you think there's a fortune here, think again. The only reason I have allowed Mrs Harker

to rent this property is because I am virtually bank-
rupt. I can't prove that my husband is dead, and I
don't believe for one minute that it's true, but I can
neither sell the property nor touch any monies that
are in his bank account.'

Julian's mouth dropped open. 'But once you have
proof of his sad demise you'll be a wealthy woman,
Daisy. Let me help you through this difficult time.'

'Thank you, Julian,' Daisy said, subduing the
desire to laugh in his face. 'But I really can manage
on my own. Now, if you'll excuse me, I'll go indoors
and make sure that the footmen aren't fighting a
duel and that the cooks have managed to make
breakfast without drawing blood.'

She walked off without giving him a chance to
argue, but she had a feeling that this time Julian
would not give up easily: there was too much at
stake, for him at least. Although he came from a
moneyed family she knew that he favoured an
extravagant lifestyle, and judging by the expensive
cut of his clothes he would not be satisfied with
second best. He had once told her that he had
developed a passion for the gaming tables while
he was at university, and it was possible that what
had started out as an amusing way to spend an
evening might have become an addiction. But it
was none of her business and, as far as Daisy was
concerned, her relationship with Julian was well
and truly over.

She entered the house through the scullery and

crept past the kitchen door, but the only sounds were those of hurrying footsteps, the clatter of pots and pans and the occasional comment from Mrs Pearce. There was no sign of Mrs Salt, and Daisy had a fleeting vision of Marjorie's cook locked in the linen cupboard by her rivals, but as she passed the housekeeper's parlour she could hear Mrs Salt's aggrieved tones and Mrs Ralston's measured answers, with Mrs Jones chipping in the odd remark. It did not bode well, but Daisy decided not to meddle in below-stairs politics until it was absolutely necessary.

She sighed and hurried on. Her next task was to help Charity get ready to make an entrance at breakfast, and to convince Patience that it would be bad manners to bolt her food and rush off to the stables without making an effort to be civil to her mother's guests.

Finally, when everyone was settled in the dining room, Daisy managed to snatch a quick bite of food and a cup of tea before Mrs Ralston burst into the morning parlour brandishing a sheet of paper.

'Mrs Harker's instructions for a soirée, to be held in a week's time. Did you know about this, ma'am?'

Daisy put her cup down and took the list. A quick glance was enough to make her shake her head. 'Impossible. We need more time to organise something like this.'

Mrs Ralston stood arms akimbo. 'Indeed we do, Mrs Tattersall. This is ridiculous. For one thing, Mr

Keyes won't have half of those items in his shop. We would need to go to Maldon or even further afield to find such luxuries, and who will pay, I'd like to know?'

'Mrs Harker is footing the bill for everything, but I need to speak to her about this. Leave it with me, Mrs Ralston.'

'Perhaps you could put that Mrs Salt in her place, too, ma'am? She's driving me mad with her airs and graces and her references to the military dinners and the high standard they achieve, even in the middle of the battlefield – although I don't believe that for one second. And that stuck-up Dorcas Jones sides with her against me. It's more than a body can stand.'

'I'll have a word with both of them, Mrs Ralston.'

'Thank you, ma'am.' Mrs Ralston sniffed and tossed her head as she stalked out of the room.

It was mid-morning by the time Daisy had a chance for a few words with Marjorie, who was showing the Woodwards round the great hall, recounting the history of the manor house with obvious enthusiasm, although neither Charity nor Patience seemed to share her feelings. Letitia Woodward was looking mildly interested, but she kept gazing out of the window as if she wished she were anywhere but here.

'And the portraits are my husband's ancestors,' Marjorie continued blithely. 'As you can see he comes from a long line of illustrious people who served their country in varying ways.'

Daisy knew that this was untrue, and that the late Squire Tattersall had purchased the paintings at auction sales in order to convince the villagers of his own pedigree, which was probably no more prestigious than that of Colonel Roland Harker. But it was time to put a stop to Marjorie's fairy tales. 'Excuse me, Mrs Harker.'

'What is it, Tattersall?' Marjorie demanded, rolling her eyes and casting a meaningful look in the Woodwards' direction.

'I need to speak to you urgently about a pressing matter, Mrs Harker.'

'Oh, really? I pay you to handle day-to-day matters, Tattersall. Can't it wait?'

'I'm afraid not, ma'am.'

'I'll be back with you in a minute, Letitia,' Marjorie said with an air of martyrdom. 'You'll have to be quick, Tattersall, because our next guests are due to arrive at any moment.' She followed Daisy into the morning parlour. 'This is very bad timing on your part.'

'Not to put too fine a point on it, Mrs Harker: As I've said before, I am not your servant – you don't pay me a salary. I am here as part of the arrangement we made, and if your new friends knew the truth I doubt if they would be impressed.'

'Are you threatening me, Tattersall?'

'I'm stating a fact, Marjorie. We are equals socially,

or perhaps I am more equal than you, as I'm lady of the manor, but I've allowed you to take on the privileges it brings.'

'For your own benefit, you insolent bitch. I could tell our guests that your husband, the so-called lord of the manor, was a criminal and he served a sentence in prison.'

'This isn't about me or my husband. This is about you and your daughters and your husband's promotion. I assume that the next guests to arrive will be something high up in the military.'

'That is none of your business.'

'Maybe, but this is.' Daisy held up the list. 'What you want is impossible. It would take over a week to prepare these dishes, and most of the ingredients are not available locally. You need to send out invitations . . .'

'Of course I thought of that before I moved into this crumbling pile of bricks and mortar. I invited all the top people in this part of the county. There will only be twenty couples and I expect you to see that the evening runs smoothly, otherwise our agreement is off. You can threaten me, but you have more to lose. I have the money, and I haven't paid off your debts as yet, nor will I unless you co-operate fully. Do you understand?'

'It can't be done.'

'You will ensure that it is,' Marjorie said firmly. 'There will be music and dancing, with good food and fine wine. If not I'll leave here and you will have to find the money to pay your debts, and the servants' wages.' She was about to march off, but Daisy was not going to allow her to get away so easily and she barred her way.

'You agreed to settle them.'

'And I will, but only if you keep your part of the bargain.' Marjorie glanced over her shoulder at the sound of footsteps and George approached them.

'Excuse me, madam, but the guests' carriage has just drawn up outside.'

'Then go and stand by the door, you stupid fellow.' Marjorie shooed him away. 'Come with me, Tattersall. I want you to show the major-general and his wife to the chinoiserie room.'

Daisy hurried after her. 'If you mean the Chinese room, why not say so?'

Marjorie paused for a moment, turning her head to give Daisy a scornful glance. 'It's the fashion in London. Don't you know anything, you country bumpkin?'

'I know that you were lying to the Woodwards,' Daisy said in a low voice. 'And they're watching us now, so if you want to keep them believing that this is your ancestral home perhaps you'd better treat me with a little more respect.'

'Don't get hoity-toity with me, madam. I still have the upper hand and a written contract to rent the manor house for a year, so I can still throw you and your friends out onto the street.' Marjorie stalked off to greet the major-general and his wife, who had been admitted by Molesworth, with James and George vying with each other to take their outdoor garments and their luggage.

Daisy sighed and walked dutifully behind Marjorie, who was advancing on the Tighe-Martins with her hands outstretched.

'Major-General Tighe-Martin and Mrs Tighe-Martin, how good of you to come to my country residence.'

'It's our pleasure, ma'am.' The major-general bowed over her hand. 'I believe we met briefly in Delhi, but you haven't met my wife, Felicia.' He turned to the small bird-like woman who stood just a step behind him. 'This is our hostess, my dear. Her husband was once my aide-de-camp, and is now a colonel.'

'How do you do, Mrs Tighe-Martin?' Marjorie said hastily. 'I'm delighted to meet you at last.'

'I remember your husband,' Felicia said shyly. 'A charming man.'

'Yes, indeed, and it's such a pity that duty prevents him from joining us, but I hope you will enjoy the entertainments I have arranged.' Marjorie shot a sideways glance at Daisy. 'My personal secretary will show you to the chinoiserie room, which I selected especially for you. It's quite the most attractive and comfortable bedchamber in the manor house, although, of course, there are many to choose from.' She gave Daisy a sly pinch. 'Now, please, Tattersall.'

'Of course, Mrs Harker,' Daisy said, biting back

a sharp reply. 'Follow me, please.' She led the way to the grand staircase and when she had settled them in their room she used the back stairs to visit the kitchens, where amazingly there appeared to be a temporary truce as Cook and her minions prepared luncheon. Satisfied that everything was running smoothly, Daisy made her way to the housekeeper's parlour in the hope of finding Mrs Ralston there alone, and she was in luck.

'Oh, madam, I'm glad to see you.' Mrs Ralston had been seated behind her desk, but she rose to her feet on seeing Daisy.

'Please sit down.' Daisy pulled up a chair. 'I was hoping to catch you on your own.'

Mrs Ralston sank back on her seat. 'Mrs Jones has taken the list of foodstuffs required for Mrs Harker's party to the village shop. I told her that Mr Keyes couldn't possibly get hold of such exotic things, especially at such short notice.'

Daisy frowned thoughtfully. 'You'd think she would know that. I have a feeling that she wants this entertainment to fail.'

'It would look bad for us, madam. Perhaps that's what she wants. I know she doesn't like having to work with me, although I have tried my hardest to get on with the woman, and that Mrs Salt is a difficult person, to put it mildly.'

'It's hard for all of us, Mrs Ralston, and I do appreciate the effort that all my servants are making.'

'Thank you, Mrs Tattersall. I'll tell the others.'

Daisy glanced at the pile of papers on the desk. 'Have you a copy of the list?'

'I have, as it happens. I don't trust that Mrs Jones, so I spent an hour last evening, copying it out in my own hand, as well as the one listing the names of the guests.' Mrs Ralston passed two sheets of paper to Daisy. 'But I don't see what we can do.'

'Leave it with me. I have an idea, and there are only a few days until this party, which I foresee being a disaster.'

That evening when the children were tucked up in bed, Daisy, Mary and Hilda sat round the table in the cottage kitchen, frowning over Mrs Ralston's barely legible handwriting.

'It's lucky I've known Ida for so many years,' Mary said, chuckling. 'I used to tell her that her writing looked as if a spider had fallen into the inkwell and crawled across the page.'

'Even so, most of these things are impossible to get round here, especially at such short notice.' Daisy sighed and ran her hand through her hair, which she had unpinned and allowed to cascade over her shoulders. It was such a relief to be away from the manor house and able to relax with her mother-in-law and Hilda. They had been through so much together and now there was an even stronger bond between them. Daisy knew that she could not think of letting them down, no matter how badly she was treated up at the big house. No doubt it would give

Marjorie enormous satisfaction to evict them from the small cottage that they had made their home, but Daisy was not about to give her the opportunity to carry out her threat.

'Cook could make better dishes than those anyway,' Hilda said stoutly. 'I'd back Mrs Pearce against Mrs Salt any day.'

Mary shook her head. 'I know, but it's Marjorie Harker we're up against.'

'You're right there,' Daisy said, nodding. 'Marjorie is a very stubborn woman. She refused to give up even when Cook told her that the village shop couldn't get any of the exotic foods she wanted. She said she would send George to purchase them from Fortnum and Mason, but I wouldn't trust him to post a parcel, let alone travel back to Little Creek with a hamper filled with expensive food-stuffs. Anyway, he'd probably get lost in London and we'd never see him again. That, at least, would please James.' Daisy pulled a face. 'Those two don't get on.'

'That's as maybe, but it seems to me that Mrs Harker is trying to be something she's not.' Hilda reached for the teapot and refilled their cups. 'Some people don't know their place, that's all I can say.'

'She's trying to prove that she would do well as the wife of a future brigadier, and she's out to find rich husbands for her daughters.' Daisy leaned her elbows on the table, gazing thoughtfully at the two lists. 'I recognise some of the names she's written down, and I'm certain those people live in London. I can't imagine them travelling all this way for an evening's entertainment.'

'They'd do better down at the village pub with Constable Fowler singing "Little Brown Jug" and accompanying himself on the grand piano – he's got a lovely voice, as you'll remember from the wedding party,' Mary said, giggling. 'Do you think madam would approve?'

Hilda nearly choked on a mouthful of tea. 'We know that Mr Keyes plays the concertina, and Fuller plays the fiddle. I'm sure the London guests will never have seen or heard the like.'

'Well, it might come to that,' Daisy said, laughing. 'But seriously, I need to check how many guests have actually accepted, and if any of them are staying the night.'

'I don't think there is enough linen in the cupboard to make up all the beds.' Mary frowned. 'But that's not my problem now. I'll leave that worry to the two housekeepers. How are they getting along?'

'It's not easy,' Daisy said, sighing. 'The trick is to keep them apart as much as possible.'

'Better you than me.' Mary sipped her tea. 'Maybe you could bring us a lump of sugar tomorrow, Daisy. Speak nicely to Cook and I'm sure she'll oblige.'

'I will, but I'll have to wait until Mrs Salt isn't within earshot. I don't trust that woman – she's mean.'

Hilda drained her cup and stood up. 'Well, I wish

I could be there to help you, Daisy, but Mrs Harker has told me and Mary very firmly that we aren't welcome at the big house. Although she might change her mind when they're rushed off their feet. Anyway, I'm going to my bed and I just hope Judy doesn't kick too much tonight. I'm black and blue from where she's so restless.'

'It's not for ever, Hilda,' Daisy said hastily. 'And if Marius makes a good profit we might be able to leave here sooner. The money he paid to charter the *Lazy Jane* has settled the most urgent debts.'

'He might make off with the ship and you'll never see a penny.' Hilda paused at the foot of the narrow staircase. 'You don't know the man, Daisy. They ain't all honourable gents like Jay.' Hilda trudged up the stairs, her shoulders hunched and her head bent so that Daisy could not see her face, although she suspected that Hilda was remembering her own late husband's failings.

'Poor soul,' Mary said softly.

Daisy rose to her feet. 'Perhaps I'd better go after her.'

'No, dear. She's better off upstairs with her nippers. They're the one thing that's kept her going since the accident. She'll be all right.'

'How did you get to be so wise, Mary?' Daisy sank back on her chair.

'I don't know about that,' Mary said with a wry smile. 'After more than twenty-four years married to Lemuel I learned how to survive. We'll come through this, all of us, and you're a strong young woman. Jay would be proud of you.'

'He's not dead, Mary. I just know it. He'll come home one day, and if he doesn't then I'll go looking for him.'

Daisy arrived at the manor house even earlier than usual next morning, and she went straight to Marjorie's bedchamber. She knocked on the door and it was opened by Ada Wendell, who stared at her in surprise.

'What do you want this early? I've just brought madam a cup of coffee. I brew it myself, just the way she likes it.' She barred the doorway. 'Come back later.'

'No,' Daisy said firmly. 'This is urgent and important. I need to speak to Mrs Harker now.'

'Who is it, Ada?' Marjorie called faintly.

Daisy was in no mood to be trifled with and she pushed past the maid. 'Marjorie, I need to speak to you about this soirée you've planned. It's in less than a week, unless you've forgotten.'

Marjorie pulled the covers up to her chin. She looked small and helpless as she sat propped up by several pillows, with a white lace cap pulled down over her ears.

'This isn't the right way to behave, Tattersall. Can't you see I'm still in bed?'

'Of course I can, but you need to stop pretending that everything is fine and listen to what I have to say.'

'Ada, show Mrs Tattersall out. I'll see her in the morning parlour after breakfast.'

'Miss Wendell, if you take a step nearer I won't be responsible for my actions,' Daisy said angrily. 'Go away and come back in fifteen minutes. I am going to speak to your mistress and I'm not leaving this room until she listens to me.'

'What shall I do, ma'am?' Ada backed towards the doorway.

'Go away as she says,' Marjorie said wearily. 'Say what you have to say and then leave me in peace, Tattersall.'

'Your demands regarding the menu are impossible to meet. That's the first thing, and the second is that I need to know how many people are coming, and who, if any, are staying the night?'

Marjorie slid further down the bed, almost disappearing beneath the starched white sheets. 'I don't know,' she said in a small voice.

'You don't know how many people are coming?'

'Not exactly.'

'But you have a list of those who accepted your invitation.'

'Not really.'

Daisy sank down on the nearest chair. 'Heaven help us. What do you mean by that? Do you know who's coming or don't you?'

'Stop shouting at me, Tattersall. I can't deal with these matters when I've only just awakened.'

'Well, you'd better give it some thought,' Daisy

insisted. 'Can you give me a rough idea how many have accepted? Is it twenty couples, as on your list?'

Marjorie shook her head.

'Fifteen?'

'No, I don't think so.'

'Ten couples, then? That would make life easier, even if you don't remember their names.'

'Not ten, exactly.'

'Have any of them replied to your invitations?' Daisy asked suspiciously.

'Not yet.'

'But that means no one is coming. You must cancel.'

'I can't,' Marjorie said miserably. 'My guests are looking forward to the entertainment. I can't tell them it's not going to happen. They were promised a social event to remember, and my husband's promotion depends on whether or not Major-General Tighe-Martin adds his recommendation. If he does then the others will follow. And Mr Carrington seems quite taken with Charity and she with him. This is a disaster – what will I do?'

Chapter Nine

Daisy stared at Marjorie Harker in amazement. This scheming but pathetic creature had caused upset and misery to two households in her crusade to further her own personal ambitions. Daisy did not believe for a moment that Colonel Harker was desperate for promotion. She knew Charity was a romantic girl who dreamed of true love, while Patience was only happy when she was in the stables or out riding. Even so, Daisy felt a stirring of pity for Marjorie, who had tried desperately to climb the social ladder, but seemed to have become stuck on the bottom rung. With no such ambitions herself, Daisy could see that Marjorie had gone about it in quite the wrong way, and antagonising people who might have been able to help her was not the best start.

'What do you want me to do, Mrs Harker?' Daisy

said calmly. 'Shall I tell the guests that due to unforeseen circumstances the party has been cancelled?'

Marjorie covered her face with her hands. 'I'll look such a fool. It's not just the social gathering that will have to be cancelled.'

'What else have you promised?'

Marjorie peeked at her through her fingers. 'I might have mentioned a fishing trip for the gentlemen, and perhaps a treasure hunt for the ladies.'

'How important is all this to you, Marjorie?'

'I wouldn't be able to face my husband or his company again if this were to become general knowledge. My girls will look foolish and be left on the shelf, or they'll become part of the fishing fleet, and that's a disgrace in itself.'

Daisy stared at her, puzzled. 'The fishing fleet?'

'Young women who would otherwise end up as spinsters are sent out to India to find husbands. It's been going on for a hundred years or more, but I'd rather that my girls didn't marry into the army. It's a hard life for military wives, as I know very well.'

Despite her frustration, Daisy's curiosity was aroused. 'Was that how you met Colonel Harker?'

'No, not exactly.' Marjorie eyed her over the edge of the coverlet. 'My grandparents were wealthy and they expected Mama to marry someone of equal wealth, but my father was just a clerk with the East India Company in Leadenhall Street. They met by chance and it was love at first sight, but they were forbidden to marry and so they eloped. I think they were happy enough at first, but Mama had been used to the good things in life and we were poor. She wanted better for me and she persuaded Papa to take a position in the Bombay office. It was on the voyage out that I met Roland, and we were married by the army chaplain soon after we landed.'

'That sounds very romantic,' Daisy said tactfully.

'I was so young, and I knew nothing of life, but I did my duty and I followed my husband from one army post to another, living in miserable married quarters and suffering from the heat and poor sanitation. I lost five babies before Charity was born, and then I had Patience.'

'I don't understand. You are a wealthy woman, so why did you put up with a life like that?'

'My parents succumbed to typhoid fever, and when my grandparents died within months of each other I inherited a fortune that enabled me to bring my daughters back to England. We moved into Four Winds, which had belonged to my family for many years. I want them to marry well, but I really don't want them to be army wives.'

'I understand, but that doesn't help us out of the present situation.'

'Felicia Tighe-Martin will tell everyone if this goes wrong. She's the sort of woman who would take pleasure in destroying my reputation, and my husband's chances of promotion would be forfeit.'

Daisy had been prepared to be unsympathetic and had expected a stream of excuses, but now she experienced a genuine feeling of empathy. Her own background was not dissimilar to Marjorie's – they were both from respectable working families, and they were ambitious, although in different ways. Daisy would not have chosen to be the lady of the manor, although she was quite happy to take on the role and enjoy the privileges it brought, but there were also responsibilities, and she did not take these lightly. She could see that Marjorie was in a genuine state of distress, and she knew she must put aside her own feelings.

'Will you leave this to me?' Daisy said gently. 'I know this means a great deal to you, so I'm willing to help.'

Marjorie's grey eyes opened wide. 'You are? But what can you do?'

'If you are prepared to leave everything to me, including the choice of food, and the guests, I'll do what I can to make the party a success.'

'You'd do that for me? After all the indignities I've inflicted upon you.'

'Well, we can't have your girls sent out on the fishing fleet, can we?' Daisy smiled and left the room. She knew exactly what she was going to do, but there was very little time left to make the necessary arrangements. For the first time since Jay's disappearance she felt she had a purpose in life and she went straight to the kitchen and called all the servants together.

There was a great deal of shuffling and whispering as the kitchen staff and chambermaids elbowed each other in an attempt to get to the front. George and James stood at the back with Molesworth, who glared at them if they made the smallest sound, and the two housekeepers stood side by side, giving each other covert glances.

'Ladies and gentlemen,' Daisy began, receiving a few sniggers from the upstairs maids, who were silenced by a glowering look from Ida Ralston. 'I have an important announcement to make. We have a crisis on our hands and I want us all to work together.'

'Are we at war, madam?' George grinned cheekily and was immediately elbowed in the ribs by James.

'No, George, not exactly, although this is a matter of some urgency and only you can save the situation – all of you. Everyone is just as important as the next person. As you know, Mrs Harker was planning a large assembly, but there have been complications. It's going ahead but it will be slightly different from what was planned. Mrs Ralston and Mrs Jones will work together to make sure the house is ready to receive a large number of guests – we'll say forty or fifty provisionally. Bedchambers will be aired and beds made up for those who need to stay the night – I leave that to you, ladies. The great hall will be made ready for dancing and the dining hall will be set up ready for the supper.'

'But we can't get the ingredients that Mrs Harker requested, madam,' Mrs Pearce said plaintively.

'No, that's true, and so we're going to provide a

supper fit for a queen, by using your best recipes and produce from the estate. I trust Mrs Pearce and Mrs Salt to work together to make this feast the talk of the county, and everyone must give a hand. Mr Molesworth will be in charge of the wine, ale and cider, and anything else he considers suitable.'

Molesworth cleared his throat. 'Might I ask who will be attending, madam?'

'I'll let you have the guest list as soon as it's ready.' Daisy looked round at the expectant faces and smiled. 'If we all work together we can make this the best social event that Little Creek has ever seen. Thank you all.' She left the kitchen to a round of applause.

Molesworth followed her into the great hall. 'Shall I inform the outdoor servants, madam?'

'Yes, of course. We'll need flambeaux lit to guide the carriages, as it will be dusk when they arrive, and unless there's a full moon it will be pitch-dark when they leave. The grooms will have to be on hand to show the coachmen the way to the stables, and refreshments will be laid on in the tack room for them. We need everything to be perfect.'

'It will be done, ma'am.' Molesworth's eyes twinkled although his expression was carefully controlled, as always.

'And another thing, please, Molesworth. Would you send for my horse to be saddled and brought round to the front entrance? And I'd like Jack Fox to ride out with me.'

'Really, madam? Jack Fox – he's just a boy.'

'And I want him with me.'

'Certainly, madam.' Molesworth hurried off just as Marjorie's maid appeared from the direction of the back stairs.

'Miss Charity is calling for you, Mrs Tattersall,' she said breathlessly. 'And Miss Patience isn't in her room. I think she might have gone to the stables.'

'Tell Miss Charity that she'll have to dress herself this morning, Ada, and I'll deal with Miss Patience when she returns from her morning ride.'

Daisy took the stairs two at a time, hitching up her skirt. At last she was doing something positive and it was a challenge that she would enjoy. She had been forced to give up her room for the guests, but she had been allowed to keep her clothes in a tiny bedchamber on the third floor, just below the attic rooms where the servants slept. The room was sparsely furnished but adequate, although the iron bedstead with its thin, flock-filled mattress did not look welcoming, and so far she had not had to put it to the test.

Daisy changed into her riding habit, safe in the knowledge that the nipped-in waist flattered her figure, and the severe cut of the jacket made her look even more feminine. She was on a mission and nothing was going to stop her. She tucked her hair into a snood, and fixed the smart little hat, based on a gentleman's topper, in place. A quick glimpse in the mirror gave her further encouragement and she left her room with a feeling of growing confidence. She was about to take to the stairs when Julian called out to her.

'Daisy, where are you going so early in the morning?' He strolled up to her, eyeing her up and down with a look in his eyes that she had seen before. Once it would have set her pulse racing, but at this moment she merely felt irritated.

'I'm sorry, Julian, I can't stop to talk. I'm in a hurry.'

'If you'd told me last night that you liked to ride out before breakfast I would have joined you.'

'This isn't a pleasure jaunt. I have business in the village.'

He threw back his head and laughed. 'What could be so important in such a godforsaken place?'

'You'd be surprised, Julian. Life isn't all about London or Paris.'

'But you could have both if you came with me, Daisy. I thought I had put aside my feelings for you, but seeing you again makes me wish I hadn't been such a fool.'

'I really haven't time to stop and talk now.'

'What are you up to? I know that determined look.'

'You'll find out in due course.' Daisy descended the stairs as quickly as was possible when hampered by long skirts, but Julian followed more slowly. James had been standing by the porter's chair, but he leaped to attention as she made her way across the great hall and opened the door. She acknowledged him with a wisp of a smile as she left the house, and it was a relief to see Jack waiting outside, holding the reins of her horse and a smaller pony. She greeted him with a cheery word and a pat on the shoulder.

'Where are we off to, Daisy?' Jack demanded, grinning.

She cuffed him gently round the ear. 'Remember your manners, young man. You might be my brother-in-law, but I'm "Mrs Tattersall" or "ma'am" to you when we're in company.'

Jack held Cinders while she mounted. 'Don't worry about Jim, he don't count.' He winked at James, who closed the door with a resounding thud.

'One day you'll go too far, Jack.' Daisy reined in her frisky mount as she waited for Jack to clamber onto the pony.

'Where are we going, ma'am?'

Daisy shot him an amused glance. 'We are going to the village on a special mission.'

'Really? You mean like spies?'

'No, better than that. But first I'm going to see my aunt and uncle, and if you're lucky Linnet will have made a cake – she's almost as good as Hattie now, but not quite.'

Daisy encouraged Cinders to a trot and headed across the deer park towards the ferry boat, which cut the distance between the manor house and the village by several miles.

Jack caught her up. 'That ain't the half of it, I'll bet.'

'You're right. We've got an important job to do and you can help by taking round the invitations that I'm going to write when we get to Creek Cottage.'

'What are you up to, Daisy? You've got that look on your face.'

She chuckled. 'I don't know what you mean, but the truth is we're going to invite the whole village to the manor house. It will be a party they'll never forget.'

'Does *she* know what you're planning?'

'She has a name, Jack. Yes, Mrs Harker knows that I'm about to save her from a great embarrassment because none of her chosen guests has accepted her invitation, so we're going to provide company who will appreciate a good meal and enjoy a night out.'

'She won't like it.'

'She hasn't much choice.' Daisy urged her horse to a canter. 'Come on, Jack. We've no time to lose.'

Linnet opened the door and her surprised look was wiped away by a wide smile. 'Mrs Tattersall, and Jack, too. Come in.'

Daisy stepped over the threshold followed by Jack, who was immediately enveloped in a sisterly hug. He suffered it for a few seconds and then pulled free from her grasp.

'Don't be soft, Linnet. I ain't a baby now.'

'You'll always be my little brother,' Linnet said, ruffling his already tousled mop of curly hair.

'Is my aunt at home, Linnet?' Daisy peeled off her riding gloves and laid them on the hallstand.

'She's in the parlour, madam.'

Daisy frowned. 'Linnet Fox, you are my sister-in-law. You never need to be formal with me.'

'Except when other people are listening,' Jack added with a mischievous grin.

'Not even then.' Daisy tried to sound severe, but Jack always made her laugh and she shook her head. 'Go with Linnet and I'll call you when I'm ready to leave.'

'Won't you stay for luncheon, Daisy?' Linnet shooed her brother in the direction of the kitchen.

'Maybe something very quick because I'm running out of time, but if you're free next Friday evening I'd like you and Elliot to come to the manor house. Wear your best clothes, it's going to be an amazing party.'

'Really?'

'Yes, I'm going to ask your sister and Nick, Mrs Bee and everyone who fancies a night out.'

'What are you up to, Daisy?'

'You'll find out then, and if I were you I'd go and check on your cakes. I wouldn't let Jack loose in the kitchen when there's good food to be had.'

'Oh, heavens!' Linnet dashed off, leaving Daisy to enter the parlour unannounced.

Eleanora raised herself from her chair by the window and rushed over to embrace her niece. 'Daisy, what a lovely surprise.' She held her at arm's length, her smile fading. 'You look tired, dear. Is that woman working you too hard?'

'It's not easy, but I'm coping well enough. That's not the reason for my visit, though.'

'You don't need a reason to come and see us, my love. Your uncle is out on the river, as usual, but he'll be back in time for luncheon.'

'I need to speak to him about arranging a fishing trip for some of Mrs Harker's guests. Do you think he'd be interested?'

'Any excuse and he's knee-deep in water, and he'll stay out all day, regardless of whether or not he catches anything.'

'That's just what I need.' Daisy went to the escritoire on the far side of the fireplace. 'Do you mind if I use some of your paper? I'm going to write invitations and young Jack is going to hand them out. Unfortunately it's short notice, but I want you and Uncle Sidney to come to the manor house on Friday evening. I'm organising a party such as the village has never seen before.'

'Good gracious! Whatever next? Tell me more, dear.'

Daisy worked hard writing the invitations and Jack was sent out to deliver them, but after a quick luncheon and a few words with her uncle, who was only too delighted to arrange a fishing trip for Marjorie's guests, Daisy set off on her own to visit Creek Hall. She was greeted by Mrs Bee, who always managed to make her feel welcome, and after a brief chat Daisy went to find Nick. His smile was genuine when she walked into his study, and he rose to his feet.

'Daisy, it's good to see you. I've been meaning to call at the manor house, but I've been otherwise occupied.'

'You seem to be doing well,' Daisy said, smiling. 'Mrs Bee tells me that the hospital is paying its way.'

Nick pulled a face. 'My late father would say that was the last thing he cared about, but you're right, the running costs have to be met and, at the moment, they are. The trust that Mrs Harker set up after the cholera epidemic has proved a boon, and the well-off in the wider community aren't afraid to surrender their sick relatives to my care. Although I have to admit that it will make my life easier when your tenants are able to return to their cottages.'

'It shouldn't be long now, Nick. As soon as Marjorie hands over the money I'll make sure that the renovations are completed.'

'It's not that they haven't been useful,' Nick added hastily. 'They've transformed the gardens and planted vegetables. The trees in the orchard have been pruned and are covered in blossom, and the old house has never been so clean.'

'Well, they say it's an ill wind that blows nobody

any good. But that's not why I'm here today, Nick.'

He pulled up a chair. 'Sit down and tell me all about it. I suppose that woman is running you ragged.'

'Yes, I know I look tired. Aunt Eleanora told me that this morning, and I suppose I am, because being treated like a servant in my own home is not easy. I'm the first to admit it.'

She sat down and Nick perched on the edge of his desk, eyeing her thoughtfully. 'Jay has a lot to answer for.'

'You can't blame this on Jay. You were always hard on him, Nick.'

'I'm sorry, Daisy, but it's the truth. He was always a charmer, but he was unreliable to the last.'

'The Dorning brothers are to blame for what happened to Jay.'

'Maybe, but he should never have left you, especially on your wedding day. He ought to have sent one of his crew to sort out problems with the wretched vessel, and now look at you. You're working all hours for a selfish, self-seeking woman, who wants to elevate her position in society. Jay put you in this situation, and for that I can't forgive him.'

Daisy shifted uncomfortably in her seat. 'Let's not talk about him, Nick. We'll never agree.'

'I'm sorry, Daisy, but I have to speak as I find, and I'm still very fond of you. If things had been different . . .'

'Yes, well, they aren't. I'm neither a wife nor a

widow, and much as I want that to change, I don't know if it ever will.'

'But if he doesn't return – and it looks very much as if that's the case – you can have him declared dead and you'll be a free woman.'

'I'll never be free, Nick. I love Jay and that won't change – ever. Anyway, I didn't come here to discuss my future.'

'We'll agree to differ when it comes to Jay. But is there anything I can do for you?' Nick straightened up and walked round his desk, taking a seat and becoming coolly professional.

'Yes, as a matter of fact there is.' Daisy handed him the invitation. 'I'm inviting you and Dove and Mrs Bee to a party that Mrs Harker is throwing at Creek Manor, on Friday evening.'

Nick studied it, eyebrows raised. 'She requests the pleasure of my company plus guests. Is this a joke, Daisy?'

'No, on my honour, it's deadly serious. I'm inviting everyone of note in the village, and of course that means you. Next to the vicar you hold the most prominent position in Little Creek.'

A reluctant smile curved his lips. 'Flatterer.'

'You know it's true, and you'll be helping me if you accept.'

'I'll think about it, but only if you tell me everything.'

* * *

Daisy left Creek Hall with three definite acceptances, and Dove's promise to make sure that all those who were fit enough to go to the party were given an invitation. Daisy headed for the vicarage, and was fortunate to catch Grace Peabody before she went out distributing calf's foot jelly and jars of honey to the sick and needy.

Grace's eyes lit up when Daisy explained the reason for her visit.

'My dear, how exciting. I haven't been inside the manor house since that woman took over. I'll give her a piece of my mind when I see her. It's shameful the way in which she's turned you into a lackey, but then Marjorie Harker was always a social climber, and a frightful snob.'

'I'm not exactly a servant, Mrs Peabody. But it is a difficult situation.'

'And very Christian of you to help her out in this way.' Grace eyed Daisy suspiciously. 'Does she know that you're inviting nearly all the village to this gathering?'

Daisy smiled. 'No, not yet, but she will when they arrive *en masse*. I'm off to the post office to send a telegram to my brother. I think Toby and Minnie would both enjoy themselves and boost the numbers, and maybe Minnie will invite some of our old friends from Mrs Wood's lodging house. That would be most amusing.'

'I do hope you know what you're doing, Daisy. You might have felt sorry for Marjorie Harker but she's not the sort of person to forgive a slight. If she looks a fool in front of her London guests she'll never forgive you.'

'That's a chance I'll have to take,' Daisy said, chuckling. 'But I'm not doing this out of spite. In an odd sort of way I'm quite sorry for her.'

Grace shook her head. 'I think you are the one who deserves sympathy, my dear. I suppose there's been no news of your husband?'

'No, not a word, but I refuse to give up hope. He'll come home one day, I know he will.'

'I do hope you're right, for your own sake, of course, but also for the poor people who were depending on Jay's money to renovate their dwellings.'

'Yes, I know, and I hadn't forgotten them. I was just saying something similar to Dr Neville. The work had to cease temporarily, but when Marjorie pays what she promised, and if Marius is right and we make a good profit, I'll put the money to good use. Moving into that tiny cottage on the estate has opened my eyes to the way our tenants have been living, and we're luckier than most.'

'I suppose so, but I wouldn't have accepted Marjorie Harker's terms.'

'I had no choice, Mrs Peabody. At least our roof doesn't leak and the floor is tiled rather than left as compacted earth, which is dusty in dry weather and can easily turn to mud when it's wet.'

'You've learned a lot from this experience, Daisy. I wish I could say that it was worth it, but you'll need a great deal of money if you're going to put things right. I'm afraid that life will always be harsh for some members of the community.'

'Maybe, but if I can make things better in the future, that's what I'll do.'

Grace smiled. 'You always had ambition, Daisy. Your aunt told me that at one time you wanted to train as a doctor.'

'One day it will be possible for women to do just that, but for now I think I can do more good by ensuring better living conditions for my tenants.' Daisy handed her the invitation. 'Can I count on you and Mr Peabody to attend?'

Grace smiled. 'I wouldn't miss it for the world, Daisy.' She picked up her basket. 'Would you like me to take some with me? I'm visiting several cottages, including Widow Egerton, who rarely goes anywhere. That long-suffering sister of hers might be only too happy to have a night out.'

'I haven't met either of them, but everyone is welcome.' Daisy went to open the front door. 'I must go, because I have a lot to do. Thank you so much, Mrs Peabody. I'm very grateful for your help.'

'I hope I do my Christian duty, dear.'

Daisy's next call was at the village shop and post office where she sent a telegram to her brother and another to Minnie. She knew Toby well enough to be confident of his acceptance, provided that a trip to the country did not interfere with his duties at the hospital, and the same went for Minnie. It would be good to see them again, anyway. Daisy realised suddenly that she had rather cut herself off from those who were closest to her, although it had not been deliberate, and now was as good a time as any to put things right.

'I hear there's to be a big party at the manor house,' Mr Keyes said hopefully as Daisy handed him the money for the telegram. 'I had them two cooks here ordering such an amount of food that it would feed an army. They almost cleared the shelves.'

'Have you and Mrs Keyes received an invitation?'

'No, Mrs Tattersall. I didn't imagine the likes of us would be invited to such a do.'

'Then you're wrong.' Daisy handed him a folded sheet of paper. 'It was an oversight and you are both more than welcome.'

His wrinkled face creased into a wide grin so that his eyes almost disappeared in folds of flesh. 'Why, thank you, ma'am. Most kind, I'm sure.'

'And I was going to ask you a favour.'

His eyes widened and his mouth dropped open. 'A favour, ma'am?'

'You played the concertina so beautifully at our wedding reception that I wondered if you would perform again, together with Constable Fowler and Tom Fuller.'

'I'd be honoured, ma'am. What had you in mind exactly?'

'Perhaps you could play some country dances or a few jigs, as before? It's going to be a splendid party and you would have a large audience. May I count on you?'

'You may indeed, ma'am. I'll call Mrs Keyes and tell her to get her best frock aired and ironed. We'll be there for certain.'

'I haven't been invited.'

Daisy turned to see Miss Creedy, the village seamstress who played the organ in church, very badly. Daisy had not forgotten the crashing discords at her wedding, but somehow it had added to the charm of the ceremony.

'I was coming to you next, Miss Creedy.' Daisy handed out yet another invitation. 'If you have a gentleman friend you would like to bring, he will be more than welcome.'

Lavender Creedy simpered and blushed. 'Oh! You do go on so, Mrs Tattersall. I put all that nonsense behind me when my fiancé was killed in the Crimea. He died a hero and there'll never be another like him.'

'Yes, of course. I'm sorry, but if there's anyone you'd like to bring with you, it will be quite all right.' Daisy tried not to listen to village gossip, but Hilda seemed to absorb it like a sponge. She knew the history of virtually everyone in Little Creek, and was eager to share the knowledge. It was well known, according to Hilda, that Lavender's fiancé had been shot for desertion, although his family had sworn that he was killed in action at Sebastopol. Daisy herself preferred to believe that version. She hurried from the shop, almost bumping into Jack, who was beaming from ear to ear.

'Well?' she said eagerly. 'How did you get on?'

'Got rid of all of 'em. Most say they'll come. They'll go anywhere for free grub.'

'Well done, Jack. Have you been to the pub?'

Jack shook his head. 'Abel Perkins didn't get on with the old man. He cuffed me round the ear last time I saw him.'

'What about the Shipways and the Greens?'

'All done, and Danny and Alfie want to come, too.'

Daisy eyed him warily. 'All right, but you'd better behave. No larking about.'

'Who, me?' Jack said with a saucy wink.

'Wait for me with the horses, Jack. I'll just have a word with Abel, and we've still got the farms on the estate to visit, so it will take the rest of the day.'

It was late afternoon when Daisy dismounted outside the front entrance of Creek Manor. She handed the reins to Jack.

'Thanks for your help. I couldn't have done it without you, Jack.'

'I can be useful at times.'

'Take Cinders back to the stable, and don't make me regret allowing your friends to attend the party. They'd better be on their best behaviour.'

'You won't know we're there.' Jack nudged his pony into a walk and rode off, leading Cinders towards the stable block.

Daisy sighed as she climbed the steps. It had been a tiring day and now she would have to face whatever had happened at the house during her absence. George let her in, his features impassive as always, and it occurred to Daisy that Marjorie must have chosen him to be her footman because of his height and extreme good looks. He was not very bright and he was grumpy at the best of times, but he looked the part. Daisy walked past him, but then she noticed a telegram on the silver salver. She picked it up and saw that it was addressed to her. Her heart sank: telegrams usually meant bad news.

Chapter Ten

'When did this come, George?'

'Not long ago, madam.'

Daisy opened it, fearing the worst and her fingers were shaking, but it was a reply from Toby and her relief was so great that she forgot to reprimand George. It was obvious that the delivery had completely slipped his mind. It was well-known below stairs, or so Hilda said, that George was sweet on one of the chambermaids, who in turn was only interested in James. The romantic triangle did not make for efficient servants.

'Is there a reply, madam?'

'It's a little late for that, George. The messenger must have left ages ago.' She tucked the piece of paper into her skirt pocket. It was good news. Toby and Minnie would be arriving in time for the party.

'I'm sorry, madam,' George said sulkily.

'There's no harm done.' Daisy made her way upstairs to the small bedchamber. The austere setting reminded her of her time in Mrs Wood's lodging house for young ladies. There had been scant comfort there, but she had enjoyed the friendship of the other residents, and especially Minnie. Daisy smiled as she thought of her friend, who would soon become her sister-in-law, and she was delighted that Toby and Minnie were able to attend the party. With that happy thought, she changed into a plain grey tussore afternoon gown, but a quick glance in the small fly-blown mirror made her change her mind. She looked like a drab and that was not how she wanted to present herself to the world. Her conversation that afternoon with Nick had brought back memories of the time when she had thought herself to be in love with him. The emotions she experienced then had been nothing compared to the way Jay had made her feel, and their brief months of marriage had been like heaven on earth, but that had made losing him even more painful. If she was wrong and he was gone for ever, she might end up a creature to be pitied, like Lavender Creedy, who was doomed to play the organ at festive occasions and funerals, but a spinster barely existed in the eyes of the world. As a widow Daisy knew that she would command some respect, but she had no desire to sink into obscurity, nor had she any intention of allowing Julian Carrington to gloat over her present position.

She undid the tiny pearl buttons on her bodice,

frowning at her reflection in the mirror, and she allowed the gown to fall to her feet. She was not yet twenty-one, and she had the figure of a young girl. Jay's memory was tucked away safely in her heart, but she was very much alive and she would take control of events. Marjorie must not be allowed to dictate terms any longer. Daisy went to the chest and selected another gown from the trousseau that Jay had insisted on purchasing for her, even though it went against tradition, but Jay had never been afraid to break the rules. She smiled as she selected a creation in emerald-green faille with a frilled skirt and ruffles at the neckline, which revealed a little more than Marjorie would think appropriate. It had been Jay's favourite and Daisy knew that it suited her dark colouring and rose-petal complexion. She took out the small casket that contained her jewellery and selected a gold brooch and the gold drop earrings that Jay had given her as a wedding present. Satisfied at last with her appearance, she left her room ready to take anyone on, and she knew she had succeeded in making an impression when she met Mr and Mrs Woodward as they took off their outdoor clothes and handed them to a maidservant.

Mr Woodward's eyebrows rose at least an inch and his mouth dropped open. 'G-good afternoon, Mrs Tattersall. Lovely day.'

His wife elbowed him in the ribs. 'Don't be ridiculous, Harold. It's just started to rain, which is why we hurried indoors.' She looked Daisy up and down and her lips pursed with disapproval. 'Are we dressing for dinner early today?'

Daisy smiled benevolently. 'Only if you wish to, Mrs Woodward. But it is a little early.'

'Yes, quite.' Harold recovered himself sufficiently to give Daisy a smile. 'You look remarkably well today, ma'am. If you don't mind me saying so.'

'Hush, Harold. It's rude to make personal remarks. You, of all people, should know that.' Letitia tucked her hand in the crook of his arm. 'We would like to take tea in the drawing room.'

'I'll pass the message on to the parlourmaid, ma'am.' Daisy glided off in the direction of the great hall, but was met by Julian and his colleagues from the Foreign Office.

'Good afternoon, Mrs Tattersall.' Julian bowed from the waist. It was an exaggerated gesture and his friends chuckled appreciatively.

Daisy remained unruffled. 'Good afternoon, gentlemen,' she said, smiling at each one in turn. 'I hope you're all looking forward to the entertainment later this week.'

Edwin Flanders puffed out his cheeks, and his jowls wobbled unattractively. 'Will the young ladies be present, ma'am?'

'Of course. They're counting the hours until the dancing begins.'

'Dancing!' Norman Jenkins flushed and ran his finger round the inside of his stiff collar. 'I'm not much of a dancer, I'm afraid.'

Daisy laid her hand briefly on his sleeve. 'Don't worry, sir. There will be plenty of other entertainments to keep you occupied. For one thing,' she added, improvising wildly, 'there will be night fishing in the lake.'

Norman's eyes shone with enthusiasm. 'Oh! That's splendid. I haven't fished since I was a boy, but that sounds exciting.'

'Night fishing?' Edwin echoed. 'Are you sure? Isn't it dangerous?'

'That only adds to the thrill, sir,' Julian said casually. 'Will you be joining us, ma'am?'

'Maybe, or maybe not.' Daisy smiled at each in turn. 'Now, if you'll excuse me, I have many things to do. Perhaps you would like to join Mr and Mrs Woodward for tea in the drawing room?'

Julian drew her aside. 'I'm trying to avoid that woman. Did you know that she's a distant relation of mine?'

Daisy smiled sweetly. 'The guest list was compiled by Mrs Harker. I am merely her secretary.' She walked on without waiting for a response, but she knew instinctively that Julian was staring after her and she could picture his bemused expression. In their past relationship she had been the one who waited eagerly for him to notice her – a governess did not put herself forward – but that was then, and now she was the lady of the manor, whatever Marjorie Harker might say to the contrary.

Daisy made her way to the kitchen and the heat

from the giant range hit her like a physical blow as she entered the room. Both cooks were working, but far enough apart so that their paths did not cross, and the kitchen maids rushed around, obeying the orders barked at them by their superiors. The aroma of baking filled the air and through the open door of the cold room Daisy could see fruit jellies shimmering like stained glass in the sunlight, and bowls of trifle studded with ruby-red glacé cherries and spiked with toasted almonds. It was obvious that Nell Pearce and Phoebe Salt had taken the challenge personally, each vying with the other.

Nell looked up from the mixture she was beating with a wooden spoon. 'Did you want something, madam?'

Daisy shook her head. 'No, I came to see how you're getting on, but I won't disturb you.'

'We'll be working until all hours,' Nell said complacently. 'You can't rush this sort of thing.' She shot a sideways glance at Phoebe. 'Although some might try.'

'I'm sure you are all doing your very best,' Daisy said hastily.

'We could do with more help.' Phoebe raised her voice to make herself heard above the general hubbub and clatter of pots and pans.

'I could use young Judy,' Nell added eagerly. 'She knows how I work and I don't have to watch her every minute in case she does something wrong.'

Marjorie had made it clear that she did not want

Mary, Hilda or even Judy interfering with the running of the household, and Daisy had been forced to agree, but now things were different. The servants had received the wages they were owed and Daisy had taken charge.

'You shall have Judy and Hilda, and Mary will come back to make sure that the housekeepers work together.'

Nell pulled a face. 'Begging your pardon, madam, but Mrs Ralston and Mrs Jones won't like it.'

'Old rivalries and differences must be put behind us,' Daisy said firmly. 'We must all work together to make this party a great success. It will be the talk of the county for years to come. Well done, everyone.' She hurried away to check on the housekeeping arrangements and to inform Ida Ralston and Dorcas Jones that Mary Tattersall would be in charge from now on. Daisy had expected a rebellion, but to her surprise both housekeepers seemed to be quite relieved to think they had a superior to turn to when things did not go to plan. Daisy left them discussing the turn of events quite amicably, and her last call was on Molesworth, whom she found in the cellar. It was while she was in the stuffy, dank atmosphere below ground level that the suggested treasure hunt came to mind. She had posed the idea without giving it any serious thought, but what could be better and more exciting than a lantern-lit walk through the secret tunnel, culminating in a romantic moonlit stroll on the beach.The prize could be hidden in the undergrowth. The traffic in contraband had come to an abrupt end after the death of the old squire, and there was no reason now to keep the passageway a secret. That particular episode could be consigned to the history books.

Daisy emerged from the cellar, and was walking through the maze of corridors back to the main part of the house when she almost bumped into Patience, who, judging by the windswept state of her hair had just returned from a ride.

'Where were you this morning when we needed you?' Patience demanded. 'I can dress myself, but Charity was in a state because she wanted to look her best for Julian Carrington, although I don't like him. I think he's sly.'

'I had business in the village,' Daisy said casually. 'It's all for your mother's party. You will be attending that, I hope.'

'I doubt if I have much choice.'

Daisy smiled. 'Probably not, but I have a job for you and your sister, which I think you will enjoy.'

'Really?' Patience eyed her curiously. 'What is it? Do tell.'

'Let's find Charity and I'll take you somewhere you've never been before, but it's a secret and you mustn't tell a soul.'

Patience's eyes sparkled with excitement. 'I promise.'

* * *

They found Charity in the drawing room seated beside Julian on the sofa, but she ignored her sister's attempts to draw her away. In the end it was Daisy who had to summon Charity, telling her that the seamstress had arrived with her new gown. Charity responded instantly, but Daisy did not answer her questions until they were out of earshot.

'I know you don't have a new gown, Charity,' Daisy said patiently. 'We're going on a secret mission and it wouldn't be a secret if I had told you in front of everyone.'

Charity's sulky expression was wiped away in an instant. 'Really? What are we going to do?'

'I've fetched your shawls; you'll need them because it's very chilly where we're going. Come with me.'

With the two sisters chattering away behind her, Daisy led them outside, taking the path beneath pergolas covered in cascades of mauve wisteria and a shower of pale pink roses. She stopped when they reached the summerhouse.

'Is this it?' Charity demanded crossly. 'Have you dragged me away from Julian when we were just getting to know each other to visit this old pile of bricks and mortar?'

Daisy ignored this remark and mounted the steps. She bent down to lift the trapdoor and felt inside for the lantern and the matches she had had the forethought to place there earlier. Having lit the wick Daisy held the lantern above her head.

'Who's brave enough to follow me?'

Patience was the first to rush forward, followed more slowly by Charity.

'Is it a cellar?' Patience demanded eagerly. 'What's hidden down there?'

'Come with me and you'll find out. It's perfectly safe, although it might be a bit slippery. Just do what I do and you'll be fine.'

Charity peered into the darkness. 'I'm not sure I want to.'

'Stuff and nonsense,' Patience said crossly. 'You are such a baby. I'm going with Daisy and you can do what you like.'

'Oh, all right. I'll come, but if I don't like it I'm turning back.' Charity edged her sister out of the way. 'I'll follow you, Daisy. You do know what you're doing, don't you?'

'Of course I do. I've been this way several times, and I thought it would be a wonderful end to the treasure hunt. The guests will all be provided with lanterns or candles and the prize will be at the other end. Let's see what you two think of the idea.'

Daisy climbed down the steps with Charity following so close behind that she could feel her hot breath on the back of her neck. Daisy held the lantern in one hand and picked her skirts up with the other. Maybe she ought to have changed into something more sensible, but the guests would be wearing their best gowns, so it was important to judge whether or not they would appreciate getting their party shoes wet. Charity grumbled at first, but her protests died away as they neared the end of the underground passage, and Patience uttered squeaks of pleasure and excitement.

'This is wonderful,' Charity breathed, as they emerged on the foreshore. 'I had no idea we were so near the creek. How did you discover this, Daisy?'

'By chance,' Daisy said casually. 'Anyway, what do you think, girls? Would this make an exciting treasure hunt?'

'Oh, yes.' They spoke in unison, ending up giggling like a couple of schoolchildren.

'What will the prize be?' Charity asked after a pause. 'It will have to be something that either a lady or a gentleman would appreciate.'

'A bottle of champagne,' Patience said excitedly. 'You must ask Molesworth if he has one in the cellar, Daisy.'

Daisy smiled at their enthusiasm. 'That's a good idea, but who will organise the treasure hunt on the night? I'll be too busy to do it myself.'

'I will.' Once again Charity and Patience spoke at the same time.

'Then I think you should both do it,' Daisy said seriously. 'I'll leave it to you, and I want you to make it as exciting as possible. Remember that it will be almost dark by the time the guests set off, so you'll need to find enough lanterns to light their way.'

'There are plenty of them in a cupboard next to the tack room. I saw them only yesterday.' Patience glanced up at the sky. 'I hope it will be a fine day. It's going to be so exciting.'

'We'd best get back.' Daisy checked the lantern to make sure there was enough oil in the chamber. 'But remember, don't breathe a word of this to anyone. It's our secret.'

After dinner that evening, Daisy found a quiet spot in the morning room and was writing a list of things to be done next morning. Everything was going reasonably smoothly thus far, but her heart sank when Marjorie burst into the room, her cheeks flushed and her expression one of near panic.

'Is anything wrong?' Daisy rose to her feet.

'Major-General Tighe-Martin has been asking questions about the guest list for the party. I tried to put him off but he was very persistent, and I haven't received any replies to my invitations. I can't think why.'

'Don't worry. It's all in hand. Your party will be remembered for years to come.'

'What do you mean, Daisy? How can we have an elegant assembly without guests of a certain calibre?'

'Do you consider Dr Neville a person of the right calibre?'

'Yes, of course.'

'And my brother, Toby, who is a doctor at the London Hospital?'

'Yes, but—'

'They are but two of the guests I've invited. All the preparations are in hand, so I suggest you enjoy the rest of your evening, and leave everything to me.' Daisy folded the list and put it into her pocket. 'I'm going to the cottage now, but I'll be here first thing in the morning.'

'Thank you, Daisy,' Marjorie said meekly. 'I do appreciate what you're doing, and my husband will be grateful, too. I just hope that Major-General Tighe-Martin and his wife enjoy themselves to-morrow. Roland's promotion depends upon good relations with his superior.'

Daisy smiled and left the room. She had done all she could for now, and she was tired. It was a long walk to the cottage, but she had good news to pass on to her little family. It was a fine evening and the air was heady with the scent of bluebells that carpeted the nearby wood, and with the fruity fragrance of damp earth. When she reached the cottage she found Mary and Hilda waiting for her with the kettle bubbling on the range, and the aroma of baking filled the room.

'How did it go today?' Mary asked eagerly.

'We feel so cut off from the goings-on in the big house.' Hilda rose to her feet and warmed the Brown Betty teapot with a dash of hot water from the kettle. 'Sit down and tell us all about it.'

'I can do better than that,' Daisy said, smiling as she took off her bonnet and laid her shawl over the back of the chair. 'You are both needed desperately, and so is Judy. Is she in bed?'

'Yes, she went up ten minutes ago. Poor child, she's been getting bored stuck here with just the two of us and the little 'uns.' Hilda spooned tea leaves into the pot, topping it up with boiling water.

Daisy sat down and stretched her weary limbs. 'Cook asked for her personally. Judy has made herself indispensable.'

'I'll be glad to have something to do,' Mary said cautiously. 'But what brought about this sudden change?'

'Mrs Harker hasn't had much choice. She's too busy trying to entertain the guests she has without troubling herself with arrangements for the party, but I have it all in hand.'

'Who's coming?' Hilda placed a cup of tea on the table in front of Daisy. 'I thought you said that madam hasn't received any replies to her invitations.'

Daisy chuckled. 'I've seen to that, with Jack's help.'

'What has my Jack done now?' Mary asked anxiously.

'Nothing bad, I promise you. He came to the village with me and we've handed out invitations to everyone who can struggle up the hill from the ferry.'

Mary's eyes widened in surprise. 'No! You didn't.'

'Wait and see,' Daisy said, sipping her tea. 'It really will be an evening to remember.'

'Does Mrs Harker know what you've done?'

Daisy shook her head. 'No, Mary. I'm keeping it as a nice surprise.'

'Heaven help us,' Mary said, throwing up her hands.

At noon on the day of the party Daisy was at the railway station waiting for the London train to arrive. She had not seen her brother and his fiancée since the traumatic events on her wedding day, and now she was quivering with anticipation. She saw Toby first – there was no mistaking his tall figure as he stepped out of the first-class compartment and helped Minnie to alight. Daisy was about to rush forward when she realised that Toby was holding his hand out to someone else, and to her surprise it was Flora Mackenzie who stepped down from the train, followed by Ivy Price. Flora's flame-red hair marked her out amongst the rest of the passengers, as did her flamboyant clothing, but Ivy was small and sparrow-like, her plain grey mantle and linsey-woolsey skirt making her almost invisible as the engine let off steam and they were enveloped in a great white cloud.

Toby and Minnie emerged, arm in arm as they hurried towards Daisy and she broke into a run, embracing Toby first and then Minnie.

'I'm so glad you could come.' Daisy glanced over Minnie's shoulder. 'And Flora and Ivy, too. This is wonderful.' She shot an anxious glance along the platform behind them. 'I hope you didn't bring Myrtle.'

Flora tossed her head. 'Don't mention the brat.

She's still making our lives a misery. I've been hoping that my latest gentleman friend would propose marriage and take me away from Mrs Wood's house of torture and her hateful daughter, but no such luck.'

'It's not that bad, Flora,' Ivy protested. 'We're like a family really. Isn't that true, Minnie?'

'In a way,' Minnie said tactfully. 'We have our differences, and I will miss you all when Toby and I are married.'

'Well, I'm delighted to see you.' Daisy seized her brother's hand. 'I've brought the barouche to take you to the manor house, although it will be a bit of a squeeze.'

'I'll sit on the box with Fuller,' Toby said cheerfully. 'Come on, ladies, there's plenty of time to catch up on all the gossip.' He signalled to a porter, who approached at a measured gait, pushing a trolley, and Toby pressed a coin into the man's hand. 'The barouche is outside in the lane.'

'Aye, sir. Thank you.' The porter tipped his cap and they left him piling the bags and cases onto the trolley.

'Now, Daisy,' Toby said firmly. 'Are you going to tell me what this is all about?'

'I'll tell you on the way to the manor house.' Daisy glanced up at the lowering clouds. 'It looks as if we're going to have a shower, so we'd best hurry.'

* * *

The manor house was decked out with greenery and vases spilling over with bluebells and cherry blossom. Bowls of early roses were placed on side tables and their scent wafted around the great hall as the servants bustled to and fro, carrying piles of china and baskets of cutlery to the dining hall. Molesworth had a martyred look as he let Daisy and her party in, and he directed a passing maidservant to take their outdoor garments. George was sent to fetch the luggage from the barouche and Daisy went outside to have a quick word with Fuller, in order to make sure he knew what time he should arrive for a practice with Constable Fowler and George Keyes. Having satisfied herself that there would be music for dancing, Daisy went back into the house to find Toby in conversation with Major-General Tighe-Martin, and to her surprise they seemed to be on friendly terms.

She approached cautiously. 'Good afternoon, General.'

Toby turned to her with a smile. 'Isn't this the most amazing coincidence, Daisy? I was at school with the general's son. Tubby Tighe-Martin and I were the best of friends, but I haven't seen him since I began my medical studies. How is old Tubby, sir?'

'As a matter of fact you'll be able to see for yourself. He should be arriving this afternoon. It was my wife's idea and Mrs Harker kindly agreed. In fact she was more than happy to have another bachelor in the party. I suspect that she is eager to find a suitable husband for her elder daughter – a dashed pretty girl, but I see that you are suited, sir.' The general bowed to Minnie, who had just joined them, and flashed her a smile.

'May I introduce my fiancée, Miss Minette Cole? Minnie, darling, this is Major-General Tighe-Martin – I was at school with his son, who coincidentally is arriving later today.'

Minnie blushed rosily and bobbed a curtsey as if being introduced to royalty. 'How do you do, General?'

He bowed over her hand. 'Delighted to make your acquaintance, Miss Cole. I must introduce you to my wife, but I believe she's in the drawing room with Mrs Harker at present. I think they're discussing ladies' matters, so I'm keeping well out of the way.'

Daisy caught sight of Flora, who was approaching with a purposeful look on her face. Daisy recognised the danger signs and she waylaid her.

'Don't even think of it, Flora. He's married and his wife is a guest here.'

Flora pouted and fluttered her eyelashes. 'I wouldn't think of it, Daisy. But did I hear him mention his son? I love a public school chap. They're always so innocent when it comes to the ways of the world and women in particular.'

'Don't say that in front of my brother, and anyway, it was only a minor public school that Toby attended. Our aunt and uncle couldn't afford Harrow or Eton.'

'I don't care,' Flora said crossly. 'I like a man who can read and write and earn a lot of money, but I'm not a snob.'

'No, you're what they call a gold-digger.' Ivy rolled her eyes. 'And you teased me when I stepped out with Jonah Sawkins, just because he was different.'

Flora turned on her, scowling. 'The creature was an evil gnome with a crooked back. You must have been desperate to go out with the likes of him.'

'He could be nice when he tried.' Ivy's brown eyes filled with tears. 'You can be very hurtful sometimes, Flora.'

Daisy slipped her arm around Ivy's shoulders. 'Never mind her. She's just cross because she hasn't been introduced to the general.'

'That will change,' Flora said casually. 'We have a party to go to and I'm very good at socialising, especially when there are handsome men involved.'

'And money,' Ivy added in a low voice. 'She can smell money a mile off, but it hasn't done her much good.'

'What do you mean by that?' Flora demanded.

'I don't see a ring on your finger. You haven't snared a man yet, Flora.'

Daisy stepped in between them. 'Hush, both of you. Do you want the general to hear you going at each other like a couple of cats?'

'It must have rubbed off from living with Rex, Mrs Wood's spiteful pussycat,' Flora said, laughing. 'He is worse than ever nowadays. I'm sure she trains

him to attack anyone who upsets her.' Flora gave
Ivy a hug. 'Fainites, Ivy, old thing.'

Ivy shrugged. 'I suppose so, but you could try to
be nice to me.'

'I will, I promise – cross my heart and hope to
die.'

'And I want you to promise to behave, Flora,'
Daisy said severely.

'My dear, of course I will.' Flora glanced over
Daisy's shoulder and her red lips curved into a
delighted smile. 'Who is that handsome man?'

Daisy turned her head. 'That's Julian Carrington
– you don't want to have anything to do with him,
Flora.' But it was too late, Flora was sashaying across
the tiled floor, heading purposefully towards Julian.

Chapter Eleven

Daisy was about to follow her when Charity
appeared as if from nowhere, carrying a trug filled
with painted pebbles, which she and Patience had
been placing at strategic places in the garden as clues
in the treasure hunt. Although she could see it
coming, Daisy was too far away to do anything to
prevent the clash. Charity seemed to sense that she
had a rival, and the result was almost inevitable. As
Flora drew nearer to her prey, Charity allowed the
trug to slip and a shower of brightly coloured stones
clattered to the ground in front of Flora, who skidded
and slid like an ice skater and fell in an ungainly
heap at Julian's feet.

There was a moment of silence as everyone stared
helplessly at the unfortunate Flora. Daisy recovered
first and rushed to her aid, but Julian was nearest
and he bent down to help Flora to her feet.

'Are you hurt, Miss, er – I'm sorry, I don't know your name.'

'It was a stupid accident,' Charity said hastily. 'Who are you, anyway?'

Daisy reached them in time to silence Charity with a stern look. 'Are you all right, Flora?'

'Yes, no thanks to her. That was deliberate.'

'Was it, Miss Harker?' Julian eyed Charity with an amused grin. 'Have I the honour of two young ladies fighting over me?'

Charity tossed her head. 'You flatter yourself, sir.' She thrust the trug into Daisy's hands. 'Make sure the mess is cleared up, Tattersall.'

'You tipped them out in front of me,' Flora said angrily. 'You pick them up.'

'Do you know who I am?' Charity demanded.

'No, and I don't care to be friendly with a spoilt child, who has the manners of a street urchin.'

'You can't speak to me like that. I'm Charity Harker and my mama is the lady of the manor.'

'As I heard it, Miss Harker, your ma is just renting this old pile of bricks, and my friend Daisy owns the house. Isn't that right, Daisy?'

'Yes, but we won't go into that now, Flora. I'll show you and Ivy to your rooms. As for you Charity, I'm sure you have better things to do than hurling insults at your mother's guests.' Daisy beckoned to James, who was hovering in the background. 'Will you please send for someone to clear up this mess?'

Julian proffered his arm to Charity. 'I'd like to see the treasure hunt trail.'

'Isn't that cheating?' Flora demanded with a pert smile.

'Why don't you come, too, Miss, er . . . ?'

'Flora Mackenzie, and I'd love to.'

Daisy caught her by the wrist as she was about to follow Charity and Julian. 'I think you'd better see your room first, Flora. I have a great deal to do today so I might not have time to spare later.'

'Oh, I suppose so.' Reluctantly Flora stood aside and watched Charity walk away, leaning on Julian's arm. As they reached the door Charity turned to give her a triumphant smile.

'You won't win there, Flora,' Ivy said, chuckling. 'You've met your match.'

'We'll see about that.' Flora turned her back on Charity and Julian. 'Lead on, Daisy. This place is a bit better than Mrs Wood's lodging house, I must say.'

'Stay there while I rescue Minnie from the general's clutches. He seems to have taken a fancy to her.' Daisy crossed the floor and waited for a break in the conversation. 'I'm sure you would like to see your room, Minnie.'

'It's a pleasure to meet you, Miss Cole. We'll continue this conversation later,' Major-General Tighe-Martin said gallantly.

'Thank you, Daisy,' Minnie whispered. 'He's very charming, but he does rattle on.'

'Don't let Marjorie Harker hear you say anything against the general. She's depending upon him to recommend her husband for promotion.'

'Is that what all this is about?'

'I don't want to say too much in front of Flora. She's already caused an incident with Charity and Julian Carrington.'

'Surely he's the man who jilted you? What is he doing here?'

'I'll tell you when we're on our own.'

Having settled the guests in their rooms, Daisy checked with Mary and was satisfied that everything was being done to make the party a success, and at six o'clock the guests started to arrive. Molesworth announced that carriages were drawing up outside and Daisy went to fetch Marjorie. She met her coming down the stairs, looking resplendent in a cream satin evening gown, sparkling with diamanté, and a French paste tiara nestled in a coronet of curls, skilfully coiffed by Hilda. Daisy had chosen to wear a more modest creation. It had come from the House of Worth and had cost Jay an exorbitant amount of money, but he had sworn that the peacock-blue silk gown showed her slender figure off to perfection. The cut was deceptively simple, but the overall effect was that of timeless elegance. Daisy had not intended to outshine Marjorie, but she knew from the admiring glances she received that this was the unpremeditated result.

'The first guests have arrived,' Daisy said urgently.

Marjorie looked her up and down, pursing her lips and frowning. 'Stand behind me at the door when I welcome them,' she said crossly. 'I am the lady of the manor this evening, not you.'

'Perhaps it would be better if your daughters stood by your side,' Daisy suggested tentatively. She had found out to her cost that Marjorie was unreceptive when it came to suggestions that questioned her decisions.

'No, certainly not. I want Charity to make an entrance when the guests are assembled. I've instructed Molesworth to serve champagne to each one as they arrive, and then Charity will descend the stairs looking like an angel in her white Valenciennes lace gown. What Patience does is up to her but I fear she might clump down the stairs in her riding habit and boots. You haven't done a very good job of turning my younger daughter into a lady.'

'I'm not a miracle worker, Mrs Harker.'

Marjorie's attention was elsewhere and she laid her hand on Daisy's arm, staring over her shoulder. 'Who is that young man? I don't recognise him.'

Daisy turned her head to look. 'I think that must be my brother's friend, Tubby Tighe-Martin, the general's son.'

'What? Why didn't anyone tell me that he was coming? You'll have to introduce me.'

'I thought you wanted me to go make myself scarce.'

Marjorie's grip tightened so that her fingernails pinched the skin of Daisy's arm. 'Don't try to be clever. You know what I mean. Smile, for goodness' sake, and follow me.' She glided ahead with her head held high, leaving Daisy little choice other than to follow her.

'Captain Ned Tighe-Martin,' Molesworth announced in a sepulchral tone.

Marjorie pushed Daisy forward. 'Do as I asked,' she hissed.

'Captain Tighe-Martin,' Daisy said, extending her hand. 'I believe you know my brother, Toby Marshall?'

Captain Tighe-Martin raised her hand to his lips. 'You must be Daisy. I've heard so much about you.'

Daisy met his direct gaze with a smile. 'Toby is here with his fiancée. He'll be delighted to see you again.'

Marjorie cleared her throat, giving Daisy a sharp poke in the back. Daisy moved aside. 'Mrs Harker, may I introduce Captain Ned Tighe-Martin?'

'How do you do, Captain? I'm so glad you were able to join us this evening.'

'How do you do, Mrs Harker? The pleasure is all mine.'

'I'll tell your father that you're here.' Daisy could see a group of villagers heading up the steps with Miss Creedy at the forefront, followed by Farmer Johnson, his wife and daughter, and three of their sons. The time had come to retreat before Marjorie realised that she was playing hostess to almost the entire village.

'Don't put yourself out, Miss Marshall,' Ned said with an easy smile. 'I can wait until my parents join me.'

'It's Mrs Tattersall,' Daisy said hastily.

'I'm sorry, I didn't know. Will I meet your husband this evening?'

'I'm afraid not.' Daisy turned away. There were times when she could put her heartbreak behind her and carry on as if nothing had happened, and at others the pain of loss overwhelmed her in a wild black tide of grief.

'Daisy, please go and find the major-general and his wife,' Marjorie said impatiently. 'Where is the champagne, Molesworth? Guests are arriving.' She turned to greet Miss Creedy and her face fell. 'Who are these people, Daisy? They were not on my guest list.'

'Your guests didn't reply, Mrs Harker,' Daisy said sweetly. 'I had to think quickly, but that is Miss Creedy, the church organist, and I see the Johnson family behind her. They are tenant farmers on the Creek Manor estate.'

'How splendid.' Ned smiled enthusiastically. 'What a grand gesture, Mrs Harker. Does my father know what a generous woman you are?'

Marjorie's angry expression melted into a confused half-smile. 'I – er – I'm not one to boast, Captain.' She turned with a start as Miss Creedy grabbed her by the hand, pumping her arm up and down.

'How very kind of you to invite me, Mrs Harker.

205

The old squire would have slit his throat rather than entertain we commoners from the village.'

Daisy laid her hand on Miss Creedy's shoulder. 'Come with me, Lavender. I'm sure you could do with some refreshment after that long walk from the ferry.'

'I'm dry as a bone, my dear. How nice of you to think of me.'

'We can't have the church organist going thirsty, and maybe you would like to give us a tune on the pianoforte later in the evening.'

Lavender Creedy's pale grey eyes filled with tears and she took off her steel-rimmed spectacles to wipe her eyes. 'So kind, Mrs Tattersall, and you're so brave bearing up to the loss of your husband. Jay was a nice boy in spite of what people say about him. I remember a time when he carried my basket all the way from the village shop to my cottage.'

'Take her away,' Marjorie whispered through clenched teeth. 'Put her in a corner somewhere.' She gazed blankly at the Johnson family, who were all spruced up in their Sunday best. 'Who are you?'

'Josiah Johnson, ma'am. And this is my missis, Edna, and my daughter Janet, and three of my boys, Eddie, Wilfred and William, but young Lewis insisted on going to sea on that coffin ship, the *Lazy Jane*.'

'Oh, all right,' Marjorie said faintly. 'Follow the others. There should be refreshments in the great hall.' She shot a venomous look at Daisy. 'If you feed my best champagne to these peasants I'll charge you for every single bottle.' She turned back to greet Nick, Dove and Mrs Bee, who were closely followed by Daisy's aunt and uncle. 'At least I know you, Dr Neville,' Marjorie hesitated, adding with a sigh, 'and I see you've brought your servants with you.'

Daisy did not wait to see the expression on the faces of Dove and Mrs Bee, and she hurried off, leading Miss Creedy and the Johnson family to the great hall where side tables were groaning with bottles of wine and cider, as well as barrels of beer. The money available had not run to champagne, which was just as well, although there was sherry for those who wanted it, and port for others, as well as a fruit punch laced with brandy. Molesworth must have emptied the cellar in order to provide such a variety, but at least it would make the evening go with a swing.

Having settled the new arrivals, Daisy returned to the entrance hall to greet her aunt and uncle. She found them chatting to Toby and Minnie, who had been joined by Ned Tighe-Martin. Ivy seemed to have been forgotten and she hovered awkwardly in the background – there was no sign of Flora.

Daisy placed her arm around Ivy's shoulders. 'Come with me. I think there's someone you might like to meet.'

'Oh, Daisy, before you disappear again.' Her uncle broke away from the group and hurried to her side. 'I wanted to tell you that Abel Perkins is down at the lake with all the fishing gear, and I'm going to join him, so if any gentlemen are interested we'll be ready to help them enjoy an evening's sport.'

'That's splendid, Uncle. I'll inform all those who might enjoy that, but right now I'm just going to introduce Ivy to someone and then I'll be back.' Daisy propelled Ivy in the direction of the great hall.

'I don't want to take you away from your family, Daisy.'

'Nonsense. There's someone I'd like you to meet. Eddie Johnson is the eldest son of one of my tenant farmers, and he's a fine upstanding young man.'

Ivy blushed prettily. 'I'm not looking for a husband.'

'Of course not, but a partner for the evening will make the party much more enjoyable.' Daisy caught her by the hand as Ivy was about to turn back. 'Come on, he won't bite.'

The Johnsons were grouped together, looking decidedly out of place and uncomfortable, but Daisy was not going to be put off. She approached them with a bright smile.

'Mr and Mrs Johnson, may I introduce my good friend Ivy Price. She's from London and she doesn't know many people, so I thought perhaps you might look after her.'

Ivy opened her mouth to protest, but Josiah stepped forward. 'How do, miss?'

'You're very welcome to bide with us,' Edna said eagerly. 'Eddie, step forward and get a glass of something for Miss Price.'

Eddie shot a warning look at his two brothers, who were grinning at him. 'What's your pleasure, miss?'

'I believe the fruit punch is very refreshing,' Daisy suggested when Ivy seemed at a loss.

'Yes, thank you. That would be nice,' Ivy said shyly.

Eddie filled a glass cup from the punchbowl and handed it to her. 'Do you like dancing, miss?'

'I do,' Ivy said enthusiastically.

'Then will you keep the first dance for me?'

'Oh, yes. Thank you.' Ivy smiled up at him. 'Where is your farm, Mr Johnson?'

'It's not far away. If you're here tomorrow morning I'd be pleased to show you round.'

Ivy's smile made her look almost pretty and Daisy left them to get to know each other. She returned to the entrance hall feeling pleased with herself. Now all she had to do was to keep Flora under control and hope that the rest of the evening went off well. But one look at Marjorie's face was enough to convince her that there would be trouble ahead. She rejoined her family group and was pleased to see that Nick had introduced Dove to Toby and Minnie, while Mrs Bee looked on, smiling benignly. The hall was getting crowded and guests were still arriving, although Marjorie's smile had turned into a rictus grin, and she shook hands like an automaton. Daisy almost felt sorry for her, but then Marjorie had brought it on herself, and if she would just relax a little she might even begin to enjoy the party.

Patience had slipped in unnoticed and had stationed herself beside Fuller, who was tuning up his fiddle. George Keyes had arrived, bringing with him his wife as well as his prized concertina. Daisy was pleased to see that Patience had made an effort to look presentable, probably aided by Hilda, who would not stand for any nonsense. But it was Charity who caused a stir, exactly as her mother had planned.

The moment the door closed after the last guest had been admitted, Marjorie held up her hand for silence and Charity paused at the top of the stairs before descending slowly with one hand trailing on the banister rail. All eyes were upon her but then disaster struck as she caught her heel in the hem of her long, floaty white lace gown and she clutched wildly at thin air and tumbled down the last six or seven steps. She would have hit the floor with a resounding thud had it not been for Ned Tighe-Martin, who leaped forward and caught her.

There was a moment of silence and then a ripple of applause turned into an ovation as he set Charity on her feet. They gazed into each other's eyes and Daisy held her breath. She felt that she was witnessing a relationship that was truly love at first sight, and it brought a lump to her throat. However, it was obvious that Marjorie did not feel the same and she bustled over to them, placing herself between Ned and Charity.

'That was well done, Captain,' Marjorie said briskly. 'Come with me, Charity. We have our duties to perform.'

Dazed and still gazing at Ned over her shoulder, Charity allowed herself to be led to the great hall.

'Music, Tattersall,' Marjorie snapped as she surged past Daisy. 'Get them to play now.'

Torn between amusement and annoyance at the brusqueness of Marjorie's tone, Daisy went over to Fuller and George Keyes. 'Is Constable Fowler here?'

'I believe so, Mrs Tattersall,' George Keyes said politely. 'I think I saw him heading for the great hall. I expect he wants to try out the pianoforte.'

'That's good, because Mrs Harker would like you to start playing as soon as you're ready. Perhaps a country dance would get people in the mood, or maybe a jig.'

Fuller played a few notes on his fiddle. 'Will there be plenty of ale, madam? Playing is thirsty work.'

'As much as you can drink without spoiling your performance, Fuller.'

'Say no more,' Fuller said, chuckling. 'Come on, George. Let's show them how it's done.' He strolled off in the direction of the great hall with Mr Keyes following him, and Patience was not far behind them.

Daisy looked round for Ned. His height made him easy to spot in a crowd. She moved swiftly to his side. 'I'm sure Mrs Harker didn't mean to be rude, Captain. She was probably in a state of shock.'

Ned smiled. 'I'm a soldier like my father, Mrs Tattersall. I'm not easily frightened.'

'I'm glad to hear it. Charity needs someone strong to help her stand up to her mother.'

'I've never seen such a beautiful girl in my whole life.'

'She seems to like you, too.' Daisy eyed him thoughtfully. 'There's a treasure hunt later. I don't think Charity has a partner for it, as yet.'

'Thank you for telling me. I'll make sure I put myself forward.'

Just at that moment, Daisy spotted Julian and his Foreign Office colleagues heading for the great hall. She grasped Ned by the arm. 'I'm sorry, I don't mean to be familiar, but you see those three gentlemen who are about to disappear into the great hall?'

'I do, indeed. Are you telling me that they are the enemy?' Ned's blue eyes sparkled with amusement.

'Two of them are merely hopefuls, but Julian Carrington is the one to watch. He's a fortune-hunter, Captain. I know from experience that he is not trustworthy.'

'Thank you for the warning. I think this calls for strategy.'

'Maybe you ought to ask Charity for the first dance. If you hurry you might get to her before Julian does.'

'Just one thing, Mrs Tattersall. Do you know why Mrs Harker might object to me paying my respects to her daughter?'

'She doesn't want Charity to marry a soldier. It's as simple as that.'

'I see. Well, we'll see about that. Charity might not agree with her mother.'

Daisy watched him stride off purposefully and she smiled. Perhaps Marjorie Harker had met her match, but that was the least of her concerns. She checked to make sure that her aunt was being entertained and found her in the great hall, chatting happily to Mrs Bee over glasses of fruit punch. Judging by the rosy colour on their cheeks and the smiles on their faces, the punch was laced with a generous amount of brandy. Molesworth was standing by to top up the bowl when needed. Farmer Johnson and his two younger sons were quaffing ale from pint tankards, while Edna sipped sherry and her fourteen-year-old daughter, Janet, was sharing a glass of punch with Patience, and both had reached the giggling stage.

The noise level rose and the band struck up a lively jig, which Daisy knew would have been frowned on by those who attended formal balls, which would inevitably begin with the grand march, followed by the first waltz. However, the residents of Little Creek did not seem to care and they seized their partners and danced with more energy than elegance.

Marjorie stood beside Charity, gazing at the scene with undisguised horror. She seemed to be struck dumb by the noise and the cavorting, and when Ned approached Charity and asked her to dance with him, Marjorie merely nodded wordlessly and turned away as her daughter laid her hand in Ned's and allowed him to lead her onto the floor. They remained together when the music stopped, and melted into each other's arms for the waltz. Daisy was about to make her way to the dining hall to check on the arrangements for supper, when Nick approached her.

'May I have the pleasure of this dance, Daisy?'

'Shouldn't you be asking Dove?'

'I'm asking you. Don't you want to dance with me?'

She laid her hand in his. 'Yes, but—'

'No buts, Daisy. We are old friends, are we not?'

She laid one hand on his shoulder as he whirled her round in time to the music. 'We are,' she said breathlessly. 'But Dove is sitting there on her own. This doesn't feel right, Nick.'

'It's the only chance I have to speak to you in private, Daisy.'

She stared up at him, trying to gauge his mood, but he was staring straight ahead as he steered her through the crush of enthusiastic dancers. 'What is it you want to say?'

'Only that I still love you. I tried to tell you the other day, but I didn't get very far.'

'Nick, you know it's impossible. Even if I knew for certain that Jay wouldn't be coming home, I still love my husband.'

'I'm prepared to wait. If there's a chance that you could return my feelings I'll let Dove down gently. I should never have taken up with her anyway, and I only turned to her because I was lonely.'

'If you don't love her then you must tell her so, because it's not fair to keep her dangling, but don't throw away what you have with Dove in the hope that I'll change my mind. I won't, Nick. I'm very fond of you, but that's all.'

'Maybe in time . . . ?'

'No, never. I have to be blunt if that's the only way I can make you understand.'

'But we work together so well. Remember the cholera epidemic – we were a team, Daisy. We conquered the disease together.' His grip on her hand tightened and he held her so that she could not break away without causing a disturbance.

'Stop this now, Nick. I won't be bullied into saying something I'll regret. Let me go, please.'

Just at that moment Julian spun Flora to a halt at their side. 'Is this person bothering you, Daisy?'

'No, I'm all right, thank you,' Daisy said icily.

'I'll thank you to mind your own business, sir.' Nick glared at Julian. 'I know who you are.'

'Come away, Julian.' Flora tugged at his arm. 'Leave her alone.'

Daisy broke free from Nick's grasp. 'I'm sorry, but I have things to do.' She edged her way through the couples and found herself face to face with Marjorie.

'Well, what sort of display was that?' Marjorie demanded angrily. 'Do you flirt with every man you meet?'

'My private life has nothing to do with you, Mrs Harker. Now, if you'll excuse me I need to go and check that everything is laid out ready for supper.'

'This is my house now,' Marjorie said in a low voice. 'I'll thank you to remember that, and as such I expect you to behave with decorum.'

Daisy did not dignify this with an answer and she walked away, but Marjorie followed her.

'I was speaking to you, Tattersall.'

'My name is Daisy or Mrs Tattersall. You've rented my home but you haven't bought me, Mrs Harker. I'm doing what you wanted me to do, so please allow me to get on with my task.'

'You haven't shown me the menu, and I don't know if you've followed my orders or not. I want to see for myself.' Marjorie followed Daisy through to the great dining hall where the servants were putting the finishing touches to the spread laid out on the long refectory table, and several smaller tables. Silver platters were piled high with meat pies, and golden-brown fried sausages. Joints of roast ham, pork and beef were ready to be sliced and baskets of freshly baked rolls were placed at intervals along the table, together with huge pats of buttercup-yellow butter. Several types of cheese were arranged on boards decorated with rosy-red apples from the fruit store, and sparkling jellies wobbled temptingly together with blancmange and bowls of trifle. The aroma was intoxicating and Daisy was delighted with the effort that all the kitchen staff had made. She turned to Marjorie with an expectant smile.

'Oh, my dear Lord!' Marjorie covered her face with her hands. 'This is peasant food. It looks like a harvest supper. It's not what I ordered, Tattersall. Did you do this to make me look foolish? I'll be the laughing stock of the officers' mess, and Roland can say goodbye to his promotion. Get out – I've had enough of you, and your wretched family. You can vacate the cottage tomorrow, and I never want to see you again.'

Chapter Twelve

Daisy stared at Marjorie in disbelief. After all the hard work that each and every member of the household had put in to make this party a success, and this was all the thanks that she was to receive for organising the event. She was tempted to walk out there and then, but the cottage was home to Mary, Hilda and the children as well as for herself, and to be evicted at such short notice would be a disaster. She knew that she would always have a home at Creek Cottage with her aunt and uncle, but Mary and the others depended upon her, and she could not let them down.

'Well! Don't stand there staring at me like a codfish,' Marjorie stormed. 'Get out now, or do I have to get Molesworth to throw you out bodily?'

Daisy looked up at the portrait of the late Squire Tattersall, Jay's natural father, and for a moment she thought she saw him wink at her. The old squire was notorious for being a bad employer, a bad landlord and an extremely bad father – but he would not have stood for any nonsense, especially from a social-climbing nobody like Marjorie Harker.

Daisy took a deep breath. 'Mrs Harker, you are the most ungrateful, ungracious person I have ever met. Your servants and mine have slaved night and day to make this party a success. What you demanded was impossible and you must know that, unless you are extremely stupid. This is my home and you cannot throw me out – in fact it should be the other way round. You never thought to obtain a legal contract with me, so it's my word against yours, and I have the whole village here, who will back me up.'

Marjorie opened and shut her mouth several times, reminding Daisy of a fish landed on the river-bank. Then, before Marjorie could think of an appropriate response, the double doors opened and guests flooded in with the general, his wife and son at their head.

'By Jove!' Major-General Tighe-Martin exclaimed, gazing round with an appreciative smile. 'What a feast you've laid on for us, Mrs Harker. Just the smell of that roast beef is making me hungry.'

Mrs Tighe-Martin nodded enthusiastically. 'How clever of you to keep to the country theme, Marjorie. This is much more appetising than some of the fancy food served up at the military balls. I must compliment you on your originality.'

Marjorie's pale cheeks flooded with colour and she took a deep breath. 'Thank you, Felicia. I'm so pleased that you approve.'

'I should think anyone would want to dig into such a spread,' Ned Tighe-Martin said enthusiastically. 'Daisy – I may call you Daisy, may I not? – would you care to partner me at supper?'

Shaken, but also dizzy with relief, Daisy smiled and nodded. 'That would be delightful, sir.'

He proffered his arm. 'It's Ned to my friends.'

'Thank you, Ned.' Daisy caught sight of Nick, who was with Dove and Mrs Bee. She could only hope that he had taken her seriously. There was no future for them – she belonged to Jay, and always would – but that did not mean she would go into a nunnery. It was very pleasant to have the company of someone like Ned, who was good-looking, charming and had a sense of humour, although she had a feeling that she was second best. Julian had managed to escape from Flora and he had somehow persuaded Charity to sit with him at one of the smaller tables. Ned's eyes kept straying that way during the meal, although he took pains to be entertaining and attentive to Daisy. She suspected that not only had Charity fallen into his arms, she had also stolen his heart. Marjorie was eyeing Julian warily, as if trying to decide whether or not he was a good prospect as a son-in-law, but she would definitely not approve of her daughter marrying into the army – even if Ned was the major-general's son.

Daisy turned her attention back to Ned. 'You like her, don't you?'

'Is it so obvious?'

She smiled. 'I'm afraid so, at least it is to me.'

'That fellow seems to be monopolising her.'

'Then do something about it, Ned. As soon as everyone has finished their meal I'm going to announce the treasure hunt. If I can arrange a diversion so that Julian is out of the way, you might like to take advantage. It's a moonlit night and it will be very romantic in the garden, and Charity loves romance.'

Ned raised his glass to her. 'You are a devious woman, Daisy.'

'Thank you, Ned. I'll take that as a compliment.'

'Would you like some trifle, or do you prefer jelly?'

'Trifle would be lovely.' Daisy sat back in her chair, planning her next move while Ned went to fetch a bowl of trifle. Flora's flame-red hair made her stand out in the crowd and she was seated at a table on the far side of the room with Ivy and the Johnson family. Judging by their raucous laughter they were all thoroughly enjoying themselves, and very merry from imbibing the ale and cider. Although that applied to most of the male guests, Mr Peabody excepted, but then it would not do for the vicar of Little Creek to be seen the worse for wear. Grace, on the other hand, was sitting next to Eleanora and their flushed cheeks and bouts of girlish giggles suggested that they had been enjoying the sherry and fruit punch. There was no sign of Uncle Sidney, but Daisy had sent James to the lake with a hamper of food and George had accompanied him, carrying a crate of bottled beer. Toby had declined the offer of a moonlit fishing trip, stating that he wanted to be with Minnie, and Daisy was pleased to see that her brother and his fiancée were sharing a table with Nick, Dove, Linnet and Elliot. What was even more satisfying was the fact that all three couples seemed to be getting along really well. Perhaps Nick had taken her rejection in the spirit it was intended and had turned to the young woman who obviously adored him.

Daisy's attention was diverted by Ned, who returned with two bowls of trifle. 'I couldn't resist it, Daisy. You obviously have a splendid cook at Creek Manor.'

'Yes, Nell Pearce has been here long before I married Jay.'

'My mother told me what happened to your husband. I'm so sorry.'

'Thank you, but I know he's out there somewhere. He will return, I'm sure of it.'

'I certainly hope so.' Ned was silent while he ate the dessert. 'That was delicious. But one thing puzzles me.'

Daisy resisted the temptation to scrape the last scrap of sherry-soaked sponge from the bottom of the glass dish. 'What is that?'

'One of your servants told my mother that you

own Creek Manor, so why is Mrs Harker living here? It's well known in the regiment that she's a wealthy woman with a property of her own.'

'Does the general know about this?'

'I don't know if Mama has told him, but it's only a matter of time before he finds out. Why the deception?'

Daisy leaned forward, her elbows resting on the table as she gave him a searching look. 'If I tell you in confidence, will you promise not to say anything to your father?'

'Of course.'

'Marjorie Harker is ambitious for her husband, and I can't fault her for that, but she saw an opportunity and took it.'

'You mean the fact that your husband is missing?'

'Yes, exactly that. She thought that living here would create a better impression on your father, and the prospective suitors for her girls, although in my opinion Patience is far too young to consider marriage.'

'And she doesn't want Charity to marry a soldier?'

'That's right.'

He leaned back in his chair, fingering the stem of his wine glass. 'Well, if I play my cards correctly she might have lost that particular battle.'

'Charity is a nice girl, if a little spoilt, and she's very naïve when it comes to men. I hope you won't break her heart, Ned.'

'You have my word on that.'

Daisy glanced across the room to where Patience had risen to her feet and was dancing with Will Johnson without the benefit of a musical accompaniment. Their energetic gyrations were causing some amusement, and several more of the younger guests joined in. Miss Creedy leaped to her feet and waddled into the great hall where she began to thump away on the piano. Daisy could hear her from where she was sitting, and after a few seconds there was a bemused silence with the guests listening in disbelief at the crashing discords.

Constable Fowler rose from his seat, his cheeks puffed out with indignation, causing his mutton-chop whiskers to flap as if they were a bird attempting to spread its wings and fly off. Clearly agitated, he marched into the great hall, followed by the rest of the company who had abandoned the supper table, leaving dirty crockery, empty glasses and most of the serving dishes empty except for a few scraps. Fuller grabbed his fiddle and rushed after the constable with George Keyes, who was clutching his concertina to his chest as he ran.

Daisy jumped to her feet and hurried after them. She was in time to see Constable Fowler wrestling with Miss Creedy as she resisted his attempts to raise her from the piano stool.

'Leave me be,' she screamed. 'I was playing the piano when you were in petticoats, Mick Fowler.'

'Don't make me arrest you for disturbing the peace, Miss Creedy.'

'Come on, my duck,' Fuller said gently. 'Get up, there's a good girl.'

'Get away from me, Tom Fuller. I'm not a girl and I'm not your duck.' Miss Creedy stuck both feet under the piano, closed her eyes and screwed up her face as the two men tried to prise her from her seat.

Daisy watched in horror but she was galvanised into action when she saw Marjorie approaching. Daisy hurried over to the piano, pushing her way through the people who had crowded round to watch the spectacle.

'Let me try,' she said in a low voice, and Miss Creedy's tormentors moved away, albeit reluctantly. Daisy placed her arm around Lavender's shoulders and eased her to a sitting position. 'That was an excellent performance, Lavender, but you mustn't tire yourself.'

Miss Creedy opened her eyes, staring blearily at Daisy. 'They were trying to bully me.'

'They meant no harm.' Daisy raised her head to glance at the expectant faces surrounding them. 'I'm sure everyone would wish to give a round of applause for your performance, Lavender.'

'Most certainly.' Ned Tighe-Martin began to clap his hands together and gradually everyone took the hint and joined in.

'There,' Daisy said triumphantly. 'You see how people appreciate you. Why don't you take a bow?'

Blushing furiously, Lavender Creedy struggled to her feet and curtsied. 'Thank you all.'

'And now shall we let the gentlemen have a turn?' Daisy suggested gently. 'I'm sure you would like some refreshment after that performance.'

Edna Johnson stepped forward. 'A glass of fruit punch will revive you, Lavender, dear. Come with me and we'll sit together for a while.'

'You were always a sweet child, Edna,' Miss Creedy said tearfully. 'Always thinking of others.' She turned to Constable Fowler. 'I can't say the same for you, Michael Fowler. You were a very naughty boy, always scrumping apples and throwing fire-crackers to frighten my poor little pussycats.'

Constable Fowler ran his finger round the inside of his collar. 'I've grown up since then, Miss Creedy. But you taught me to play the piano, so I'm very grateful.'

Daisy could see that the crowd had become bored with the scene and they were melting away. Now was an ideal time to start the treasure hunt. She spotted Charity, who seemed to be lecturing Patience and Janet Johnson, no doubt telling them off for their riotous behaviour. Daisy moved swiftly to Ned's side.

'I'm going to announce the treasure hunt. If you want to partner Charity, now is the time to ask her. Flora is clinging onto Julian for all her worth, so you'd better hurry.'

Ned saluted her and strode off in Charity's direc-tion. The smile Charity gave when she saw him was enough to convince Daisy that she had done the right thing. If a romance blossomed between Charity and Ned Tighe-Martin, Marjorie would simply have to put up with having her daughter wedded to the regiment.

Daisy turned to Constable Fowler, who had regained the piano stool and was flexing his fingers while Fuller tightened the strings on his fiddle.

'Constable Fowler, will you play me a chord so that I get people's attention?'

'Yes, Mrs Tattersall, and thanks for helping with Miss Creedy. She's a determined little body and a better piano teacher than a player.' He played the piano equivalent of a trumpet fanfare and it had the desired effect of gaining everyone's attention.

Daisy moved to the middle of the floor to announce the start of the treasure hunt. 'If you will choose your partners . . . and you will need to wrap up as it's a bit chilly outside. Good luck, everyone.' She left the great hall and made her way to the front door where James handed her a woollen shawl. 'Thank you, James. That's very thoughtful.'

'It was Hilda who suggested it, madam.'

'Well, thank you anyway. I'm going to make sure all the lanterns are lit. We don't want any accidents.' She stepped outside and took a deep breath of the scented air. The cool breeze was welcome after the fug indoors, but she wrapped the shawl around her shoulders and made her way round the side of the house to the rose garden. It was a moonlit night, and that combined with the flickering light of the flambeaux made it easy to see the coloured pebbles that Charity and Patience had laid down as a trail leading to the summerhouse. She could hear footsteps not far behind her, together with excited chatter and laughter. It seemed that the treasure hunt was proving popular. She broke into a run and was able to open up the trapdoor before anyone came into sight. Jack had been given the task of lighting lanterns and placing them at intervals along the underground passage, but Daisy wanted to make sure that they were all in good working order. A fall or a sprained ankle would mar the evening for all concerned, and she was almost at the end of the tunnel when the sound of someone running made her stop and turn around. She lifted a lantern and raised it above her head.

'Julian, you're the first,' she said cautiously. 'Where is your partner?'

'I'm blooming well coming,' Flora said breathlessly. 'You're no gent, Julian Carrington. A decent man would wait for the lady to catch him up, or at least hold her hand. What's the matter with you?'

Julian rounded on her. 'Hold your tongue, you red-headed harpy. I have business to discuss with Mrs Tattersall.'

'Don't speak to her like that,' Daisy said angrily.

'She latched onto me. I didn't ask her to come on this wild-goose chase.'

'If you feel like that what are you doing here?'

'I want to speak to you, but you're always surrounded by people indoors.'

'I have nothing to say to you, Julian.'

Flora pushed past him to stand next to Daisy. 'Is this cove the man you were engaged to, Daisy? The swine who jilted you at the altar.'

'Yes, but it wasn't quite like that, Flora,' Daisy said hastily.

'It was a mistake.' Julian made a grab for Daisy's hand. 'You've forgiven me, haven't you, my dear? You know it was my parents who put pressure on me to marry someone of my own class.'

Daisy backed away from him. She could feel the cool air coming from the mouth of the tunnel and the one thought in her head was to escape. 'It was over a long time ago and things have changed since then.'

'But I haven't,' Julian whined. 'I want you, Daisy. I always did.'

'Be honest with her, you pathetic rat.' Flora faced him, arms akimbo. 'You're a fortune-hunter. I saw you gawping at that young girl, Cherry or Charity or whatever her name is, but she don't want you either. You're a sad case, if ever I saw one.'

'You were keen enough on me at the start,' Julian said, curling his lip. 'If I'm a fortune-hunter, it takes one to know one.'

'Yes, cully. That's why I've got your measure. Now clear off. Daisy don't want you and neither do I.'

Julian seized her by the shoulders and pushed her aside. 'You're nothing but a trollop. I don't have to listen to you.'

The slap that Flora gave him echoed around the damp walls of the passageway, and Julian's hand flew to his sore cheek. Daisy made a run for it, her only aim now was to escape into the fresh air, and put Julian Carrington as far behind her as possible.

She emerged onto the path through the undergrowth to the welcome sound of the waves sucking on the pebbles and the soft breeze rustling the fresh green leaves on the surrounding trees, but she could also hear Julian's irate voice and he was intent on following her. She fought her way through the bushes and brambles, heading for the beach. She could only hope that Toby would be one of the first to follow the clues and arrive in time to put a stop to Julian's unrelenting pursuit. Julian was not far behind her and Flora was still screaming at him. Daisy covered her ears with her hands and broke into a run, instinctively heading towards the water. Clouds had scudded across the moon, and the lanterns that Jack, aided by Judy, had placed along the foreshore twinkled like fallen stars. But there was another sound that Daisy recognised instantly and she came to a halt as a wooden keel grated on the stony foreshore. A dark figure leaped into the water and hauled the jolly boat onto the beach.

'Daisy. Is that you? For God's sake, what are you doing out here at this time of night? And who's that shouting like a lunatic?' Marius waded through the shallows and was at her side in an instant. He took off his cloak and wrapped it around her.

She leaned against him, breathing in the comforting scent of bay rum and the tang of salt. 'What are you doing here, Marius? I thought you had gone on a long trip.'

'Let her go,' Julian said breathlessly as he skidded to a halt beside them. 'Who the hell are you, anyway?'

'I have every right to be here, but who are you?' Marius placed his arm protectively around Daisy's shoulders.

'What's going on?' Flora demanded, gasping for breath. 'Is this part of the treasure hunt, Daisy? If so I'll take him – he looks like a good sort.'

Marius inclined his head, laughing. 'I don't know what sort of party you're having at the manor house, but it seems to have got out of hand.'

Daisy broke away from him, but she kept his cloak wrapped around her. 'Mr Carrington was escorting this young lady on a treasure hunt, Marius. It's a party I had to organise for Mrs Harker.' She glanced towards the bushes from where some of the other treasure seekers were beginning to emerge.

'Come on, you stupid man,' Flora said, tugging at Julian's sleeve. 'You're not wanted here and we've still got time to win the prize. I hope it's worth it.' She dragged him away, still muttering beneath his breath.

'Nice company you keep,' Marius said drily.

'He's someone I used to know.'

'But you don't want anything to do with him now?'

'It's all in the past, Marius. But more importantly, why are you here? I wasn't expecting you to return quite so soon.'

'We had fair winds and we landed the cargo without any delays. I came to give you your share of the profits.'

The clouds that had obscured the moon moved on and for the first time she could see his features clearly. 'That's wonderful.'

'It's not a fortune, but it's a start and we'll go on from here, if you're willing to trust me to find cargoes for the *Lazy Jane*.'

'I am, of course, but are you sailing again right away?'

'No. I persuaded Guppy to put into the creek so that I could see you and give you your dues. I thought you might be in need of the money.'

'More than you know,' Daisy said with a wry smile. 'I'm not sure if I have a home at the moment. Mrs Harker wanted to evict us from the cottage, but she might have changed her mind after the success of the party.'

Marius patted the pocket of his great coat and coins clinked together. 'I'm not saying that this is a fortune, but it will help.'

He produced the leather pouch and handed it to her. It was satisfyingly heavy and Daisy experienced a glimmer of hope. Maybe there was a chance that they could survive financially without having to rely on Marjorie's money. The thought made her smile.

'I'd love to stay and see you safely back to the house,' Marius said hastily. 'But I should get back on board.'

'Of course. I mustn't keep you.' Daisy followed him to the water's edge. 'I don't suppose you learned anything that might be of interest.'

He stopped and turned to give her a steady look. 'If you mean have I heard anything about your husband – I'm afraid not. Although I have people making enquiries all along the coast. Occasionally a person is rescued from the sea and they can't remember who they are or how they got there, but no such reports have come my way.' He took her hand in his and kissed it. 'But if I hear anything you can be sure that I'll pass the news on to you straight away.'

'Thank you, Marius.' Daisy wrapped her fingers around his hand, unwilling to let go of the one person who might bring her news of Jay, either good or bad. 'But you don't think there's much hope, do you?'

'Never give up hope, Daisy.'

She released him reluctantly. 'Will you sail with them on the next voyage?'

'No. I only went to see how the ship was being run, but I'm satisfied that Guppy and Ramsden have a good crew and can be trusted with the cargoes. My job is to make sure that the holds are never empty – that's business.'

'Yes, I see that.'

'I have an office in Maldon now, and a couple

233

more in the north, which I visit on a regular basis, but if you need me, send word to my clerk in Maldon. He'll make sure that I receive the message and I'll come as quickly as I can.'

'Thank you, Marius. I just need to keep in touch – for business reasons, of course.'

He pushed the jolly boat into the water and climbed into it. 'Don't worry. I'll let you have the figures as soon as they're ready and I'll call on you whenever possible.'

Daisy stood on the foreshore watching him row back to the *Lazy Jane*, and despite the comforting weight of the money pouch, she felt a sense of loss – as if she had just said farewell to an old friend.

'Who was that, Daisy? Are you consorting with smugglers?'

She spun round at the sound of her brother's voice, and she laughed. 'Toby, you made me jump.'

'Seriously, though. Who was that?'

'Marius Walters is my business partner, Toby. I haven't had time to tell you about it, but he's a shipping agent, and he's chartered the *Lazy Jane*. He came to bring me my first share in the profits.'

'Deuced funny time to call on a lady,' Toby said, frowning.

'Leave her alone, Toby.' Minnie clutched his arm. 'This is a party. You can cross-examine your sister in the morning.'

'I think it is the morning already,' Daisy said, chuckling. 'Have you found the treasure?'

'We're not seriously looking.' Toby glanced along the narrow beach. 'I say we build a fire and get the fiddler and the chap who plays the concertina to join us. Dancing in the moonlight would be just the thing.'

'And it's such a lovely night,' Minnie added, looking up at the myriads of stars. 'Do say yes, Daisy.'

'It's a splendid idea. I'll go and fetch the musicians.'

'Stay here, Daisy,' Toby said firmly. 'Send the boy who's been skulking in the shadows. He looks lost.'

Daisy followed his gaze. 'Oh, it's Jack.' She beckoned to him and called his name. 'You remember him, Toby. He's Jay's younger brother.'

Jack responded eagerly, rushing over to join them like an excited puppy. 'You wanted me, Daisy?'

'Yes, Jack. We're going to build a bonfire on the beach, and I'd like you to fetch the musicians to play for us so that we can dance in the moonlight.'

'Can I bring Judy and my mates?'

'Yes, but if they misbehave they'll be sent home. They can collect brushwood and dried leaves for the fire.' Daisy smiled to herself as he scampered off towards the mouth of the tunnel. This would be a party to remember – but she dreaded to think what Marjorie would say if she learned that it had ended with a moonlit frolic on the beach.

Chapter Thirteen

Not only did Jack bring the three musicians and Judy – who was supposed to be looking after her younger siblings, but had somehow managed to escape her mother's eagle eyes – he also brought his friends Danny Shipway and Alfie Green. They were followed by so many of the other guests that the narrow strip of beach was soon crowded. A huge bonfire was constructed and lit, and flames darted up into the night sky, putting the moon to shame. Ned and Charity had arrived soon after Toby and Minnie, followed by Nick, Dove, Linnet and Elliot, but to Daisy's astonishment the last people to emerge from the underground passage were the general and his wife. Daisy glanced behind them, instinctively crossing her fingers in case Marjorie had followed them, but they seemed to have come on their own. Patience and Will were already searching for the prize and the rest of the Johnson family joined them. Somehow crates of beer arrived as well as bottles of wine and cider, and at this point Daisy would not have been surprised to find the punchbowl and glass cups laid out on the sand, but evidently these had been left behind.

Then to her surprise she spotted the house servants having a party of their own further along the beach, together with the grooms and stable boys. What surprised Daisy even more was the fact that the rivalry between the Manor and Four Winds servants seemed to have been forgotten, and the housekeepers were chatting amicably, as were the two cooks, while the kitchen staff set out a picnic with the leftovers from the house party.

Music filled the night air and Constable Fowler serenaded the ladies in his beautiful baritone voice, with the partygoers joining in the choruses of the various popular songs. Couples held each other close, whether the tune was a waltz or a jig, dancing cheek to cheek, and others wandered off into the shadows, free to do as they pleased without chaperones putting a stop to anything they considered inappropriate.

Daisy stood at the water's edge, staring at the inlet where the moonlight created a silver path across the rippling waves. It lured her like the song of a siren and she felt compelled to step onto it and glide towards horizon – out there it seemed possible that she might find Jay and bring him back to shore. Everyone had a partner to share the wonder of the

starry night, everyone except herself. Daisy placed
one foot into the water, but was restrained by a
strong hand.

'You can't dance with wet feet, Daisy.'

'Marius – how did you get here? I saw you row
away.'

'I changed my mind. The tide doesn't turn for
another three hours. I couldn't leave you on your
own, especially on such a beautiful night.'

This made her giggle. 'I'm hardly alone, Marius.
Virtually everyone has joined us on the beach.'

'You were alone in your heart. I couldn't bear to
see you suffer like that.' He held out his hand. 'Will
you dance with me, Daisy?'

She hesitated. 'I don't know. It wouldn't be proper.'

'When was the last time you danced?'

'On my wedding day.' Her voice broke on a
suppressed sob.

'But you are not in mourning, Daisy. It isn't a sin
to enjoy yourself once in a while.'

Marius took her in his arms and whirled her
round to the strains of a waltz. She looked up and
met his sympathetic gaze with an attempt at a smile,
and she did not argue. Waltzing on damp sand and
rough pebbles was not like gliding around a highly
polished dance floor, and at times it was necessary
for Marius to hold her close in order to prevent her
from falling or twisting an ankle. Daisy moved stiffly
at first, but the canopy of stars and the warmth
from the bonfire created a mystical and magical

atmosphere that seemed to affect all those present, and gradually she began to relax and allow Marius to take control. She had borne the problems that beset her since Jay's disappearance and now, for the first time, she allowed someone else to guide her footsteps, even if it was just a waltz.

But the spell was broken by the sound of a harsh voice, one that Daisy knew only too well.

'What do you think you're doing, Tattersall? You've ruined my party and I'll never forgive you for this.' Marjorie glared at Marius, who had come to a halt as the music ceased. 'And who may you be, sir?'

He acknowledged her with a curt nod of his head. 'Marius Walters, ma'am.'

'Marius is my business partner,' Daisy added hastily.

'Business? What business? What have you been keeping from me, Daisy Tattersall?'

'You'll pardon me saying so, ma'am,' Marius said in a low voice, 'but this is neither the time nor the place for such a conversation.'

'You will keep out of it, sir. This has nothing to do with you.'

'Marius is right,' Daisy said angrily. 'We will talk about this later, Mrs Harker, but for now I suggest you join in the party, or risk making yourself look foolish.'

Marjorie raised her hand as if to strike Daisy, but Marius was too quick for her and he caught her by the wrist. 'That won't solve anything.'

'I don't know how you came to be here, but I want you to get off my property.' Marjorie's face was white in the moonlight and her eyes dark pools, her lips twisted into an ugly grimace.

Daisy glanced over Marjorie's shoulder. 'This is my land, Mrs Harker, and I suggest you moderate your tone if you wish to make a good impression on the general, because he and his wife are coming this way.'

Marjorie turned her head to look and her whole demeanour changed so dramatically that she might have become another person.

'General and Mrs Tighe-Martin – I do hope you're enjoying my party.'

'It's wonderful.' Felicia Tighe-Martin grasped Marjorie's outstretched hand. 'Thank you so much for all your hard work in organising this amazing evening. We've never enjoyed ourselves so much, have we, Hereward?'

'No, my dear, I don't think we have. The treasure hunt ending on the beach was an inspiration. I feel twenty years younger.'

His wife dug him playfully in the ribs. 'I'll remind you of that tomorrow when you're stiff and aching from all this exercise. But, seriously, Marjorie, I must congratulate you. Your husband is a lucky man to have such a clever and charming wife.'

Marjorie simpered and cast her eyes down. 'You flatter me, Felicia.'

'On the contrary,' the general said firmly. 'You

may rest assured that I will put in a good word for Roland when his promotion comes up for review. In fact, I could do with you on my staff, Marjorie. With your organisational skills I'm sure we would win every battle.'

Marius grasped Daisy by the hand. 'Now is as good a time as any to make our escape.'

She needed no second bidding and she followed him towards the folly. At that moment a great shout went up, followed by clapping and cheering.

'Someone has found the prize,' Daisy said breathlessly.

'What did they win?'

'A bottle of champagne – the last one in the cellar. Marjorie will be furious because she wanted to impress her guests by serving unlimited champagne. She simply didn't understand that the funds wouldn't stretch that far. Anyway, she'll be the centre of attention now so she won't notice that I've gone.' Daisy held her hand out to Marius. 'Thank you for everything. I'd better return to the house and make sure that all is well.'

Marius shook his head. 'You've done enough for that woman. I'm going to see you safely back to your cottage.'

'You don't have to do that. I'm quite capable of making my own way home.'

'Of course you are, but it's the middle of the night and you never know who might be wandering around the grounds. I won't take no for an answer, Daisy.'

It was obvious that he had made up his mind and it was useless to argue, besides which, she was exhausted and more than ready for bed. They negotiated the underground passageway in silence and walked arm in arm through the rose garden, across the deer park and over the field. When they reached the cottage Marius saw her inside, but he did not follow her in. He leaned over and kissed her on the cheek.

'Get some sleep, Daisy.'

'Will you get to the ship in time?'

'Yes, don't worry, but if I should happen to miss the tide I can always ask Mrs Harker to put me up for the night.'

His dry tone and wry smile made Daisy giggle, and the slight tension that had arisen between them was eased.

'Good night, Marius. Or should I say good morning?'

'I think it's almost dawn, so I'd better get going. I'll see you again very soon, Daisy.'

'Thank you for everything.'

She waited until he was swallowed up by the shadows before closing the door. The cottage was quiet, with no sound coming from the room that Judy shared with her mother and three siblings. It had been an eventful evening, but Marjorie had been incandescent with fury. If she carried out her threat to evict them it would be the start of a bitter battle for Creek Manor, and one that Daisy intended to win. She climbed the stairs to her room, undressed as far as her chemise and stowed the pouch of money under the mattress before she fell into bed. She slept so heavily that she did not hear Mary when she entered the room.

Breakfast next morning was a subdued affair. Daisy was still exhausted, but Mary and Hilda were suffering from the after-effects of drinking the fruit cup and several glasses of wine. Judy took the little ones into the garden to see if the hens had laid eggs, and there was a brief period of peace.

'Are you going up to the house this morning?' Mary asked, sipping her tea and wincing each time she moved her head.

'Yes, of course.' Daisy tried to sound more positive than she was feeling.

'We heard the way she was speaking to you on the beach,' Hilda said warily. 'Do you think she'll evict us all?'

Daisy shook her head. 'No, of course not. I've told her before that without a contract it was simply a verbal agreement. I own the manor house and this cottage.'

'But she can afford a good lawyer,' Mary added grimly. 'That woman is ruthless. I've a good mind to go there and have a word with the general. If he knows what she's really like he'll have nothing more to do with her.'

'It's the girls I feel sorry for.' Hilda nibbled at a

piece of bread and butter, swallowing with difficulty. 'Charity and Patience were really enjoying themselves on the beach, and that young man, the general's son, is ever so good-looking.'

'But he's a soldier, Hilda.' Mary pulled a face. 'That won't suit madam.'

Daisy rose to her feet. 'I'd better go and face her. Let's see what she has to say today.'

'Well, we can't go on like this for too long,' Mary said wearily. 'It's not the first time she's threatened us. That woman needs to be taught a lesson. Just because she's rich, she can't rule other folk's lives.'

Before going to the manor house Daisy went to the beach. She told herself it was to see what state the revellers had left it in, but she also wanted to make sure that Marius had reached the *Lazy Jane* in time for her to sail. She half expected to see him camped out on the foreshore, but the only signs of the previous night's merrymaking were the ashes of the two fires and some empty bottles that had been missed during the general clear-up. Daisy shielded her eyes and gazed out to sea, but there was no sign of the ship, and the *Lazy Jane* must be well on her way to Maldon. She sighed: it was time to face Marjorie and find out what mood she was in this morning. One thing was certain as she made her way back through the narrow tunnel – the secret passage was no longer a secret.

She emerged into the rose garden and walked

briskly, taking deep breaths of the keen sweet-scented air. The day promised to be fine and that would suit the guests, although Daisy had no idea of how long they intended to remain at the manor house. Julian and his colleagues must surely have to return to London, or wherever they were based, and that would be a relief. Julian Carrington was trouble and she was well rid of him. She could only hope that Charity had seen through his charming manner. It had seemed that she had a preference for Ned Tighe-Martin, but Charity would have to contend with her mother's disapproval should she choose him as her suitor.

Daisy entered the house with a feeling of dread, but Molesworth greeted her with a pleased smile.

'Good morning, Molesworth. Do you know where I'll find Mrs Harker?'

'Good morning, madam. I believe she's in the drawing room. Miss Wendell said she was asking for you earlier.'

'Then I'd better go to her.' Daisy hesitated, turning to him with a smile. 'How do you think it went last evening?'

'It's not for me to say, but in my opinion it was the best party ever held in Creek Manor. The old squire would have been proud of you.'

'Thank you, Molesworth. I hope you all enjoyed it.'

'We did, thank you, madam. A good time was definitely had by everyone.'

James nodded in agreement and she thought she

saw a glimmer of a smile in his eyes. She suspected that his evening had proved to be more than enjoyable, and judging by George's downcast expression she sensed that he had been the loser in the game of romance. However, as she approached the drawing room she was beginning to wish that the party on the beach had not happened. Marjorie had been very clear that she wanted them out of the cottage, and Daisy was prepared for a fight. She knocked on the door, opened it without waiting for a response and walked in, head held high.

'Good morning, Mrs Harker. I believe you wanted to see me.'

Marjorie was seated at a rosewood escritoire, pen in hand, but she placed it back on the silver inkstand. She turned her head to give Daisy an inscrutable look.

'I've come to a decision.'

Daisy clasped her hands tightly in front of her. 'And that is?' She was expecting the worst, but to her surprise Marjorie's expression lightened into a semblance of a smile.

'Last evening, despite your attempts to make me look foolish, was an enormous success.'

'That was not my intention,' Daisy said icily. 'We worked miracles considering how little time we had in which to prepare, and very little money for such a big event.'

'Tra, la, la,' Marjorie sang in an irritatingly high soprano. 'Don't try to make excuses, Mrs Tattersall.

All I would say was that your efforts, whatever the intention might have been, received the highest praise from the general and his wife, and indeed all the guests who came and thanked me for a wonderful party. Not that I would normally mix with the landlord of the village pub or the tenant farmers, but by some miracle they had a wonderful time, and the general has promised to recommend my husband for promotion.'

'Then I'm very glad,' Daisy said warily.

'And Charity is very taken with Ned Tighe-Martin. Of course, it's early days, and not what I had planned, but I can see definite advantages to being related by marriage to the major-general. Although Mr Carrington has good prospects in the Foreign Office, and his family are moneyed, Felicia has told me things about them that are quite shocking.'

Daisy decided that she had nothing to lose by being honest. 'Julian Carrington is a philanderer. I know that from personal experience.'

Marjorie stared at her intently. 'I don't listen to gossip.'

'If he married your daughter he would go through her fortune and abandon her. Believe me, I know Julian only too well.'

'I always thought you had a past, Mrs Tattersall, and now I'm certain of it. I don't think I want my girls to associate with you.'

'So you want me to leave the manor house? I was prepared for that.'

'On the contrary. I'm tired of living in this mausoleum, and it's served its purpose. I've instructed my servants to start packing and we'll leave after the guests have departed, which will be tomorrow.'

'I can't repay the money you laid out for my servants' wages at the moment, but I can assure you that I will . . .'

Marjorie held up her hand. 'It was nothing. I'm a very wealthy woman and our stay here has served its purpose. There is no reason to prolong the experience, and I'm eager to return to the comfort of my own home.'

'That's very generous of you,' Daisy said cautiously. 'Might I ask the reason for your change of heart?'

'Despite your efforts to embarrass me, everything has worked out well. However, you may continue to earn your keep by managing the servants until we leave, and I expect you to assist my daughters with their toilettes as before. I pride myself in being a fair woman, but I'm not a fool. We will maintain the mistress servant relationship until I depart.'

'I understand.' Daisy waited to be dismissed.

'You may go,' Marjorie said grandly. 'And make sure that the servants' work is up to standard. There was a great deal of uncalled-for carousing on the beach last night.'

Daisy had no answer to this and she left the room, pausing outside the door to take a deep breath. Was it true? Did Marjorie Harker actually say that she would be leaving the manor house so soon? Daisy pinched her left arm to make sure she was not dreaming – it hurt. She smiled and resisted the temptation to do a little jig as she made her way to the back stairs. Today she was a servant but tomorrow or the next day she would be mistress of the house once more, and she would not have to use the back stairs or keep order between the two rival sets of servants. She could hardly wait to tell Mary and Hilda, though they were probably already aware of the coming change. News travelled fast below stairs.

Charity was already up when Daisy entered her room. She looked ethereal in a white organdie wrapper, trimmed with lace, but her eyes were shining and there was a delicate flush to her cheeks. She danced up to Daisy and spun her round the room.

'What do you think of him?' Charity asked eagerly. 'Isn't he the most handsome man you've ever seen?'

'I can't think who you mean,' Daisy teased.

'Yes, you do. I'm talking about Ned, of course. He's such good company and so funny, he makes me laugh, and he's a wonderful dancer, too.'

'Yes, I agree with you, Charity. He is all those things.'

'Mama doesn't approve, but she'll come round. I always get my own way in the end.' Charity stared at Daisy, a frown puckered her brow. 'Who was that stranger you were dancing with on the beach last night? He was holding you very close.'

'I'm surprised that you noticed.' Daisy steered

Charity to the bed. 'Sit down and tell me which gown you want to wear this morning. You don't want to miss the Tighe-Martins at breakfast, do you?'

'Heavens, no! I'll wear the Indian muslin, or should I wear the pink poplin? Which do you think, Daisy? I can't decide.'

'Pink is perfect – it's very becoming, and you want to make a good impression on Mrs Tighe-Martin. Her husband already thinks you're a very pretty young lady.'

'Does he really?'

'Oh, yes. I heard him say so.'

'Then the pink it is. I was afraid I was looking like an old hag after dancing nearly all night.'

'You're eighteen, Charity. No one looks haggish at your age.'

'How old are you, Daisy?'

'I'm not quite twenty-one.'

'And already a widow. How sad.'

Daisy let this go – she was too happy to argue. She would be mistress of Creek Manor once again, and she had the money that Marius had given her. She'd counted it this morning and found it was a considerable sum, which would keep them going for a month or maybe more, and she hoped it was the first payment of many.

She went to the clothes press and took out the gown in question, shaking out the creases as she laid it on the bed.

Charity stood up and allowed the wrap to fall to the ground. 'Lace me up as tightly as you can, Daisy. I'm sure I ate far too much last evening.'

After much heaving on the strings of the corset, punctuated by squeals of complaint, Daisy managed to whittle Charity's waist to little more than a hand-span, and the gown fitted perfectly. Daisy was just finishing Charity's coiffure when Patience burst into the room, dressed as usual in her riding habit.

'You might wear something different, just for a change,' Charity said crossly.

'I wore a dress last evening.' Patience flung herself down on the bed. 'Anyway, I'm going riding today. Will Johnson is going to call for me and he's going to show me round their farm.'

'I always said you ought to marry a farmer,' Charity said, chuckling.

'At least a farmer doesn't get shot at by tribesmen.'

'Ned is a soldier, that's his job.'

'So is Papa, and Mama hates it when he's away fighting battles on the North-West Frontier. She'll be horrified if you choose Ned Tighe-Martin.'

'Don't be silly, Patty. We've only just met and he's leaving later today. I might never see him again.' Charity's voice broke with emotion.

'Don't think like that,' Daisy said, patting her on the shoulder. 'What will be, will be. Just let things take their course. If he's the one for you then nothing will keep him away.'

'Do you really think so?'

'Yes, I do.' Daisy stepped back to admire her handiwork. She had coiled Charity's tresses into a becoming style, taming her naturally curly hair except for a few stubborn tendrils that caressed her forehead and cheeks. 'That looks splendid. Now off you go, both of you.' She reached out to catch Patience by the hand before she could escape. 'And you, young lady, be nice to your sister. She really cares for Ned, so don't say anything that will embarrass her.'

Patience pulled a face. 'As if I would. Anyway, I rather like Will Johnson, so maybe I'm not such a hoyden after all.'

'I never thought you were. You're just young and full of life,' Daisy said, smiling. 'And Will is a nice young man. His family are decent, hard-working people, so don't let anyone tell you that he's not good enough for you.'

Patience stared at her in amazement. 'You really mean that, don't you?'

'Happiness should be grasped with both hands whether you are young or old. Anyway, you'd better go down to breakfast.'

Patience shook her head. 'I've got a better idea. I'm going to the stables to have my horse saddled and I'll ride over to the farm. If I have breakfast I know that Mama will try to prevent me from going out.' She ran to the door. 'You won't peach on me, will you, Daisy?'

'I won't say a word, although if your mother starts

to fret later I might have to tell her that you went riding in good company.'

'That's all right. Do that anyway, then she won't worry. But please wait until I've had a chance to get away.' Patience hurried from the room, allowing the door to close on its own.

Daisy tidied up Charity's clothes. She would miss the girls when they returned to Four Winds, but it would be wonderful to move back into her home again. She would once again be mistress of Creek Manor – all she needed to make life perfect was news that Jay had been found alive and well, and would soon return to his loving family. She came to a halt by the cheval mirror, and the young woman who gazed back at her looked anything but a grieving widow. Daisy had heard whispers in the village from gossips who wondered why she was not wearing full mourning, but neither she nor Mary were willing to give Jay up to the sea – not yet, anyway.

Chapter Fourteen

Toby and Minnie were the first guests to leave, accompanied by Ivy, but Flora had somehow managed to persuade Julian to take her back to London, although Daisy could see that his colleagues were not too keen on the idea. The barouche was kept busy plying to and from Little Creek station, and Mr and Mrs Woodward had no choice other than to await their turn, but when Molesworth finally announced that it had come for them, Letitia drew Daisy aside.

'You may think it's amusing to throw that red-haired trollop in Julian's path, but wait until my cousin Agnes hears about this. She won't be best pleased, and I wouldn't be surprised if you hear from Mr Carrington.'

Daisy shrugged. 'It had nothing to do with me, Mrs Woodward. Julian is free to choose his friends, and quite frankly it's his business, not yours, and certainly not mine.'

'Oh!' Letitia bristled with indignation. 'I won't be spoken to in that tone of voice by a mere servant.'

'My connection with your family ceased a long time ago, and for your information I am not a servant. I am the lady of the manor and Mrs Harker has been renting the property to impress gullible people like you, but she's leaving tomorrow and I am taking back control of my property. Now, I think your husband is calling to you. The carriage is waiting to take you to the station. Goodbye, Mrs Woodward – I hope we won't meet again.'

'Well, I never did.' Letitia bustled over to her husband. 'Harold, I've just been insulted by that woman.' She pointed a shaking finger at Daisy.

'Never mind that now, my dear. We need to hurry if we're to catch the London train.' He ushered his wife out of the house, but he paused before following her and doffed his hat to Daisy. She thought he winked at her, but he was too far away for her to be certain.

'Have they gone?' Marjorie appeared suddenly at Daisy's side. 'Dreadful people. I don't know why I invited them here.'

'They've gone now and I doubt if either of us will be seeing them again.'

'For once I agree with you, Daisy.' Marjorie surged forward at the sight of the general and his wife as they descended the grand staircase. 'Your stay has been all too brief – I'll miss you both.'

The general smiled benignly. 'I have a feeling we will be seeing more of you, my dear. Quite apart from the fact that I'm personally recommending your husband for promotion, it seems that my son and young Charity have come to an understanding.'

'Yes,' Felicia added hastily. 'Although, of course, it's early days and they're both very young. We'll have to see what transpires in the future.'

'Yes, indeed,' Marjorie said graciously. 'He's a charming young man, and he's more than welcome to visit us at Four Winds.'

The general eyed her curiously. 'You have another property, Marjorie?'

'She told us last evening,' Felicia said impatiently. 'Have you forgotten already?'

'Er – no, of course not.' He looked from one to the other as if seeking inspiration.

'I'll tell you again when we're on our way home.'

'I believe your carriage is waiting outside.'

Marjorie walked to the door with them, but Daisy hung back. She was pleased for Charity's sake that the general and his wife seemed happy to consider her as a future daughter-in-law, and Marjorie would have to accept the fact that her daughter had fallen in love with a soldier. However, it might be a different story should Patience choose to associate with Will Johnson, and she might not receive much support from her mother, even though Will was a decent, hard-working young man. The Johnsons would probably welcome her into their family, but Daisy could not imagine Marjorie taking kindly to the idea of her daughter as a farmer's wife. However, Patience was only sixteen, and there was plenty of time to think of marriage.

Daisy glanced out of the window and smiled as she spotted Charity and Ned in a close embrace – which did not look like a goodbye kiss. She turned away, resolutely crushing the niggling pangs of envy that suddenly beset her, and she headed for the servants' quarters.

Mrs Ralston popped out of her office like a jack-in-the-box just as Daisy was about to walk past.

'Oh my goodness,' Daisy gasped, clutching her hands to her bosom. 'You gave me such a fright.'

'I'm sorry, madam, but I need to speak to you urgently.' Mrs Ralston held the door open, leaving Daisy little alternative other than to enter the small room, which served as an office and a private parlour for the housekeeper.

'What is it, Ida? Is something bothering you?'

'What is going on, madam? I know I oughtn't to be so forward, but there are rumours flying around the servants' hall like a swarm of angry wasps.'

'What is being said?'

'That we're all to lose our jobs and we must start packing.'

'Who told you that?'

'Won't you take a seat, madam?'

'No, Ida. Not until you tell me who is responsible for spreading this rumour.'

'Miss Wendell was overheard speaking to Dorcas Jones. I've tried to get some sense out of her, but I think she's enjoying my discomfort. If it gets out amongst the rest of the servants there'll be out-and-out war between us and them.'

Daisy sank down on the nearest chair. She had to bite her lip to prevent herself from laughing.

'I don't see anything amusing in the situation, Mrs Tattersall.'

'No, Ida, it isn't. I'm sorry, but it is so ridiculous. Miss Wendell might well have been telling Mrs Jones to pack up their belongings because Mrs Harker and her daughters are moving out tomorrow. They and their servants will be returning to Four Winds.'

'Do you mean that, madam? You're not just saying it to keep the peace.'

'Certainly not. I know it's come about suddenly, but Mrs Harker has done what she set out to do. Miss Charity has met a young man who seems to be genuinely taken with her, and the general is going to recommend Colonel Harker for promotion. There is no need for them to remain here any longer.'

A series of expressions flitted across Mrs Ralston's small features, but her smile was wiped away by one of suspicion. 'Does that mean we have to pay back the wages she gave us?'

'No, most definitely not. You earned that money and so did I.'

Mrs Ralston reached for her hanky. 'I can't tell you how happy I am. Nell and I were thinking we would be cast out on the street, and who would take us on at our age?'

'Anybody with any sense would value two such hard-working, experienced and capable women, as I do. In fact, when my finances are settled I will be giving you a rise in your wages.'

'I don't know what to say.'

'Say nothing at the moment. How many people know about this?'

'We've tried to keep it from the others, madam. Nell thought it best.'

'Very wise. I'll go and tell her not to worry. Tomorrow we will get the manor house to ourselves.'

Daisy hurried to the kitchen to pass on the good news and Nell Pearce's pale blue eyes filled with tears.

'Oh, madam, I'm so relieved. I just can't tell you how much this means to me and to Ida. We really thought the end had come for us.'

'Far from it. This is just the beginning, but please keep it to yourself until after Mrs Harker and her daughters have left tomorrow.'

'I will indeed, and to celebrate getting my kitchen back to normal, I'll make a special dinner . . . after they've gone, of course.'

Daisy felt the atmosphere in the kitchen lighten perceptibly despite the fact that the maids were rushing around in the endless circle of preparing, serving and clearing up after meals. They all seemed oblivious to the coming changes, except for Cook, who was grinning broadly, and she even managed a smile when Phoebe Salt marched up to her and demanded more bacon for the dining room. Daisy left them to get on as best they could and she decided that Marjorie could manage without her for an hour or two. She was no longer at her beck and call.

Daisy walked back to the cottage and found Hilda and the children weeding the vegetable patch in the back garden, while Mary pegged washing on a line strung between two trees.

'Why are you here?' Mary asked anxiously. 'Is anything wrong?'

'On the contrary. Mrs Harker has decided to go home. They'll be leaving tomorrow and we can move back to the manor house.'

Hilda straightened up, wiping her grubby hands on her apron. 'What made her change her mind?'

'She's done what she set out to do, Hilda. We can live in comfort again.' Daisy gave her a steady look. 'What's the matter?'

'Don't you want to go back to the manor house?' Mary demanded, frowning. 'I can't wait to have a room of my own again.'

'I like it here,' Hilda said softly. 'It feels more like home to me and the nippers. I'm sorry, Daisy, I don't mean to sound ungrateful, but I love the cottage and the garden. I feel like myself for the first time since . . .' she broke off with a catch in her voice, and Judy gave her mother a hug.

'I love it here, too,' Judy said eagerly. 'I like working for Cook, or I did before the other kitchen maids turned up, but this little house is cosy and I don't mind the walk to the big house.'

'Neither do I,' Hilda added hastily. 'I can manage the walk providing I carry a walking stick. What do you say, Daisy? The cottage belongs to you.'

Daisy smiled. 'It's yours for as long as you want it, Hilda. You work as hard as anyone and harder than most, and there's always someone willing to keep an eye on the little ones. You deserve to have your own place.'

Hilda buried her face in her apron and Judy hugged her mother, while Molly comforted Nate and Pip, who had both started to cry.

'Don't take on like that,' Mary said, sniffing. 'You'll have me crying next, girl.'

'And Molly should go back to school,' Daisy added. 'Everything has been topsy-turvy since the Harkers moved into the manor house, but now we must get back to normal.'

'Well, I, for one, will be glad to have my own bed again,' Mary said firmly. 'You know I love you, Daisy. I couldn't wish for a better daughter-in-law, but you take up more than half the bed and some-times you talk in your sleep.'

Daisy smiled. 'And you snore, Mary. The feeling is mutual. Anyway, we'll move our things to the manor house tomorrow, but now I'd better get back and make sure that everything is running smoothly.'

Mary followed her to the garden gate. 'When will you find out how much money that fellow has made for you, Daisy?'

'I don't know. I've been relying on Marius to keep me informed, but that will have to change.'

'What will you do?'

'I'm going to ride to Maldon. I need to talk things over with Marius and I intend to take a more active part in managing my own affairs. I don't intend to be caught out again as I have been with the bank. There's money in Jay's account, but I can't touch it unless he's . . .' Daisy broke off, shaking her head. 'You know what I mean, Mary.'

Mary laid her hand briefly on Daisy's shoulder. 'I know, I feel that way too. If we say the word it feels as if we're admitting that he's gone for ever. You do what you must, dear. You have my blessing.'

'Thank you,' Daisy said simply, but she walked away with a more confident step. She knew that the manor house was important to her mother-in-law for many different reasons, and it meant a great deal to Daisy herself, if only because it belonged to Jay. She would do everything she could to protect his inheritance, and Mary's question had reminded her that the *Lazy Jane* was an asset she must make full use of, at least until Jay returned.

* * *

Two days later Daisy had Cinders saddled and she set off for Maldon with Jack riding beside her. She had chosen him as her companion over the more experienced grooms because she wanted better things for the boy than a life spent in the stables. Jack was intelligent and eager, if undisciplined, and although he was only eleven, Daisy knew that Jay would have wanted his younger brother to broaden his education, and she was fond of the boy. Besides which, he was an excellent rider and it would not do for the lady of Creek Manor to be seen riding unaccompanied. She urged Cinders to a canter, and Jack gave a whoop of joy as he encouraged his pony to keep up.

After a while Daisy reined in Cinders. 'We don't want to wear them out, Jack.'

He followed suit. 'Why are we going to Maldon? Is it to see that Marius fellow?'

'Mr Walters to you, unless he says differently. And, yes, I have a business proposition to put to him, and I don't want to wait until he finds time to visit me at the manor house.'

'Don't you trust him?'

She shot a sideways glance at Jack, taken by surprise. 'What makes you say that?'

'It's a long way to go just for a chat,' he said, chuckling. 'Or do you fancy him, Daisy?'

'You cheeky little monkey. Don't say such things or you'll set tongues wagging, and in answer to your question – no, I don't fancy him, but I like and trust him.'

They rode on, stopping occasionally to allow the horses to drink from a stream and take a brief rest. It was a warm start to the day, promising to become even hotter later on. The trees were in full leaf with the freshness of early summer, and the meadows were bright with buttercups, dandelions and moon daisies. Skylarks sang overhead and Daisy had a feeling that the day would go well, even though there was no guarantee of meeting up with Marius. She knew he travelled the country, but even if he was away she would leave a message with his agent, asking him to contact her urgently. All this could have been done by letter, but if she went in person she could be sure that the request was received, and at least she was doing something positive; simply sitting around and doing nothing was not something that appealed to her.

It was late morning when they rode into the small town and Daisy headed for the quay where the tan sails of Thames barges flapped idly in the gentle breeze. She realised that she and Jack were attracting curious looks, but she ignored them and dismounted close to the office where Marius employed a clerk.

'I'm hungry and thirsty,' Jack said crossly. 'May we get something to eat and drink afore I die of starvation?'

'Don't die yet.' Daisy glanced at him over her shoulder. 'You'll live for another half an hour or so and then we'll go to the inn.' The memory of her first meeting with Marius came back to her with vivid intensity, when the landlord of the inn had refused to serve her because she was a woman on her own. Marius had come to her rescue then – but now things were different. Her brief time with Marjorie had convinced her that she must take control of her own future, and that was what she wanted to discuss with Marius.

'Great heavens! What are you doing here in Maldon, Daisy?'

Startled out of her reverie, Daisy looked up and saw Marius walking towards them.

'You're here,' she said dazedly. 'I was hoping to find you.'

'Then you're in luck. I was just about to leave.'

'We come all this way and we're starving,' Jack added plaintively.

Marius chuckled and slapped him playfully on the back. 'We can't have you expiring from lack of nourishment, young man. It's Jack, isn't it?'

Jack pulled off his cap. 'Yes, sir.'

'We'll have a drink and a bite to eat in the Jolly Sailor. Take the horses to the stable, Jack, and then join us in the taproom.'

'Aye, sir.' Jack took the reins and led both horses to the stables at the rear of the inn.

Marius proffered his arm. 'Allow me, madam. This is an unexpected pleasure, I must say.'

'It's purely business, Marius.' She laid her hand on his sleeve and they entered the inn together.

The air was thick with tobacco smoke and men sat smoking clay pipes with tankards of ale on the tables in front of them. Despite the warmth of the day there was a fire in the inglenook, but Marius found them a table overlooking the busy quay and the neat weatherboard houses that lined the street.

'Well, now, Daisy, why have you come all this way?' He pulled up a chair and sat down beside her.

'Marjorie Harker has moved out. The party, strangely enough, was very successful, and her husband's promotion is almost assured. Charity has caught the eye of the general's son and Marjorie decided that it was time to leave. We have our home back.'

'I'm delighted to hear it, but how does that involve me?'

Seated close to him and with a view of the trading barges preparing to set sail, Daisy was suddenly assailed by doubts. 'Well, I thought that I could do more to help you run the business. I mean, you share a clerk with other companies – how do you know that he's being completely honest with you?'

'You think I'm being cheated?'

'Oh, no,' she said hastily. 'At least, not exactly, but the temptation would surely be there. You need someone who has your best interests at heart.'

'What had you in mind?'

'You could have an office in the manor house, and as I've a vested interest in the *Lazy Jane*, you could trust me to handle matters while you're away on business.'

The landlord chose that moment to appear at their table, and after a brief discussion with Jack, who had come in from the stable, they ordered meat pies and a jug of shandygaff, which Daisy discovered was a refreshing mixture of ale and ginger beer. When their plates were cleared away and the last drop of shandygaff had disappeared down Jack's throat, he rose from the table.

'I'd like to go and look at the barges, if you don't mind, Daisy.'

'That's all right, Jack. Don't fall in or your mother will have something to say about that.'

He grinned and sauntered out of the inn. Daisy sat back against the wooden settle.

'Well, Marius? You haven't said whether or not you like my suggestion.'

'I'm delighted that you want to help, but I'm afraid it wouldn't be very practical. Creek Manor is too far from any port to make it work.' He laid his hand on hers as it rested on the table. 'Not that I'm doubting your ability, Daisy.'

She withdrew her hand. 'Yes, I see that now. It was just an idea.'

'You need something more to occupy your mind.'

'I suppose that's true. I love the manor house and the people of Little Creek, but . . .'

'But you still miss your husband.'

'It's not the same without him. When Marjorie took over I didn't have time to think about my loss, but I need to find a way to earn money to supplement whatever profits we make from the *Lazy Jane*. I went through the accounts with Mrs Ralston, and the figures don't add up. No wonder the old squire turned to smuggling.'

'I trust you aren't thinking of following his example,' Marius said, laughing.

'I might very well if I knew how to go about it.' Daisy smiled reluctantly. 'But it's not your problem, Marius. I must think of another way, and I mustn't waste any more of your time.' She rose to her feet. 'Thank you for the pie and shandygaff. I must remember that drink, it's quite refreshing.'

Marius placed a handful of coins on the table and stood up. 'Do you have to go so soon?'

'I've done what I came to do.' Daisy walked through the taproom and out into the courtyard. The smell of tar, oil and the river mud brought back memories of a trip on the *Lazy Jane* when she had been a reluctant passenger and Jay had been the captain. She could see Jack standing on the quay wall, gazing at the Thames barges and he looked so much like his brother that she might have been looking at Jay when he was a boy.

'I hate to be the one to say this, Daisy, but it must be two months since Jay went missing. Perhaps you ought to face the fact that he won't be coming back.'

She spun round to glare at Marius. 'Don't say such things.'

'I'm sorry, but it's true. If he'd been rescued that night he would have been brought ashore somewhere along the coast, and he'd have made his way home. Or if he was injured he would have sent word.'

'I know what you say makes sense, but I'd know in my heart if he were dead. I won't rest until I know what happened that night.'

'You may never know.'

'I won't give up.'

'Be realistic, Daisy. You could go to court and let them decide on the likelihood of his return. I know you don't want to hear this, but if the verdict is death *in absentia*, as his widow you will gain access to the funds you need to run the estate. You're young, you have the rest of your life to lead – don't bury your heart in the grave.'

'I could only do that if he were dead, and I don't believe it.' Daisy turned her back on Marius and marched over to where Jack was standing. 'Fetch the horses. We're leaving.'

Marius had made no effort to stop them, and Jack had kept up a cheerful banter during the long ride back to Creek Manor, until eventually he seemed to realise that Daisy was not listening. After that they continued in silence. She was still angry when they arrived home, but she thanked Jack for accompanying her and he took the horses to the stables for a well-earned rub down and rest.

Daisy went straight to her room and stripped off her dusty riding habit. She lay down on her bed and closed her eyes, but Marius's words kept repeating over and over in her head, and eventually she got up and went to fling the window open. It was early evening and the scent of flowers and newly scythed grass floated on the gentle breeze and birdsong filled the air, but the peaceful scene below only served to make her more agitated. Common sense told her that life must go on, that Marius had been right and he had been speaking as a friend, but her heart was set against him, and she clung to the instinctive feeling that Jay was still alive.

She turned away from the window and went to the washstand where she rinsed away the dust from the road, and then she selected a pale blue taffeta gown and a gauzy lace shawl that Jay had bought for her during one of their trips to London. She recalled the day when they left their hotel in Dover Street and visited the major fashion houses as well as a foray into Peter Robinson, the exciting department store. It had been winter then, but she remembered it as if the sun had been shining down from an azure sky, instead of the reality of a cold, wet and windy day, when Jay wrapped his overcoat around her shoulders to keep her warm. She sat on the stool in front of the dressing table and picked up her hairbrush. If she had him declared dead it would be an end to the dream of the life they had planned together. The children that they had both longed for would never be born, and she would end up old, alone and embittered. There was only one person to whom she could unburden herself, and that was Jay's mother. Mary was suffering in her own quiet way, and she had endured many losses in her time.

Daisy and Mary dined in the small dining room that evening. Hilda had taken the children to the cottage and the house was quiet without Marjorie and her daughters. Daisy toyed with her food but Mary ate with obvious enjoyment. She laid her napkin aside, gazing at Daisy with a worried frown.

'Are you going to tell me what's bothering you, Daisy? Or do I have to guess? I'm assuming it must be something that occurred when you visited Marius today. Am I right?'

Daisy pushed her dessert away, barely touched. 'I've always been such a positive person, Mary. But this time I'm at a loss. I really don't know what to do for the best.'

'Perhaps you'd better tell me, dear?' Mary said gently. 'You know what they say – two heads are better than one.'

'I'm not so sure in this case.' Daisy hesitated, searching for the right words. Mary had been so brave, but hearing a court declare her elder son dead might be too much, even for her.

'What is it, Daisy? You know you can tell me anything.'

Daisy opened her mouth to speak, but just then the door burst open and James entered without knocking. He thrust a silver salver at her on which was a small envelope.

'I'm sorry, madam, but the telegram boy has just delivered this for you. He wants to know if there's an answer.'

Chapter Fifteen

Daisy's hand shook as she plucked the telegram from the tray and ripped it open.

'What does it say?' Mary asked anxiously.

'Is there a reply, madam?'

Daisy leaped to her feet. 'Yes, James.' She went to the escritoire, took a pen from the inkstand and dipped it in the inkwell, writing her reply on the back of the telegram. 'Will catch the first train tomorrow morning.' She handed it to James. 'That's my answer. Please give it to the delivery boy.'

James acknowledged her with a nod and hurried from the room.

'Where are you going, Daisy? What's wrong?' Mary rose from the table, her face as white as the damask cloth.

'It's from Toby,' Daisy said hoarsely. 'He thinks Jay might have been admitted to the hospital. I wouldn't be in time to catch the last train this evening, but I'll go to the station first thing in the morning. Do you think it's him, Mary? Could it be, after all this time?'

Mary moved unsteadily to the sideboard and picked up a decanter. 'I just hope and pray that your brother is right.' She poured two generous tots of brandy and handed one to Daisy. 'Drink that and sit down for a moment. It might be a false alarm, just keep that it mind.'

'I know it's Jay. Marius tried to persuade me to apply to the court for an order of death *in absentia*, but I knew in my heart that Jay was still alive.' Daisy took a sip of brandy and felt the alcohol burning its way to her stomach. 'All I know is that I won't sleep a wink tonight.'

Daisy arrived at the London Hospital next morning after a tedious journey during which the train stopped at every small station and halt. She had been up at dawn after a long night when, as she had predicted, she had barely slept for more than an hour at a time, but she was not tired. Buoyed up with hope, she entered the reception area and the familiar smell of carbolic filled her nostrils. A subdued buzz of conversation from the patients waiting to be seen was accompanied by the sound of sensible shoes clattering on the tiled floor, as nurses and probationers moved purposefully along the rows, taking details and escorting patients to the cubicles where they would be examined. It was not long since Daisy had worn the same uniform, but it was another life and she was no longer part of this establishment. She hurried to the reception desk and was told to wait – Dr Marshall would see her when he was free – but that was not good enough. Daisy thanked the clerk and when he turned his attention to the next in line she went in search of her brother. Of course she knew the hospital well and she recognised some of the nurses who had been fellow probationers, but she did not stop to chat. Long explanations would only delay her search for Jay, and the most important thing was to find Toby.

It was then that she spotted Minnie, who was now a fully-fledged nurse, and she looked angelic despite the severity of the starched uniform. Her blue eyes shone with pleasure when she saw Daisy and she rushed over to give her a hug.

'Are you all right, Daisy?' she asked anxiously.

'Yes, but I'll be better when I've seen Jay. Do you think it is him?'

'It's hard to tell. I only met Jay a couple of times and this fellow is very poorly.'

'What happened? How did he get here?'

'I only know what Toby told me. The patient was brought in by a crewman from his ship. Toby will tell you the rest, but you'll want to see him straight away.' Minnie glanced over her shoulder. 'Sister Benson isn't looking – I'll take you to the ward. Toby should be there.'

275

Daisy clasped Minnie's hand. 'Thank you. I can't believe this is happening.'

'Don't get your hopes up, just in case it's a complete stranger.'

'But Toby thinks it's Jay, so it must be.'

'There's only one way to find out.' Minnie led the way to the male medical ward, which was familiar ground to Daisy.

Nothing had changed since she worked there as a probationer. The huge room was lined on both sides with iron bedsteads, each one had a small locker and all the beds were occupied.

'We've been spotted,' Minnie whispered as the ward sister advanced on them.

'Who is this, Nurse Cole? I cannot allow the routine to be interrupted by visitors out of hours.'

'Mrs Tattersall is Dr Marshall's sister, and it's possible that she can identify the unnamed patient.'

The sister looked as if she were about to refuse permission but her expression changed subtly when Toby rushed into the ward.

'I'm sorry, Sister,' he said breathlessly. 'I forgot to warn you that I'd sent for someone who might establish the patient's identity.'

'That's quite all right, Doctor. The patient is awake, but he isn't very responsive.'

'He was given a large dose of laudanum,' Toby explained as he ushered Daisy towards a bed at the far end of the ward. It was screened off from the rest of the patients, and Toby came to a halt. 'He was in a distressed state when the mate from a merchant ship brought him to us last evening. I didn't see the fellow, so I didn't get the full story. Anyway, I think it's Jay, but I can't be certain. He's unshaven and very emaciated.'

'But Jay disappeared two months ago.'

'Don't expect too much, Daisy. The poor fellow can't even remember his own name.'

'You mean he's lost his memory?'

'Exactly, and he seems to have been suffering from some kind of fever, so be prepared for a shock when you see him.' Toby drew back one of the screens and Daisy moved closer to the bed.

The patient's eyes were closed and his hair was matted and darkened with sweat, but the lower part of his face was disguised by a thick ginger beard.

'Jay,' Daisy said in a hoarse whisper. 'Jay.'

The man opened his eyes, and they were a startling shade of blue against his tanned skin, but there was no recognition in his gaze. He stared at Daisy for a moment and then his eyelids fluttered and closed. Daisy turned to her brother with a strangled sob.

'It is Jay, but he didn't recognise me.'

Toby placed his arm around her shoulders. 'I couldn't be sure, but you know him better than anyone.'

'He's so thin, and he looks so ill.'

'It's hard to make an exact diagnosis, and he isn't very responsive to questioning, but it's early days.'

'Will he regain his memory?'

'I can't say at this stage. Only time will tell.'

'Can he be moved? I could look after him if we could get him home to Creek Manor.'

Toby frowned thoughtfully. 'Not at the moment. I'd like to keep an eye on him for a few days at least, and then we can work out what's best for him.' He gave Daisy a searching look. 'You are sure it's Jay, aren't you? I know you want it to be him, but this man might be a complete stranger.'

'I'd know him anywhere, Toby. When he opened his eyes I knew for certain that it was Jay.' Daisy felt in her reticule for her hanky and mopped her eyes. She did not know why she was crying, but perhaps it was the sheer relief of knowing that her husband was still alive. He might be a shadow of his former self, and if he never recognised her it would be tragic, but she loved him none the less.

'Come away, Daisy,' Minnie said gently. 'Come to the nurses' room and I'll make you a cup of tea. You can't do anything for him at the moment – he's in good hands.' She smiled and nodded to the ward sister, who sniffed and pulled the screens back into place.

'You may visit at the appropriate time, Mrs Tattersall.'

'Thank you, Sister,' Daisy murmured as she followed Minnie from the ward.

'I'll make sure he has the best possible treatment,' Toby said as he walked beside her. 'I have to leave you now, but we must find you some accommodation close to the hospital.'

'She must stay with me,' Minnie hesitated in the doorway. 'That's if the lady of the manor doesn't mind sharing a room with her soon-to-be sister-in-law. I'm sure that Gladys will be delighted to see you again, as will the abominable Rex, and Mrs Wood is always keen to make more money.'

'I'd love to share a room with you again, Minnie. And I can put up with Gladys for a while, although I don't know how you've stood those lodgings all this time, especially that wretched cat.'

'Toby and I are looking for somewhere to live when we're married. We want a house with a garden, maybe in one of the squares. You can help me look, Daisy. It will be fun.' Minnie's smile faded. 'Of course, I know you'll want to spend as much time as possible with Jay, but perhaps you ought to give him time to get used to you.'

Daisy stared at her in dismay. 'But he's my husband.'

'He doesn't remember that at the moment.' Toby patted her on the shoulder. 'You'll have to accept the fact and be patient, Daisy. I've only seen a couple of similar cases, but it could take a long time for him to regain his memory, if ever.'

'You mean he might never remember me?'

'I don't know. We can but hope that in time he will, but I can't guarantee anything.' Toby linked his arm through hers and they followed Minnie to the staff canteen, where she rushed off to get a cup of tea. She returned moments later and placed the cup on the table in front of Daisy, together with a plate of bread and butter.

'I don't suppose you've had any breakfast, so you must eat something. We don't want you fainting away and ending up on a ward, do we?'

Daisy managed a smile. 'Yes, Nurse. I'll do as you say.'

'I have to get back to work,' Toby said, leaning over to brush Daisy's cheek with a brotherly kiss. 'Visit the patient at the appropriate time, but don't expect too much.' He blew a kiss to Minnie and strolled off.

'He can't bring himself to admit it's Jay,' Daisy said sadly. 'But I'd know him no matter what state he was in.'

'I hope so, for your sake.' Minnie sat down beside her. 'I can't stay long or I'll be in trouble, but you can go to Fieldgate Street when you're ready. I'm sure Mrs Wood will be pleased to see you. The wretched woman is always pleading poverty.'

Gladys opened the door and her eyes bulged in surprise, adding to her frog-like appearance. As Flora had once remarked, Gladys must have been hiding behind the door when good looks were handed out.

'I never thought we'd see you again, miss.'

'It's Mrs Tattersall now, Gladys. May I come in?'

Gladys moved aside but her curious gaze never wavered. 'If you're married, what are you doing back in London?' She stuck her thumb into her mouth, sucking it like a baby.

Daisy took a deep breath. She was tempted to tell the nosy girl that it was none of her business, but she knew from past experience that it was best not to get on the wrong side of Mrs Wood's only child. Gladys was not only a gossip, she had a spiteful tongue and she was a sneak, who went through the lodgers' belongings when they were out of the house, and helped herself to any trifle that took her fancy.

'I'm here to visit my brother and Miss Cole. She said I could share her room again, if it's all right with your mother.'

Gladys unplugged her thumb, eyeing Daisy slyly. 'I could put a good word in for you, miss, but it would cost you sixpence.'

Daisy put her valise down on the polished floorboards. 'Oh, look. There's dear old Rex. He's such a fine specimen. No wonder your mother thinks the world of him.'

'I hate that cat,' Gladys said with feeling. 'One day he'll end up in the river with a brick tied round his skinny neck.'

'I wouldn't let your mama hear you speaking of her pet like that, if I were you,' Daisy said pointedly. 'What were you saying about money, Gladys?'

Gladys had many failings but she was far from stupid, and her sallow skin flushed darkly. 'I was joking, miss. You know where the room is, but don't ask me to take your bag up them stairs.' She stomped off in the direction of her mother's private parlour, leaving Daisy to find her own way to the room she had once shared with Minnie.

She climbed the stairs, noting that nothing had changed. She was sure she recognised the large cobweb that hung from the candle sconce on the second floor, and the big fat spider that lay in wait for yet another juicy victim. And Minnie's room was just the same as before, although the second bed was covered in a pile of clothes, waiting to be folded neatly and placed in the tallboy. Minnie was not the tidiest of people, but Daisy was relieved to have somewhere to lay her head that night. She spent the next hour tidying the room and unpacking. She knew from experience where the clean linen was kept and she went to the cupboard and helped herself to bedding, but all the time she was working, her mind was occupied with thoughts of Jay.

The man lying in the hospital bed bore little resemblance to the man she had married, but at least he was alive, and the relief on finding him was overwhelming. She would have to be patient and abide by Toby's advice, although she knew that it was going to be hard. Her first instinct had been to take Jay home where he would receive all the love and attention he needed to bring him back to them, but it was obvious that he was a sick man. She had seen enough tragedies during the cholera outbreak last year, and she knew that Jay was in the best place – for now.

She visited him again during the hours specified by the hospital. There was no change in his condition, but there was no deterioration either, and Daisy had enough nursing experience to know that this was a good sign. She returned to the lodging house that evening with hope in her heart. Toby had warned her that it would be a long road to recovery, but Daisy was certain that the worst was over, and things could only get better.

She walked into the parlour and was greeted by Ivy, who rushed over and threw her arms around Daisy as if they were long-lost friends.

'How is that handsome footman?' Ivy demanded, blushing. 'I mean George, of course. I had a few dances with him on the beach and he was very romantic, but I haven't heard from him since I returned to London.'

'He's Mrs Harker's servant, Ivy. They've returned to their old home so I don't see them now.'

'Oh!' Ivy's bottom lip trembled. 'I don't seem to have much luck with gentlemen. There must be something wrong with me.'

'Nonsense, Ivy. You're a nice person, you just haven't met the right man yet.'

Ivy shrugged. 'Flora seems to do very well for herself. She's seeing that Julian Carrington, the one she met at your big house. I thought she hated him, but it seems not.'

Daisy pulled a face. 'He won't marry her. In the end he'll find someone that his parents approve of, and I'm afraid it won't be Flora. She'd do better to look elsewhere.'

'At least she has a gentleman friend to take her to the theatre and nice restaurants. Even Gladys has found someone.'

'But she's only sixteen, if that. Does her mother know?'

Ivy grinned wickedly. 'You'll never guess who the silly girl has been seeing.'

'Don't tell me it's Jonah Sawkins. I wouldn't wish that on Gladys.'

'It is. I saw them together the other evening when Flora and I were buying ham rolls from Old Joe's stall.' Ivy covered her mouth to suppress a giggle. 'Just imagine what ugly children Gladys and Jonah would have if they got married.'

'I'd rather not, thank you, Ivy. But it won't happen. When Mrs Wood realises what's going on beneath her nose it will be the end of Gladys' relationship with Jonah.'

'I wish I could live in the country,' Ivy said sadly. 'I was born in Hoxton, and I've lived all my life in London, but I did have a good time at your lovely house, and I met such nice people.'

At this point Daisy was wishing that someone would come in to rescue her from Ivy's self-pitying company. 'I'm tired,' she said, yawning. 'I don't think I'll wait up for Minnie. She went out to dinner with my brother.'

'The party at the manor house was the best time

I've ever had,' Ivy continued dreamily. 'At supper I sat with a dear old lady, who was ever so kind to me.'

Daisy stared at her in surprise. 'Who was that?'

'Mrs Guppy, I think she called herself. She said her son was a sea captain and very important. We really got on well.'

A vision of Clem Guppy's aged, bad-tempered, witch-like mother made Daisy stare at Ivy in amazement. 'Mrs Guppy? Are you sure?'

'Oh, yes. She said I was to call on her any time I was in the neighbourhood.'

Daisy was struggling to think of a suitable remark when Minnie and Toby breezed into the room.

'We've come to take you to the music hall,' Minnie said, smiling. 'Toby and I thought you needed cheering up, after the day you've had.'

Ivy leaped to her feet. 'Oh, I love all that singing and dancing. Can I come, too?'

Minnie and Daisy exchanged wary glances, but Toby smiled benignly. 'Of course you can, Ivy. But we'll have to hurry or we'll be too late.'

Daisy rushed up to her room to fetch her bonnet and shawl, and despite her worries about Jay's health and welfare, she felt ridiculously light-hearted. It was good to be back in London, despite the noxious smells from the drains and the manufactories along the river. The heady mixture of aromas from imported spices, roasting coffee beans and burnt sugar from the mills in Wellclose Square was familiar and brought back memories of childhood. The constant noise of horse-drawn traffic thundering and rumbling across cobblestones, and the babble of raised voices from costermongers, draymen and working women who could hold their own against the fiercest opponent were in sharp contrast to the relative silence of the countryside. But it had been home for the best part of her life and the past was bathed in a glow of nostalgia. She hurried downstairs to join the others and they set off for the Pavilion Theatre.

The show was enjoyable and Flossie and Ethel, the two dancers who lived on the top floor in Fieldgate Street, now had their own spot and were no doubt heading for top billing. Daisy forgot all her problems as she watched the various performers. Tumblers, singers, comics and dancers took their turn in front of the appreciative audience, and by the end of the performance Daisy's hands were sore from applauding enthusiastically. After the show they stopped at a stall and bought plates of jellied eels, which they ate with relish, and then it was time to return to the lodging house. Daisy was so exhausted that even the lumpy mattress could not spoil a good night's sleep, and she awoke next morning filled with hope for the future.

After a week devoted almost entirely to visiting the hospital and sitting at Jay's bedside, Daisy's mood had changed and she was beginning to worry. She had brought a small sum of money with her, but it would not go very far, and Jay was showing little sign of improvement. He was recovering slowly from the bout of fever that had nearly cost him his life, but he did not respond to Daisy. They might have been total strangers, and she found it frustrating and upsetting in equal measure. Toby and Minnie did their best to keep her spirits up, but by the end of the second week Daisy was beginning to despair.

One evening when she returned to Fieldgate Street after a long and difficult session with Jay, she arrived at the lodging house at the same moment as Julian.

He alighted from a hansom cab and stared at her in amazement. 'This is an unexpected pleasure, Mrs Tattersall. What brings you to London? I'm surprised that Mrs Harker can do without your services.'

'I don't work for Marjorie Harker,' Daisy said impatiently. 'You know that very well.'

'I'm sorry. That's what I understood when I visited Creek Manor.'

'I own the manor house. Mrs Harker was renting it from me.'

'It had slipped my mind. I'm afraid I still think of you as being in service, my dear. However, I assume that your errant husband has not turned up.'

'Don't pretend to care, Julian. It doesn't suit you.' Daisy rapped urgently on the door, praying silently that someone would answer it quickly, but it seemed that Julian was not going to give up so easily. He paid the cabby and came to stand beside her.

'My offer still stands. I was a fool to let you go. Have the brute declared dead and marry me.'

She shot him a sideways glance. 'My husband is very much alive, thank you, Julian.'

'So where is he?'

The door opened and Flora's smile faded when she saw Daisy. 'Why are you two together?'

'We are no such thing.' Daisy stepped over the threshold and came face to face with Gladys and Jonah Sawkins.

'This is my gentleman friend,' Gladys said proudly. 'We're stepping out together.'

Jonah gave Daisy a crooked grin, exposing a row of yellow teeth. 'It's your loss, Miss High and Mighty.'

'She's married now,' Gladys said, jabbing him in the ribs.

'I like married women.' Jonah licked his lips in a suggestive manner. 'They're grateful for a bit of attention.'

Daisy tossed her head and ignored him. She made for the staircase and did not look back, but Rex caught her as she reached the first landing. He took a leap and with a vicious swipe of his unsheathed claws he tore at her arm, leaving a row of bleeding scratches on her wrist. It was the last straw and Daisy stumbled up to the room she shared with Minnie, blinded by tears. She flung herself down on the bed and gave vent to her pent-up emotions. It felt as if everything was against her, from Jay's total lack of memory, to the shadows from her own past, from which there seemed to be no escape. After a while she grew calmer and she raised herself from the bed and went to the washstand to splash cold water on her face. She put her hair up and pinched her cheeks to bring back the colour, but as she did so there was a knock on the door.

'Miss Marshall, there's a gentleman who's come to see you. I shouldn't have to climb the stairs to give you a message, particularly when you know that I don't hold with my ladies entertaining persons of the opposite gender in my front parlour.' Mrs Wood sighed loudly and thumped again on the door panel.

Daisy hurried to open it. 'I'm not expecting anyone, Mrs Wood.'

'Well, he's refusing to leave and he's standing in my entrance hall, bold as brass.'

'I'm coming.' Daisy said hastily.

'And you'll inform him of the rules.'

Daisy hurried down the stairs. 'Yes, Mrs Wood, and kindly restrain your feline friend. He attacked me earlier.'

Mrs Wood followed her. 'My Rex is the gentlest creature imaginable. You must have provoked him.'

Daisy came to a halt and turned on her landlady. 'He's a dangerous animal and he should be in the Zoological Gardens.' She continued downstairs closing her ears to Mrs Wood's tirade of abuse.

'And tell that fellow if he comes here again I'll slam the door in his face.'

Daisy leaned over the banisters to see who could be calling on her. She could hardly believe her eyes when the man looked up and met her curious gaze with a disarming smile.

Chapter Sixteen

Daisy ran down the rest of the stairs and grasped his outstretched hand. 'Marius. I can't believe it. What are you doing here?'

Mrs Wood strutted past them, her head held erect. 'I trust that he'll be leaving promptly. No gentlemen callers.'

Daisy waited until Mrs Wood slammed the door to her private parlour. 'I apologise for my landlady, Marius. But how did you know where to find me?'

'Are you all right, Daisy? You look pale.'

'I'm fine, thank you. But you haven't answered my questions.'

'I called at the manor house to see you, and Mary told me that you'd rushed up to London because Jay had been found, so I caught the next train to London, and I went straight to the hospital. Toby gave me your address.'

'I expect he told you that Jay has lost his memory. He doesn't even remember his name, let alone mine. In fact, it's like talking to a complete stranger.'

'I'm sorry, Daisy. After all the waiting it must be very hard to bear.'

She gave him a grateful smile. Marius was sympathetic without being maudlin, and that was a comfort. 'Yes, it is.'

He glanced at the parlour door. 'Your landlady is a bit of an ogress. Shall we take a walk?'

'Yes, anything to get out of here. Just give me a minute to fetch my bonnet and shawl.'

Seeing a friendly face from home raised Daisy's spirits so that she barely felt her feet touch the ground as she went upstairs to fetch her outdoor things. She joined Marius minutes later, wearing her best straw bonnet trimmed with cream silk roses and a fine woollen shawl so delicate that it was like a cobweb. He gave her an appreciative look, but he did not comment on her appearance and they stepped outside, closing the front door firmly. The flutter of a lace curtain gave Mrs Wood away, and Daisy waved to her as they walked past.

'Why did you choose to stay there, Daisy? I'm sure you could find better accommodation.' Marius gave her a speculative look. 'Are you in need of money?'

'No, at least I'm managing, but I came away in such a rush that I didn't think to bring more with me. Nor did I expect to be here for such a long time.'

He took her hand and held it in a warm grasp. 'I am sorry, Daisy. I can imagine how hard that must be for you.'

'It is. He just lies there and stares at the ceiling. Sometimes I think he's lost the will to live. It's so unlike the Jay I know.'

'I can only imagine how you must be feeling.' He gave her fingers a sympathetic squeeze. 'I went to Creek Manor to tell you that I've procured two large cargoes for the *Lazy Jane*, and she'll be sailing as soon as they're loaded. There'll be a good profit in this trip, and I can give you an advance, if that will help.'

'No, thank you. I can manage.'

He shot her a sideways look. 'Are you sure?'

'Well, it will be very difficult if I have to remain here much longer.' She came to a sudden halt. 'I can't see the end to it, Marius. Jay isn't his old self and I don't know how to bring him back.'

'What does your brother say?'

'Toby doesn't know and neither do the other doctors. All they can tell me is that it's a matter of time. But how long? I can't remain in London indefinitely.'

He set off again, leading her towards the nearby churchyard, where they perched on a stone wall. 'I'm not a medical man, Daisy, but I wonder if taking Jay home might be the answer. If he is surrounded by people who love him, in a place he knows well, he might recover far more quickly than he would in a hospital bed.'

'I think you may be right,' Daisy said thoughtfully. 'He seems to have shut himself off from the world at the moment, but if I took him home . . . ?'

It was arranged so swiftly that Daisy was left feeling breathless. Marius, it seemed, was not the sort of man who would stand back and allow things to happen in their own time. Daisy did not know how he managed it, but he persuaded the doctors to discharge Jay, and he produced clothing suitable for travelling, which replaced the baggy shirt and trousers that Jay had been wearing when he was brought to the hospital. Marius also provided socks and shoes, having somehow guessed what size would fit Jay, and he helped him to dress. Daisy was nervous as she waited for them in the hospital foyer. There was no certainty that Jay would accompany them willingly, but although he was a little dazed by the sudden change of scene, he appeared to be calm and compliant, although he hesitated when they reached the outside door.

'Where are we going?'

Daisy laid her hand on his arm. 'We're going home, Jay.'

'I don't know where that is.'

'Perhaps you'll recognise it when we get there,' Daisy said eagerly. 'The doctors think that something familiar might make you remember something.'

'Who are you?' Jay gazed at her, frowning. 'I know you keep telling me, but your name slips my mind.'

'Just call me Daisy,' she said gently.

Marius nodded. 'That's right, and I'm Marius. I'll hail a cab, Daisy. Just wait here.'

Daisy glanced round at the sound of someone calling her name and she smiled when she saw Toby hurrying towards her.

'So you're off, then?' he said breathlessly. 'Let me know how matters progress when you get back to Little Creek.'

'I will, and thanks for everything you've done. I'll miss you, Toby.'

'We'll try to visit you before the wedding, but I can't guarantee to get time off.' Toby took a small bottle from his pocket and pressed it into her hand. 'If Jay gets upset or anxious when you're travelling just give him a couple of drops of this.'

She tucked it into her reticule. 'What is it?'

'Laudanum. He might need some at night, too. Don't be surprised if he is restless, and confused. Call Nick if you're worried.'

'Yes, of course.'

'Marius has found a cab.'

Daisy stood on tiptoe to kiss her brother's cheek. 'Thank you once again for everything you've done for Jay.'

'I don't know where I'm going,' Jay muttered, backing away. 'I'd rather stay here.'

Toby linked arms with him. 'Come on, old chap. You're going to the country to get well. I'll come and see you as soon as I can.'

Jay nodded wordlessly and allowed Toby to take him to the cab, where Marius helped him onto the seat. Daisy joined them, but she was apprehensive. Perhaps it was too early in Jay's recovery to take him away from the hospital.

'He'll be fine, don't worry.' Marius gave her a reassuring smile.

Daisy sat in between Jay and Marius as the cab plunged forward into the chaotic traffic. She knew that Marius meant well, but the prospect of nursing her husband back to full health was daunting, and she wondered how Mary would react when her son did not recognise her.

After a relatively easy train journey they arrived back at the manor house. Mary was obviously upset when Jay failed to recognise her, but as Daisy had discovered long ago, Mary was not the sort of woman to give in to despair. She smiled at Jay and patted his hand.

'I've had your old room made ready for you, my dear. I thought you'd prefer to be somewhere familiar.'

He gazed round dazedly. 'I don't remember this house.'

'Never mind that now,' Mary said firmly. 'I'm sure it will all come back to you in time, but I dare say you'd prefer to have your meals in your room for the time being.'

'I'm not very hungry.'

'You see how it is, Mary,' Daisy said in a low voice. 'He doesn't recall a thing.'

'We'll be fine after a good rest.' Mary spoke to her son in the tone she might have used when he was a small child. 'Cook knows what your favourite foods are, Jay. I'm sure she'll do her best to tempt you to eat.'

He shook his head. 'I don't know.'

'You will when you taste them,' Mary said, taking him by the hand as if he were a five-year-old. 'Come along now. Don't dawdle. I have other things to do than wait on you, young man.'

Daisy exchanged amused glances with Marius, and for a moment she thought that Jay was going to refuse, but he merely nodded and allowed his mother to lead him from the drawing room.

Marius chuckled. 'Obviously his mother knows best.'

'She's had a lifetime of dealing with difficult men,' Daisy said, sighing. 'If anyone can help him, it's Mary. I wish I could do something, but I can't seem to reach him.'

'Don't upset yourself, Daisy.' Marius patted her on the shoulder. 'This is just the start and you'll have to be patient.'

'Yes, I know, but it's not easy.' Daisy sighed heavily. 'I suppose you'll have to go now, but thank you for everything you've done.'

'Are you sending me away?'

The irrepressible twinkle in his dark eyes made

her smile. 'No, of course not, but you must have business matters that need your attention.'

'Which is a polite way of asking me to leave.' His eyes darkened and he gave her a speculative look. 'I don't want to intrude, Daisy. But I do want to help, and I think I might have an idea that will shock Jay into remembering something from the past.'

'You're not intruding. I'm sorry, Marius. I suppose I'm just tired and worried about Jay, who seems to be making so little progress.'

'I understand, and I will go now, but I'll be back soon.' He stood up. 'I left my horse in your stables when I travelled up to London. I hope you don't mind.'

'Why would I mind? You're almost like one of the family.'

He gave her a long look. 'Thank you, but I'll never be that, I'm afraid. Anyway, I must go now – it's a long ride to Maldon. I'll see myself out, Daisy.'

He left the room and Daisy sank back on the sofa. Marius had made everything seem possible, although she sensed that there was something he could not, or would not, share with her, and she suspected that his feelings for her ran more deeply than simple friendship. But she was a married woman and she loved her husband; Marius was a business partner only, and that was the way it had to be.

Daisy rose to her feet and went in search of Hilda, who was always a source of good common sense and practical advice. She found her in the still room, preparing rose petals to make rose water. Sunshine poured through the windowpanes and a glorious scent filled the air.

'I heard that you'd brought him home,' Hilda said gravely. 'How is he?'

Daisy leaned against the work table. 'I don't know. He looks like Jay, and he sounds like Jay, but he doesn't know me and he doesn't seem to remember anything of his old life.'

'Well, he's in the right place. If the magic of Little Creek doesn't cure him, then nothing will.'

'Magic?' Daisy stared at ever-practical Hilda, not knowing whether to laugh or cry. 'You don't believe in magic, do you?'

'Of course I do. Doesn't everyone? At least a little tiny bit anyway? There's magic when you hold your baby in your arms for the first time, and magic when it smiles. There's magic in a beautiful sunrise and a flaming sunset, and when you fall in love. You do love Jay, don't you?'

'Why, Hilda, I didn't know you were a poet at heart. That's really beautiful, but I still don't know what to do for the best. And of course I love Jay, but I'm afraid I've lost him.'

'I think you should go and talk to Dr Neville. He's your friend, isn't he? And he's known Jay since they were boys. If anyone can help and advise you, it will be the doctor.'

'Yes, of course, you're right. I suppose I'm just

tired, and it's good to be home.' Daisy picked up a red rose and inhaled its delicate perfume. 'I'll call on Nick tomorrow.'

'You might like to have a word with young Jack before you do anything. He's more upset about his brother than he lets on, and he might make matters worse if he starts bombarding Jay with questions.'

'Yes, that wouldn't do at all. Mary is the best one to be with him at present. I'll take a walk to the stables, and I'll try to make Jack understand that he must be careful what he says in Jay's presence.'

'We'll all do what we can, Daisy. Nell has been baking jam tarts because she says they're his favourites, and everyone will do their best to act naturally.'

'I'm sure he'll be very touched, when he's in a fit state to realise how much everyone cares for him. Jay was so used to being branded as the "bad boy" in the village, I don't think he knows how well respected he's become.'

'There's another thing, Daisy. I know it's not my place to say so, but maybe your money worries are over now.'

'How so?'

'Your husband isn't dead. He might have forgotten who he is, but he's still the rightful owner of Creek Manor. If I was you, I'd take him to the bank and make them pay out – then you won't have to have the likes of Marjorie Harker calling the tune.'

'It hadn't occurred to me, but you're right.' Daisy gave her a hug. 'If we can get the money I can run the estate until Jay is fully recovered, and I can pay the servants. Hilda, you're a genius.'

Creek Hall was bathed in early summer sunshine as Daisy rode into the stable yard. Billy, the stable boy, came running from the tack room to hold Cinders while Daisy dismounted.

'It's good to see you again, miss.'

'Thank you, Billy, but I'm no longer "miss" – I'm a married woman now.'

He pushed his cap to the back of his head. 'Yes, missis. Sorry, I forgot.'

'Is the doctor at home?'

'Well, he ain't taken his horse or called for the pony and trap, so I suppose he must be.'

'Thank you.' Daisy walked across the cobblestones to enter by the scullery door.

Mrs Bee was in the kitchen, assisted by a couple of young village girls. She looked up from rolling out a sheet of pastry and smiled.

'Welcome back, madam. We heard that you'd gone to London.'

'Thank you, Mrs Bee. It's good to be home.'

'How is Jay? Dove has been so worried.'

'He's been very ill, but he's on the mend now. Anyway, I need to speak to her before I see the doctor.'

'Dr Nick is in his study, I think, and you'll find Dove upstairs. She gives her all to the patients.' Mrs Bee glanced at the two kitchen maids, but they were getting on with their chores and did not appear to be listening. 'Between you and me – and I don't say this lightly because I think the world of the doctor – but I don't think he really appreciates how much she does for him. He had his sights set elsewhere, if you know what I'm saying.'

'I do, and I agree with you, Mrs Bee. Dove is a young woman in a million.'

'I hope that he'll come to realise that before it's too late.'

Daisy patted Mrs Bee's floury hand. 'It will sort itself out, so try not to worry. I'll go and find Dove and keep her up to date on her brother's progress.'

'You must stop for a cup of tea and a slice of seed cake before you go. I doubt if you bothered to have breakfast.'

Daisy smiled. 'I had a slice of toast, but of course I'd much rather have some of your cake. I'll call in before I leave.' She left the kitchen and went in search of Dove, almost bumping into her as she emerged from a patient's room.

Dove's serious expression melted into a welcoming smile. 'You're back. Is Jay with you?'

'He's at home with your mother.'

'But he's all right? It seems like a miracle that he's come back to us after all these weeks.'

'He's unhurt physically,' Daisy said carefully, 'but he's still weak from the fever he'd been suffering from, and he's lost his memory. He doesn't even know his own name.'

'He will get better, won't he?'

'I hope so, but no one seems to know. I'm going to speak to Nick now, but I wanted to tell you first.'

'May I visit him, Daisy?'

'Of course, and maybe seeing you and Linnet will bring back some memory from the past. Mary was going to allow Jack five minutes with his brother this morning.'

'I'll ask Nick if I can accompany him when he visits Creek Manor. I assume that's why you're here, Daisy.'

'Yes, I need to ask Nick for his medical opinion. I'm hoping he might be able to help.'

'I'm sure he will. He's an excellent doctor.'

Daisy eyed her curiously. 'I hope he realises how lucky he is to have you.'

'I don't know about that.' Dove's pale cheeks flamed with colour. 'I would probably be a kitchen maid if it weren't for Nick.' She hesitated, biting her lip. 'I know he still has feelings for you, Daisy, but he's fond of me and I'm prepared to accept that.'

'You have nothing to fear from me, Dove. But don't be second best – you're worth more than that. Nick should think himself very lucky to have someone like you.'

'He might even make an honest woman of me one day.'

'Are you telling me that he's taken advantage of you? He should be ashamed of himself.'

'I was more than willing, Daisy. I love him.'

'As I said, he doesn't deserve a woman like you. I want words with Dr Neville.'

Dove laid a restraining hand on Daisy's arm. 'Don't tell him what I said. He would be very angry if he thought I'd spoken to you about something so personal.'

'I won't make things worse, I promise you that. You are my sister-in-law, Dove. If Jay were himself and he found out that Nick has been playing fast and loose with your affections there would be trouble.' Daisy broke free from Dove's grasp and she headed for Nick's study.

'Good heavens, Daisy.' Nick dropped his pen and rose hastily to his feet. 'What on earth is the matter?'

She folded her arms, glaring at him. 'You are the trouble, Nick Neville. I've been talking to Dove and she let it slip that you two are more than just colleagues.

'It's a private matter.'

'Not if it affects my sister-in-law. This is family business, Nick. If my husband was fit and well he'd settle this in a matter of minutes.'

An amused smile flitted over Nick's handsome features. 'Are you calling me out in his stead, Mrs Tattersall?'

'Don't make a joke of it. I'm not in the mood for silliness. I came to see you to ask for your help with Jay because he's lost his memory and doesn't even know his own name, but it seems that you need some sisterly advice.'

'I'm glad that Jay has been found, and of course I'll do my best for him, but you aren't my sister, Daisy. You know how I feel about you.'

'So you say, and yet you take advantage of a nice young woman who obviously worships you. For shame, Nick.'

He slumped down on his chair. 'I know, you're right, and my father would be ashamed of me if he were here. I'm very fond of Dove and she's an excellent nurse.'

Daisy leaned over the desk, fixing him with a hard stare. 'You know what you must do. It's not up to me to tell you, but if you make that girl unhappy you will have me to deal with.'

'Now I am afraid,' Nick said, chuckling. 'I should marry a rich widow or an heiress, but not too many wealthy women want to live in a small village like Little Creek.' He met Daisy's angry look with a smile, holding his hands up in a gesture of submission. 'I know I've lost my chance with you, and we would probably have made each other miserable. I like to be in control and I can't change my nature, but I will try to mend my ways.'

'You'll treat Dove properly?'

'I was going to ask her to marry me at some point, I suppose.'

'Then do it before things go too far and you ruin her reputation.'

'I will, I promise.' Nick rose to his feet and reached for his medical bag. 'You came to ask my opinion regarding your husband, Mrs Tattersall, so I suggest we leave now.'

'And you'll invite Dove to accompany us. She needs to see her brother, and I'm hoping that having his family around will bring back his memory.'

'I don't pretend to be an expert in such matters,' Nick said ruefully. 'But I'm glad that Jay survived, and I'll do what I can for him.'

Jay's physical condition improved quickly with good care and the food prepared to tempt his poor appetite, but despite visits from his brother and sisters, Jay remembered nothing of his past. He seemed to enjoy Daisy's company, but there was nothing remotely lover-like in his attitude towards her. She suspected at times that he was more comfortable with Dove and Linnet than he was with his own wife, although she would have died rather than admit such a disheartening fact. Mary was the only person to whom he turned during his dark spells of depression, and Hilda was able to persuade him to wash and shave when he seemed to have given up entirely. Daisy was increasingly desperate and Nick seemed unable to help. However, life was made easier when a visit to the bank proved successful, and with Jay there to sign the necessary papers, funds were released, enabling Daisy to pay the servants and the outstanding household bills.

After a few weeks of resting and eating well Jay was allowed to venture into the grounds, and this seemed to brighten his mood. Daisy's uncle suggested that Jay might like to take up fishing, and he came one sunny June morning bringing all the gear needed for a day of sport at the lake. Jack was allowed to accompany them, and he was his brother's shadow. Daisy never needed to worry as long as Jack was with Jay, and when she took a picnic hamper to the lake she was delighted to see Jay almost back to his former self. She had not heard him laugh since he came home and the happy sound echoed across the water, but then it came back to mock her when her husband thanked her politely for the food, as if she were a servant.

Daisy managed a weak smile and she made her way back across the neatly cut lawns, wiping tears from her eyes. It was not until she reached the parterre garden that she realised someone was waiting for her.

'Marius.' She quickened her pace, tears forgotten. It was a huge relief to be greeted warmly by someone on whom she could rely. 'I wasn't expecting to see you today.'

He held out his hand to help her over the low ornamental wall and she grasped it as if it were a lifeline.

'What's the matter, Daisy? You look upset.'

She tucked her hanky into her pocket. 'I had something in my eye – a bit of dust.'

He gazed into the distance. 'Is that Jay by the lake?'

'Yes, my uncle thought he might enjoy a day's fishing, and Jack is with him. That boy has been wonderful. I wouldn't have credited him with so much good sense, but he looks after Jay as if he were the elder brother.'

'But there's still no sign of Jay recovering his memory?'

'No, sadly not. His mother and sisters have tried everything they can, as have I, but with no success. I'm at a loss as to what to do next.'

'I have an idea, it might not work, but I think it's worth a try.'

'Anything, Marius. I'll do anything if it will help to bring Jay back to the real world. At the moment he still feels like a stranger amongst us, and I know he's not happy.'

'Then this is worth a try. Actually, it was Guppy's idea.'

'Clem? What did he suggest?'

'The thing that Jay loves best in the world, next to you and his family, of course. What is that, Daisy?'

She met his intense gaze and she smiled. 'The *Lazy Jane*.'

'Precisely. They sailed from Maldon and by our reckoning they should reach the creek early this evening. We had a little delay in getting one of the cargoes to the quay, but that happens more often than not. Anyway, she's ready to sail for the Channel Islands, but one night moored in the creek won't pose a problem. I suggest a walk to the cove after dinner might prove beneficial. It's worth a try, isn't it?'

Daisy flung her arms around his neck and kissed his cheek, but realising what she had done, she moved away quickly, her cheeks burning with embarrassment.

'I'm sorry, Marius. It's just that there's been so little hope, and I think you might have hit on the one thing that could bring Jay back to us.'

'Don't apologise. I don't often get rewarded in such a charming manner.'

'Well, it's a brilliant idea. Have you had luncheon? We were about to eat and my aunt is here. I'm sure she'd like to see you again. You met so briefly.'

He caught her by the hand. 'That would be splendid. I barely had time to snatch a bread roll for breakfast, and that was stale.' He squeezed her fingers. 'Take heart, Daisy. We can beat this together – we are partners, after all.'

'I hope your idea works, Marius. This evening can't come quickly enough.'

Chapter Seventeen

The walk to the beach had to be kept a secret from the rest of the family or everyone would have wanted to accompany them. Daisy's aunt and uncle had been invited to join them for dinner, and Eleanora monopolised the conversation. There was a brief pause when the maid brought the desserts, which were bread-and-butter pudding, glistening with crisp buttery sugar, and a lemon tart. Jay ate with obvious enjoyment, but contributed very little to the general conversation, and Daisy was too excited to care much about food. She kept her eye on the dainty gilded clock, which had pride of place on the mantelshelf, flanked by silver candlesticks and a cut-glass spill jar.

'Have some more pudding, Jay,' Mary said gently. 'This one was always your favourite, although we rarely had such a treat when you were a boy.'

Jay smiled vaguely. 'Thank you. It's very nice, but I can't eat another morsel.'

Eleanora pointed to the lemon tart. 'Cut me another slice, please, Mary. It's almost as good as the one Hattie used to make. Dear Linnet tries hard, but she can't compete with Hattie when it comes to baking.'

'I suppose you'll lose her when she marries the schoolmaster.' Mary served a generous portion and passed the plate back to Eleanora. 'Would anyone else like some? What about you, Mr Walters?'

'Not for me, thank you.'

Mary eyed him warily. 'Are you staying in the village tonight, Mr Walters?'

He shook his head. 'It's Marius. I hope you count me as a friend, Mrs Tattersall, and no, I intend to ride back to Maldon.'

'You mustn't think of it, Marius,' Daisy said quickly. 'We have plenty of spare rooms.'

'Of course,' Mary added. 'And it's Mary to my friends, Marius.' She smiled and he responded with a chuckle.

Daisy had to wait while her aunt finished her food, and then there was the slight possibility that Eleanora and Sidney might want to accompany them on their walk. At any other time they would have been more than welcome, but Jay was even more silent than usual when in their company, and he might decide to go to his room. Never a keen reader, Jay had suddenly become interested in books, and he had

311

developed the habit of retiring early to bed with a novel, or a travelogue. Daisy tried hard to accommodate the stranger who inhabited her husband's body, but she was finding it increasingly difficult.

Eleanor ate the last crumb, folded her napkin and rose from the table. 'That was a delightful meal, but it's time we were making our way home. The ferryman won't work after twilight, and I can't say I blame him.'

Sidney was already on his feet. 'Yes, excellent food, Daisy. My compliments to Cook.'

'Thank you, Uncle. I'll pass them on.' Daisy gazed pointedly at Jay, who was about to leave the table. 'I thought it would be nice to go for a walk.'

'I was going to my room, Daisy.'

'Nonsense,' Mary said firmly. 'You need to get some fresh air, my son. Go for a walk with your wife and don't be a misery.'

'You could walk to the ferry with us,' Eleanora suggested.

'I was thinking of the cove, but we could go part of the way with you.' Daisy turned to Marius. 'Would you care to accompany us?'

'Yes, of course.'

'Then that's settled.' Daisy opened the door for her aunt and uncle. 'What will you do about your fishing tackle, Uncle?'

'I've left it with one of your groundsmen, Daisy. I'll be back tomorrow to give Jay another lesson. I think he rather enjoyed himself today.'

'I did, thank you, sir,' Jay said automatically.

Daisy gave him a curious look. She could not imagine the old Jay saying such a thing. He would never have had the patience to sit by the lake all day, hoping for a bite. His former self would have laughed at such a suggestion, and he would have taken Sidney off to the village pub for a glass or two of ale and a chat with the locals.

She sighed. 'I'll fetch my shawl.'

After saying good night to her aunt and uncle, Daisy led the way to the summerhouse and opened the trapdoor. She glanced at Jay, but his expression was unreadable and it was impossible to tell whether or not he remembered the secret passage. She lit a lantern but Jay took it from her as she was about to descend into the tunnel.

'I'll go first. You might slip.'

'Do you remember the way?'

'I don't know, but it's dark below ground and you aren't suitably dressed for climbing down ladders. Maybe you ought to remain here.'

'Certainly not,' Daisy said coldly. 'I've been this way many times. You're the one who should be careful.'

Marius gave her a warning look. 'Let him go, Daisy. Perhaps it's instinct or maybe he does remember something.'

'The ground is very uneven and the stones are slimy. I don't want him to fall and injure himself.' Daisy followed, taking care not to slip. Her heart was thudding against her ribcage and her palms were damp with excitement. Surely this was a good sign. Maybe the passage that had once been the secret way to the manor house would work a miracle, and the memories it evoked would bring the old Jay back to her.

They emerged into the briny freshness of a June evening, lulled by the sound of the waves caressing the shore. The sun was low in the sky and the shadows deepened, but Jay ran through the trees to the water's edge and was pointing at the ship as it bobbed gently at anchor. He turned to Daisy with an excited smile.

'*Jane*.' His voice cracked with emotion. 'It's the *Lazy Jane*. My ship.'

'You remembered,' Daisy said excitedly. She grasped him by the shoulders, giving him a gentle shake. 'Do you know who you are?'

Jay drew away from her, frowning. 'I'm Jay Tattersall – so you all keep telling me. But I know that vessel – she's mine.'

'Yes, you're right, but do you know who I am?' Daisy asked eagerly.

'You're my wife, and your name is Daisy.' Jay recited the words like a child repeating a set of rules, but it was obvious that his thoughts were elsewhere. He walked to the water's edge, gazing at the *Lazy Jane*, basking in the glow of the evening sun.

'Jay.' Daisy raised her voice. 'Come back and talk to me.'

'Leave him alone, Daisy,' Marius said gently. 'Give him time.'

'It's obvious what is more important to him.' Daisy turned away. If she saw pity in Marius's eyes she knew she would not be able to hold back tears of bitter disappointment.

Marius laid his hand on her shoulder. 'Perhaps the memories will return slowly, and this is just the start.'

'He recalled the name of his ship, but he doesn't know me. Let's see if he remembers the way home.' Daisy stormed off in the direction of the tunnel. Jay's sudden recollection of the *Lazy Jane* felt like betrayal. She could have understood his blind devotion better had it been for another woman, but to love an object created from wood and canvas more than the wife he had professed to adore, seemed like the worst kind of treachery. She reached the mouth of the passageway and paused for a moment to catch her breath.

'Are you all right, Daisy?' Marius came to a halt at her side. 'I can imagine how hard this must be for you.'

'I need to be alone, Marius. If you want to help please make sure that Jay gets home safely. I don't trust myself to speak to him yet.'

'Of course, if you're sure.'

'Yes, I am. I'll be fine, I just need some time to think.' Daisy picked up the lantern and headed into the darkness.

* * *

When she reached the house Daisy would have gone straight to her room if it had not been for Marius, but it would look odd if she left Mary and Jay to entertain him. Reluctantly she went to the drawing room where Mary was seated by the window, darning one of Jay's socks.

'You were a long time. Where are Jay and Marius?'

'We went to the cove. They'll be here soon.' Daisy hesitated in front of a wall mirror, patting her hair into place.

'You look flustered, dear. What's the matter?'

There was no avoiding the truth. 'The *Lazy Jane* was at anchor and Jay recognised her. He knew her name.'

Mary dropped the sock and her hands flew to her mouth. 'Oh, my God. His memory has come back.'

'Not entirely.'

'What do you mean?'

'He still doesn't know me.'

'I'm sorry, Daisy. But perhaps it will happen slowly. We'll have to be patient.'

'Yes,' Daisy said dully. 'I suppose you're right.' She looked round at the sound of the door opening, and Jay entered the room, followed by Marius.

'I remembered the ship, Mother,' Jay said triumphantly. 'The *Lazy Jane* is mine.'

'That's wonderful.' Mary rose to her feet and crossed the floor to embrace him. 'Do you recall anything else?'

'It's like walking in a fog. The only thing I can

see clearly is the ship, and I know that I'm the master and owner.' Jay sat down suddenly. 'But if I'm the owner, why is she moored in the cove? Do you know, Mother?'

Mary shot a wary glance in Daisy's direction. 'You must ask your wife, Jay. She's handled our affairs in your absence.'

'Daisy? What have you to say for yourself?'

'You disappeared on our wedding day and I was left without funds. I couldn't even pay the servants and I wasn't allowed to draw money from the bank. I was desperate and the *Lazy Jane* was doing nothing, so I decided to put her to work and I went in search of a cargo.'

'But you know nothing about the shipping business.' Jay leaped to his feet. 'Why did you have to interfere?'

'What would you have done in similar circumstances?' Marius asked. 'Why don't you sit down and allow your wife to explain?'

'Mind your own business,' Jay said angrily. 'I don't know how you came to be so well known to my family, and you seem to be a little too friendly with my wife.'

'But you don't remember me, do you, Jay? I'm nothing to you.' Daisy faced him, searching his face for a spark of recognition and finding none. 'You loved me, or you said you did. How could you forget what we had?'

He turned away. 'I'm trying hard to place everyone,

but Marius hasn't answered my question. Who are you, sir?'

'Marius is my business partner,' Daisy said icily. 'Ask your mother, if you don't believe me.'

'I'm a shipping agent.' Marius looked Jay squarely in the face. 'My relationship with your wife, whom I might add is a woman I admire and respect, is purely based on business. We met by accident and our partnership is proving beneficial to both parties.'

'Perhaps, but I've returned now, and the *Lazy Jane* is my business. From now on your dealings will be with me, should I decide to continue with the so-called partnership.'

'But that's not fair,' Daisy protested. 'You have no idea what we've been through in your absence. You can't walk in and take over without a by-your-leave.'

'Yes, I can. I don't remember living here or even being married to you, but I do know how to sail a ship and manage a crew. From now on you will have nothing to do with business matters, Daisy. You will leave everything to me, as a woman should.'

'Do you remember how you made a living from the ship?' Daisy asked angrily. 'Do you recall the father who led you into the world of smuggling? That's how the squire made his fortune and he duped you into working for him.'

'I don't believe it.' Jay stared at her in disbelief. 'You're lying.'

'Daisy, please. This isn't the right time,' Mary protested. 'Let his memory return gradually.'

'I'm not saying any more, but I suggest you'd better talk to your son, Mary. Tell him how it was and how it is now. He won't listen to me.' Daisy walked towards the doorway. 'I'm sorry, Marius. I seem to have had matters taken out of my hands, so I'll say good night.'

He followed her from the room. 'We'll talk in the morning, but in the meantime I'll have a few words to say to your husband. The only excuse I can make for his behaviour is that the bump on his head has affected more than just his memory.'

She smiled reluctantly. 'Thank you for everything, but it looks as though this is goodbye.'

'We'll see about that. Good night, Daisy.'

She paced her bedroom floor until she was too exhausted to take another step, and she sank onto her bed. The feather mattress welcomed her into its soft folds, but she could not relax. All she could think of was the way that Jay had behaved towards her. The months of worry and hard work, the humiliation of being treated like a servant in her own home, and the struggle to survive financially had counted for nothing in Jay's eyes. All he cared about was the *Lazy Jane*. He had once warned her that he was a wanderer, and now she could see that it was true. She closed her eyes and eventually drifted off into a fitful sleep.

She awakened with a start to find the room flooded with early morning sunlight. It was the beginning of another day, but nothing was certain. She rose from her bed, washed and dressed and prepared herself for whatever might happen. She checked her appearance in the mirror before going downstairs to face any problems that might arise. Daisy Tattersall was not a woman to give up easily, and the sooner Jay realised that, the better.

To her surprise she found him seated at the dining-room table, eating a hearty breakfast of bacon, eggs and devilled kidneys. He made to stand, but she motioned him to remain seated.

'I think we need to talk, Jay.' Daisy sat down and filled a cup from the silver coffee pot. She added a dash of cream and took a sip, eyeing him warily over the rim of the cup.

'I realise that I should have been more considerate last evening,' Jay said reluctantly. 'You have to under-stand that I'm struggling to overcome this loss of memory, and it's far from easy.'

'I try to, but it doesn't give you the right to belittle me in front of others.'

'If you mean Marius, then I agree. He pointed out my shortcomings in no uncertain terms after you had gone to bed last night. I know I was a little harsh, but the one thing that has become clear to me is that the *Lazy Jane* holds the key to my past and to my future.'

'What are you saying?'

'I've been up all night trying to decide what is best for all of us. I accept that I married you for love and probably with the best of intentions, and Mary told me about the old squire, my father. It still seems like a story about someone else, but I know it must be true.'

'You accept the fact that Mary is your mother?'

'She has no reason to lie, and I feel something for her. I can't explain it, but I know that I can trust her.'

Daisy put her cup down, gazing at him intently. He was obviously sincere, but that did not make his words any easier to understand. 'So where does this leave me? Are we still married?'

He smiled ruefully. 'You are a beautiful woman, and from what other people tell me, you are brave and resourceful and a wife that any man could be proud of.'

'But you feel nothing for me?'

'I wish I could say that I did, and it's for that reason in particular that I'm leaving.'

'Leaving? You don't mean it.'

'Marius informed me that the *Lazy Jane* will be sailing on the tide.' He glanced at the clock on the mantelshelf. 'I have to hurry or I'll be too late.' He pushed his plate away and stood up. 'I've written to the bank, giving you authority to draw money as and when you need it. I know that you've been running the estate in my absence and I'm asking you to continue to do so.'

'You're abandoning your family, to say nothing of your responsibilities.'

'It's better this way. I don't know if I'll ever regain memories that mean anything to me.'

'You're a coward, Jay Tattersall,' Daisy said angrily. 'You're too afraid to stay and take up where you left off.'

'Perhaps you're right, but it's the only way for me. I have tried, believe me, but I can't go on like this. I know when I feel the deck beneath my feet that I'll be the person I was.'

She followed him from the room. 'What about Marius? He's invested money in the business.'

'He'll be paid as any shipping agent would be. I know what I'm doing, Daisy.' Jay strode into the main entrance hall where Molesworth was waiting with a large valise at his feet.

'Your luggage, sir.' He picked it up, his expression carefully controlled, but Daisy knew the butler well enough to detect a note of satisfaction in his voice.

Jay took the bag, acknowledging Molesworth with a casual nod of his head. James opened the door and Jay stepped outside without a backwards glance.

'I assume that the master will not be back in time for dinner, madam?'

Daisy met Molesworth's knowing gaze with an attempt at a smile. 'Not today, anyway.' She turned away and came face to face with Marius.

'You knew that he was going,' she said in a low voice.

'We had a long talk last evening, Daisy. I know this is hard for you to understand, but I think he's right.

Perhaps he'll find himself when he's at sea, which is something he might never do had he decided to stay.'

'I can't agree.'

'You might in time.' He gave her a searching look. 'Have you eaten?'

'I'm not hungry.'

'Well, I am and it's a long ride back to Maldon. Will you at least keep me company?'

'I will, but only if you promise to tell me exactly what was said last evening after I went to my room. I want to know where I stand.'

Later, after Marius had ridden off in the direction of Maldon, Daisy was in the morning parlour with Mary and Hilda.

'I can't believe he would treat you this way,' Hilda said, collapsing onto the nearest chair. 'After all we went through with that woman here.'

'He's my son, but I'm ashamed of him,' Mary added, sighing. 'Of course he's like his father. The squire was unpredictable and selfish. I don't like to say it of my son, but he should have stayed and taken his responsibilities seriously.'

'We managed on our own before,' Daisy said firmly. 'We can do it again, but this time there won't be a problem with the bank.'

'Will we see that nice Mr Walters again?' Hilda asked eagerly. 'He's such a gentleman, and he gave my nippers bags of toffee when he arrived yesterday. He came to the cottage to see them.'

'I don't think he'll be back. Jack has taken the one thing that Marius and I had in common as business partners.' Daisy looked from one to the other. 'We're on our own, but we can manage. However, I think we need a plan.'

'I agree,' Mary said, nodding. 'What do you suggest?'

'You know the running of this house better than anyone, Mary. Would you be happy to resume your duties as mistress of Creek Manor?'

'Would I be taking over from you entirely?'

'Of course.'

'Then yes, I will gladly.'

'That's excellent, and I must learn to run the estate properly. We can't afford to pay the land agent, so I will make it my business to visit the tenant farmers and collect rents. I also intend to make sure that the renovations of the cottages owned by the estate are completed quickly. You lived in one for long enough, Mary, so you know what they were like.'

'What about me?' Hilda said plaintively. 'Have I got a part in all this? I know I'm lame, but I can manage.'

Daisy eyed her thoughtfully. 'You've done so well with your small plot, I think you ought to be put in charge of the kitchen garden. Mountjoy is getting old and I don't think his eyesight is as good as it was. I think he would be grateful to have someone take over from him.'

'He's been a gardener here since I was a girl,'

Mary said hastily. 'You're not going to retire him, are you?'

'No, but I'd like Hilda to make the important decisions and to supervise the work. I've noticed that the beds aren't being weeded properly and we aren't getting as much fresh produce as we should. Besides which, the roses need deadheading and the hedges need trimming, and I think it needs a house-wifely approach. Poor Mountjoy is too tired to cope any longer and the under gardeners take advantage of him, but I'm sure they would respect you, Hilda, and should you get any trouble, refer them to me. I was used to dealing with difficult patients at the hospital.'

'Do you include me in that?' Hilda asked, laughing.

'No, my dear, you were a model patient. Anyway, I know you'll be kind and sympathetic to Mountjoy and his rheumatics. He was telling me all about it the other day.'

'He passed on his knowledge to me, and I'll be glad to help him now. I can do it without upsetting him, and I love being out in the fresh air. I could never be a house servant, or a cook like my Judy.'

'If we get surplus fruit and vegetables we might be able to do a deal with Mr Keyes in the village shop, or even take them to market in Maldon.' Daisy warmed to the subject. 'I don't know much about farming, as yet, but I'm thinking of fencing off the deer park and replacing the deer with sheep.'

'You can't get rid of the deer,' Mary protested.

'Of course not. I'll simply move them to another part of the estate, and I think there's an old pigsty at the back of the barn. Keeping a pig or two would be handy and they could eat up all the scraps, but I need advice, and I'm going to start right away by going to see Farmer Johnson. He's a sensible man and I know I can trust him.'

'Well, I never did!' Hilda said, chuckling. 'Who would have thought that the elegant young lady from London would take up farming?'

Mary sighed, shaking her head. 'When I was a young skivvy, terrified of the master and all those above me, I couldn't have imagined that one day I would be the one in charge, or that the child I was carrying would be the rightful heir to all this. I just wish that Jay would recover and become his old self.'

Daisy reached out to pat Mary's hand. 'He told me that he felt something for you and he believed that you were his mother, despite the fact that he remembered nothing of his old life.'

'Apart from the blessed ship,' Hilda added drily.

Daisy rose to her feet. 'That's true, but we're not going to sit here and complain. We're going to bring Creek Manor Estate back to its days of glory, and we're going to do it on our own.'

Chapter Eighteen

When Daisy rode into the farmyard later that week she was surprised to see Patience Harker chatting to Will Johnson.

Will broke off the conversation to greet her. 'Good morning, Mrs Tattersall.'

'Good morning, Will.' Daisy dismounted. 'Good morning, Patience. It's nice to see you again.'

'And you, Daisy,' Patience said with a cheeky grin. 'Or should I call you Mrs Tattersall now?'

'I'm quite happy with Daisy. How are your mother and sister?'

'Mama is on tenterhooks waiting to hear if Papa has got his promotion, and Charity is utterly boring. All she can talk about is Tubby Tighe-Martin. I like calling him that because it infuriates her. Anyway, she mopes around all day with his letters tucked into her blouse. I wish they'd elope and get it over and done with.'

'And your mama is well, I trust?' Daisy said, changing the subject. She was not in the mood to listen to Patience grumbling about her sister.

'She is as always.' Patience shrugged and turned her attention to her horse.

'What might we do for you, ma'am?' Will asked hastily.

'I'd like to speak to your father, if he's not too busy.'

'He's in the dairy, miss. Shall I get him for you?'

'No need, I'll find him, but I'd be grateful if you would look after Cinders for me – I wasn't sure where to tether her. I won't be long.' She handed him the reins and picked her way carefully across the muddy farmyard, taking care not to tread on any of the fluffy golden chicks that puttered about, copying the mother hens as they pecked at tiny insects and crumbs of food. A cockerel displaying his gaudy plumage to the hens gave Daisy a malevolent look as she walked past, and she quickened her pace.

In the brick-built coolness of the outbuilding Josiah Johnson was in the middle of berating two dairymaids, whose faces were flushed and eyes downcast. They were standing over large bowls of creamy milk with skimming ladles in their hands, but, judging by the scolding they were receiving, they had not been performing their work to Josiah's satisfaction.

'And if you two spent more time concentrating on your task in hand than in gossiping we would not be having this conversation,' Josiah said angrily. 'Get on with it, and not another word from either of you.' He turned his back on them and led Daisy out into the yard.

'This isn't the place for you, Mrs Tattersall. Shall we go into the house?'

'Actually I was hoping you would have time to show me round the farm. I'm going to take much more of an interest in running the estate now that my husband has gone back to sea.'

Josiah nodded wisely. 'I could see it coming, if I might be so bold, ma'am. My Lewis begged me to let him go back to sea until I gave in just to get some peace and quiet. He sailed on the *Lazy Jane* with Clem Guppy and Eli Ramsden. So Master Jay has gone along as well, has he?'

'Yes, and I am in charge now, but I will need some advice and I couldn't think of anyone better qualified than you, Mr Johnson.'

He puffed out his chest and the colour in his ruddy cheeks deepened. 'Well, that's very nice of you, ma'am. I do pride myself on being the biggest and best farmer in the area.'

'And I'm not setting up in competition with you, Mr Johnson. I'm happy to buy our dairy produce from you, as always, but I intend to keep pigs and sheep, and put the fields to good use. I'll get to know all my tenant farmers and maybe I can help them out in times of difficulty. I'm sure we would all profit by co-operating with each other.'

'You've set yourself a hard task, ma'am, if you don't mind me saying so, and you being a townsperson into the bargain.'

'I can learn, Mr Johnson, and that's why I've come to you in the first place. I'll do it stage by stage, season by season, but you'll find me an eager pupil and a quick learner.'

He inclined his head in acknowledgement. 'I dare say you won't remember it, but you took care of my dear old mother when she suffered from the cholera. You pulled her through when everyone said she was a goner. She's still with us; a bit older and more crotchety, but she has a wise old head on her shoulders.'

'I do remember her,' Daisy said, smiling. 'I'm glad she's recovered fully.' As far as Daisy could remember, the old lady was one of the most difficult patients she had nursed, and now she was well again she probably spent her days bullying her poor daughter-in-law.

'Well, let's start by showing you the piggery.' He led the way out of the dairy and across the muddy yard to a row of brick pigsties, the occupants of which were snuffling around for food or sleeping peacefully under cover.

'Is there much work involved in keeping pigs?' Daisy asked, eyeing the boar nervously. He was in a separate pen and he looked as if he could be fierce, if annoyed.

'They need to be fed and kept clean,' Farmer Johnson said, chuckling. 'A bit like human beings, and they don't like being dirty, as some folk think.'

'We have an old pigsty amongst the outbuildings. It wouldn't take much to renovate it.'

'A bit like them old cottages the squire owned,' Farmer Johnson said, with a wry smile. 'I hear as how you're doing a fine job there, Mrs Tattersall.'

'I'm new at being a landowner, Mr Johnson. I am trying hard to do what's right.'

He eyed her speculatively. 'Talking about what's right, ma'am, I think you know what happened to young Benny Sykes on board your husband's ship.'

Daisy shuddered at the memory of the patient brought into the London Hospital suffering from severe burns, which proved fatal. 'I'll never forget him, poor fellow.'

'Well, his mother lives in that cottage.' Farmer Johnson pointed at a small house a little further down the lane. 'Poor soul, she struggles to survive on what little I can afford to pay her, but there's not much she doesn't know about pig keeping. I'm sure she would be more than eager to help you, and the extra money would make all the difference.'

'I'll wait until we have the sty habitable, and then I'll call on her and see what she says.'

'An excellent idea, ma'am.' Farmer Johnson frowned thoughtfully. 'We're haymaking at present, and you'll need winter feed for your horses. The ten-acre field above the creek should yield enough hay to last the season.'

'I don't think we've any farm equipment,' Daisy said, frowning.

'All you need is some strong men with scythes and the ability to press the hay into bales and you'll be ready to harvest, although you don't want to leave it any later.' Josiah tapped his chin with his forefinger, gazing at her thoughtfully. 'We've almost finished haymaking, so as a thank you for saving Ma from death's door, I'll send the labourers I've hired to help out. I don't hold with the work gangs organised by men who treat them worse than slaves. My lot are good workers and hand-picked.'

'Thank you. I'm most grateful.'

'My boys will make a start later today, if that's convenient, ma'am.'

'Yes, that will suit me very well.'

'You'll also need to check your barns and make sure they don't leak, so that the dried bales can be stored.'

'I'll do that, Mr Johnson, and thanks again, but I mustn't keep you any longer. I'm sure you have a lot to do.'

'You'll discover what it's like running a farm soon enough, ma'am. But you must come into the house. Mrs Johnson will be very upset if you leave without seeing her, and Ma.'

'Of course,' Daisy said, making an effort to sound enthusiastic. Her mind was buzzing with all the information that Josiah had given her, and she was eager to make a start on making the future of Creek Manor secure. It could no longer be left to chance.

Almost before she knew it, Farmer Johnson's labourers were busy scything the grass in the ten-acre field, tying it into sheaves and leaving them in the sunshine to dry. Daisy sent two of the housemaids with jugs of homemade cider and hunks of bread and cheese to feed the workers when they took a break in the late afternoon. She walked to the edge of the field to see their progress for herself, and was amazed at the speed with which they worked. These men were itinerant labourers, who went from farm to farm at harvest time, getting work wherever they could, sleeping in barns or sometimes out in the open. They were a tough breed, used to hard labour, and stripped to their waists they were all bone and muscle. Daisy smiled to herself as she watched the housemaids moving between the men, who had slumped to the ground, snatching a short rest. The two girls eyed the gleaming muscular torsos and the men's sinewy arms with barely concealed admiration, and they giggled self-consciously as they handed out the food and drink. Daisy could hear the deep drone of the men's voices, but judging by the girls' reactions, she could imagine that the remarks were suggestive, although meant to be taken in good part and the girls did not seem to be upset.

Daisy set off for the house with a feeling of having achieved something. Until this morning the hay harvest was something she had heard of, but had never thought much about, and now it was part of her plan to bring Creek Manor estate back into profit. Years of neglect by the old squire had taken their toll, but now the land was under new management and if Daisy had her way it would prosper.

Molesworth met her by the front entrance. 'Well done, madam,' he said smiling.

'Thank you, Molesworth. So you think I'm doing the right thing? And please don't say it's not your place to give an opinion.'

'I think you are doing splendidly, madam. Would you like me to bring a tray of tea to the drawing room?'

'Thank you, Molesworth, but I'm on my way to the kitchen. I'm thinking of getting some chickens and a couple of pigs, and I need to find out if there will be enough scraps to feed them.'

'A very laudable idea, madam.'

'I thought so,' Daisy said smugly. She continued on to the kitchen where she sat at the table and shared a pot of tea with Cook, while they discussed the possibility of feeding pigs and chickens on kitchen scraps.

'It's what we always used to do in the old days,

madam,' Cook said with a nod of approval. 'The late mistress was very sensible, like yourself, and all the table leftovers were saved and all the vegetable peelings and the like were tipped into a bin, and fed to the animals, fresh each day. But the late squire wasn't interested in that sort of thing, and the pigs and hens went to their Maker – well, at least they made a few roasts and some savoury stews.'

Daisy drained her teacup and rose to her feet. 'Thank you, Cook. We'll do as you say when the animals arrive. Now all I have to do is make sure that the piggery and henhouse are in good order and we'll go ahead.'

'If I might make a suggestion, madam?'

'Yes, Cook, what is it?'

'You'll need someone to look after the animals. We used to employ a pig man and someone to clean the henhouse.'

'Of course. I hadn't thought of that.'

'My nephew is looking for work, madam. He's young and healthy and he could do both jobs.'

'That sounds promising,' Daisy said hopefully. 'Ask him to come and see me.'

'Yes, madam. I will.'

The next few weeks passed so quickly that Daisy was left wondering exactly how she had occupied her time before she became a farmer, a land agent and generally someone to whom all the local people suddenly brought their problems. She divided her time between visiting the tenants and collecting their rents, although these visits generally turned out to be sessions where she learned about their families and the diseases of plant and animal, let alone the sniffles and snuffles of the children, which might turn out to be one of the dreaded sicknesses of childhood that took so many lives. Everyone knew that Daisy had trained as a nurse in London, and that she had helped to care for the victims of the cholera epidemic, and she found herself giving medical advice, examining rashes, tending to sprained ankles and other minor ailments, which were considered too trivial to take to the doctor, who charged a fee. Daisy's opinion was respected, and it was free.

Then there were the renovations on the cottages owned by the estate. These had been put on hold while Daisy could not access Jay's bank account, but now she had authority to write cheques and draw cash she was able to hire craftsmen to complete the work while the weather was fine. All this helped to keep her mind off Jay's sudden departure. Once again she had been left in a state of limbo, neither a wife nor a widow, and yet still legally tied to a man who seemed to have forgotten her existence. There had been no news of the *Lazy Jane* and Daisy had not seen Marius since the ship sailed. He would have no reason to contact her as they were no longer partners, and she was too busy to even think of travelling to

Maldon on the off chance of finding him there. She tried not to think about him, but he was a link to Jay, and somehow his continuing absence felt like a betrayal of their friendship. If she were being honest she had to admit that she missed his company, and his sense of humour. Marius had a way of putting what had seemed to be an insurmountable problem in perspective. But he had obviously moved on and was fully occupied making new business contacts, and she had enough to keep her busy.

Then there was the wedding. Toby and Minnie had originally opted for October, but they had brought the date forward, having found a suitable house in Sidney Square, just a short distance from the hospital. An invitation arrived from Minnie's parents and the wedding was to take place in her father's church at Little Threlfall in Hertfordshire.

Daisy had barely finished reading it when her aunt arrived, flushed with excitement and breathless.

'Have you received your invitation, Daisy?' Eleanora slumped down on a chair in the morning parlour, fanning herself vigorously. 'I've walked all the way from the ferryboat, and I couldn't wait for your uncle to come home. I'm so excited, Daisy. Of course we'll go together to Hertfordshire, and Minnie's parents have kindly offered to put us up in the vicarage, providing they have room or they'll book us accommodation at the local inn. Does your invitation say that, too?'

'Yes, Aunt. I've only just finished reading it.'

'Of course I'll have to have a new bonnet for the occasion, no matter what your uncle says. He'll spend any amount of money on fishing tackle, but if I want anything I have to practically go down on my knees and beg.'

Daisy knew that this was an exaggeration, but she did not want to spoil the drama of the occasion for her aunt. She rose to her feet to tug at the embroidered bell pull. 'We'll have some tea, or would you prefer coffee?'

'Tea, I mean coffee, please, dear. Perhaps we could have a day's shopping in London before the wedding. I want to purchase a new bonnet, and maybe some lace gloves, too. I can't let Toby down by looking like a drab.'

Daisy resumed her seat. 'You would never look like that, Aunt. You are one of the smartest ladies in Little Creek. I'm sure everyone envies you.'

'I don't know about that, dear,' Eleanora said with a smug smile. 'Although Grace did cast covetous looks at the mousseline afternoon gown I wore to evensong. The vicar is quite penny-pinching when it comes to buying clothes, so I believe. If I had a new bonnet bought from one of those smart shops, it would be the talk of Little Creek.'

'Then that's what we must do. I've been working hard, and I think I've earned a day off.'

Eleanora gave her a searching look. 'And still no news of Jay?'

'Not a word, Aunt.'

'But it's weeks since the ship sailed.'

'Yes, I know, but I'm no longer in contact with Marius, so I have no news of the *Lazy Jane*.'

'But surely his crew live in the village, dear.'

'You're right, Aunt. I've been so busy that it simply didn't occur to me. I'll visit Eli Ramsden's wife – she might know something – and there's always Clem Guppy's mother. Although I'd rather avoid her, if possible.'

'Excellent, Daisy. Now when will we go to London? I'm excited by the prospect of a day out, and perhaps we could stay the night at an inn? Could we afford such an extravagance, dear?'

Daisy smiled. 'I think we deserve a treat, Aunt.'

Eleanora beamed at her. 'Maybe we could have tea at Gunter's? I love ice cream.'

'Whatever you want, Aunt. It will be my treat. After all you've done for Toby and me, it's the least I can do.'

'It's been a pleasure and a privilege, my love. Your uncle and I weren't blessed with children of our own, but we couldn't love you more.'

Daisy gave her a hug.

Later that day, after seeing her aunt off on the ferryboat, Daisy called on Eli Ramsden's wife, only to find that she knew nothing. She had not heard from Eli since the *Lazy Jane* last set sail. It was disappointing, but Daisy decided that if Mrs Ramsden had no knowledge of the ship's progress, there was little likelihood of Mrs Guppy having any more information. Daisy returned home feeling puzzled and ill at ease. It was not unusual for voyages to take longer than expected, but Jay had not been himself and she could not help wondering if he had been well enough to take back command of the vessel. She comforted herself with the knowledge that Eli and Clem were experienced seamen, and they would not allow Jay to endanger the ship.

The trip to London was organised. Daisy had contacted her brother, letting him know that they would be in town for a few hours, and Toby had replied by telegram, inviting them to stay in Sidney Square. The house had been renovated and he was living there on his own until after the wedding. It was an invitation that was too good to refuse, and Aunt Eleanora's almost childish excitement was contagious. Toby was at Bishopsgate Station to meet the train and they took a hackney carriage to his new home, where they left their overnight bags. A quick tour of the four-storey terraced town house was followed by luncheon. Toby had taken on a cook-housekeeper, who proved that she was as adept in the kitchen as she was at keeping house. Eleanora was full of praise and she insisted on meeting Mrs Fulton, to compliment her personally on the lamb collops and braised peas, not to mention the strawberry tart. The housekeeper bustled off to make coffee, and Toby blew his aunt a kiss.

'You could give the Diplomatic Corps a few lessons, Aunt. I'm sure Mrs Fulton will try to outdo herself every time Minnie and I entertain from now on.'

'Where is the dear girl?' Eleanora asked, wiping her lips on a spotless white table napkin.

'She's gone to stay with her parents until the wedding,' Toby said ruefully. 'Thank goodness it's only for a month. I miss her so much.'

Daisy reached out to pat his hand. 'She is a lovely girl. I know you'll be very happy together.'

He smiled and squeezed her fingers. 'I agree, Daisy. I'm the luckiest chap alive to have met someone like her. I only wish you could be as fortunate.'

Daisy withdrew her hand swiftly. She knew that Toby meant it kindly, but criticism of Jay still had the power to hurt her. 'It wasn't Jay's fault,' she said stiffly. 'It was the accident that robbed him of his memory.'

'And she still hasn't heard from him,' Eleanora added crisply. 'The ship might have sunk, for all we know.'

'What does Marius say?' Toby looked from one to the other. 'Haven't you heard from him, Daisy?'

'No, and I'm not likely to,' she said, sighing. 'Jay made it clear that I had nothing to do with the business. He wanted to deal with Marius himself. I don't expect I'll see him again.'

'He has an agent in Maldon, hasn't he, Daisy?'

Toby said thoughtfully. 'You could visit him and ask for Marius's address. You did well in Jay's absence, and Marius is a friend.'

'Yes, indeed.' Eleanora said, nodding. 'He seemed such a nice young man, and I don't wish to be unkind, Daisy, but I think that Jay behaved badly, even allowing for his lack of memory.'

'It's all in the past now, so may we change the subject?' Daisy rose to her feet. 'I'll go and tidy up, if you don't mind. We have a lot of shopping to do this afternoon, Aunt.'

'Yes, dear, I know. I'll be ready as soon as I've had my coffee.'

Toby stood up and went to open the door for Daisy. 'I'm off duty at six o'clock, so I suggest we go somewhere nice for dinner – my treat, of course.'

'That would be lovely,' Daisy said, smiling.

Toby's words and those of her aunt had unsettled Daisy, but she put her worries behind her as she and Eleanora explored the shops in Oxford Street. They tried on bonnets and hats trimmed with feathers, flowers and seductive veils. Eleanora put aside a confection of pink roses and ostrich feathers, opting instead for a more matronly blue silk bonnet. Daisy had already picked a dashing straw hat for herself, and a more conservative style for Mary. They left the hat department laden with bandboxes and moved on to where shawls were displayed. There was a dazzling array and so many that it was almost impossible to choose between creations in delicate lace, fine wool and exotic Indian prints, shimmering with gold thread. Eleanora did not need much encouragement when it came to purchasing a particularly fine example of the French lacemakers' art, and Daisy purchased a more practical, but still luxurious woollen shawl for Hilda. Then, having exhausted the possibilities in that department, they turned their attention to gloves. They were shown woollen mittens and gloves made of peccary leather, embroidered silk and glossy satin. Then the shop assistant produced a range of fur hats and tippets, although it was still midsummer, but she assured them that these would sell out quickly at the first sign of autumn. Daisy purchased scarves and woollen mittens for Judy and Molly, and gloves for the tiny hands of Pip and Nate.

Exhausted by several hours of shopping, Daisy and her aunt made their way to Gunter's and treated themselves to a selection of cream cakes and bowls of delicious ice cream. They returned to Sidney Square laden with packages and bandboxes. Eleanora paid the cabby and Daisy could tell by the way he grinned and doffed his cap that the tip had been generous. Laughing and chattering like a couple of excited schoolgirls, Daisy and her aunt took their purchases upstairs to Eleanora's room. They tried everything on again, admiring themselves in the dressing-table mirror.

'May I try your hat on again?' Eleanora said

eagerly. 'I know it's too young for me, but it is so pretty.'

Daisy fingered the black lace shawl that Eleanora had purchased, acting on impulse. She wrapped it around her shoulders. 'What do you think of me in this, Aunt?'

Eleanora abandoned the hat with a rueful smile. 'I may be too old for such a confection, but black lace is too matronly for you, my dear.'

'That's just the trouble,' Daisy said, shaking her head. 'I'm a married woman, but I might just as well be a spinster.'

'Well, Daisy, I'm afraid you will have to bear it, no matter what. There's no escaping your fate after you've taken your marriage vows. We married women are very much at the mercy of our husbands. I count myself very lucky to have a good man like your uncle.'

'I suppose I'm fortunate in a way,' Daisy said reluctantly. 'I might not have a loving husband, but I am free to do things my way. I would find it quite hard if Jay were to return suddenly, especially if he wanted to take over the running of the estate.'

'That right, Daisy. Better an absent husband than one who is addicted to drink or the gaming tables, and worse still to be tied to a womaniser. The only rival I have for your uncle's affections is the river, and I can bear that, even if I do get tired of eating fish.'

Daisy was trying to think of a suitable answer when there was a knock on the door.

'May I come in?' Toby asked.

Daisy stood up and went to open the door. 'You're home early.'

'Not really, it's nearly half-past six. I have some good news for you, Daisy.'

Chapter Nineteen

'What is it?' Daisy asked eagerly. 'Don't keep me in suspense.'

'One of my patients today came in from the docks. He'd sustained a serious injury to his left arm while unloading a vessel.' Toby hesitated, as if choosing his words carefully.

'Come to the point, dear,' Eleanora said sharply.

'Well, I don't want to give you false hope, Daisy, but the ship was the *Lazy Jane*.'

Daisy leaped to her feet. 'Why didn't you say that in the first place? Where is she berthed? I must go there immediately.'

'I'm sorry, but it's too late.'

'What do you mean?' Daisy stared at him in dismay.

'I finished early and I went to the wharf where she was docked, but she'd sailed.'

Daisy sank down on the bed. 'I wish you hadn't told me now.'

'Yes, Toby, that was thoughtless,' Eleanora scolded. 'You've upset your sister.'

'I'm sorry, but it's not all bad. I saw Marius coming out of a shipping office and I caught up with him. We had a long chat and he's joining us for dinner this evening.'

'That's good,' Daisy said dully. 'But was Jay on board?'

Toby shook his head. 'That's the odd thing. I asked Marius, of course, and he said that Clem was acting as master. He was about to tell me more when he was called away, but not before we'd made arrangements to meet for dinner at the Ship and Turtle in Leadenhall Street at eight o'clock. Will that suit you, ladies?'

'Yes. Most definitely,' Daisy said eagerly. 'Maybe I'll get some answers at last.'

Marius was there waiting for them when they arrived at the Ship and Turtle. He handed Eleanora from the hackney carriage first and then Daisy, while Toby paid the cabby.

Marius held onto Daisy's hand a little longer than was necessary. 'It's been too long since we last met. I've wondered how you were getting along, Daisy.'

The warmth in his eyes and the sincerity of his smile sent a *frisson* of pleasure down her spine and she knew she was blushing. 'I've taken on the management of the estate and I've been very busy,' she said in an attempt to sound casual.

'I look forward to hearing about it, but first I suggest we go inside before we get soaked to the skin.' Marius glanced up at the darkening sky as the first raindrops hit the dry pavement, hissed and evaporated.

Eleanora held her hat on as she made a dash for the doorway. Daisy followed her aunt, but came to a halt in the shelter of the portico. 'You must tell me what Guppy said, Marius. I want to know why Jay wasn't on board.'

'I'll tell you all I know when we're inside,' Marius said firmly. 'This isn't the place to discuss private matters.'

Daisy waited until they were all seated at their table, and the waiter had poured the wine, before she put the question to Marius for the second time.

'Where is Jay?' she asked. 'Why wasn't he with the others?'

Marius swirled the wine round in his glass, gazing into its depths. 'Guppy said that Jay was still not quite himself and had opted to stay ashore.'

'That sounds odd,' Toby said, frowning. 'Why didn't he return home where he would be cared for?'

'I can't answer that.' Marius looked up and met Daisy's anxious gaze with a sympathetic smile. 'I'm sorry, Daisy. All I know is that the *Lazy Jane*'s last port of call was Weymouth in Dorset.'

'What business could they have had there?' Daisy took a sip of wine.

'For some time we've been doing business with Keiller's, who make marmalade, amongst other confections. The *Lazy Jane* transports a cargo to St Peter Port in Guernsey, where they unload before taking on a consignment of marmalade, which they take to Weymouth and it travels onward by rail from there.'

'Marmalade?' Eleanora stared at him in amazement. 'That sounds very odd.'

Marius shrugged. 'The sugar tax in Guernsey is a fraction of what it is on the mainland and the Scottish firm built a factory there. Anyway, that's not the point. Jay remained in Weymouth, and that's as much as either Guppy or Ramsden would tell me.'

'His mind must be wandering,' Eleanora said briskly.

'We don't know that, Aunt.' Toby picked up a menu and began to study it. 'I'm sure there's a perfectly simple explanation. What do you think, Marius?'

'There's only one way to find out,' Marius said solemnly. 'I have contacts with agents in Southampton and Poole, and I was planning a trip to that part of the country. I could make a detour to Weymouth and see if I could locate Jay.'

'Would you, Marius?' Daisy had been silent during the latter part of the conversation. The details of the *Lazy Jane*'s cargo held no interest for her, and all she could think about was her errant husband. She collected her thoughts with difficulty. 'Jay might be in trouble.'

'It didn't sound like that,' Marius said carefully. 'I couldn't get much out of either Guppy or Ramsden, but they didn't seem to be worried. Apparently Jay is very familiar with that part of the country.'

'It's all a bit odd,' Toby said, frowning. 'If Jay's condition is deteriorating it makes me wonder if he's fit to command a ship.'

'I wouldn't have allowed her to sail if I thought he wasn't able to do his job.' Marius gave Daisy an encouraging smile. 'It's a mystery, but I'm sure we'll find there's a simple explanation.'

'When do you plan to go to Dorset?' Daisy asked eagerly.

'I was thinking of travelling tomorrow.'

'Would you take me with you, Marius?'

'Of course, but wouldn't it be better if you went home and waited for him there?'

'Yes, Daisy,' Eleanora said anxiously. 'You don't want to go traipsing about the country on a wild-goose chase. Jay might be on his way home as we speak.'

'Leave it to Marius,' Toby said, nodding.

'No, that won't do,' Daisy said firmly. 'There's something very wrong and I need to know the truth.'

* * *

Eleanora was wary about travelling home to Little Creek on her own, but Toby gallantly offered to accompany her, and with a little persuasion from Daisy, he offered to take the parcels and bandboxes containing their purchases to Creek Manor. This left Daisy free to accompany Marius to Weymouth with the minimum of luggage.

They set off next day, leaving London from Waterloo Bridge Station, travelling westwards. It was a long and often tedious journey, although the scenery was lovely, and Daisy spent much of the time gazing out of the window, but her mind was elsewhere. Jay had never mentioned any connection with Dorset, and there seemed to be no reason why he would have chosen to remain in a small coastal town so far from home. If Marius had any ideas he was keeping them to himself, and after a failed attempt to draw him on the subject, Daisy did not mention it again. It was only when they were nearing their destination that she began to feel more hopeful.

'Have you any idea where Jay might be staying, Marius?' she asked eagerly.

He stood up to take their luggage from the rack above his head. 'Guppy wasn't very forthcoming, but he mentioned a village a mile or two from the town. He was quite vague and I had the feeling my questions weren't welcome.'

'That's very odd. I can't understand why Jay would want to stay away.'

Marius placed their valises on the floor. 'Neither

can I. Let's hope we find him and then he can explain.'

Daisy glanced out of the window. 'I think we're pulling into the station.'

'I've been here once before. There's a decent hotel on the seafront. I'll book us in there.'

Daisy turned to him, frowning. 'But we're supposed to be looking for Jay. This isn't a holiday, Marius.'

'Of course not, but it's getting late and we don't stand much chance of finding him today. We'll make some enquiries this evening, and first thing in the morning we'll hire some sort of transport to take us to the village Guppy mentioned.'

'Oh dear!' Daisy said with a wry smile. 'My reputation will be ruined if anyone finds out that we've stayed in the same hotel. It's fortunate that Aunt Eleanora didn't think that far ahead. Poor dear, she was so eager to get home that she didn't give it a thought.'

'No one knows us here, so I think you can relax, Mrs Tattersall. I can always pass myself off as your brother, if that would put your mind at ease.'

'No, don't do that, Marius. I think it would be fun to watch the other guests eyeing us suspiciously, even if we aren't doing anything wrong. More shame on them, I say.' Daisy rose to her feet as the train ground to a shuddering halt. 'Is it far to the hotel you mentioned?'

'No, just a pleasant walk along the seafront, with

a beautiful view of the bay.' Marius opened the carriage door and hefted their luggage to the ground. He helped Daisy to alight and a porter rushed up to carry their bags out onto the station forecourt. Marius tipped him, and as the porter walked away they were accosted by a youth, offering to carry their luggage to their destination.

'Obliging lot, these Dorset people,' Marius said, smiling as he watched the lad stride off with a valise in each hand. 'Look, you can see the sea. I don't think I could ever live inland.'

'Me neither,' Daisy said, taking his arm as they set off, heading to the Esplanade in the wake of their luggage. 'I have to keep reminding myself that we're here for a serious reason.'

'Don't feel guilty for wanting to enjoy yourself, Daisy. You are young and you don't deserve to go through all this. I know this is a serious mission, but that doesn't mean we have to be miserable.'

She stopped as they came to the Esplanade with its elegant terrace of Georgian houses and hotels. The sweep of the bay was ahead of them and the blue summer sky reflected on the water in varying shades, from deep ultramarine at the horizon to sparkling light turquoise closer to shore.

'It's beautiful,' Daisy said breathlessly. 'I love the saltings at home, but the North Sea is never quite this colour, and the air here is so fresh and clean.'

Marius squeezed her hand gently as it rested on his sleeve. 'We'd best follow our young guide. I think he's almost reached the hotel. We can take a walk after dinner.'

'After we've made arrangements to go to the place where Jay is supposed to be living,' Daisy added hastily.

'Yes, of course. Don't worry, Daisy. We'll find him.'

That evening they ate in the hotel dining room, seated at a table in the window. The view of the bay at sunset was breath-taking, and the meal was excellent. Daisy knew they were attracting the attention of the other guests, and she was amused to see them smiling benevolently.

'They think we're on our honeymoon,' she whispered, giggling.

Marius smiled and blew her a kiss. 'There, that should convince them,' he said, laughing.

'Don't do that,' Daisy said with an attempt at a frown. 'You're making it worse.'

'Nonsense, my love. We're making them happy for us.'

'Marius, be serious for once. Did you get any sense out of the concierge?'

'He said the village we're looking for is probably Osmington or Osmington Mills, although he said we'd best avoid the latter.'

Daisy was about to take a mouthful of roast chicken, but she paused with the fork halfway to her lips. 'Why?'

'He said the inn had a bad reputation in the past.'

'In what way?'

'Smuggling, I think, although the fellow wouldn't be drawn on the subject.'

Daisy pushed her plate away, the food half eaten. 'I hope Jay hasn't gone back to his old ways, Marius.'

'Don't jump to conclusions,' Marius said gently. 'There's only one way to find out. I'll go on my own, if you don't feel you can face it.'

'I'm not a weak little woman. I'm going with you, no matter what.'

'The concierge promised to find a carriage to take us there after breakfast tomorrow.'

Daisy took a sip from her wineglass. 'I'll be ready.'

Next morning, they had an uncomfortable journey in a dilapidated barouche that had, according to their driver, once been the pride and joy of two maiden ladies who had fallen on hard times and been forced to sell the family home and the contents of the coach house and stables. Their retired coachman now made a living by hiring himself and the carriage out to anyone willing to pay enough to keep him in baccy and beer. He was a gloomy soul, not given to talking, and the ageing cart horses plodded along the country lanes and negotiated the steep hills slowly and painfully. Daisy imagined she could hear the animals' joints creaking and she was tempted to get down and walk; it would certainly have been quicker. However, they reached their destination eventually, and the horses grazed on the long grass at the top of the cliff, while the coachman sat on the box, smoking a clay pipe.

Daisy held onto Marius's arm as they negotiated the steep steps down to the inn, which nestled in a narrow valley a stone's throw from a small, sheltered bay. It was a secluded spot and so it was easy to understand how it must have proved ideal for smugglers in days gone by, giving the revenue men an almost impossible task. A stream meandered past the inn and several small cottages before trickling onto the stony foreshore. It was a picturesque view, but Daisy had seen poverty in Little Creek and in London, and she knew that this idyll was on the surface only. The dwellings were small and the thatched roofs were in desperate need of repair. Barefoot children eyed them suspiciously, and the young woman who stood in the doorway of one of the cottages was unkempt and poorly dressed.

'Perhaps we should make enquiries in the pub?' Marius suggested hastily. 'The landlord will have a good knowledge of what goes on locally.'

Daisy shook her head. 'You do that, Marius. I think I'll have a word with that person.'

'She looks scared,' Marius said doubtfully. 'Maybe they don't get many strangers here. It is a bit out of the way.'

'Nevertheless, I have a feeling about this. It's better if I talk to her on my own.' Daisy walked off without giving him a chance to argue, but the woman had gathered up her children and retreated into the cottage. Daisy was not going to be put off so easily, and she had to knock several times before the woman opened it just enough to peer out.

'I'm sorry to bother you, ma'am,' Daisy said politely. 'But I'm seeking some information.'

'I don't know nothing.' The woman tried to shut the door, but Daisy was too quick for her and she put her booted foot over the sill.

'I won't keep you for more than a couple of minutes,' Daisy said gently. 'May I come in?'

The door opened and the young woman stepped outside.

'What d'you want, missis?'

Now that they were face to face Daisy could see traces of beauty in the pinched face. Dark smudges underlined large eyes, which were a shade of blue comparable to the summer sky, but her fair hair was unwashed and scraped back into a bun at the nape of her neck. Beneath the crumpled and dirty folds of the cotton gown, it was obvious that the woman was pregnant. One of the grubby children emerged from the house and clung to his mother's skirts.

'Is this your little boy?' Daisy asked, smiling down at the child, who immediately hid his face.

'Go inside, Robin.' The mother shooed the little boy into the cottage and closed the door.

'You named your boy after a bird?' Daisy's heart missed a beat and she felt suddenly light-headed.

'It were his pa's idea, not mine. Who are you, missis?'

'My name is Daisy. What do I call you?'

'It don't matter what my name is. What do you want?'

Daisy opened her reticule and took out her silk purse. 'I'm prepared to pay for information.'

'I don't take charity. Say what you came for and then you can go. We ain't on show here.'

'I'm Mrs Tattersall and I think my husband might have stayed here recently.'

'You'd best ask the landlord. I dunno nothing.'

'His name is Jay,' Daisy said softly. 'A bird's name, like your son's.'

'There ain't no law against it, is there?'

'No, of course not.' Daisy struggled to think of a way to get the information she desperately needed. She was certain that this woman knew something.

'Then stop wasting my time. I got nippers to feed.'

'I was told that Jay Tattersall was here. He's the captain of the *Lazy Jane*.'

'That ain't his name. You got the wrong person, missis.'

'Might I ask who you are?'

'I'm Bessie Fox and Jay is my husband, but I don't know this Tattersall fellow. Is that all you want to know?'

Daisy felt as though her heart was being dragged from her body. The pain was physical and it was severe. 'Your husband is Jay Fox, the master of the *Lazy Jane*?'

'That's right, missis. We was wed in the local

church five years since, and I got the marriage certificate to prove it. What is it to you, anyway?'

'And the children?' Daisy said faintly. 'They are
from your marriage?'

'What are you saying? Are you calling me a
whore?'

'No, indeed,' Daisy gasped. 'I wouldn't dream of
such a thing.'

'Anyway, who are you? What right have you got
to come here making out that I'm no better than I
should be?' Bessie held onto the door as the elder
of the two children attempted to open it. 'Wait a
minute, Robin. Go and sit with Dove.'

Daisy backed away. Only Jay would have chosen
such names for his children, and she did not doubt
the truth of Bessie's claim to be Jay's wife. 'Where
is your husband now, Mrs Fox?'

'He's on his ship, of course. I told you he was the
master of the *Lazy Jane*. He goes off on sea voyages
all the time.'

It was obvious that Bessie believed that Jay was
on board the vessel, but Daisy knew this was not
true. That left her with even more questions than
answers. The little boy had begun to snivel and the
other child was sobbing loudly.

'I can't tell you nothing more,' Bessie said crossly.
'Ask the landlord if he knows the fellow you're so
keen to find.'

'Thank you, Mrs Fox,' Daisy said hastily. 'I won't
trouble you any longer.'

Bessie hesitated as she was about to open the door. 'Why did you think it was my Jay that you was looking for, anyway?'

'I'm sorry to have bothered you. It was obviously a mistake.' Daisy could not bring herself to tell the poor creature of her husband's duplicity. Jay Fox or Jay Tattersall, as he was known now, was a bigamist and she herself was an innocent victim, as was Bessie. They had both been taken in by a charming rogue, whose real love was the *Lazy Jane*, and the call of the sea was stronger even than the sound of his mother's voice. Daisy walked away, but she sensed that Bessie was watching her, and she quickened her pace as she reached the steps. All she wanted to do now was to get far away from the place where Jay must have spent the missing months.

'Daisy, wait a moment.' Marius caught up with her. 'What's the matter? You look as if you've seen a ghost.'

She shook her head. 'Let's get away from here.'

'Of course. Take my arm.'

When they reached the top of the steps Daisy came to a halt. 'I need to catch my breath, Marius.'

'Let's stroll to the top of the cliff and admire the view, just like any other visitors.'

Daisy glanced anxiously at the coachman, but he had fallen asleep with his billycock hat pulled down over his eyes and his arms folded over his portly belly.

She took a deep breath and told him what Bessie had said. 'So you see, Marius. I'm not legally married to Jay. It was all a sham.'

'If he was here at this moment I'd throttle him,' Marius said angrily. 'Are you sure that she was telling the truth, Daisy? Did you see the marriage certificate?'

Daisy shook her head. 'She didn't know who I was and she had no reason to lie. The worst part is that Jay was living here while we were frantic with worry, not knowing whether he was alive or dead. Guppy and Ramsden must have been party to the deception.'

'Not necessarily,' Marius said thoughtfully. 'But they have some explaining to do when we get home.'

Daisy stared out across the water, but the sight of merchant ships under sail and smaller fishing vessels only served to fuel the maelstrom of emotions that she was experiencing, from anger to humiliation and the pain of betrayal.

'How could he do this to me?' she said softly. 'What will Mary say when she finds out, and how will I tell her?'

Marius slipped his arm around her shoulders. 'Let's take it one step at a time, Daisy. First of all I suggest we go to the village church and check the records, just to make certain that the woman wasn't lying.'

'Yes. I took her word for it, but I suppose she could have been duped. I thought I knew Jay, but all the time he was leading a double life.'

'Let's go and wake the coachman up. There's nothing to be gained by staying here,' Marius said calmly.

'Yes, of course.' Daisy turned her back on the view and started walking, but she paused. 'Do you think Jay really had lost his memory?'

'I can't answer that, Daisy. Only Jay can give you the reasons for his extraordinary and cruel deception. We'll go to the church first,' Marius said firmly. 'Then we'll know one way or the other.'

The village proper was about a mile and a half away, and the old carriage bumped and rattled its way back through the narrow lanes and lush hedgerows, coming to a halt outside the lychgate. Marius helped Daisy to alight, but halfway up the path leading to the church door, she came to a halt.

'I don't think I can do this, Marius.'

'We can leave now, but then you might never know the truth.'

'You're right – I must find out.' She braced her shoulders and entered the church. It took a few seconds to accustom her eyes to the relative gloom of the interior after the brightness of the summer day, but before she had a chance to look around the verger came bustling to meet them.

He greeted them cordially, and Daisy asked to see the parish register. She did not give any further explanation and the verger did not enquire. He glanced from one to the other, smiled and led them into the vestry, where after a short wait, he brought the register for them to study at their leisure. Daisy's hand shook as she turned back five years of records, and the names seemed to jump out at her. She took a step backwards.

'She spoke the truth, Marius. It's here in black and white.'

He placed a protective arm around her shoulders. 'I'm so sorry, Daisy.'

'No one must know.' She reached out and snatched a Bible from a shelf. 'Swear on the Bible that you won't breathe a word of this, Marius.'

He stared at her in disbelief. 'You don't mean that, Daisy.'

She thrust the Bible into his hands. 'I've never been more certain of anything. I'm not going to tell anyone at home about this, and neither will you.'

'But the truth will out eventually. Guppy and Ramsden must know some part of Jay's cruel lies.'

'I'll see them when I return to Little Creek. I refuse to become the laughing stock of the village. Swear on the Bible that you won't tell a soul, please, Marius.'

Chapter Twenty

Despite Marius's attempts to persuade her otherwise, Daisy was adamant that no one at home must find out the shocking truth. Jay had married her bigamously, and if reported to the law he could go to prison, but Daisy was not out for revenge. During the journey back to London she kept her thoughts to herself, but she was still struggling to accept the fact that the man she loved had lied and cheated his way into her affections. The story about his rescue at sea had never been fully explained, due to Jay's amnesia, but his condition when he was admitted to the London Hospital had been severe enough to convince the doctors that his illness was genuine. As to Jay's loss of memory – it had been very convincing. Daisy racked her brains to think of signs that she might have missed: subtle indications that he was beginning to recall names and faces, or even that he was simply play-acting. If that had been the case, he had been frighteningly convincing.

'Daisy, we're nearly there.' Marius leaned over to pat her hand. 'Are you all right?'

She dragged herself back to the present, gazing out of the window as the familiar landmarks came into view. It was raining – an apt welcome, considering the circumstances.

'Yes, I am, and you didn't need to come all the way to Creek Manor, Marius. I could have managed quite well on my own.'

He sat back in his seat and smiled. 'Yes, I'm sure you could, but I have to go to Maldon. The *Lazy Jane* should be there in a day or so.'

'You think that Jay might be back on board, don't you?'

'It's a possibility. He wasn't in Weymouth, and I'm wondering if he caught the train to London and joined the ship there.'

'Why would he do that?'

Marius leaned forward, giving her a straight look. 'It seems that Jay has been leading a double life, for how long is anyone's guess. Don't ask me why he'd do such a thing, because I think the fellow is mad, but that's just my opinion.'

'I'm confused and I'm angry, but I still want to keep it from everyone at home, at least until I've heard Jay's side of things.'

'How do you think he could justify marrying you bigamously?'

She shook her head. 'He can't, but I still want to speak to him. This affects more than me. There's his mother, who has been through enough pain and distress in her lifetime, and the rest of the family. Jack is just a boy, and he hero-worships Jay.'

'You can't keep it from them for ever, Daisy.'

'I know that, but for the time being I want it to be our secret.'

Daisy rose to her feet as the train slowed down and came to a juddering halt. Their arrival in Little Creek had put an end to the conversation, but Daisy knew that her problems were only just beginning. For the foreseeable future she would have to present a confident face to those around her, but she knew that at any moment her whole world might crumble away to nothing. If Bessie should discover that her husband was a wealthy landowner she would be within her rights to claim her place in society, and Daisy knew where that would leave her. She would be humiliated, homeless and an object of pity, maybe even derision. She could imagine Marjorie Harker relating the story to her society friends with a certain amount of satisfaction.

Marius opened the carriage door and placed their valises on the platform. He held out his hand to help her to alight. 'Are you all right?'

'Yes, I'm fine, thank you.' She smiled and nodded to the porter as he picked up their luggage.

'Your carriage is waiting for you in the lane, Mrs Tattersall.'

Daisy turned to Marius with an enquiring look. 'How did they know we'd be on this train?'

'I sent Mary a telegram last evening. You'll be home in no time, Daisy.'

'But you must come with me. You can't travel on at this late hour.'

'I need to be in Maldon tomorrow when the ship docks.'

'Then leave first thing in the morning. I can guarantee you a good meal and a comfortable bed, which is more than you'll get in a wayside inn.'

'If you put it like that, how can I refuse?'

She linked arms as they set off in the porter's wake. 'You've been a good friend to me, Marius. I can never repay you for your kindness.'

'It's not kindness, Daisy. I care about you.'

She shot him a sideways glance, but he was staring straight ahead, and before she could think of an answer, they were accosted by a group of women who had alighted from a third-class carriage.

'Good afternoon, Mrs Tattersall.' Nancy Noon rushed up to Daisy and bobbed a curtsey. 'I wanted to thank you for the repairs your men done to our cottage. It's so much more comfortable for Ma, who's getting on in years, and suffers from her rheumatics something chronic. We're enjoying life now, and it was all your doing.'

'I'm glad it's an improvement, Nancy.' Daisy was about to walk on when Miss Creedy barred her way.

'Will we see you at evensong on Sunday, Mrs Tattersall?'

'Yes, you will, Miss Creedy. I trust that you'll be accompanying the congregation on the organ.'

'Yes, indeed, ma'am. It's very kind of you to ask.' Miss Creedy lowered her voice. 'There are some who don't appreciate good music.'

'More shame on them,' Daisy said, keeping a straight face with difficulty. Miss Creedy's individual style of thundering away on the church organ in a series of wrong notes and discords was little better than her attempts to play the piano.

Annie Maggs, the local midwife, who appeared to be sober for once, grinned toothlessly at Daisy. 'We've had a ladies' day out, missis. Very enjoyable it were, too.'

'That's nice, Mrs Maggs. Now, I'm sorry I can't stop to chat, ladies, but they'll be expecting us at home.'

Nancy Noon eyed Marius curiously. 'We mustn't keep you and your gentleman friend, ma'am.'

Marius doffed his top hat. 'It was a pleasure to meet you, ladies.' He took Daisy by the arm and propelled her towards the waiting carriage.

Daisy glanced over her shoulder in time to see the ladies with their heads together. She knew they were talking about her, and she could imagine the sensation it would cause when the truth about her marriage to Jay became known. The old squire had been notorious and now it looked as though Jay, his natural son, was following in his father's footsteps. Daisy climbed into the carriage and settled down on the luxurious padded leather squabs. Two days ago this had been her property – now it belonged to Jay and the woman he had chosen to marry. Daisy sat back and closed her eyes. The future, which had once looked so bright, was now shrouded in uncertainty.

Marius had taken his seat next to her and he was holding her hand. She opened her eyes and was met with a sympathetic smile.

'Chin up, Daisy,' he said softly. 'You don't have to fight this particular battle on your own.'

Mary leaped to her feet when Daisy entered the drawing room, followed by Marius.

'Daisy, you're home at last.' Mary rushed over to Daisy and enveloped her in a hug. 'Eleanora told me that you'd gone to Dorset, looking for Jay. Did you find him? I hope you gave him a piece of your mind.'

'No, Mary. We must have missed him. Marius thinks he probably rejoined the ship in London.' Daisy shot a warning glance at Marius.

'I'm sure there's a reasonable explanation, Mrs Tattersall,' Marius said casually. 'I hope to catch up with him tomorrow when the *Lazy Jane* arrives in port.'

Mary resumed her seat on the sofa and picked up a small garment that she had been mending.

'Well, I will have something to say to my son when he turns up again. It was quite all right when he was younger and unattached, but he's a married man now, and he has responsibilities.'

'I've invited Marius to stay tonight, Mary.' Daisy walked over to the fireplace and tugged on the bell pull. 'I'll ask Mrs Ralston to have a room made up for him.'

'Yes, of course, and Cook will need to know that there's one more for dinner.' Mary folded Nate's breeches and set them aside. 'Now tell me all about your trip to London. Eleanora said that you'd been shopping. I could do with a new bonnet for the wedding, but I'll have to trim one of my old ones.'

'No need,' Daisy said, smiling. 'I might have just the thing for you. Aunt Eleanora and I chose it with you in mind, and as my aunt will tell you, she has excellent taste. It will be in one of the bandboxes that Toby was kind enough to bring home.'

'Oh, really?' Mary's eyes shone with pleasure. 'I haven't had a new bonnet for years.'

'I'm sure you'll like the one we chose. I'll show you later.' Daisy glanced over her shoulder at the sound of a timid knock on the door. 'Come in.'

'You rang, madam?' Judy bobbed a curtsey, managing to keep her balance despite the long black skirts of the uniform that Hilda had cut down to fit her.

'Yes, Judy. We'd like a tray of tea and perhaps

some cake or biscuits, and please tell Cook that there will be one extra at table for dinner. Oh, and please ask Mrs Ralston to see that a room is made ready for Mr Walters.'

'Yes, madam.' Judy backed towards the doorway, but she caught her heel in the hem of her dress and stumbled, but managed to save herself by catching hold of the door handle. She giggled nervously and scuttled into the passageway.

'What is that child doing in such a ridiculous costume?' Daisy demanded as the door closed. 'She's only ten, much too young for a housemaid.'

'She's very sensible and tall for her age,' Mary said firmly. 'Would you rather keep her a slavey in the kitchen?'

'No, certainly not. She's a bright girl, and she could better herself, given half a chance.' Daisy frowned thoughtfully. 'I'll have a word with Hilda. There must be something we can do for young Judy.' She turned to Marius. 'What do you think?'

'It's not my field of expertise, Daisy. I leave my housekeeper to run the house while I'm away.'

Daisy was curious and for a moment she forgot the problems that were uppermost in her mind. 'Where is this house, Marius?'

'It's in White Lion Street, Spitalfields. I bought it some years ago.'

'And yet you choose to stay at hostelries.' Daisy met his amused gaze with a frown. 'That doesn't seem very sensible.'

'It's none of our business, Daisy,' Mary said primly. 'I'm sure Marius has his reasons.'

Daisy opened her mouth to reply, but there was a thud on the door, and the sound of teacups rattling on their saucers made Daisy leap to her feet and rush to Judy's aid. She took the tray from her. 'Thank you, Judy. That will be all for now.'

Judy eyed her warily. 'I'm supposed to put the tray on the tea table in the window, madam. I got me instructions from Cook.'

'Consider it done,' Daisy said, smiling. 'That will be all, thank you, Judy.' Daisy carried the tray to the table and set it down. It was good to be home amongst her family, but once again the truth hit her with the force of a body blow. She did not belong here – her life could be shattered at any moment if the truth became known. She gazed out of the window at the sunlit grounds, with the creek visible in flashes of shimmering water through the foliage of the trees.

'Are you all right, Daisy?'

She turned to find Marius standing behind her, a frown wrinkling his brow.

'Yes, I was just admiring the view. Do you take sugar in your tea?'

'No, thank you.' Marius moved a little closer. 'You could come to Maldon with me tomorrow. If he's on board you would be able to talk to him in private.'

'What are you whispering about?' Mary demanded

peevishly. 'I want to know why you thought that Jay was in Dorset. What's going on, Daisy?'

Daisy handed a cup of tea to Marius and poured another, which she handed to Mary. 'It turned out to be a wild-goose chase. Jay wasn't there.'

'But what made you think he would be in that part of the country? Is there something you aren't telling me?'

'Of course not.' Daisy handed round the plate of cake. Mary refused, but Marius took a slice.

'It's all very strange,' Mary said crossly. 'I'll have a few words to say to my son when he shows his face here.'

'Me, too,' Daisy added hastily. 'And for that reason I've decided to accompany Marius to Maldon. The ship is due to arrive tomorrow, weather permitting, and I'll see Jay then.'

'You're going away again? But Toby and Minnie's wedding is in a week's time.'

'I'll only be gone for the day. I'll take the carriage and Fuller will see that I get home safely.'

Mary frowned as she placed her cup and saucer on the table at the side of the sofa. 'I'm very cross with Jay. My son can be so thoughtless at times. You must insist that he comes home with you, Daisy. Then we can attend Toby's wedding as a family.'

Daisy had been about to sit down, but just the mention of Jay's name filled her with dread. It was all so different now, compared to the blissful early months of their marriage. Even when he was missing she had clung to the belief that he would return home, but she could never have imagined the situation in which she found herself. She made a move towards the doorway.

'Shall I show you to your room, Marius? I'm sure Mrs Ralston will have our best bedchamber ready for you by now.'

'I'll come with you.' Mary rose from her chair. 'I'd like to see your purchases, Daisy.'

'I've got a better idea,' Daisy said lightly. 'Why don't you sit there and have another cup of tea, and I'll bring the gifts I bought down here. If Hilda and the young ones haven't gone back to the cottage they could join us, and it will be like Christmas all over again.'

'What a nice idea.' Mary smiled as she rang the bell. 'Be quick. I can't wait to see what you have for me.'

Daisy opened the door and Marius followed her from the room. When they were out of earshot, he caught Daisy by the hand.

'You are sure about tomorrow, aren't you, Daisy?' he said anxiously. 'I didn't mean to force you into something against your better judgement.'

'You ought to know me well enough by now, Marius. I don't allow anyone to force me to do anything if I think it's a bad idea. I must find Jay, and it would be better to say what I have to say away from the family.'

* * *

Fuller had the carriage waiting outside the manor house early next morning and they left before Mary was up and about. Daisy had a long list of messages for Jay from his mother, but she doubted if she would find time to pass them on. The question she wanted to put to him was simple and could be summed up in one word – why? She sat in the corner of the carriage with Marius seated opposite her, although she was not in the mood for conversation. As always, he seemed to understand, speaking only when spoken to and respecting her need for silence.

It was late morning when they arrived at Hythe Quay, and through a forest of sailing-barge masts Daisy could see the familiar outline of the *Lazy Jane*, moored in the channel. She turned to Marius, who was standing beside her.

'There she is. What do we do now?'

'I suggest we visit the taproom of the Jolly Sailor first. If the crew have come ashore it's the first place they'll make for, unless they live locally.'

'But Jay might be on board.'

'If he is we'll hire a boat to take us out to the ship.' Marius proffered his arm. 'Are you sure you want to do this, Daisy? You could wait in the carriage while I make enquiries.'

'No, I'm quite calm – I won't make a scene, if that's what worries you.'

Marius smiled. 'It isn't. I know better than that.'

'So stop worrying about me, Marius. I just want the truth, no matter how much it hurts. Then I can move on. But until I know exactly what Jay thinks and feels I'm caught in a spider's web of lies and deceit. I can't live like that much longer.'

He laid his hand on hers as it rested on his sleeve. 'You're the bravest woman I've ever met, Daisy. I want you to know that I'm here to support you, should you need it.'

'I know you will, and I'm grateful. I just want to get this over and done with.'

'I understand.'

Marius led the way into the pub, protecting Daisy from the curious glances of the locals. Daisy followed him, looking anxiously around to see if she recognised anyone, but to her disappointment there were no familiar faces.

Marius made enquiries at the bar and he returned to Daisy moments later. 'The landlord knows the crew. He said Guppy is in the snug, having a meal, so I've ordered food and we'll join him, if that's all right with you.'

Daisy nodded. 'I know Clem quite well. I'm sure he'll tell me anything he knows.'

The landlord came out from behind the bar to show them into the snug, and to Daisy's relief she found Guppy on his own. He was seated at a table eating a large meat pie. He looked up and jumped to his feet, knocking over the bench on which he had been sitting.

'Mrs Tattersall, ma'am.'

'I'm sorry to startle you, Clem. Do you mind if we join you?'

Guppy righted the bench and dusted it with a none-too-clean rag that he produced from his pocket.

'Please, take a seat, ma'am. You, too, sir.' Guppy waited until they were settled before sitting down opposite them.

'You'll be loading the next cargo today, Guppy,' Marius said evenly. 'Is the captain on board?'

Guppy eyed Daisy warily. 'Er, no, sir. He didn't sail with us this trip.'

'Why not?' Daisy demanded, unable to keep silent any longer.

'I dunno, ma'am. It weren't none of my business to enquire.'

'But you must have some idea, Clem,' Daisy said gently. 'I know you're very loyal, but I need you to tell me the truth.'

'Of course, ma'am.' Guppy pushed his plate away. 'That pie ain't one of their best. I'd have the beef stew, if I was you.'

'Thanks, I'll bear that in mind,' Marius said casually. 'You haven't answered Mrs Tattersall's question, Guppy.'

'I can't, sir. What the captain does is his affair. I keep me nose out of other folk's business.'

Daisy turned to Marius, laying a hand on his sleeve as he was about to reprimand Guppy. 'I'd like to speak to Clem in private, Marius. Would you leave us for a few minutes, please?'

Marius glared at Guppy. 'I'll go and order the food, but you'd best mind your manners when you're speaking to Mrs Tattersall.'

'Aye, sir.' Guppy waited until the door closed on Marius. 'I'm sorry, ma'am. I didn't mean any offence, but the captain has been good to me, and I don't talk out of turn.'

'I realise that, Clem. But I am faced with a predicament. No one seems to know where my husband might be. Can you give me any information?'

Guppy shook his head. 'He was in Weymouth when us left, ma'am.'

'Do you know his exact whereabouts?'

'No, ma'am. I can't help you there.'

Daisy decided to change her method of persuading him to talk. 'I was in London a little while ago, and I was talking to a young lady who met you at the party given by Mrs Harker. You might remember Miss Price.'

Guppy's sulky expression was wiped away by a wide grin. 'I should say I do, ma'am. Ivy is a lovely girl, too good for the likes of me.'

'I don't know about that, Clem,' Daisy said earnestly. 'I believe she gets on very well with your mother, and I'm sure Mrs Guppy is a very good judge of character.'

'Ma did take to her; that I do know.'

'And Ivy was asking about you, Clem.'

Guppy's weathered face reddened and his eyes shone. 'She did? Are you sure it were me she was asking about?'

'Very sure, Clem. I could invite her down to Creek Manor at a time when you have shore leave.'

'You'd do that for me, ma'am?'

'I would, of course, and I'm sure you would try to oblige me, if I needed some information.'

Guppy's eyes narrowed. 'You want me to peach on the captain?'

'I wouldn't put it like that, Clem. I am concerned for Jay's welfare and any information you can give me would be of enormous help.'

'And you'd ask Ivy to the manor house?'

'If you so wished.' Daisy leaned her elbows on the table and met his gaze with a searching look. 'Tell me the truth, Clem. Where is my husband now?'

Clem looked away, staring out of the window. 'We left him in Weymouth, ma'am.'

'Why did he stay there? His home is in Little Creek.'

Daisy glanced over her shoulder, sending Marius a warning look as he walked through the door. 'Go on, Clem,' she said gently. 'You can speak in front of Mr Walters. It won't go against you. Tell me if you know what happened to my husband after the boat sank.'

Chapter Twenty-One

Guppy took a deep breath. 'Me, Ramsden and Lewis were picked up by a fishing boat, but I swear we didn't know what happened to the captain. It was only recently we learned the truth.'

Marius took a seat beside Daisy. 'Go on, Guppy. Tell us what you know.'

Guppy wiped the back of his hand over his mouth. 'I'm powerful thirsty, sir. Could I have a pint of ale?'

Marius nodded. 'When the potman brings our food, I'll order your drink.'

'Thank you, sir.' Guppy took a deep breath. 'Well, as I was about to say – the captain was picked up by a merchant ship. He'd lost his memory so he couldn't tell them where he came from, and he had no choice but to stay on board while they was on patrol. He said he didn't remember much about his time at sea and he went down with a fever, which nearly done for him.'

'That's what we were told,' Daisy said, nodding. 'Jay was still very poorly when we brought him home, and he couldn't remember anything or anyone.'

'That's right, ma'am.' Guppy eyed her warily. 'I might be speaking out of turn, but the truth is that the captain recovered his memory much sooner than he let on.'

'That doesn't make sense. Why would be keep up the pretence?' Daisy asked, frowning. 'Did he tell you anything more, Clem?'

'He should be the one to tell you all this, ma'am. It's not my place to repeat what he told us in confidence.'

'Stop prevaricating, man,' Marius said impatiently.

'That won't help, Marius.' Daisy turned to Guppy with an attempt at a smile. 'We don't know where Jay is. I'm hoping that you will be able to help us.'

The potman entered at that moment, carrying a tray laden with bowls of stew, a platter of bread and a large pat of golden butter. He placed it on the table, together with cutlery, and two glasses of cider.

'A pint of ale, please.' Marius handed the man a tip and was rewarded by a wide grin.

'I'm starving,' Daisy said, picking up a spoon and fork. 'You can tell us the rest when you've had your drink, Clem.'

'This smells good,' Marius said, sniffing appreciatively. 'Have a think, Guppy. Try to remember everything that Captain Tattersall told you.'

They ate hungrily, and were halfway through the generous helpings of beef stew when the potman returned with Guppy's tankard of ale. Marius paid the fellow, who bowed and backed out of the room as if in the presence of royalty.

Guppy took a long drink and sighed with pleasure. 'The best ale in the county. Now where was I?'

'You hadn't got very far,' Daisy said patiently. 'You said that my husband's memory had returned but, for some reason best known to himself, he didn't tell us.'

'He didn't let on because he was desperate to get back to Dorset. He often left me and Ramsden to sail the ship while he went ashore, and we guessed that there was a woman involved. There always was, even when we was boys.'

Daisy's appetite suddenly deserted her. 'What do you mean by that, Clem?'

Guppy took another swig of his drink. 'Begging your pardon, ma'am. I don't like to say it in front of his missis, but the captain always had an eye for a pretty face.'

Daisy recalled the pale, thin woman with two young children and another baby on the way. Bessie must have been pretty once. How many deserted women and babies had Jay left in his wake? The temptation to get up from the table and rush outside to vent her feelings was almost too much to bear, but somehow she managed to keep an outward appearance of calm, although inwardly she was raging at Jay's infidelity.

'Go on, Clem,' she said slowly.

'You don't have to listen to this.' Marius patted her hand.

'Yes, I do,' Daisy said firmly. 'It's time all this came out in the open. I won't have things said behind my back.'

Guppy put his tankard down with a thud. 'Your name has never been mentioned, ma'am. Neither for good nor for ill.'

'That's not important now, but I've met the young woman you speak of, Clem. I know that my husband has another family to support, but he must be getting money from somewhere. Has Jay gone back to his old ways? You know what I mean.'

'I wouldn't like to say, ma'am. When the old squire was alive we done a lot of things that was against the law, but we didn't have much choice, being as how we was his tenants.'

'I know all about that,' Daisy said slowly. 'What I don't understand is why Jay went to Dorset in the first place? It's a long way from Little Creek, and I never heard him mention a connection.'

'The squire owned a property not far from Weymouth, ma'am. He inherited it from some distant relation, so I was told.' Guppy glanced out of the window. 'I should be getting back on board.'

'You're on my time,' Marius said firmly. 'You'll go when I say so. Is there anything else you can tell us?'

'The old squire had been dealing with the Chance family at the Crown Inn, Osmington Mills, more than thirty years ago. They was notorious smugglers and in league with some chap called French Peter. That's how Squire Tattersall managed to set hisself up with the estate back home, at least that's what I heard. There was fortunes to be made free-trading in them days, if you was prepared to risk the hangman's noose.'

'So Creek Manor was bought with ill-gained profits,' Daisy mused. 'I always knew the squire was a thoroughly bad man, but I can't believe that Jay has taken after him.'

'Is there anything more you can tell us, Guppy?' Marius eyed him sternly. 'You know that I don't hold with law breaking in any form, don't you? If I thought that anything like that was going on to this day I would sever my connection with the *Lazy Jane* and her captain.'

'Aye, sir.' Guppy scrambled to his feet. 'But what I will say is that the captain never involved the *Lazy Jane* after the old squire died. What he does when he's in Dorset is his own business, not ours. We just do our work and keep our mouths shut.'

'Thank you, Clem,' Daisy said hastily. 'You've been very helpful, and I'll have a word with Miss Price. I'm sure she'd enjoy a few days in the country.'

Guppy hesitated in the doorway, grinning at her. 'Thank you, ma'am. Much obliged.'

Marius waited until the door closed on Guppy. 'What was all that about?'

'Guppy is in love,' Daisy said, sighing.

'Never mind him. Are you all right, Daisy? You don't have to believe everything Guppy said. He might be mistaken.'

She shook her head. 'He has no reason to lie. I spoke to Jay's wife and I saw her children. You and I saw the entry of the marriage in the parish register, but I want Jay to tell me to my face. I've tried to hate him, Marius, but the person we brought home from the hospital was a stranger. He wasn't the man I fell in love with.'

'I'll go to Dorset and find him, and I'll bring him back with me, whether he wants to come or not.'

'No, don't do that. I want him to come voluntarily, otherwise it's no good.'

'What will you do now?'

'I don't know. Jay's put me in an impossible position. I'm not legally married to him, but I can't just walk away and leave Mary to cope with the estate on her own. Everyone, including the tenants, depends on me.'

'It's time he faced up to his responsibilities, and I'll tell him so. Although, speaking personally, I'd like to throttle him for what he's done to you.'

'I don't want anything said until I've had a chance to talk to him.' Daisy rose to her feet and gathered up her gloves and reticule. Talking it over with Marius only made her feel worse, and she needed to be on her own. 'I think it's time I was on my way home. There's nothing more I can do here.'

Daisy had fallen asleep several times during the journey back to Little Creek, but her dreams had been disturbing. It was a relief to awaken and find the sun shining through the carriage windows, and as they neared the village she had an undisturbed view of the saltings. The spiky clumps of salt marsh grasses, glasswort and the occasional clump of sea lavender were a familiar and welcome sight. The brackish smell of the marsh mud mingled with the scent of garden flowers as they passed through the village, and Daisy received smiles and waves from the people she had come to know and like, some more than others.

Marjorie Harker and Charity were about to climb into their carriage as they left the vicarage, and Grace Peabody stood with her husband, waving them off. Daisy wondered if they had been discussing wedding plans for Charity and Ned Tighe-Martin. Daisy acknowledged them with a wave, but she looked the other way when the carriage drove past the church where, not so long ago, her own marriage ceremony had taken place. She closed her eyes and tried to erase the memories, but they intruded on her thoughts like unwelcome visitors, and she had to force herself to think of something more pleasing.

It was late afternoon by the time Daisy arrived at the manor house and the sight of the mellow red-brick Tudor mansion basking in the sunshine filled her heart with happiness. It was good to be home.

Fuller leaped off the box to open the carriage door and he put the step down to enable Daisy to alight.

'Thank you, Fuller,' she said with a tired smile. 'It's been a long day.'

'It has indeed, ma'am.' Fuller climbed back on the driver's seat and drove off in the direction of the stables, but as Daisy mounted the steps to the front entrance she was surprised to see Molesworth waiting for her in the doorway.

'Is everything all right, Molesworth?'

He shook his head. 'You're needed in the drawing room, ma'am. Urgently.'

She stepped over the threshold and handed her cape and gloves to the maid. 'Whatever is wrong, Molesworth?'

'It's not for me to say, ma'am. Best beware, though.'

Intrigued and unnerved by Molesworth's unusual display of emotion, Daisy hurried to the drawing room, but the sight that met her eyes made her gasp. Mary was deathly pale, but she rose from the sofa and rushed over to throw her arms around Daisy.

'Tell me that it isn't true. This woman is lying, isn't she? She says that she's Jay's wife and these are their children.'

Daisy turned her head to see Bessie Fox glaring at her.

'What are you doing here?' Daisy demanded angrily.

Bessie deposited the younger child on a chair and the small girl opened her mouth, emitting a high-pitched screech that made the lustres on the candlesticks tinkle.

'I'm the rightful mistress of Creek Manor,' Bessie said with sly grin. 'You knew that when you come poking your nose into my business. Well, you'll be sorry you did, because I made Jay tell me everything.'

Mary released Daisy and she spun round to face Bessie. 'You're a liar. I don't believe my son would have married a trollop like you.'

'I ain't no trollop,' Bessie said angrily. 'You take that back, you old cow. You may be his ma but you're nothing to me, and this is my house. I can throw you out any time I like.'

'This is ridiculous.' Daisy felt her knees about to give way beneath her, but she braced her shoulders and forced herself to stand stiffly erect. 'What are you doing here, Bessie?'

'Ho, that's rich, that is. What am *I* doing here? What are *you* doing here, missis? I'm the legal wife and you're his bit of stuff.' Bessie put her hand in her skirt pocket and pulled out a crumpled sheet of paper. 'This is our marriage certificate, all legal and proper, and I know you've seen the parish register because my pa told me he drove you to the church.'

'The driver was your father?' Daisy stared at her aghast as she tried to remember the conversations she had had with Marius during the carriage drive from Weymouth. What had the man overheard?

'Yes, he is. You should be careful what you say in front of people you think are beneath you, missis,' Bessie said with a self-satisfied smirk.

Mary sank down onto the nearest chair. 'That hussy thrust the marriage licence at me the moment she walked into the room.'

'I'll thank you to keep a civil tongue in your head, Ma-in-law,' Bessie said spitefully. 'I got the upper hand, and your son ain't going to do nothing about it, because if he steps out of line I'll have him up for bigamy. I know too much, and I could have him put away in the blink of an eye.'

'Where is Jay?' Daisy asked warily. 'Does he know you're here?'

'Not yet, but when he gets home and finds the cottage locked up, he'll go next door to the pub, and he'll find out soon enough because the landlord is a friend of mine. He'll tell Jay where I've gone and why.'

Mary covered her face with her hands. 'Oh, Jay! What have you done?'

'He married me, missis,' Bessie hissed. 'And these kids are his, and the one in me belly. I come to claim what's due to me, and she can sling her hook. You can too, if you don't like the way things are now. I'm the mistress here.'

The children were sobbing loudly and Bessie seemed to lose some of her bravado. She sat down suddenly. 'I ain't eaten since breakfast. What do you have to do round here to get something to eat? And me kids are starving, too.'

Mary sent Daisy a helpless look, but Daisy had had enough. She tugged on the bell pull.

'I'll send for some food, but you can't stay here, Bessie. The coachman will take you to the village inn and you can put up there until Jay returns.'

'Who do you think you're talking to?' Bessie rose to her feet and faced Daisy with a belligerent out-thrust of her chin. 'I've wiped the floor with people twice your size, missis. I'm not going anywhere.'

'Sit down,' Daisy said sternly. 'Look after your children and we'll talk about this later. If you've got any sense you'll keep quiet in front of the servants, unless you want the whole village to know your business.'

Bessie sat down again, and this time she attempted to comfort her two children, who were both sobbing loudly.

It was Hilda who answered the bell, and Daisy moved swiftly to her side. 'I need to speak to you in private,' she whispered, holding the door so that Hilda had little choice but to step back into the passage.

'Who is that woman?' Hilda asked anxiously. 'It's all round the servants' hall that she claims to be Jay's wife.'

Daisy closed the door. 'Oh dear! I was hoping to keep it quiet for a while. I don't know what to do with her and her children. I was going to send them to the village inn, but I realise now that would be fatal. It would the gossip of Little Creek before dark.'

'Is it true, then? Is she Jay's wife?'

'I was going to tell you and Mary, but I was hoping to see Jay first and have it out with him. Unfortunately he wasn't on the *Lazy Jane* when I visited Maldon this morning.'

'But she can't be married to him,' Hilda insisted. 'You're his wife. Heaven knows you was married twice, both times in church.'

Daisy shook her head. Suddenly she was overwhelmed with fatigue and a deep, nagging sorrow, as if mourning for the loss of a loved one. But Jay was far from dead, and he was the architect of all her problems. 'They were married several years ago. I've seen the parish register, Hilda, and there's no question about it.'

'Well, I never did!' Hilda stared at her in a mixture of horror and amazement. 'What are you going to do?'

'I wish I knew, but the most important thing at the moment is to give them some food, and find them somewhere to stay for the night.'

'I'll get them something to eat.'

'And I'll take them to the morning parlour, where they'll be out of the way while we organise a room for them. I suppose we could put them in the old nursery suite, for the time being, anyway.'

'Shall I send Mrs Ralston to you?'

'No, you can tell her what's happened. Ask her to make the necessary arrangements and to keep it to herself as much as possible, Hilda.'

'Don't worry. You can rely on me.'

Later that evening, having managed to persuade Bessie to make herself and the children comfortable in the nursery suite, Daisy and Mary ate in the dining room, but it was a subdued meal and most of the food remained untouched on their plates.

'How could a son of mine put you in such a terrible position?' Mary said gloomily. 'I thought better of Jay.'

'I find it hard to believe, too.' Daisy drank deeply from her glass of claret. 'I believed him when he said he loved me, Mary.'

'And I'm sure he did – I mean I'm sure he still does, but Jay is selfish and greedy, like his father. He takes what he wants without a thought of what it does to others. I'm ashamed of him.'

'He could go to prison for bigamy,' Daisy said tiredly. 'Although that wouldn't solve anything, but he has to set me free. Our marriage must be legally annulled.'

'You won't leave here, will you?' Mary's bottom lip trembled ominously. 'This is your home as much as it is mine.'

'It isn't in the eyes of the law. I suppose I'll have to go sooner or later, but you must stay.'

'I started out as a servant in this house, and that's how I'll end up, if she has her way.'

'Nonsense, Mary. You were married to the squire, and if I have to move on, you must take charge. Don't allow her to push you aside.'

'I don't know how you can be so calm and rational, Daisy. I'd want to tear the woman's hair out, and I can't tell you what I'd like to do to a man who betrayed my trust in such a way.'

'I'm furious and I'm hurt, and my instinct is to do all the things you mention, but it won't help. I have to survive somehow, and I care about you. I don't want to see you beholden to that woman. I know she's been badly done by, but somehow I don't care, and simply tolerating her takes all my energy.'

Mary folded her table napkin and laid it neatly on the table. She rose from her seat. 'A good night's rest is what we both need, although I doubt if I'll get a wink of sleep.'

'You're right,' Daisy said firmly. 'Things will seem better in the morning. At least that's what I keep telling myself.'

When Daisy entered the dining room next morning she came to a sudden halt. Seated in her place at the head of the table, Bessie was snapping orders at Judy. The two small children wailed miserably, wiping their runny noses on the white tablecloth.

'What sort of establishment do you run, missis?' Bessie demanded, dismissing Judy with a wave of her hand. 'That girl is an idiot. I could do better standing on me head.'

'It's all right, Judy,' Daisy said gently. 'I think we're in need of a fresh pot of coffee and some toast.'

'Yes'm, right away.' Judy bolted from the room, leaving the door open in her haste to escape.

Daisy gave Bessie a withering look. 'You don't speak to servants like that in my house.'

'It's my house, don't forget. And there's going to be some changes made round here.' Bessie attacked a plate of bacon and eggs, shovelling the food into her mouth as if she had not eaten for days, and ignoring the sobs of her children.

Daisy marched up to her and snatched the plate away. 'What sort of mother are you? Your babies are obviously hungry and you're gobbling food like a hungry dog. And you can get out of my chair. You're not mistress of Creek Manor yet.'

Bessie grabbed her plate from Daisy's hand in an undignified tussle, which had the effect of startling the small children into silence. They stared at their mother wide-eyed and open-mouthed.

'You won't get the better of me, missis,' Bessie said triumphantly, and as if to prove her point she forked the remaining shards of bacon into her mouth. 'This is my seat now. I'm in charge here.'

'That's what you think, missis.' Hilda strode into the room and before Bessie could do anything to defend her position, Hilda tipped her onto the floor and stood over her, arms akimbo. 'Now we'll have a bit of respect for Mrs Tattersall and the rest of us. You're a guest here, even if you're an unwelcome one, so just bear that in mind afore you go throwing your weight around.'

Bessie scrambled to her feet, her normally pale face flushed with rage. 'You wouldn't dare behave like this if the master was at home.'

'Neither would you,' Hilda said angrily.

'That's enough.' Daisy picked up the small girl and gave her a comforting cuddle. 'You are not a good mother, Bessie Fox. The little ones need bathing, clean clothes and something to eat and drink. Is this how you carry on normally?'

'I'm the lady of the manor now,' Bessie said sulkily. 'I started in service when I was twelve, and I know how things work. You got to find me a nanny for me kids, and I need to put me feet up and rest. I might miscarry thanks to her.' She shot a resentful look in Hilda's direction.

'You can do as you please, but keep out of my way.' Hilda took the child from Daisy and held her hand out to the boy. 'Come with me, little 'un. We'll make breakfast especially for you and your sister.' She turned to Bessie. 'I take it you've got no objection, missis?'

'No, she hasn't,' Daisy said firmly.

Bessie took a seat at the table. 'Do as you please. They give me a headache, anyway.'

Daisy waited until the door closed on Hilda and the children, before helping herself to bacon and buttered eggs from the silver serving dishes on the sideboard. She took her seat at the head of the table.

'Let's get one thing straight, Bessie. I am the lady of the manor now, and I will continue to run the estate until Jay returns. When he decides to show his face here we will sort this mess out in a grown-up, dignified fashion. I don't want any repeat of the sort of behaviour you've exhibited. Do I make myself plain?'

Chapter Twenty-Two

Daisy had been looking forward to her brother's wedding, but now it was almost upon them she had a problem, and that was Bessie Fox. With Hilda's help and plenty of encouragement from Mary, Daisy had managed to keep Bessie from installing herself as mistress of Creek Manor, but allowing her to have free run of the house during their absence spelled disaster. Left to her own devices Bessie would be certain to establish herself as lady of the manor, and Daisy shuddered to think of the chaos she might find on her return. There was still no sign of Jay and not a word from Marius, which left Daisy in a quandary. Bessie could not be allowed to destroy everything that Daisy had worked so hard to establish, and she called on the family for much-needed help.

Linnet and Jack moved into the manor house the day before Daisy and Mary were due to leave for

Little Threlfall, and with Hilda's assistance they were confident they could keep Bessie in her place, and put a stop to any hint of gossip. Molesworth, Mrs Ralston and Cook were also involved, with back-up from Fuller and Faulkner, the head groom, should things get out of hand.

Dove was now officially engaged to Nick, who was Toby's best man, and they left for Hertfordshire a day earlier than the rest of the party. This left Eleanora, Sidney, Daisy and Mary to travel together.

The journey to Little Threlfall took the best part of the day, even travelling by train, as the journey involved several changes and long waits on draughty railway stations. Sometimes there was a reasonably comfortable waiting room where they could relax, but at smaller stations they spent up to an hour seated on wooden benches. Despite the tedium and discomfort, Daisy was so relieved to be away from the difficult situation at home that she felt she could put up with almost anything. Once again she had sworn everyone to secrecy. Toby would be upset and extremely angry when he discovered that his brother-in-law was a bigamist, and Daisy wanted to keep it from him, at least until after he and Minnie returned from their honeymoon. Mary had said very little during the journey and even the prospect of wearing her new bonnet and shawl did not seem to excite her. Daisy gave up in the end, and if it had not been for Eleanora's constant chatter, they might have spent the entire journey in silence.

Toby met them at the station when they arrived at Little Threlfall. He had hired a carriage to take them to the inn where he was staying, as well as some of the guests. Minnie's previous invitation for Daisy and the family to stay at the vicarage had been withdrawn, due to the number of her relations who needed a bed for the night. Minnie was the eldest of nine children, and Daisy could only imagine how cramped the vicarage must be; she herself was grateful for a quiet room at the back of the old coaching inn. At dinner that evening Daisy was delighted to find Ivy and Flora seated at the next table, which the waiter obligingly moved closer so that they could chat while enjoying the simple, but excellent meal.

After dinner they sat in the inglenook, where in winter there would have been a log fire blazing up the chimney, but now it was filled with colour and the sweet scent of garden flowers arranged in a brass urn. Daisy was careful to avoid any mention of her own problems, and it was a relief to sit and chat with her friends, though everyone agreed that it had been a tiring day and the party broke up early. As they made their way to their rooms Daisy drew Ivy aside.

'I was in Maldon recently,' Daisy said in a low voice. Flora was watching them with interest, but this piece of news was for Ivy's ears only. 'I saw

Clem Guppy, and he told me that he would like to see you again, Ivy.'

Ivy blushed furiously and giggled. 'Well, I never did. Are you sure?'

'Yes, of course. I said you might be visiting me at the manor house, so we'll have to arrange it for when the *Lazy Jane* is in port.'

'How exciting.' Ivy clapped her hands, attracting a curious glance from Eleanora as well as Flora. 'I could visit his mother. She was so nice to me at your party. She's a lovely lady.'

'Hmm, yes, of course,' Daisy said doubtfully. 'Well, I'll say good night now, Ivy. I'll see you at breakfast, no doubt.'

'Oh, yes. I must tell Flora that I've got a gentleman friend. She's never let me forget about Jonah. She calls him "the beastly little gnome".'

'She's not far wrong,' Daisy said with a wry smile. 'I think the description fits him perfectly.'

'Thank you, Daisy.' Ivy gave her a hug. 'You're a good friend.'

'Good night, Ivy.' Daisy stood aside and Ivy raced up the narrow oak staircase that led to the rooms on the first floor of the seventeenth-century inn. Daisy smiled to herself – no doubt there would be much chattering and giggling in the girls' room that night.

'What was that about?' Aunt Eleanora demanded as she urged her husband to go upstairs ahead of her.

'Nothing, Aunt. I was just doing a bit of match-making.'

'You need to sort your own affairs out, Daisy, dear. Never mind matchmaking for others.'

'Guppy is a decent chap, and Ivy is a sweet girl, but a very bad judge of men.' Daisy sighed. 'Maybe that's my problem, too.'

Aunt Eleanora shook her head. 'That's foolish talk, my dear. Jay loves you and he'll turn up again when he's ready. I've no doubt you'll both be very happy.'

'Good night, Aunt,' Daisy kissed her aunt's soft cheek, inhaling the sweet woody floral scent of the violet perfume that Eleanora always wore. This was not the time to break the bad news to her aunt, but keeping it secret was no easy matter.

The day of the wedding dawned fine and clear with the promise of heat later on, and after breakfast Daisy returned to her room to put the finishing touches on her attire. She had chosen a morning gown in pale pink silk faille, worn with a perky hat trimmed with full-blown tea roses and a short veil. As she gazed at her elegant reflection in the mirror she thought of Bessie in her ragged dress, and the two small children, who were pale and undernourished. A quiet rage had been simmering in her bosom ever since she had discovered Jay's betrayal, not only of herself, but also his cavalier treatment of the woman he had married and their two offspring. But this was not the time for self-pity; this was her brother's wedding day and as such it should be joyful. Daisy adjusted the veil so that it covered the top half of her face and she plucked her lace mittens and reticule from the bed. Now she was ready, and she would keep her secret hidden from those she loved until it became necessary to reveal all. She left her room and went downstairs to join the rest of the party, and was pleased to find Mary looking rested and even a little excited.

It was only a short walk to the church, which was set within a well-kept graveyard where the tombstones gleamed in the sunshine as if polished especially for the occasion. Ancient yew trees had been clipped to neat shapes and these gave much-needed shade on a hot day. There was a large crowd of onlookers waiting outside the lychgate, and the air buzzed with excitement as they waited to see the bride and her retinue arrive. It was obvious to Daisy that the vicar and his family were well respected and well liked.

Daisy walked a step or two behind her aunt and uncle, with Ivy and Flora following as they entered the cool interior of the church. Dove was already there, seated on the bridegroom's side of the aisle, and Nick was standing beside Toby, who kept glancing over his shoulder. Daisy could see beads of perspiration standing out on her brother's forehead and she knew that he was nervous, but all she could do was give him an encouraging smile.

The organist was playing music that seemed very appropriate for a wedding and he could actually hit the right notes, unlike Lavender Creedy. The pews filled rapidly and Daisy saw Toby run his finger round the inside of his starched collar as the organist launched into the 'Bridal Chorus' from the opera *Lohengrin*, the verger energetically pumping the bellows.

The whole congregation turned their heads simultaneously to see Minnie walking up the aisle, clutching her father's arm, with her younger sisters following behind as bridesmaids. She caught Daisy's eye as she processed towards the altar, and she smiled.

There was a sudden rustle amongst the people seated at the back of the church as the door opened to admit a latecomer. Daisy was more interested in watching her brother and Minnie, and she paid little attention to the disturbance, but when a man edged his way into the pew to stand next to her, she turned to give him a warning look, and she froze.

'Jay!'

He smiled. 'Sorry I'm late, darling.'

'Shhh.' Eleanora turned round, giving him a stern look.

Daisy stared at him in disbelief. Jay was immaculately dressed in clothes that must have cost a great deal of money, judging by the cut and fit of the jacket and the tailored pin-stripe trousers. His face was tanned and lean, and his blue eyes gleamed with amusement as he met Daisy's astonished gaze. He put his finger to his lips, and his generous mouth widened into a mischievous grin.

Daisy looked away. She had to take a firm grip

on her emotions or she might have slapped his face and brought the ceremony to a halt, but she resisted the impulse and the even greater temptation to push past him and run from the church. She took a deep breath and stared straight ahead, but she heard nothing of the ceremony. Her actions were purely mechanical: she kneeled when the congregation went down on their knees to pray and she stood when everyone rose to their feet. She was in a state of shock, while Jay seemed to be enjoying himself. He sang the hymns in a loud, clear voice, and responded at the end of each prayer with a clear 'Amen'. If looks could quite literally kill, Daisy would have slain him there and then.

Afterwards, when everyone congregated outside the church to throw rose petals at the happy couple, Daisy found Jay once again at her side. He took her hand and tucked it into the crook of his arm, despite her attempts to pull away.

'You might look happy to see me, my love,' he said soulfully. 'I've returned to you, fully recovered and ready to start afresh.'

Daisy looked round at the happy faces and the radiant smile on Minnie's face as she emerged from the church on her new husband's arm. This was not the time to make a scene. Daisy forced her lips into a smile.

'I'll deal with you later,' she hissed, but her heart sank when she saw Mary threading her way through the crowd.

'Jay, my boy.' Mary hurried over to throw her arms around him. Then she stood back and slapped him hard on the cheek.

His hand flew to cover the red finger marks on the side of his face. 'What's that for, Ma? I thought you'd be pleased to see me.'

'Please don't tell everyone, Mary,' Daisy said in a whisper. Luckily only a few people had witnessed the scene as most of the guests were concentrating on the newlyweds.

'All right, but you deserve to be horse-whipped, Jay. I love you, son, but I can't forgive you for what you've done to Daisy, and that poor, silly girl from Dorset.'

Jay threw his head back and laughed. 'Oh, Ma! You don't change, do you? But where did you learn that right hook? You could do a few rounds with the champion.'

'Stop it, both of you,' Daisy said anxiously. 'Please keep this to yourself until we get home, Mary. Then we can sort it out quietly and in private.'

'You're right.' Mary shot an angry glance at her son. 'But you take after your father, Jay. I hoped that you wouldn't inherit any of the squire's bad traits, but I see that I was wrong. I won't say any more now, but I'm ashamed of you.' With her head held high, Mary stalked off to talk to Minnie's mother and father.

Sidney had been eyeing them with a pleased grin and he rushed over to pat Jay on the back. 'Glad you could make it, old chap. Daisy's had a lot to contend with while you were away. I hope you appreciate what she's taken on in your absence.'

Jay smiled confidently. 'Yes, sir. Indeed I do. I'm a very lucky man.'

Daisy waited until her uncle was out of earshot and she snatched her hand free. 'Your luck has run out, Jay Tattersall, or should I say Jay Fox. That's the name you go by in Dorset, isn't it?'

'Let's forget that for today, shall we, my love?'

'Why did you come here, Jay? What do you want?'

'I came to support you, my dear. After all, it is a family wedding.'

She stared at him in amazement. 'You expect me to act as if we're still married?'

'We are, aren't we? I seem to recall going through the ceremony twice.'

'But you already had a wife and children.'

'Oh, that!' He shrugged. 'Bessie and I were very young when we tied the knot, and her father insisted that I make an honest woman of her. She's a good sort, but you are the love of my life, Daisy mine.'

'If you say that once again I swear I will tell everyone here what you've done.'

'Do you mean to say that no one knows?' Jay glanced round at the guests, who were strolling off in the direction of the vicarage, eager to sample the delights of the wedding breakfast.

'Do you think my uncle would have spoken so pleasantly to you had he known the truth?' Daisy demanded crossly. 'I've been keeping it a secret until you put in an appearance, but I certainly didn't expect to see you here. How did you find out that the wedding date had been changed, and how did you know where to come?'

'That's simple. I went home to Creek Manor, but I received an icy reception from James and Molesworth. When I refused to leave they sent for Linnet, and she told me what had happened and where you'd gone – so I'm here to support my wife.'

Daisy clenched her fists at her side. 'Stop it, Jay. You know very well that we're not legally wed. Bessie is your wife – I've seen the entry in the parish register – and, what's more, she turned up at home demanding to be treated as lady of the manor.'

Jay threw back his head and laughed. 'That sounds like my Bessie. I knew you'd found out about us because old man Coker, Bessie's pa, was the driver who took you to Osmington. He gave me a detailed description of you and Marius, and he said you stayed together at the hotel on the seafront. What's going on there, Daisy?'

She rounded on him. 'How dare you ask me that? Marius was going to Weymouth to find you and I travelled with him, otherwise I might never have discovered the truth.'

'You were with another man and no chaperone.' Jay put his head on one side, giving her an impish grin. 'Tut-tut, my love. What will the village gossips say about that?'

Daisy walked off, following the last of the guests to the vicarage. If she stayed with Jay a moment longer she was afraid she might strike him, and that really would create a stir. She quickened her pace and caught up with Ivy and Flora, who, as usual, were dawdling along, chatting and giggling.

'When can I come to Creek Manor?' Ivy asked eagerly. 'Do you think the *Lazy Jane* will put into port soon?'

Daisy composed herself with difficulty, but she managed a vague smile. 'When I find out I'll let you know, Ivy. We can make arrangements then.'

'You don't want to get tied to a sailor,' Flora said, curling her lip. 'He'll go off to foreign parts, and you'll have to bring up the nippers on your own. Why not go for someone like my Hubert?'

Daisy eyed her curiously, momentarily diverted from her own problems. 'Who is Hubert? I thought you had your sights set on Julian Carrington.'

'He thought I was easy game, and he lost interest when he discovered that I wasn't.' Flora tossed her head. 'Then I met dear Hubert. He's a clerk in the City, and he's due for promotion soon. What's more, he's madly in love with me, and we plan to get married and have a nice little terraced house somewhere respectable.'

'I'm happy for you, Flora,' Daisy said equably. 'But Ivy must make up her own mind. She could do a lot worse than Clem Guppy. He's a good, honest man, and he wouldn't let her down.'

'Oh, look!' Ivy cried excitedly. 'They've set out tables on the lawn. Isn't that delightful? I do love being away from the smoke and dirt of the city. I think I'd be quite happy to live in a village.'

Daisy left them to make their way to a table while she went to congratulate her brother and Minnie. But Jay was never far away and he, too, offered his congratulations to the happy couple, although Toby received them coolly and turned his attention back to Daisy. He waited until Jay wandered a little way off to speak to Eleanora.

'Is everything all right, Daisy?' Toby asked anxiously. 'You look upset.'

She decided quickly that a lie would only make things worse. 'I didn't know that Jay was coming today. It was a surprise, and I'm annoyed that he left everything to the last minute.'

'If you want me to have a brotherly word with him, I will.'

'No, thank you, I can handle Jay. You enjoy your day, Toby. I know you'll be very happy with Minnie.'

He leaned over and kissed her on the cheek. 'I hope Jay does right by you, Daisy. He's a charmer, but he's unreliable. Quite honestly, I think he exaggerated his memory loss and traded on your good nature. I don't trust him and I worry about you.'

'There's no need, Toby. I can look after myself and you must concentrate on Minnie – she's a treasure.' Daisy glanced at Minnie, who turned to give her a sunny smile. Behind her Daisy could see

Nick, and he was beckoning to her. 'I think Nick wants a word,' she said hastily, and walked over to him.

Nick was frowning ominously. Daisy could only suppose that Linnet must have told her sister why she was needed at Creek Manor, and that Dove had passed the titbit of gossip on to her fiancé.

'What's Jay doing here, Daisy?' Nick said in a low voice.

'I didn't know he was coming,' Daisy said defensively.

'Dove told me everything. You should have come to me with your problems. I might have been able to help.'

She shook her head. 'It's not as easy as that, Nick. You must know that Jay's wife turned up at Creek Manor with her two children. I could hardly throw her out.'

'I'm going to have words with Jay. He can't treat you like this.'

Daisy laid her hand on his arm, alarmed by the angry look on his face. 'No, Nick. Not now, please. I can handle Jay, but this isn't the time or the place.'

'I suppose not,' Nick said reluctantly. 'I thought Jay had changed when he married you, but I was obviously mistaken. He's the same irresponsible, selfish fellow he always was. I'll say nothing today, but if he crosses my path when we return home, he'll be sorry.'

'Let's get through the wedding breakfast without any fuss. Toby and Minnie deserve a day to remember for the right reasons. I want you to promise you won't say anything, no matter how Jay provokes you.'

Nick met her anxious gaze with an attempt at a smile, which did not reach his eyes. 'You have my word.'

'Thank you, Nick. I'll deal with this my way.'

'You're a remarkable woman, Daisy. I only wish that things could have been different between us.'

'You can't choose the person with whom you fall in love, Nick,' Daisy said ruefully. 'It just happens.'

'Do you still love him, Daisy?'

She thought for a moment; it was not a simple question. 'I don't think I can answer that, Nick, because I really don't know.'

'He doesn't deserve such generosity.' Nick glanced over her shoulder and his expression changed subtly. 'Dove is coming. I won't mention the subject again, at least for now.'

Daisy turned to greet Dove with a genuine smile. No matter how badly Jay behaved it made no difference to her affection for the rest of the Fox family.

Dove wrapped her in a warm embrace. 'Daisy, I can't believe that my brother is here. I'm so sorry for what he's done. You don't deserve such treatment.'

'Let's forget it for today. This is a happy occasion, and I won't allow anyone to spoil it.'

'You always were too good for him,' Dove said in a whisper. 'I love my brother, but sometimes I despair of him.'

'I haven't eaten yet.' Daisy eyed the tables set with pies, savoury pastries and platters of cold meat, not to mention the trifles and dainty cakes. 'I think we'd better help ourselves before everything disappears. Minnie's younger brothers and sisters are obviously dying to get their hands on the cream cakes, and they're only waiting for a word of encouragement from Mrs Cole.'

Nick made a visible effort to smile. 'Why don't you two find a table? I'll brave the vicar's children to fill a plate with some of those tempting dishes.'

Dove led the way and they found a table in the shade of a stately oak tree, but any chance of a private conversation was lost when they were joined by Eleanora, who had apparently lost Sidney to a group of Minnie's uncles, who were all keen fishermen.

Somehow Daisy managed to get through the rest of the reception, and she avoided Jay, but after the bride and groom had left for the railway station the wedding party began to break up.

Fortunately for Daisy's peace of mind, Jay was staying at an inn on the edge of the village, and their paths did not cross that evening. He had gone off with a group of young men, who seemed to be related to Minnie, and were eager to escape from the restraints of their older relatives. Daisy could imagine that they would spend the evening drinking and telling bawdy jokes, and she was glad that there had been no room vacant for Jay where she was staying. She planned an early start next morning and her aunt was in agreement. Uncle Sidney would have little opportunity to argue when Eleanora eventually managed to separate him from his new friends.

Jay was nowhere to be seen when Daisy arrived at the station next morning together with Mary, Eleanora and Sidney. Daisy had been dreading the journey in Jay's company, and she sighed with relief when the train pulled away from the station and there was still no sign of him. She needed to speak to him in private, and she hoped that he would follow them on a later train, but with Jay there was never any certainty. He might have taken off in a quite different direction, and could disappear again for weeks or even months. The situation at Creek Manor was as yet unresolved, and Daisy braced herself to face the inevitable problems that would meet her when she returned. She settled back in her corner seat and stared out of the window at the summer meadows, studded with poppies, cornflowers and moon daisies, and fields filled with ripening corn, bounded by shady woodland. It was a glorious day, but what awaited her when she arrived home? She tried to put it from her mind.

It was late afternoon when they arrived at Little Creek. Daisy had sent a telegram from one of the stations en route, and Fuller was there to meet them with the barouche. They dropped Eleanora and Sidney off at Creek Cottage before making the last leg of the journey to the manor house.

Mary had been chattering happily for most of the journey, but even she was quiet as the carriage pulled up outside the front entrance. Daisy looked out of the window, expecting to see Molesworth standing in the doorway, but to her amazement it was Jay who sauntered down the steps to open the carriage door before Fuller had a chance to climb down from the box.

'How did you get here before us?' she demanded as he took her by the hand and helped her to alight.

'I caught the earliest train this morning,' Jay said casually. He proffered his hand to his mother. 'Come on, Ma. Jump down and come inside. You look tired, old girl.'

Mary accepted his help and then pushed him away. 'Less of the old girl, thank you. And you've got a lot of explaining to do, Jay.' She marched up the steps and brushed past Molesworth, who was standing to attention, staring straight ahead.

Daisy followed Mary into the house, acknowledging Molesworth with a hint of a smile. She turned to Jay, frowning. 'I want to talk to you, in private.'

He shrugged. 'There's no need for that. What I have to say affects everyone. Bessie is in the drawing room, and Hilda has the nippers under control. This is the ideal time to put things straight.'

'I don't see how you can wriggle out of this one, Jay Tattersall,' Mary said, wagging her finger at him.

'I'm going to put matters straight, Ma.' Jay strolled through the great hall, leaving them to follow him to the drawing room.

Mary hesitated, but Daisy slipped her arm around her mother-in-law's shoulders. 'We can at least hear what he has to say.'

Chapter Twenty-Three

Bessie was seated on the sofa, her work-worn hands clasped in her lap and a scowl etched on her face.

'Take a seat, please, Daisy. You, too, Ma.' Jay went to stand with his back to the empty grate, and he waited until everyone was seated. 'We have a bit of an uncomfortable situation here,' he said seriously. 'What I propose is that I take Bessie and the children back to Dorset.'

'Hold on,' Bessie said angrily. 'I ain't something you can get rid of so easily, Jay. I'm your wife.'

'How could I forget it, my little petal?'

Jay was smiling, but Daisy could tell that it was for Bessie's benefit and he was simply humouring her. She sat back in her chair and waited.

'As I said,' Jay continued casually, 'I'm taking Bessie and the children to Dorset, and we'll be living in the house that I inherited from my father. It's a mansion a few miles along the coast from Osmington.'

'What does that solve?' Daisy demanded crossly. 'What do you propose to do about our sham marriage?'

'Yes. She could have you arrested for bigamy,' Bessie added spitefully. 'And so could I, if I was of a mind to get me own back on you. You cheating bastard.'

'If I go to prison you and the nippers will starve, unless your pa takes you in, and I doubt if that would happen.' Jay turned to Daisy with an apologetic smile. 'I know I did badly by you, Daisy. If it's any consolation I did love you and I still do.'

'You can't say that,' Bessie cried passionately. 'You fathered the little ones and the babe I'm carrying now. You said you loved me.'

'And I do, sweetheart.' Jay went to sit on the sofa and he placed his arm around Bessie's thin shoulders. 'I love you and the little ones, but I also love Daisy, and my ma, of course. I'm a loving type of fellow.'

'You're a disgrace,' Mary said bitterly. 'I can't believe you're my son. Although, I'm sorry to say, you do take after your father.'

'Harsh words, Ma.' Jay nodded as if in agreement. 'But I'm trying to make amends. I want you to have the manor house. You did marry the old man, after all, so you can't have hated him that much.'

'You'll never know,' Mary muttered darkly.

'Anyway, as I said, you can have this house and

the estate. I don't see myself as a landed gentleman.' Jay turned once again to Daisy. 'I know what you've done here, Daisy. I respect you for being a superior person and you're everything I am not, so I want you to stay here with Ma, and look after her and the estate. As far as I'm concerned it's yours.'

Daisy sprang to her feet. 'But that's just the point, Jay. It isn't mine legally and never will be. You think you can wriggle out of this by making empty gestures. You've put me in an impossible position. I'm neither legally married nor am I single.'

'Come now, my love. You're a very attractive woman, and you'll be part owner of the Creek Manor Estate. I'll sign it over to you and Ma, if that makes you happy. There will be dozens of eager suitors who will marry you, regardless of the formalities.'

'But I'm not free to marry anyone else,' Daisy said furiously. 'I'm still married to you, even if it isn't legal.'

'I should be mistress of Creek Manor.' Bessie's bottom lip trembled. 'You wed me, Jay. I don't want to be shut away in an old ruin down Dorset way.'

Jay threw up his hands. 'Is there no pleasing you women? For a start, Bessie, my love, the old ruin you mention is a mansion with twenty bedrooms. My pa was an astute man when it came to property. With the money that the *Lazy Jane* brings in, as well as my other businesses, none of which you need know about, I can afford to hire servants and you'll have fine dresses and everyone will envy you.'

'I'm not listening to any more of this,' Daisy said angrily. 'I suggest you take your wife and your children back to Dorset as soon as possible, Jay. In the meantime I'm going to see a solicitor.'

'But that means Jay will go back to prison.' Mary gazed at her with tears in her eyes. 'There must be another way, Daisy, dear.'

'No, this must be settled once and for all,' Daisy said firmly. 'Tomorrow Jay and I will take Bessie and the children to Waterloo, where they will board a train for Dorset. Then we will visit my uncle's old solicitor and take advice from him. Either that or I go to the police.' She faced Jay, eyes narrowed, silently daring him to argue.

He nodded. 'Very well, Daisy. I agree.'

'But I don't.' Bessie jumped to her feet. 'I ain't going to be treated like a child. I'll go to the solicitor with you.'

'No, Bessie. You'll do as I say,' Jay snapped. 'I'm tired of your constant carping and whining. You're my wife and you'll obey me, no matter what. I'm trying to do what's right by you and the children. Go upstairs and pack your things. We'll leave in the morning, as Daisy suggests.'

'Oh! You brute. Wait till I tell Pa how you've treated me.' Bessie flew from the room, slamming the door behind her.

'What have you done, Jay?' Mary asked wearily. 'Why did you marry that person?'

'Bessie is all right,' Jay countered. 'She's not in

419

her element here, but at home she's a different person. I do love her, in my way, and I admit I've taken her for granted when I should have been looking after her and the nippers.'

'You disgust me, Jay Tattersall.' Daisy walked to the door and opened it for Mary, who left them, shaking her head and muttering beneath her breath. Daisy closed the door, eyeing Jay with a scornful curl of her lip. 'I don't know what I ever saw in you, but the sooner this is over the better.'

'Wait a minute, Daisy.' Jay held up his hands in a gesture of submission. 'You're right. I'm everything you say I am, but I need your help if we're to work this out properly.'

Daisy leaned against the door, folding her arms. 'Go on. I'm listening.'

'The truth is that there is no grand house in Dorset. There was such a place, but I sold it some time ago. I said that to keep Bessie quiet.'

'You really are a selfish swine,' Daisy said bitterly. 'Why do you treat people this way?'

'I'm not making excuses for my behaviour, Daisy. I live by my wits and always have done.'

Daisy walked slowly to the fireplace and slumped down in a wing-back chair. She fixed Jay with a hard stare. 'I think you'd best tell me everything.'

He paced the floor, hands clasped behind his back. 'I've always been honest with you, Daisy.'

'No, you haven't. Everything you said was a lie.'

'I just didn't mention the fact that I already had

a wife, but everything else I said to you was the truth.'

'Is that all you have to say? Because it's a pretty lame excuse for bigamy.'

'I know, and that was a bad mistake. Marrying you was the best thing I ever did, but I was young when I met Bessie and she was pretty then, and she was in love with me.'

'Jay, this is getting us nowhere. You've already told me all this.'

'Her father threatened me with a shotgun if I didn't do the right thing by her.' He came to a halt. 'I could divorce Bessie. If I sold the *Lazy Jane* the money would be enough to keep her and the children in comfort, and she'd be free to marry someone who would treat her better than I.'

'And I suppose you would expect me to take you back as if nothing had happened?' Daisy said angrily.

'Yes, you know you love me, as I love you. I'd turn over a new leaf and try to be a good husband and a responsible squire.'

Daisy rose to her feet, facing him with a determined lift of her chin. 'Your mother was right, Jay. You are like the old squire, and I'm glad that our marriage isn't legal. I want to be free of you for ever.'

'You don't mean that, Daisy mine. Come with me if you don't want to stay here and manage the estate. We'll sail away on the *Lazy Jane* and live abroad.'

'I was angry with you, but now I feel only pity. You are a child in a man's body, clamouring for the moon, and crying when you find out that it's far from your reach.'

His expression changed and his lips twisted into a bitter smile. 'A child, am I? Well, this estate is still mine and you are here illegally. I've a good mind to throw you out.'

'You'll find yourself in front of a magistrate on a charge of bigamy if you do anything stupid. In fact, that seems to be the only way to disentangle our affairs. Tomorrow we'll do as I first suggested and we'll go to London to see the family solicitor. It's up to you what you tell Bessie, but I don't think she'll be very happy when you admit that you lied to her about the grand house.' Daisy left the room before Jay had a chance to stop her.

Matthew Brumby's office in Lincoln's Inn Fields was small and poorly lit by a single window, the panes of which were frosted with soot and city dirt on the outside, and smeared with fingerprints on the inside. The walls were lined with shelves that were crammed with law books, files and periodicals, and these spilled onto the floor, together with documents rolled and tied with red tape. Mr Brumby's desk was an island in the midst of all this chaos and he worked by the light of an oil lamp. As long as Daisy could remember, Matthew Brumby had looked old, worn and the skin on his face was creased like a piece of crumpled tissue paper.

He peered at Daisy over the top of his steel-rimmed spectacles, his myopic blue eyes red-rimmed and watery. 'My dear girl, how did you get yourself in this invidious situation?'

Daisy shot a sideways glance at Jay, who sat beside her on a rickety wooden chair that must have come from somebody's kitchen, judging by the grease stains and congealed lumps of food sticking to the uprights.

'I thought I'd married the right man, Mr Brumby,' she said, sighing. 'I didn't know that Mr Tattersall already had a wife, and two children.'

'That must have been a shock for you, Mrs Tattersall.'

'I think I prefer to be known as Miss Marshall,' Daisy said icily. 'It seems that I never had the right to my married name.'

'Hold on, Daisy,' Jay protested. 'I married you twice, didn't I? Doesn't that show good intent?'

Mr Brumby fixed him with a cold stare. 'Not if the marriage is illegal, Mr Tattersall. What have you to say in this matter?'

'I've offered to divorce my first wife,' Jay said sulkily. 'Daisy doesn't like the idea.'

'Bessie has two children to raise and another one on the way. I don't want you now and I don't trust you, Jay. I can't divorce you, because we aren't legally wed, but I want to be free.'

'Have you anyone in mind that you wish to marry legally, Miss Marshall?'

'No, I have not.'

'What about Marius?' Jay said slyly. 'You booked into the Crown Hotel in Weymouth for two nights with him. I have a witness who will substantiate the fact.'

'I was looking for you,' Daisy protested. 'And Marius and I had separate rooms. It was all perfectly respectable.'

'So what do we do now?' Jay sat back in his seat, eyeing Daisy with a smug smile.

She ignored him, turning her attention to the solicitor. 'What can I do, Mr Brumby?'

'Bigamy is a crime, it's true, but realistically you would have to take the matter to the magistrates' court, and then to the quarter sessions. It's a costly procedure and the punishment these days is relatively light – maybe a few months' imprisonment – a year at the most. These cases are so common nowadays with divorce being so expensive, and the results are often unsatisfactory for the woman involved.'

'But I am not legally married to Jay,' Daisy said slowly. 'I have no intention of marrying anyone at the moment, but I might at some time in the future.'

'This type of case rarely comes before me, my dear.' Mr Brumby ran his hand through his mane of white hair, causing it to stand on end around his head like a halo. 'I will have to consult my associates and go through similar cases to find out what is the best advice I can offer you without, I assume, taking court action against Mr Tattersall.'

'I'm prepared to do the decent thing by both of them,' Jay said grandly.

Mr Brumby took off his spectacles and wiped the lenses on a grubby hanky. 'My dear sir, I don't think you know the meaning of decency. I suggest you go away and think about it, leaving me to deal with the legalities.'

Daisy rose from her chair. 'Thank you, sir. I'm most grateful. My uncle would have sent you his best wishes, had he known that I would be seeing you, but I wanted to keep this from my family as long as possible.'

'I quite understand. I have to say that in my opinion, since your marriage was illegal in the first place it is considered to be void, and as such there is no question of annulment. However, having said that, you may at some point desire to marry, and then you might need to prove that you were never legally married to Mr Tattersall. I'll look into it and let you know my findings.' Brumby stood up and shook her hand, but when Jay proffered his hand, Mr Brumby ignored the gesture, and he ushered them out of the office.

'Well,' Jay said as they stepped out of the building into the dazzling sunshine, 'we'd best go home and wait for him to sort the matter out.'

Daisy shook her head. 'Oh, no, Jay. You are going to follow Bessie to Dorset, and quite frankly I don't care what you do after that. I am catching the next train to Little Creek.'

Jay rammed his top hat onto his head. 'Don't tell me what to do, Daisy mine. I have no intention of following Bessie. She's perfectly capable of getting herself and the children back to Weymouth, where she will no doubt call on her father to take her home to the cottage. I have other matters to attend to.'

Daisy eyed him curiously. 'You're going to look for the *Lazy Jane*, aren't you?'

'Absolutely right, my love. She's due in port today and I intend to take up my duties as master. I'll call in to see if Marius is in the office, and make sure that he's doing his job to the best of his ability.' Jay strolled off in the direction of Fleet Street and Daisy hurried after him.

'Wait a minute, Jay. I might need to contact you.'

'I'm sure that old Brumby can manage without me, and I have no intention of giving myself up to the authorities. You heard what he said about judges being lenient on bigamists. They used to be transported to the colonies or branded, but we're a more just society now.'

'You're not getting off so easily. If you're going to Marius's office I'm coming with you. At least I know I can get some sense out of him as to how and where I can get in touch with you.'

Jay glanced over his shoulder. 'Or is it that you have Mr Walters in mind for your second attempt at matrimony, Daisy mine?'

Daisy fell into step beside him. 'Don't be ridiculous, and stop calling me that. I am not yours now, and it seems that I never was.'

Jay raised his hand to hail a passing hansom cab. 'Have you any money on you, my love? I must have given my last penny to Bessie when we left her at Waterloo Bridge Station this morning.'

'Yes, and I have my return ticket to Little Creek. I know you only bought a single, so I hope you can afford the fare to Weymouth, and I know you sent your luggage on in the guard's van for Bessie to deal with at the other end. You are not a gentleman, Jay Tattersall.'

'I have everything I need on board ship.' Jay handed her into the cab as it came to a halt at the kerbside. 'I'm banking on the *Lazy Jane* being in port. She'll come to my rescue yet again, of that I'm certain. Lower Thames Street, Cabby. Galley Dock.' Jay climbed in and sat down beside her as the cab started to move. 'Come with me on the *Lazy Jane*. You've done it before and that's when we first fell in love. Do you remember?'

'I don't want to talk about it.' Daisy stared straight ahead. The familiar London streets brought back memories of her childhood and she knew that she would always feel at home in the city, much as she loved Little Creek. She tried to ignore Jay, who talked incessantly, reminding her of the old days and the love they had shared. He was playing games with her and she knew it. Jay was very good at manipulating people, but she had no intention of falling for his sweet talk again. A small part of her would always love the wild boy and adventurer, but his deceit had hurt her more than she could say, and she would never allow herself to be taken in by him again.

When the cab dropped them in Lower Thames Street it was a short walk to Galley Dock Quay and Daisy descended the watermen's stairs cautiously. This was not the first time she had been this close to the pulsating heart of the city, where fortunes were made by trading with the rest of the world. Steam was gradually taking over from sail, but the *Lazy Jane* was all grace and beauty as she swayed gently at anchor in the late afternoon sunlight. One look at Jay's face was enough to convince Daisy of the truth she has always known – the love of his life was a sailing vessel: no woman could compete with the *Lazy Jane*.

'This way,' Jay said, taking her by the arm. 'Mind your step or you might find yourself tripping over something and pitching onto the mud below.'

She shook free from his grasp. 'I'm perfectly capable of walking along the quay without falling into the river. Where is the office?'

'Just here.' Jay stopped outside one of the low wooden buildings along the quay. Above the door was a sign bearing the name 'Marius Walters, Shipping Agent'. Jay barged in without bothering to knock.

'Marius, old chap. Glad you're here. I've brought someone to see you.' Jay ushered Daisy into the dim interior.

It took her a few seconds to accustom her eyes to the gloom, but there was no mistaking the smile of welcome on Marius's face as he came from behind his desk to greet them.

'This is a pleasant surprise, Daisy. What are you doing in London?' His expression darkened as he turned to give Jay a questioning look. 'So you've deigned to turn up, Captain. Or are you Squire Tattersall? You need to make up your mind, Jay.'

Jay shrugged. 'I'm master and owner, Marius. And I'll thank you to treat me with the respect that deserves.'

'You have to earn respect, Tattersall,' Marius said angrily. 'But Guppy and Ramsden have done a good job. Cargoes have been delivered on time and no complaints, despite your lackadaisical attitude to your position.'

'I should think so. I hand-pick my men, and I train them well.'

Daisy tapped her booted foot on the wooden floorboards. She was growing impatient with this pointless chatter. 'Jay, for goodness' sake tell Marius why we came here today.'

Marius met her gaze with a questioning look. 'Why are you here, Daisy?'

'We've just come from the solicitor's office. My marriage to Jay is null and void, according to Mr

Brumby, and he's going to let me know how to go about having it acknowledged legally.'

'So you are a free woman?'

'I always was, according to the solicitor. Jay has a lot to answer for.'

'I'm still here,' Jay said plaintively. 'I acknowledge that I was careless, and I should have told Daisy about my wife and children, but everyone makes mistakes. However, I'm being very generous. As always, the *Lazy Jane* is mine and mine alone, but I'm allowing my mother and Daisy to stay in Creek Manor and run the estate between them.'

'So Daisy will be working for you without any reward?' Marius's eyes narrowed. 'What benefit will she get from that arrangement?'

'How many women have the opportunity to be in total charge of a country estate? Daisy is a free agent now, but if she marries she will have to move out. I'll sell up and use the money to renovate the old ruin my father left me in Dorset.'

Daisy stared at him in surprise. 'But you said that the mansion didn't exist.'

'I was lying,' Jay said, grinning. 'I wanted you to feel sorry for me. The house is real enough, but it's dilapidated and needs money spending on it. I might have to draw on funds from the estate account.'

'We need to discuss this, Jay,' Daisy said hurriedly. 'This is something you should have mentioned before.'

'Don't worry, my dear. You'll have enough to live on. From what I saw you've done wonders managing things in my absence. Continue like that and we'll all be happy.'

Marius took a step towards him. 'It's none of my business, but that doesn't sound very fair, Jay. You're using Daisy.'

'She should consider herself very fortunate to be living in such a wonderful place. After all, we were never legally married so I am not responsible for her and she can walk away if she so wishes.'

'You really are a miserable bastard,' Marius said through clenched teeth.

'I suppose you'd like to sever business relations with me.' Jay chuckled as if enjoying the stir he had created. 'But you would lose money if you did that, old chap. You see, I can tell by the way the *Lazy Jane* sits in the water that she's fully laden, and I'm about to join her. We'll deliver the cargo and you will reap the rewards of our labours. I won't be back for a while, so keep an eye on Daisy and Ma for me. I've no doubt you'll be only too delighted to take my place in Daisy's affections.' Jay sauntered out of the building.

Daisy watched helplessly as he climbed down the wooden ladder to a lighter that was preparing to cast off. She was about to step outside and call out to him, but Marius moved swiftly to her side.

'Let him go, Daisy. You're better off without him.'

'Don't you think I know that, Marius? But he's left me in a difficult position. I need to be clear as to his intentions.'

'It seems to me they're glaringly obvious. He's using you to run the estate and make money, which he will no doubt fritter away. Moreover, you are looking after his mother, whom he's abandoned and he's left you to keep the rest of his family together.'

Daisy could see the lighter ploughing its way through the choppy water, heading for the *Lazy Jane*.

'I need to speak to Mary,' Daisy said firmly. 'She is a sensible woman and she has the most to lose if Jay should decide to sell the house and land.'

Marius laid his hand on her shoulder. 'I'll do anything I can to help, but for now I suggest you come home with me. It's too late for you to travel back to Little Creek tonight, and I'm sure that my housekeeper will be delighted to show off her cooking skills.'

Daisy glanced at the clock on the wall. 'You're right, it is getting late, but I don't want to put you out.'

'You won't. You need to rest and think about things before you set off for Little Creek. I'm happy to talk about it or not, as you wish, but I can guarantee you a fine supper.'

Daisy managed a smile even though she was feeling like crying. All her hopes and dreams had been shattered and for the first time in her life she did not know which way to turn, and it was not only for herself that she worried. The servants in Creek Manor and the tenants on the estate had become like an extended family, and they relied upon her. Suddenly everything was clear to her; she felt as though she had been walking in a peasouper and now she had suddenly emerged into daylight.

'Marius, I want to go on board the *Lazy Jane*.'

His eyes widened and he shook his head. 'That's impossible, Daisy. She's about to set sail.'

'The tide is on the turn. They'll wait until it's on the ebb; that gives me enough time to get on board if you can find a boat that will take me out into the channel.'

'What do you think you can achieve? Jay hasn't paid any attention to your wishes so far.'

'Then I must make him. Please, Marius, do this one thing for me.'

He hesitated, eyeing her gravely, and then he nodded. 'Wait here. I'll see what I can do.'

'Permission to come aboard.' Daisy cupped her hands around her mouth and repeated the request. A strong easterly wind had come from nowhere, backing up the sails, which were being unfurled in readiness for departure. The Jacob's ladder had been lowered and the lighterman was encouraging Daisy to make use of it as he steered the craft alongside the *Lazy Jane*.

'Mrs Tattersall.' Guppy's anxious face gazed down at her. 'Don't risk it, ma'am.'

'I'm coming on board.' Daisy reached out to grab the rope ladder and took a leap, clinging on for dear life. Her long skirts were already soaked and they hampered her movements, but she was desperate to get to safety and she raised one foot, feeling for the wooden rung, and then the other. Her arms felt as though they were being wrenched from their sockets, but she persisted, neither looking up nor down, although she could hear the water pounding against the wooden hull and she knew that if she fell the current would suck her under in seconds. Her hands were numb and she could not feel her feet. Her strength was failing and she knew that she could not cling on much longer – it would be a relief to let go and allow herself to fall into the churning water of the River Thames . . .

Chapter Twenty-Four

The next thing she knew she was hauled unceremoniously onto the deck, where she lay gasping for breath.

'Looks like I landed a marlin,' Jay said, laughing.

Daisy looked up and glared at him through the wet hair that obscured most of her vision. She brushed it back with a shaking hand. 'It's not funny. I might have died.'

'I didn't ask you to follow me. You should have known better.' Jay took her by the hand and dragged her to her feet. 'Are you hurt?'

'Much you'd care if I was,' Daisy retorted angrily.

'The missis is soaked to the skin, Captain.' Guppy took off his jacket and wrapped it around Daisy's shoulders. 'Best come below, missis. Ramsden will make you a nice hot cup of tea.'

'The wind and tide are just right. We set sail now,

Guppy,' Jay said firmly. 'Take the wheel. I'll look after my wife.'

'I am not your wife.' Daisy ignored his proffered hand. 'I know my way about the ship as well as you do. I'll get warm and then you can put me ashore downstream.'

Jay followed her to the saloon. 'You'll find dry clothes in my cabin. We've been here before, Daisy mine.' He threw back his head and laughed. 'Don't look at me like that. We were in love, once upon a time.'

'Yes, but that was then. This is now, and I don't know whether to hate you or pity you.'

'So why did you risk your life to come on board with me?'

'I didn't stop to think, but if I had I would have stayed ashore and accepted Marius's offer of a bed for the night and a good dinner.'

Jay sprawled on a chair, eyeing her with some amusement. 'Go on then, Daisy. What did you have to say that couldn't wait?'

The deck was moving beneath her feet, but Daisy walked up and down in an attempt to get warm. 'You can't just go away without settling our affairs. I don't care what you do with your private life, but I want a written statement from you, admitting that you were already married when we wed. And if I'm to stay on at the manor house I want you to employ me as estate manager with a regular wage.'

'Why should I bother? You've been doing it for

nothing while you thought we were married. I know you, Daisy. You wouldn't desert my mother or that woman you've taken under your wing.'

'That was the old me, Jay. This is me as I am from now onwards. Do you agree to my terms?'

Jay regarded her with a smug smile. 'And if I don't? What then, Daisy? What can you possibly do that would make me change my mind?'

'Maybe nothing, but I think a year in prison would sharpen your mind. If the only way I can be free from this sham marriage is to report you to the authorities, then that's what I'll do.'

'Thank you for the warning, my love. However, you've put me in a difficult position, Daisy. I can't put you ashore with that threat hanging over my head. I'm afraid you'll just have to accompany us on this trip. Anyway, you might find it interesting.'

'What are you saying?'

'We have a cargo of corn for St Peter Port, and then, who knows where we'll go?'

'What do you mean by that?'

'I'm not going to be Marius Walters' pawn from now on. He was useful for a while, but he seems to think that he's the master, and he's wrong. What I say goes, and I intend to take charge of my own destiny. Neither you nor Bessie have a say in what I do next.'

'Does she know this?'

'Not yet, but she will when I fail to return.'

'You're going to desert her?' Daisy stared at him,

her wet clothes and cold limbs temporarily forgotten. 'What about the children?'

'Old man Coker always had plenty to say for himself. Let him take care of them. I've had enough of being the domesticated sort of chap. I told you once that I'm a wanderer, and it's true.'

'What did I ever see in you, Jay?' Daisy stared at him in dismay. 'You can forget about taking me to the Channel Islands. You'll set me ashore somewhere along the river.'

'The only way you'll get ashore is if you jump overboard and swim for it, Daisy. I'm not diverting the *Lazy Jane* for you, or anyone. Now go to my cabin and find some dry clothes. I don't want a sick woman on my hands.'

'I will, but only because it suits me to do so. But you haven't heard the last of this.' Daisy left the saloon, although it was impossible to walk with dignity due to the movement of the deck below her feet. She had almost forgotten what it was like to spend time on board, but unless she could persuade Jay to change his mind, it looked as though this was going to be a long trip.

Jay's cabin was the same as it had been when she was last on board the ship, and it was surprisingly neat and tidy. She braced herself to go through the garments in the sea chest, but the scent of him clung to the clothes, bringing back memories of happier times when love was all that mattered and the future had looked bright. She selected a dressing robe and slammed the lid. Whatever happened in the next few days, she must not allow Jay to charm her into forgiving him, or even worse, fall in love with him for a second time. She stripped off her wet garments and wrapped herself in the soft woollen material of the dressing robe. The galley was her next stop, and she took her wet things to the warmest part of the ship. Ramsden was busy preparing the stew for their supper that evening and he gave her a gap-toothed grin.

'It's like old times, missis.'

'I'm going ashore at the first possible opportunity, Ramsden. Would you be kind enough to see that my clothes dry quickly?'

'Aye, missis. But you're not likely to get ashore for some time yet. We've got to take the cargo to St Peter Port. I dunno what the orders are then, but the captain will tell us.'

'We'll see about that.' Daisy left him and made her way to the saloon where she found a pen and paper, and she settled down to write the terms upon which she would remain at the manor house and the salary she might expect to receive. Having done that, she went on to write a declaration for Jay to sign, absolving her of being complicit in a bigamous marriage. She waited until the ink was dry and then folded the sheets of paper and tucked them in the pocket of the robe. She would wait until after dinner, and then hopefully Jay would be in a mellow mood after enjoying a good meal and a glass or two of wine, and she would persuade him to sign them.

However, it did not quite work out in the way she had hoped. Jay was absent from the table when dinner was served, and Ramsden announced that the captain had taken the wheel while he navigated the crowded waters of the Pool of London and beyond.

'He always does that, missis,' Ramsden said proudly. 'A finer ship-handler you'll never come across.'

'But he must eat.'

'He'll sup after he hands over to Clem, but the captain will want to take advantage of the remaining daylight so that we're well on our way when darkness falls.'

Daisy could tell by the way he spoke that Ramsden had a great deal of respect for his captain, and while she applauded his loyalty, she knew that it would make getting ashore all the more difficult. She would have to concentrate on Guppy. If he wanted to see Ivy again it might make him more amenable to helping her.

Daisy finished her meal and went up on deck, but the warm summer evening had suddenly become overcast beneath a sulphurous sky, and a flash of lightning was followed by a crack of thunder. Then the rain came down in a torrent and Daisy ran for cover. She retreated to the saloon and took a seat, holding onto the table as the ship was buffeted by strong winds. The sound of booted feet on the deck above echoed round the saloon and she could hear Jay shouting orders, his voice cracking with the effort of making himself heard above the howling wind and claps of thunder.

After what felt like an eternity, Jay put his head round the door. 'This is going to be a long night. You'd best use my cabin. I won't be getting much sleep.' He disappeared before she had a chance to respond, but Daisy could tell by the look on his face and the excitement in his voice that he was in his element and enjoying every minute of the challenge to his ship-handling skills.

She made her way to his cabin and curled up on the bunk, pulling the covers up to her chin. The pillow and the bedding smelled of Jay, and she closed her eyes, forcing herself to put him out of her mind. Jay was like a drug that once taken was hard to give up, but she was not going to allow herself to be taken in by him ever again. She needed sleep to make her clear-headed in the morning and capable of forcing Jay to put her ashore at a port close to home.

Sunlight was streaming through the porthole when Daisy awakened, and she raised herself on her elbow, gazing round in an attempt to remember how and why she had woken up in Jay's cabin on the *Lazy Jane*. It took only a few seconds for her to recall the events of the previous evening. She leaped off the bunk, still wearing Jay's robe, and when she looked for her clothes she remembered that they had been left to dry in the galley. It was an eerie repeat of the first time she had been on board this same ship, under similar circumstances. So much had happened in the intervening months that it was almost impossible to comprehend the ups and downs of her turbulent relationship with Jay. She wrapped the robe around her and tied the belt tightly about her waist. There was nothing for it but to go to the galley and retrieve her clothes. Ramsden would know how far they had travelled during the night, and if they were likely to put into port before braving the busy English Channel.

In the galley Ramsden was stirring a large saucepan filled to the brim with porridge. He shook his head when she posed the question. 'Not a chance, missis. I know the captain, and he won't put ashore for anyone, even you. Besides which, you're a lady and you shouldn't travel on your own.'

Daisy sighed. 'It seems we've been this way before, Ramsden. I'll have a word with the captain. Maybe I can make him see things my way.'

'Aye, well, good luck, missis.' Ramsden tasted the porridge and smiled. 'This is tasty, if I say so meself, and it's one of the captain's favourites.'

'Yes,' Daisy said, smiling. 'I remember.'

'Your duds are dry, missis.' Ramsden put down the spoon and reached for the garments. 'I'll put some breakfast in the saloon for you. The porridge will be cool enough to eat by the time you're ready for it.'

'Thank you, Ramsden. That's very thoughtful of you. I won't be long.'

Daisy hurried back to Jay's cabin and found him sprawled on the bunk. 'Excuse me,' she said crossly. 'I need to get dressed.'

He opened one eye. 'It's nothing I haven't seen before, my love.'

'I am not your love, and apparently I never was. But since you're here, I want you to give orders to call in at the next port. I'm going home, Jay.'

'We've just left the Thames Estuary, Daisy. Now leave me alone. I've been on watch all night and I want to get some sleep.' He turned onto his side with his back to her, leaving Daisy in no doubt that the conversation had been terminated.

'All right,' she said firmly. 'Rest now, but I'm having this cabin tonight and you can sleep where you like, but not with me. It's the least you can do, since I'm virtually a prisoner on board this wretched ship, but I want you to put me ashore at the first possible opportunity.'

Jay answered with a snore and Daisy realised that he had succumbed to exhaustion. She dressed hastily and went to the saloon to eat the breakfast that Ramsden had set out for her. If she were being realistic she knew that nothing would make Jay change his mind, and she had no alternative but to accept the situation. However, that would not prevent her from working on his better nature and making him sign the documents she had painstakingly written out. At least she would have something to show for her time on board the *Lazy Jane* when she eventually managed to get home. She resigned herself to a few days at sea, determined to make the most of the respite. When she returned to Creek Manor there would be work to do.

Two days later the *Lazy Jane* docked in St Peter Port harbour. Daisy hoped that they would unload their cargo and sail back to the mainland, but Jay had been evasive when she asked him where the ship was bound next, and neither Ramsden nor Guppy seemed to know.

It was late afternoon when they arrived and Daisy was surprised to find Jay in the cabin, which he had vacated unwillingly. He was going through his sea chest and flinging garments into a ditty bag.

'What are you doing, Jay?'

'I'm packing, my love.'

'Why? Where are you going?'

He straightened up and faced her, his lips curved in a wry smile. 'I suppose you'll find out anyway, so it's best if it comes from my lips. I have responsibilities here.'

Daisy sank down on the bunk. 'What do you mean by responsibilities?'

'You don't want to know.'

She eyed him suspiciously. 'What are you saying?

Are you telling me that you have another family here on the island?'

'I can't help it if women fall in love with me, Daisy. I try to resist, I really do, but you know how it is, but I find myself doing anything to keep them happy.'

'You have a wife here, too?'

'Well, we went through a marriage ceremony some years ago. It's really difficult to avoid such a thing when you're in love with a woman.'

'You mean you're a bigamist twice over? Who is your legal wife?'

'It has to be Aimee, although I was very much involved with Bessie at the time. Aimee is a lovely girl, but she has six elder brothers, all of them big, burly fishermen. We married when she was in the family way with the first nipper. It was convenient for all of us.'

'So you aren't legally married to Bessie?' Daisy stared at him in astonishment.

'Well, I married her in church, so that kept her happy.'

'Do these women know about each other?'

He laughed. 'Hardly. I'm not stupid, Daisy. Bessie accepted the fact that I was a seafarer, and so did Aimee. I could come and go as I pleased, and the old squire didn't mind because we did business with the Channel Islands, if you know what I mean.'

'You are as bad as he was, Jay. If it weren't so tragic and so utterly selfish, I think I would find it funny.'

'I thought you'd be furious when you found out. Why aren't you shouting at me and throwing things?'

'What good would that do? Anyway, I'm past feeling anything for you, Jay. Just tell me one thing – where did I fit in? Why did you marry me?'

'You are the love of my life, Daisy mine. Surely you believe that?'

'No, I don't. Not for a minute.'

'But I've signed the paper stating that our marriage was bigamous, and I've agreed to let you live in Creek Manor and run the estate, paying yourself a very generous salary. What more can I do?'

She rose to her feet. 'I'm speechless, Jay. I should hate you, but for some odd reason I find that I really don't care.'

He shrugged and tossed the last garment into his bag. 'I'm hurt, but I suppose it does make it easier for me to walk away.'

'One day you'll be found out and you'll get your comeuppance, Jay Tattersall, but I care about Mary and the rest of the family too much to drag the family name through the courts.'

'You are the best one, Daisy mine. If things had been different I think I might have settled down with you.' Jay gave her a long look. 'I'm telling you this in confidence because I know I can trust you, but I'm leaving the country and I doubt very much if I'll ever return.'

'What do you mean by that?'

'Just what I said. I'm taking Aimee and the nipper

to start a new life in Australia. No one outside the crew knows as yet, and I certainly don't want her father and brothers to find out until after we've sailed.'

'Why Australia? Why go so far?'

'I want to start afresh, and who knows, I might find gold and end up a wealthy man. I'm not a farmer or a landowner at heart.'

'But what about your family in Little Creek? What will I tell Mary?'

'Don't tell her anything. I'll send word when we're settled somewhere, and maybe I'll come back and visit. Tell Jack that there'll always be a home with me if he wants to see the world.'

Daisy sank down on the bunk. 'I can't believe you're doing this to the people who love you. But on the other hand, it's typical of you, Jay. You are the most selfish person I have ever met.'

He leaned over to kiss her on the cheek. 'I'll miss you, Daisy. But I have to go. You do forgive me, don't you?'

'I won't answer that. You are conceited enough without me adding to it.' Daisy rose to her feet, pushing him away. 'What will the crew do?'

'I've paid them off as they don't want to come with me. They're leaving as soon as the cargo is unloaded. Ramsden and Guppy will take you back to Little Creek. I've given them the train fare.' Jay hesitated, grinning mischievously. 'By the way, I forgot to mention that I visited the bank in Maldon before I set off for Little Threlfall. I withdrew a substantial sum of money, which is only fair. You'll soon make up the shortfall when the rents are collected.'

He was about to open the door, but Daisy caught him by the arm. 'Just a minute. Are you telling me that you've taken everything?'

'Would I be so unfeeling? I left just enough to carry you through, providing you're careful with the money.'

'You really are a bastard,' Daisy said with feeling. 'I suppose you owe Marius money, too. What shall I tell him?'

'I'm sure you'll think of something, Daisy mine. You're rarely lost for words.' Jay opened the door and allowed it to swing shut behind him.

Daisy stood for a full minute, staring at the space where the man who had once been her husband had last stood. The scent of him lingered and his presence seemed to echo round the small cabin, but it faded quickly and she wrenched the door open. The sound of his footsteps faded and she could hear him talking to someone on deck. She picked up her skirts and hurried after him, but he was negotiating the steep gangplank with the ease of long use, and he disappeared amongst a crowd of dock workers.

'He's going away for good this time, missis.'

She turned to see Guppy standing at her elbow. 'What will you do now, Clem?'

He pushed his cap to the back of his head. 'Well,

I was thinking of swallowing the anchor, missis. I'm very taken with Miss Price, and you said you'd ask her to stay at Creek Manor so that she can get to know me better.'

'I did, indeed, and she was eager to take up my invitation, but I hope you won't let her down, Clem. There seems to be too much of that going on these days.'

'I ain't like that, ma'am. I reckon it's time I got wed and looked after Ma. She brought me up on her own and she ain't getting any younger. Ma liked Ivy, and it's the first time she's took to any girl I had a fancy for.'

'That's a good start, and maybe I can find work for you on the estate,' Daisy said thoughtfully. 'You know all the farmers and tenants, and I could do with a manager I can trust.'

'You're staying on then, ma'am?'

'Like you, Clem, I don't seem to have much choice. Tomorrow morning, first thing, I'll send a telegram to Creek Manor, telling them that I'll be home in a few days, providing I can get passage on a ship going to the mainland.'

'That won't be a problem, providing you don't mind the smell of fish, ma'am. We know most of the local fishermen, and they're always looking for ways to make money.'

They landed in Weymouth late in the evening of the following day. Daisy was tired, cold and cramped after spending several hours being tossed around in a small fishing boat, and she was certain that her clothes would never be clean again. The stench of fish, some of it none too fresh, clung to her skirts and permeated every garment she was wearing. She walked to the station with Ramsden and Guppy, only to find that the last train had gone and there would not be another until the morning.

'I am not going to sleep on a bench in the waiting room,' Daisy said tiredly. 'You two can do as you please, but I am going to the hotel where I stayed with Mr Walters.'

'I ain't wasting good money on no fancy hotel.' Ramsden shot a sideways glance at Guppy. 'What about you, mate?'

Guppy nodded. 'I'm with you, but I'll see Mrs Tattersall to the hotel.'

'Meet me in the pub over the road,' Ramsden said gruffly. 'A few pints of ale and we'll sleep like babies.'

'I can find the hotel on my own,' Daisy volunteered.

Guppy, however, would have none of it and he insisted on accompanying her along the Esplanade to the same place where she had stayed on her previous visit. But as they arrived a familiar-looking equipage pulled up outside the hotel and the driver climbed down to open the carriage door. He gave Daisy a cursory glance, turned away and then looked back with recognition dawning on his weather-beaten features.

Daisy turned away. It was just her luck to arrive at the hotel at the same time as Mr Coker, Bessie's father, and he had obviously recognised her.

'I'll be all right now, thank you, Clem,' Daisy said hastily.

'I'll come for you early tomorrow, missis. We'll catch the first train to London.'

'Yes, of course. I'll be ready.' Daisy hurried up the steps and entered the hotel foyer.

The clerk on the reception desk eyed her askance, but Daisy was not in the mood for explanations. It was, of course, unusual for a young woman to be travelling on her own, and even more unusual for someone like herself to book into a hotel, and the clerk was clearly puzzled and at a loss. He summoned the manager, who looked Daisy up and down as if assessing the cost of her outfit, and he wrinkled his nose.

'Where is that dreadful smell of fish coming from, Parkes?'

The clerk shook his head. 'I can't say, sir.'

Daisy tapped the desk impatiently. 'I am trying to book a room for tonight, sir. I'm afraid I missed the last train to London.'

The manager took a spotless white handkerchief from his top pocket and held it to his nose. 'I'm afraid it's against hotel policy to allocate rooms to single ladies, madam. I'm sure you will understand that we have our reputation to think of.'

Daisy was reminded of the first time she had

visited Maldon in search of a shipping agent, where she had met with similar prejudice. 'I am a respectable married woman, and I have money to pay for accommodation. I have simply had the misfortune to miss my train.'

The manager folded his arms across his chest. 'I'm afraid I must ask you to leave, madam.'

'Yes, throw her out, Mr Troop.' Bessie's father burst in through the main entrance, waving his hand to attract the manager's attention. 'She's the one who stole my Bessie's husband.'

'I did no such thing,' Daisy protested.

'Yes, you did.' Coker pointed a shaking finger at her. 'You and that fellow over there. You hired me to take you to spy on my girl.'

Daisy spun round half expecting to see Jay, but the person walking towards her was even more of a surprise.

Chapter Twenty-Five

'Marius,' Daisy gasped. 'What are you doing here?'

He wrapped his arms around her and held her tightly for a few seconds before holding her at arm's length, as he studied her with a worried frown. 'Thank God you're all right. I've been frantic with worry since you were dragged on board Jay's ship. You might have been killed.'

Shaken by his sudden appearance and the emotion that he could not conceal beneath his usual urbane charm, Daisy was momentarily lost for words, but she knew that they were being watched and she managed a smile.

'As you can see, I'm all right.'

Mr Troop held up both hands. 'Will somebody tell me what's going on?'

'That's easy – she's a Jezebel, and that man there is her pimp,' Coker said angrily.

'You'll apologise to the lady for that, sir.' Marius took a step towards Coker, his hands fisted at his sides. 'Mrs Tattersall is a respectable married woman, and you insult me by that accusation.'

'Mrs Tattersall?' Coker roared. 'She ain't his wife. My Bessie can prove that she's married to that bastard Jay Tattersall.'

'Watch your language, Coker,' Marius snarled. 'And go about your business. This has nothing to do with you.'

'I should say it has, mate,' Coker said angrily. 'My Bessie's been badly done to and *she's* to blame.'

'Look to the man you call your son-in-law, Coker. He's the one who's culpable, not this poor lady.'

'She ain't no lady,' Coker snapped.

Mr Troop slammed his hand on the reception desk. 'I won't have this sort of behaviour in my hotel. You'll take this outside.'

Daisy held up her hands. 'Stop it, all of you. All I want is a room for the night.'

'Yes, all right. Anything to keep the peace.' The waxed ends of Mr Troop's military moustache quivered with emotion. 'And you can get out, Coker. I won't have my foyer turned into a bear garden.' He waited until the angry coachman had left the building before turning to Marius. 'As for you, Mr Walters, if you will vouch for this young person I will find her a room, just for one night.'

'Of course I will, and I think you owe Mrs Tattersall an apology, Troop.'

Troop nudged the desk clerk. 'Pass the guest register to the lady, Parkes.'

'An apology first.' Marius gave Daisy a warning look as she picked up a pen.

'I apologise for the error, Mrs Tattersall.' Troop glanced round anxiously as an elderly couple strolled into the foyer, and he forced a smile. 'I hope you both enjoy your stay.'

Daisy signed the register and Marius led her to the hotel lounge where he ordered coffee and brandy. He sat down opposite her. 'I don't know how you came to be here tonight, but it feels like a miracle, and it's wonderful to see you looking so well. I've been frantic with worry, Daisy.'

'I was quite safe on board the *Lazy Jane*. Jay isn't perfect by any means, but he wouldn't lay a finger on me.' She met Marius's anxious gaze with a steady look. 'He behaved like a gentleman, and anyway, he doesn't want me.'

'I find that hard to believe.'

'It's true, Marius. What we felt for each other is no longer there.' Daisy reached for the coffee and took a sip. 'It's almost like another life, and it's long gone.'

'Really? Are you being honest with yourself, Daisy?'

'Yes, I am. It was sweet and lovely while it lasted, but now there's no going back. Jay is moving on.' She replaced the cup on its saucer. 'You'll hardly credit this, but he married a Guernsey woman before he became involved with Bessie, and they have a child.'

'So he's a double bigamist,' Marius said, shaking his head.

'Yes, and now he's abandoning Bessie and her children to Coker's care, which I don't agree with at all, but it's really none of my business. Jay has no conscience when it comes to getting his own way.'

Marius sipped his drink. 'So is he going to make Guernsey his base from now on?'

'I know he did a deal with you, but he seems to have forgotten all about that. Jay is taking Aimee and their child to Australia, and they won't be coming back.' Daisy leaned forward to lay her hand on Marius's arm. 'I am so sorry, because I know you went out of your way to find cargoes for the *Lazy Jane*. If he owes you money I'll do my best to pay it from the estate, if Jay has left any money in the account.'

Marius gave her a steady look. 'I won't tell you what I think of Jay, because it's not your responsibility. I can stand the loss, but it sounds as if you will be struggling once again, despite all your hard work.'

'He said that he'd left enough to keep us going, and I've agreed to stay on and manage the estate. I've been doing it for the past few months anyway, and although I was born and bred in London, I really love country life.'

'So Jay has reneged on all his promises and responsibilities, leaving you, whom he treated despicably, to pick up the pieces. It's all wrong and it's an insult, Daisy. I won't pretend to condone Jay's behaviour or his treatment of you.'

'I'm fond of Mary and the rest of the family,' Daisy said gently. 'I love Creek Manor and the whole village. It's my home and I'm happy to stay on.'

'You deserve so much more, Daisy. You're a beautiful woman and you should have a home of your own, and a husband who loves you more than life itself.' Marius raised her hand to his cheek, then he released it suddenly. 'What is that awful smell?'

'It's rotten fish,' Daisy said, giggling. 'I do apologise, but I came over in a fishing boat with Guppy and Ramsden.'

'That explains it.' Jay kissed her hand. 'But Jay should be horsewhipped for treating you so badly.'

'I know he's let you down.'

'I don't care about the finances, Daisy, but I do care about you. The way he's behaved is appalling, and I can't believe that he's going to leave you with all the responsibilities that he should be shouldering.'

'I can't walk away from my friends, Marius. At least Jay has signed the papers I need to prove that our marriage was void, and he's given me a contract to run the estate with a generous salary.'

Marius drained the last drop of brandy from his

glass. 'That is an insult in itself, Daisy. You were supposed to be his wife, and he promised to love and take care of you. But somehow Jay has turned it around so that you have all the worries, and he has got away with everything.'

'What you say is true,' Daisy said, shrugging. 'But there's very little I can do about it, Marius. Anyway, you haven't told me how you just happened to be here when I needed you.'

'You might have been killed when you decided to board the *Lazy Jane* mid-channel, Daisy. I saw everything and there was nothing I could do to stop you. I knew where the ship was headed, and I also knew that Jay is on the run from the authorities and he wouldn't put you ashore. I had a feeling that he was about to do something rash, and now I know I was right.'

'I suppose you were worried about the cargo,' Daisy said slowly.

'I told you that I don't care about the money. I was concerned for your welfare, which is why I travelled by train to Weymouth. If the *Lazy Jane* hadn't arrived by morning I had a passage booked on a vessel heading for St Peter Port. It didn't occur to me that Guppy and Ramsden would take it upon themselves to see you home. But they might have chosen a craft that didn't stink of rotting fish.'

The twinkle in his eyes brought a responsive chuckle from Daisy. 'I can't wait to change out of these clothes, but I suppose there's always a bright side. Smelling like this, Guppy, Ramsden and I should be guaranteed a compartment to ourselves.'

'They can look after themselves, Daisy. I'm taking you, first class.

She looked away, the question that was burning on her lips unspoken. She had come to rely on Marius, knowing that his support would be there if she needed it, but without a shared interest in Jay's ship there would be no call now for any contact between them. When Marius returned to London he would have no excuse to visit Creek Manor, and their friendship would die a natural death. Daisy rose to her feet.

'I'm very tired, Marius. You'll forgive me if I go to my room.'

He stood up. 'Of course. I hope you sleep well, Daisy.'

She nodded, suddenly overcome by the events of the day. 'Good night. I'll see you at breakfast.'

Daisy arrived home next day having parted with Marius on Bishopsgate Station. They had shared a first-class compartment from Weymouth to Waterloo Bridge Station, and, as he had business to transact in London, Daisy travelled on to Little Creek with Ramsden and Guppy. She had leaned out of the window, waving until a blast of steam from the engine obscured Marius in a thick mist. When it cleared, he was gone.

*   *   *

459

'I don't think I'll ever see him again, Mary,' Daisy said wearily. 'After what Jay did to Marius I'm not sure I can face him again. He must have lost a considerable amount of money.'

'What a to-do!' Mary said, sipping her tea. 'I don't know what to say, my dear. I'm ashamed to call Jay my son.'

'It's not your fault.' Daisy put her cup and saucer back on the tray. 'At least we know where we stand now.'

'I'm almost sorry for that woman in Dorset,' Mary said, sighing. 'I didn't take to her, but those children are my grandchildren. I don't suppose I'll ever see them again.'

'You don't want to get involved with the likes of her.' Hilda shook her head. 'She's trouble, Mary.'

'Yes, I suppose you're right.' Mary reached out to pat Daisy's hand. 'But I am glad that you've come home.'

'Me, too,' Hilda added earnestly. 'It's not the same without you, Daisy.'

'Jay isn't all bad, Mary. In fact he asked me to look after you, and he wants me to run the estate in his absence.'

'Does he indeed? I'm afraid that Jay is just like his father and if things go awry in Australia he'll come home and take everything from us. I wouldn't blame you if you wanted to go your own way, Daisy.' Mary wiped her eyes on the crumpled hanky she had been grasping so tightly that her knuckles were like white marbles beneath her skin.

'This is my home now,' Daisy said slowly. 'When I was younger I imagined that I would become one of the first lady doctors in the country, but that wasn't to be. I think now that I can do far more good by staying on here, and running the estate for you. Jay said I could take a salary, and I have it in writing.'

Mary managed a smile. 'It's not fair for you to be tied to a man who isn't legally your husband. We could say that you're his widow.'

'Oh, no! You mustn't do that.' Daisy shook her head. 'That would be a lie.'

'He's dead to me, my dear. I don't want to hear his name mentioned in my presence, and I'll tell the girls that, and Jack, too. It's hardest on him, the poor boy, because he hero-worshipped his brother.'

'Let me tell him, Mary,' Daisy said gently. 'Jack deserves to hear the truth from me.'

Mary nodded half-heartedly. 'Make him under-stand that it's not the way to treat women, Daisy. I know Jack is a good boy, but he's young and impressionable.

'You'd best be quick then.' Mary glanced out of the window. 'I can see Guppy and Ramsden heading for home across the park. You know how word spreads, Daisy.'

'Indeed I do.' Without bothering to stop to change out of her travel-stained and decidedly fishy-smelling garments, Daisy left the house and headed for the stables. She found Jack grooming her favourite horse, and he stopped, gazing at her in surprise.

'So you're back, Daisy. What's the matter? Something must be wrong for you to come looking for me.'

Daisy beckoned to one of the older grooms. 'Would you finish Cinders for me, Hobson? I need a word with Jack.'

Hobson nodded and took the currycomb from Jack's hand. 'Yes, ma'am.'

Daisy led the way from the stable block with Jack following a couple of paces behind, but when she came to a halt on the far side of the coach house, he came to stand beside her.

'It must be serious, Daisy.'

'It's about Jay.'

'You've killed him?' Jack said, grinning.

Daisy laughed, although she was painfully aware that what she was about to say would hurt Jack. 'No, although I would have liked to on a couple of occasions. I'll come right out with it because there's no easy way to say this, but Jay has a wife and a child in Guernsey, and that makes his marriage to Bessie null and void.'

Jack whistled between his teeth. 'I don't know what to say.'

'There's more, Jack. He's decided to emigrate to Australia and he's probably set sail by now, providing he's managed to replace Guppy and Ramsden.'

'They didn't go with him?'

'No. They came home with me. They're loyal to

Jay but neither of them wanted to spend the rest of his days in Australia.'

'You don't think Jay will return?'

'I don't know, and that's the truth. I am sorry, Jack. I know you love your brother.'

Jack wiped a tear from his eyes on the back of his grubby hand, leaving a streak of dirt across his cheek. 'Why didn't he tell me? I could have gone with him and made my fortune in the goldfields.'

'Perhaps he'll send for you,' Daisy suggested hopefully.

Jack shook his head. 'No, he won't. I know my brother. He comes and goes as he thinks fit, and the devil take the rest of us. I'm glad you're not married to him now, Daisy. He wasn't good enough for you.'

Daisy could see how upset he was and she slipped her arm around his shoulders. 'You don't have to work in the stables. I need someone to help me run the estate, and I'm still learning. Besides which, if Jay doesn't return you will inherit Creek Manor.'

'Really?' Jack's face brightened. 'You'd do that for me?'

'You're still very young and I think you ought to go back to school – and I don't mean the one in the village. If you're to be lord of the manor one day, or even if you aren't, you'll need a good education so that you can better yourself.'

'But I don't want to go back to school, Daisy.'

'It will be a boys' school, and you'll do sport and

all kinds of things you haven't done before. In the holidays you can help me to run the estate. What do you say?'

'But where will you get the money?'

'Don't worry about that. I'm sure there are scholarships for a bright boy like you. I'll have a word with Elliot. He'll know what to do.'

'I'll show Jay,' Jack said, chuckling. 'When he does come back he'll find me a grown man with a degree at Cambridge and we'll be rich.'

'That's right. Go back to the stables for now, and leave everything to me.'

Jack hesitated. 'What will Ma say?'

'She'll be so proud of you, Jack. She deserves to have a son who's a credit to her.'

'You're right, and that will be me. Just wait until I tell Judy. She'll wish she was a boy and could come with me.' Jack sauntered off towards the stables, whistling happily, and Daisy returned to the house to give Mary the good news that Jack had agreed to go back to school. He would become an educated gentleman and Creek Manor would one day have a new lord.

Daisy threw herself into the daily routine of running a large estate with renewed energy, finding it the only way to conquer the heartache caused by Jay's callous behaviour. The harvest was gathered in, and each day she learned something new about farming and managing the land. She visited the bank, acting in her new official capacity, and she made certain that the money was always on hand to pay the farm workers and the servants. She had a weekly meeting with Mrs Ralston at which Daisy checked the house-keeping accounts and they discussed menus and any problems that arose in the servants' hall, which by and large were few. There were always sharps spats caused by a clash of personalities, but these were generally over quickly and peace was restored. Judy had shown great promise and although she was very young, she had been taken under Mrs Ralston's wing to train as a parlour maid.

Jack moved into the house, and when Daisy rode out to visit the tenant farmers, he accompanied her on a pony of his own, which he would soon outgrow. He was tall for his age and working in the stables had developed his muscles, so that he was a strong, well-built youth. His natural good humour and the manners drummed into him by his mother stood him well with the farmers and the servants alike, and Daisy was proud of him. She invited Elliot and Linnet to dinner to discuss Jack's future education and Elliot assured her that Jack would easily pass the entrance examination to any good school, and maybe even qualify for a bursary. He undertook to tutor Jack with that aim in mind and lessons were arranged for an hour every evening. Jack was not too keen at first, but Judy volunteered to keep him company, and Elliot was good at inspiring young people with a thirst for knowledge. He had a public school in mind, where he was certain that Jack would be accepted, but there was the question of money, and that was a serious consideration.

It was a warm September day, three weeks after Daisy had returned from the Channel Islands. She had ridden to Maldon accompanied by Jack, and she had visited the bank, expecting the worst, but the manager had been surprisingly accommodating. Even though Jay had withdrawn a substantial amount of cash, the rents had been paid and the surplus from the home farm had fetched a good price at market. At least one of Daisy's worries had proved groundless and she left the bank with a feeling of pure relief.

They had a list of groceries that could not be obtained in the village shop, and Daisy had decided to treat Jack to lunch at the pub on Hythe Quay. Perhaps it was the tasty food that drew her to the water's edge, or maybe it was the pleasant memories of eating there with Marius that influenced her decision. She had received a brief letter from him, a week after her return, although it did not reveal much of his future plans. However, he had mentioned a new project that might make it possible for him to visit Creek Manor every now and again. Daisy had written back to say that would be delightful, and she had watched for a response daily, but so far none had arrived.

Jack was starving, of course. Daisy remembered how much he had loved Hattie's cooking when he had lived with her aunt and uncle, and no one, not even Linnet, had quite come up to Hattie's standards. Daisy walked briskly towards the quay, with Jack loping along at her side. He had grown suddenly and was all gangly arms and legs, reminding her of a young colt, but his enthusiasm for everything was contagious.

'We'll set off for home when we've had lunch,' Daisy said as Jack held the door open for her. She entered the taproom, half expecting the landlord to throw them out with the excuse that he was not allowed to serve unaccompanied women, but apparently Jack was man enough to be considered as her escort, and she hid a smile as she ordered their meal.

'I'll have the beef stew,' she said firmly. 'It was really excellent last time I was here.'

'And I'll have the meat pie,' Jack added, licking his lips. 'I love a good pie. Is there gravy, Landlord?'

'Aye, master. Plenty of good gravy. It's my wife's speciality. Folks come from miles around to have their dinners here, and it's the gravy they appreciate the most.'

'I can vouch for that.' A familiar voice made Daisy's heart lurch against her ribs and she spun round with a cry of delight. 'Marius! What a coincidence, and what a lovely surprise.' She rushed forward to greet him and for a long moment they held hands, but then Daisy realised that they were the object of curiosity amongst the other customers and she broke away, blushing.

'I'm here on business,' Marius said hastily. 'I thought it was your horse I saw in the stable.'

'I had to visit the bank and we needed some supplies,' Daisy said, attempting to sound casual.

'As a matter of fact I was planning to ride over to Creek Manor tomorrow, so that I could give you my good news.'

'I can't wait to hear it.' Daisy glanced at Jack, who was standing by the bar, grinning broadly. 'Jack is my right-hand man now. We've just ordered a meal. Will you join us?'

'Nothing would give me more pleasure.' Marius strolled over to greet Jack with a friendly slap on the back. 'It's good to see you again.'

Jack nodded, apparently lost for words.

'What's your pleasure, guvnor?' the landlord asked cheerily.

'I'll have a pint of your best ale. What about you, Daisy? Will you have a celebratory drink with me, and you, Jack, of course? You're quite a man now, so I think you might have a glass of ale, if Daisy agrees.'

'I'll have a glass of cider,' Daisy said, smiling. 'And of course Jack may have what he likes today.'

Jack puffed out his chest. 'I'll have a pint of your best ale, please, Landlord.'

'Make that half a pint.' Marius laid some coins

on the counter. 'And I'll have a bowl of your wife's excellent stew.'

'Very well, sir. If you'd like to go into the parlour, I'll send the drinks through.'

'I would have come sooner, Daisy,' Marius said as they took their seats at the table by the window, 'but I've been negotiating a tricky business deal, and I didn't want to tell you about it until it was settled.'

The landlord hurried in with their order and set the glass and two pewter tankards down on the table. Marius waited until the door closed.

'I've sold all my agencies except the one here in Maldon.'

Daisy eyed him curiously. 'That sounds like a huge risk, Marius.'

'Not really,' he said, smiling. 'I've recently inherited the family business, including a house. My uncle died, leaving me a fleet of sailing barges and I intend to move here permanently.'

Daisy's breath caught in her throat, but with a death in Marius's family it would have been tactless to sound too delighted. 'He must have thought a lot of you.'

'To be honest I hardly knew him. He was a miserable, miserly old man who never married, and he cut himself off from the rest of the family. Heaven knows why he left everything to me, but I'm very grateful that he did. It means that I no longer have to travel from port to port and I can settle down at last.'

Daisy eyed him curiously. 'You never talk about your family, Marius.'

'There's not much to tell. I was an only child, and my father died when I was just a boy. My uncle paid for my education, but he wouldn't have anything to do with my mother or her family. He considered them beneath him because they were fishermen, and my mother, God rest her soul, was a simple woman, but beautiful and with a heart of gold.'

'I'm so sorry,' Daisy said softly. 'I didn't mean to pry and bring back sad memories.'

'I think fondly of my mother. She was an inspiration to me, but she's been gone for eight years or more, and I've lived a purely selfish existence since then, although that's something I would very much like to alter.'

Daisy was about to question him further, but Jack slapped his tankard down on the table, smacking his lips. 'That was good,' he said with a tipsy smile. 'I'm still thirsty, Daisy.'

'You've drunk almost all of it, Jack. You're squiffy.'

'He'll be fine when he's eaten,' Marius said, smiling. 'But how about you, Daisy? I'm sorry I haven't been in touch sooner, but that doesn't mean I haven't been thinking about you. In fact, you've been constantly on my mind.'

'I've been working hard, but everything is beginning to run smoothly.' Daisy glanced at Jack, who was dozing quietly in the corner of the settle opposite them. 'My main problem is finding the money to send Jack to a good school. He's a bright boy and Elliot says he could do well, given half a chance.'

'Elliot is your sister-in-law's fiancé?'

'That's right. I'm surprised that you remember.'

He covered her hand with his. 'I have a good memory for things that are important to me. I also recall that Dr Neville has never quite given up hope, as far as you're concerned.'

'Nick and Dove are engaged. I expect them to announce the date of their wedding very soon.'

'I'm glad. It narrows the field, giving outsiders like myself more of a chance.'

They were seated so close together that she could feel his warm breath on her cheek, but she could not bring herself to look him in the eye. Perhaps she was reading too much into what he had said, or maybe she was hearing what she wanted to hear.

'Look at me, Daisy.'

She looked up slowly and saw herself mirrored in the dark depths of his eyes. He tightened his grasp on her hand.

'There's so much I want to say to you.' He glanced over his shoulder as the landlord barged into the parlour carrying a large wooden tray laden with food.

Jack opened his eyes with a start. 'Pie and gravy. Just what I wanted.'

'What was it, Marius?' Daisy asked in a low voice.

'It will have to wait until a more appropriate moment.' His smile enveloped her in a warm embrace, but the spell was broken by the clatter of cutlery as Jack attacked his meal with enthusiasm.

'This is such good grub,' he said happily. 'Why aren't you two eating?'

Chapter Twenty-Six

Outside the hot afternoon sun blazed from an azure sky and seagulls wheeled overhead, their plaintive cries mingling with the shouts of the dock workers and the responses from the men on board the barges. Jack, now sober after eating two pies and a hefty portion of treacle pudding, had gone to fetch the horses from the stables, leaving Daisy and Marius standing on the quay wall.

'I'd see you safely home, but I have an appointment with my solicitor in half an hour,' Marius said apologetically.

'Don't worry. Jack and I will be fine.'

'May I visit you very soon?'

'Of course. You know you're always welcome.' Daisy stared into the distance, suddenly unsure of herself. They were speaking to each other like polite strangers, and the moment of intimacy earlier had dissipated like the wisps of cloud overhead scattered by a thermal wind.

'I'd like you to see my new home,' Marius said cautiously. 'I don't think my uncle was very interested in comfort and style. In fact it's a bit of a mess, but I could do with some advice as to decoration and furnishings.'

'I'd be glad to help in any way I can.'

'And I've been thinking about the boy's future,' Marius added, watching Jack as he crossed the road, leading the two horses. 'My old school has a good reputation, and I'd be happy to take him there for an interview with the headmaster, if you so wish.'

'It's a question of money, Marius.'

'We can discuss that when I come to Creek Manor, but I think Elliot is right. The boy is intelligent and determined. If he puts his mind to it, he'll succeed.'

'It would make his mother so proud.'

'What about you, Daisy?'

She smiled as he lifted her onto the saddle. 'I think that Jack would make an excellent lord of the manor when he's older. What do you say, Jack?'

He pulled a face. 'I don't know about that.'

'Daisy is right,' Marius said, nodding. 'You deserve a chance in life, Jack. I'll write to the head this evening.'

'Thank you, Marius. I really appreciate your help,' Daisy said earnestly. 'I hope I'll see you again soon.'

'You may depend upon it.' Marius turned to Jack. 'Take care of her.'

'I'm not like my brother, sir,' Jack said, vaulting onto the saddle with the ease of a circus performer. 'I appreciate Daisy, even if Jay didn't. He's a fool.'

Two days later Daisy was in the study going over the accounts when Molesworth interrupted her.

'Excuse me, madam. You have a visitor.'

She looked up, frowning. It was very early for callers and she wanted to finish what she was doing. 'Who is it, Molesworth? Tell them I'm not at home.'

'Really? I thought I was welcome at any time.' Marius put his head round the door. 'I'm sorry, Molesworth, but I was hoping to receive a warmer welcome.'

Daisy rose to her feet. 'Of course you are welcome, Marius. It's all right, Molesworth.'

'Very well, madam.' Molesworth shot a look of disapproval in Marius's direction as he left the room.

'You must have left Maldon at the crack of dawn to get here so early.'

'I spent the night in my new home, and very uncomfortable it was, too.'

Daisy gave him a searching look. 'Is anything wrong?'

'On the contrary. The other day, after we parted I decided to visit my old school rather than waste time writing to the headmaster, and he is willing to see Jack.'

Daisy sat down again, sighing. 'I do appreciate all the trouble you've gone to, but there remains the problem of financing his school fees. The estate is beginning to do well, even though Jay took such a large amount of cash when he left, but it would be difficult to raise the sort of funds we'd have to find.'

'Don't worry about that. There is a bursary available for suitable candidates and I would be happy to make up the difference.' Marius laughed and held up his hand. 'Don't look at me like that, Daisy. You could pay me back when the income from the estate improves.'

'Well, I suppose it is Jack's to inherit eventually. Although if life in Australia doesn't suit Jay there's always the chance that he might return, bringing his family with him.'

'Don't dwell on what might happen in the future. Who knows what Jay will do? The important thing is to look after you and to give young Jack a good education.'

Daisy turned away, using the pretext of placing the pen on the inkstand and closing the ledger. 'You're very kind, Marius.'

'Not at all. I have an ulterior motive.'

She shot him a sideways glance and saw that he was smiling. 'What is it?'

'I was hoping you would come with me today to view the house, and give me some advice on what to do next. I confess I am completely at a loss when it comes to such things.'

'Of course I will, and you don't have to bribe me, Marius.'

'I wouldn't dream of doing something so low.'

'Now you're laughing at me.'

'No, I'd never do that. I think too highly of you, but I would value your opinion. Are you free to come with me now?'

Daisy rose to her feet. 'I'm glad to have an excuse to leave the figures to themselves. By the way, where is this house? Is it in Maldon?'

'No, as it happens it's just outside Colneyhurst, a small village about three miles from here.'

'I'll send a message to the stables to have Cinders saddled up and ready.'

'No need. I came in my uncle's chaise. I mean, my chaise – I still can't get used to the fact that everything he owned is now mine.'

'It's a lovely day. I fancy a carriage ride. Give me five minutes, and I'll fetch my bonnet and shawl.'

Daisy hurried to her room and selected a fetching straw bonnet, trimmed with silk cornflowers and blue satin ribbons. Having wrapped a fine woollen shawl around her shoulders she paused by the tall cheval mirror to check her appearance, and tucked a stray dark curl back in place. Satisfied that she looked her best, she picked up her reticule and went downstairs.

Mary was in the hallway, talking to Molesworth, but she turned to give Daisy a curious look. 'Where are you going? I didn't think you had any appointments today.'

'Marius is taking me to see the house that his uncle willed to him. He wants my advice.'

Mary put her head on one side, smiling. 'Advice is it? It sounds like a good excuse to get you on your own to me. Oh, well, you go and enjoy yourself, Daisy. You deserve a day off.'

Daisy was about to tell her that it was purely business, but glancing through the nearest window she could see Marius waiting by the chaise, and she did not bother to argue. 'I'll see you later, Mary.'

Colneyhurst Hall was surrounded by a brick wall that stretched as far as Daisy could see. The entrance was protected by ornate wrought-iron gates, and as they approached, a man emerged from the gatehouse to let them in. He tipped his cap as Marius drove the chaise into the long carriage sweep, at the end of which Daisy saw an imposing Georgian house with a columned portico and a white stucco façade.

'It's very impressive, Marius. And it looks large, too.'

'I haven't counted the number of rooms, but there are too many for my taste. I rattle around in there like a pea in a pod.'

She chuckled, shooting him a glance beneath the shady brim of her bonnet. 'I wouldn't describe you as a pea, but I know what you mean. I felt the same way about Creek Manor after living in my aunt and uncle's cottage, and our apartment above the shop in Whitechapel was quite small.'

'I'm in two minds as to whether or not to put the place up for sale.' Marius reined in the horse outside the front entrance. 'It's far too large for me.'

Daisy was about to say that he might marry one day, but somehow it did not seem appropriate, and the thought of Marius carrying another woman over the threshold was somehow quite shocking. She waited for him to help her to alight, and a groom hurried from the stable block to take charge of the horse.

A maidservant let them into a wide entrance hall with a black-and-white marble-tiled floor, a high ceiling with an ornate plasterwork frieze and a staircase rising in a grand sweep to the first floor. In its day it must have been quite splendid, but it was obviously suffering from years of neglect and the air was filled with dust motes. There was a strong musty smell mixed with overtones of stale cigar smoke and wet dog. The walls were grubby with finger marks and the sooty remnants of coal fires going back many years. The house felt sad and neglected, but even so, Daisy fell instantly in love with the place. It cried out for someone to rescue it from oblivion, aided by a small army of cleaners.

'You can't think of selling this house, Marius,' Daisy cried passionately. 'It just needs someone to bring it back to life. It's like the story of Sleeping Beauty, just waiting for the right person to come along and rescue it from a slow and painful decline.'

'You make it sound like a person.' Marius followed her gaze. 'It reminds me of visits here as a child. It was always a gloomy house, and the old man was even gloomier.'

'Show me all of it, please. It needs lots of hard work, but this place must have been very grand when it was built more than hundred years ago. It's quite beautiful beneath the layers of dust and dirt.'

'You might not feel the same when you've seen the rest.' Marius led the way into the first reception room where all the furniture was hidden beneath holland covers. The curtains were drawn but sunlight filtered through large moth holes, and there was a dead bird in the hearth, which must have been trapped in the chimney and had succumbed to the choking soot.

'A chimney sweep is the first person to call upon,' Daisy said firmly. She walked round, lifting the covers to peer at the furniture underneath. 'Some of this is quite acceptable, but the rest will make a good bonfire.' She faced Marius with an excited smile. 'Lead on. I can't wait to see the other rooms.'

After exploring the whole house from the wine cellar – sadly empty – to the top floor where the servants slept, Daisy and Marius ended up in the kitchen, which was the only room in the house that was reasonably well kept. Their presence did not seem to suit the aged cook, who made it clear that she did not consider it proper for the master to take tea in the kitchen, let alone to entertain a lady without a suitable chaperone. She made a pot of tea for them and sliced a rather stale loaf, adding a scrape of butter and a few slivers of Cheddar cheese, which she slapped on a plate and placed in front of them as they sat at the long deal table.

'That's all I got, sir. I wasn't expecting you to have company, and the dining room is under covers. We're still in mourning for the old master.'

'I understand,' Marius said gently. 'But life goes on, Mrs Dowsett, and I am the master now. If that creates a problem for you, perhaps you would like to retire? I would ensure that you have a good pension.'

'The old master would never have given anyone a pension,' Mrs Dowsett said grimly. 'My rheumatics do get me down in the winter, but I got nowhere to go, sir.'

'I saw some pretty little cottages that looked as if they belonged to the estate,' Daisy said eagerly. 'Do you know if they are occupied, Mrs Dowsett?'

'Some are, ma'am, but most are empty, because they're damp and rat-infested.'

'I'm sure something could be done about that.' Daisy turned to Marius. 'I've recently overseen the work on the cottages in Little Creek. They were in a dire state, but now they're habitable and very comfortable.'

'I'll look into it,' Marius said seriously.

'Let's take our luncheon outside,' Daisy suggested impulsively. 'It's a beautiful day for a picnic, and I'd love to see the garden.'

'It were a fine garden once, long ago.' Mrs Dowsett rolled her eyes. 'Nothing but grass as high as your waist now, as well as nettles and weeds. You'll get bit to pieces by mosquitos and stung by wasps. No one picks the apples in the orchard these days and they rot on the ground.'

'Oh dear!' Daisy said sympathetically. 'That's very sad. But I would still like to go outside.'

Marius rose from the table. 'I'll take the tea, if you'll take the plates.'

'The girl should do that for you, sir,' Mrs Dowsett protested. 'But she's a bit simple, if you know what I mean. She'd forget her head if it weren't screwed on.'

Daisy managed to get out through the scullery into the back yard before she burst out laughing. 'Oh, Marius. You'll have to find Mrs Dowsett a nice little cottage where she can spend the rest of her days talking about the old times and grumbling.'

'I agree wholeheartedly, but I wouldn't know where to begin.' Marius led the way, balancing a tea tray in his hands as he crossed the cobbled yard. When they reached the terrace at the back of the house it was possible to imagine the tall windows open, with the sound of music and laughter echoing across what might once have been a velvet-smooth lawn, which led to the parterre garden and on to a lake seen through gaps in the trees. The paving stones were damaged in places, and dandelions pushed their golden heads through the smallest cracks. Daisy perched on a moss-covered stone balustrade and when Marius placed the tray on the ground she handed him his food.

'It really is like Sleeping Beauty's palace, Marius. You can't abandon it to someone who doesn't care about it.'

'You really mean that, don't you?'

'Of course I do.' Daisy took a bite of the bread and cheese. 'This isn't too bad. The bread is a bit stale, but it's edible. We must find you a good cook, and a housekeeper who will organise the servants for you.' She paused with the slice of bread halfway to her lips. 'But can you afford to live here? That's the question.'

'I can, but there might be a problem.'

'What is it? I'm sure it's nothing that couldn't be settled with a bit of thought.' Daisy tossed the crust to a pigeon, who had waddled up to them, looking hopeful.

Marius threw his bread untasted onto the ground and a flock of pigeons descended upon it, followed by two large crows, the birds squabbling and fighting over the unexpected treat.

'Go away, you wretched creatures.' Marius waved his arms and there was a fluttering of feathers and a flapping of wings as the birds flew up into the sky, squawking angrily.

'That was mean,' Daisy protested.

'Never mind the wild creatures.' Marius grasped both her hands, gazing into her eyes. 'I think you know how I feel about you, Daisy. I know there are still obstacles in the way, but I love you with all my heart.'

She met his ardent gaze with a tremulous smile. 'I didn't know – I mean, I thought sometimes that you cared for me, but you always seemed so much in control of your emotions.'

'It's a failing I'm trying to conquer. I find it hard

to express my deepest feelings, but I fell in love with you the first moment I saw you.' He squeezed her hands gently, drawing her closer. 'But you were married, or so we both thought, and then there was the handsome young doctor. I'm thirty, virtually middle-aged.'

She raised his right hand to her cheek. 'I don't know where you get these mad ideas, Marius. You've been my true friend throughout all my troubles, but I love you for yourself.'

'You do?'

She smiled. 'I have loved you for a long time, but I dared not admit it, even to myself.'

He kissed her hand, holding her fast as if he would never let her go. 'Daisy, my darling girl, I'd be the happiest of men if you would agree to marry me.'

Daisy's instinct was to fling her arms around him, but a cloud passed over the sun, creating a patch of shadow that made her shiver.

'I don't know if I'm free to marry you, Marius.'

'Your marriage to Jay is void. You have his written declaration that he married you bigamously. I want to love you and keep you safe for the rest of our lives. Will you marry me, Daisy?'

He drew her into an embrace; his mouth was hot on hers and his arms wrapped around her body like protective armour. She felt safe and secure for the first time in months, and she knew she had come home to where her heart truly belonged. But she was the first to pull away.

'What's the matter?' Marius asked urgently.

'I do love you, and I want to be with you more than anything in the world, but I have a responsibility to Mary and her family. They depend upon me to run the estate, and I can't just walk away and leave them to struggle on their own.'

Marius brushed her hair back from her forehead. 'Listen to me, my love. I understand how you feel, and I'm not asking you to do anything that you feel is wrong, but we need to approach this sensibly.'

'I don't feel in the least bit practical at the moment, and I'm so tired of being sensible.'

'Then allow me to help, my darling. I suggest that we take Jack to see the headmaster. If he's accepted at the school I think his mother will feel easier in her mind. We'll get the whole family together and give everyone a chance to voice an opinion on how the estate should be run. You can't devote your whole life to Jay's family, and I need you more than they do. Then we'll visit Mr Peabody and ask him if he'll marry us – if not I'll get a special licence and we'll marry in a register office.' He kissed her again, and this time she gave herself up to the sheer delight of being held in the arms of the man she adored.

Marius, Daisy discovered, was not someone to waste time, and the interview with the headmaster was arranged more quickly than she had expected. Jack was persuaded to wear the smart suit of clothes that had been purchased for Daisy's wedding, and Mary also put on her Sunday best. Fuller drove them in the barouche with Faulkner seated beside him, both of them dressed in their old and rather moth-eaten uniforms, but the effect was impressive, if viewed from a distance.

The ancient abbey, now a reputable school, was set in superb grounds and the pupils they saw were well turned out and polite. Daisy could not help but be impressed, and Mary seemed to have been struck dumb by the experience. If she spoke at all it was in a whisper, but Marius took the lead and he was obviously on the best of terms with the headmaster. Jack answered all the questions that were put to him, and Daisy gave him encouraging smiles, willing him to show himself to his best advantage. If Jack were to be accepted in this prestigious school he would be the equal of anyone, and he had the advantage of good looks and a quick wit. Daisy was so nervous for him that her mind began to wander during the long interview, and she found herself gazing out of the window to the green sweep of the playing fields and the wooded hills in the distance.

When she came back to the present she realised that everyone was smiling. Marius shook hands with the headmaster and Mary mopped her eyes with her clean hanky.

'I'm not crying,' she said when they gathered outside the head's study. 'I'm just so happy. Who would have thought that a son of mine would be accepted in a school where they educate young gentlemen?'

Jack looked round self-consciously. 'Shut up, Ma. You're making a spectacle of yourself.'

'You'll learn better manners here, young fellow,' Marius said, laughing. 'But, well done, Jack. You passed with flying colours and that was all down to you.'

Daisy gave him a hug. 'Don't grumble, Jack. Who cares what the other boys think? I'm proud of you.'

'We'd best get home,' Mary said urgently. 'We've got everyone coming to dinner this evening, although you still haven't told me why you wanted to get us all together, Daisy.'

Daisy and Marius exchanged conspiratorial glances. 'You'll find out this evening,' was all Daisy was prepared to say.

Eleanora and Sidney were the first to arrive at Creek Manor. Eleanora had dressed up for the occasion and she tried hard to make Daisy tell her the reason for the dinner party, but Daisy managed to fend off all her aunt's questions. She prayed silently that the others would arrive on time and was rewarded by Linnet and Elliot appearing next, swiftly followed by Nick and Dove. They were in the drawing room, sipping sherry and chatting, when Molesworth announced the arrival of the Peabodys. Daisy greeted them and when everyone had settled down she took the centre stage. Her heart was pounding and she could feel the colour rising to her cheeks, but it was time everyone knew the truth. She cleared her throat and waited for silence.

'I wanted everyone here to know the truth. So many wild tales fly round the village when there's a tasty bit of gossip.'

'What on earth are you going to tell us, dear?' Eleanora asked with a nervous giggle.

'Some of you already know this, but Jay and I were never legally man and wife,' Daisy said in a clear, firm voice. 'Of course, I had no knowledge of his relationship with Bessie, the woman in Dorset, when I agreed to marry him, and I've discovered since that he already had a wife and child, living in Guernsey when he married Bessie.'

John Peabody leaped to his feet and moved to her side, placing his arm around her shoulders. 'My dear girl, I am so sorry.'

'I'd have horsewhipped him if I'd known,' Sidney added angrily. 'Why have you kept this from us, Daisy? Where is the swine now?'

'That's my brother you're speaking of, sir.' Jack pushed to the front of those seated, his young face flushed and his eyes blazing.

'Sit down, there's a good fellow.' Marius sent him a warning look.

'I know Jay has done wrong,' Jack said sulkily. 'But there's no call to insult him.'

Daisy held up her hands. 'This isn't getting us anywhere. I've tried to run the estate as if I were still the lady of the manor, but I am not. Mary holds that position while Jay and his legal wife are out of the country.' Daisy turned to her aunt and uncle with an apologetic smile. 'I'm sorry I've kept it from you for so long, but Jay has taken his legitimate family to Australia, where he plans to start again.'

'You poor dear,' Eleanora said, fumbling in her reticule for her hanky.

'Why are you bringing this up now, Daisy?' Nick asked gently. 'I'm sure we all sympathise with your plight.'

'That's just it, Nick. I refuse to consider myself as a victim. I'm a free woman and I can choose the person with whom I want to spend the rest of my life.' She held her hand out to Marius. 'We plan to marry when the formalities have been settled, but that means I won't be able to help Mary to run the estate. Jack has been accepted at a very good school, thanks to Marius, but I don't want to abandon you all. I love you as if you were my real family.'

'I am shocked to the core, Daisy,' Mr Peabody said solemnly. 'But I assume you can prove that Jay was legally married to the woman he calls his wife?'

'Yes, I can,' Daisy said firmly. 'I have a written deposition from Jay confirming the fact.'

'Then I see no objection to your marrying. As a matter of fact, I knew Marius's uncle, and although he was a difficult man, he was a pillar of society, especially in his younger days.'

Marius inclined his head. 'Thank you, Vicar.'

Mary rose to her feet and went to stand beside Daisy. 'You deserve a chance to be happy, Daisy. No one deserves it more than you, and I know I can rely on both my daughters and their husbands, should I need help to run the estate.' She beckoned to Hilda, who had been sitting quietly in a corner. 'And I know that Hilda will stand by me as she has done ever since we moved into the manor house, so I won't be on my own.'

'You can rely on us if you need help, Mary.' Nick glanced at Elliot, who nodded in assent.

'Dove and I will do everything we can, Ma,' Linnet added. 'You'll have two more weddings to attend before long. Better get up to London and buy yourself more new hats.'

A ripple of laughter trickled round the room, and suddenly everyone was smiling and chattering excitedly about the future.

Marius slipped his arm around Daisy's waist. 'They've forgotten us already. Will you take a stroll with me in the twilight?'

'Yes, of course I will. It's a lovely evening. Shall we walk to the lake?'

Marius smiled and shook his head. 'I have a better idea.'

They emerged from the secret passage and walked hand in hand to the foreshore. The fiery sunset reflected on the still waters of the creek, and the melodious song of birds settling down to roost filled the soft air with music, adding sweetness to the gentle lapping of the waves on the shingle.

'I expect you're wondering why I wanted to bring you here,' Marius said, tightening his arm round Daisy's waist.

She smiled, inhaling the fresh scent of the countryside mingled with the salty tang from the sea. 'I think I know why, Marius. You rowed ashore from the *Lazy Jane* on the night of the Harkers' party. You emerged from the darkness like a knight in shining armour, and I was never so glad to see anyone in my whole life. I think it was then I knew I loved you, even if I couldn't admit it.'

'I've waited a long time to hear you say those words.' Marius took a small shagreen-covered box from his breast pocket, and he went down on one knee, despite the wet sand. 'You are now free from your responsibilities to the estate, and you know that I love you. My life was nothing until I met you, and I didn't believe that I deserved someone so young and beautiful, courageous and kind. I promise to love and care for you for the rest of my life. Will you marry me, Daisy?' He flicked open the box and the last rays of the setting sun were captured in the fiery glow of the solitaire diamond.

Torn between tears and laughter, Daisy nodded. 'Yes, Marius. I will.'

He slid the ring onto her finger and stood up, enveloping her in an embrace that seemed to last into eternity.

'This beach was the end of the treasure hunt,' Marius said softly as he curled a stray lock of Daisy's hair around his forefinger. 'I feel as though I've won the best prize of all. You are my treasure, sweetheart.'

Daisy felt the pain and anguish of the past slipping away on the outgoing tide. 'I love you, too, Marius.'

Read on for a sneak peek at
the final book in
The Village Secrets trilogy

The

Country

Bride

Chapter One

Creek Manor, Essex 1879

The old house seemed to have been awakened from a long sleep by the sound of children's laughter and the pitter-patter of scampering feet. Judy glanced anxiously at Mary Tattersall, who looked pale and tired as she sank down on the sofa, while the new parlour maid cleared up the debris left by Daisy Walters' boisterous young sons.

'Would you like me to make you a camomile tisane, Mrs Tattersall?' Judy asked gently.

Mary gave her a wan smile. 'No, thank you, Judy. I love Daisy's children, but they are exhausting. I'm always delighted to see them when she brings them over from Colneyhurst Hall, but it's a relief when she takes them home again.'

'They are very lively,' Judy conceded, smiling.

'To think that they might have been my grand-children.' Mary sighed and turned her head away. 'Jay not only cheated on Daisy and that other woman he married bigamously, he deceived me, his own mother, and that I find very hard to forgive.'

'Thank you, Lizzie.' Judy nodded to the maid, who had stacked a tray with the dirty crockery, half-eaten slices of bread and butter and cake crumbs. 'That will be all for now.'

'Yes, Miss Begg.' Lizzie backed out of the door, narrowly missing colliding with a young woman who rushed into the room, blonde curls falling loose to her shoulders, and her bonnet hanging over her arm.

'What have you forgotten, Molly?' Judy asked with a sigh. Her seventeen-year-old sister carried out her duties as nursemaid to Daisy Walters' children in a haphazard style all of her own. Scatterbrained and disorganised, Molly was disarmingly good-natured and extremely pretty – qualities that were guaranteed to make everyone forget her failings.

'I'm so sorry,' Molly said breathlessly. 'I forgot Master Henry's jacket.' She gazed round the room and her blue eyes lit up as she spotted the missing garment. 'There it is.' She pounced on it. 'I'd better hurry. They're waiting for me.' She left the room with a flurry of starched white petticoats.

'That girl gives me a headache,' Mary said feebly. 'She's exhausting.'

'She means well, ma'am.' Judy caught sight of

herself in one of the gilt-framed mirrors that adorned the walls of the drawing room. The likeness between herself and her sister was striking, but Molly was the flighty one, who could get away with anything. Judy had always been the serious, responsible older sister. She raised her hand to smooth a stray curl that had dared to escape from the chignon at the back of her neck. 'I sometimes wish I was more like her.'

'You're fine as you are, my dear.' Mary fidgeted restlessly. 'I'm not very comfortable.'

Judy plumped up the cushions, and Mary leaned back, closing her eyes. 'Where's your mother, Judy?'

'She's in the study, ma'am. It's the end of the quarter and she's getting the household accounts ready for me to check before they go to Mrs Ralston.'

'I don't know what I'd do without her, or you, come to that, Judy. I've no head for figures and when Mrs Ralston finally retires, you will take over her position as housekeeper. That is, if you still wish to do so.'

Judy hesitated. To agree to such an offer at the age of twenty seemed like condemning herself to early middle age, but what alternative was there for a woman like herself? She could remember what life had been like in London when she was a small child. The smell of poverty and the gnawing pangs of hunger were something she would never forget. Life had been so much better since Daisy, having witnessed the terrible street accident that had killed their father and crippled their mother, had brought Judy's small family to live at Creek Manor. They had nothing to complain about, although sometimes Judy found herself wondering what life would be like now if she returned to London. She had broadened her very basic education by reading as many of the books from the late Squire's library as she could, and she had had the added bonus of sharing lessons with Mary's youngest son, Jack, who had been a somewhat unwilling student. They had been close friends since childhood, although she had seen little of him since he went away to the school that educated the sons of gentlemen and the ambitious middle classes. But that friendship had changed subtly last summer, and Jack's return to university had left Judy feeling bereft. She had been counting the days until his return. She came back to the present with a start, and realised that Mrs Tattersall was staring at her with a puzzled frown.

'You do want to stay on here, don't you, Judy?'

'Yes, of course, ma'am. This is my home and my family are here in Little Creek.'

'The position of housekeeper is a worthy occupation,' Mary insisted wearily. 'You could do a lot worse, and Ida Ralston is an excellent example.'

'Yes, ma'am.' Judy shifted from one foot to the other. They owed everything to the Tattersall family, but sometimes she longed to be free. There was a whole wide world out there, although her choices were limited, and she would either opt for a life in service, or marriage to one of the village boys she had known from childhood. Jack's friends Danny Shipway and Alfie Green both vied for her attention on Sundays when everyone attended morning service, but she could never take them seriously. 'If that's all, ma'am, I'll go and check on the arrangements for Master Jack's return from university.'

Mary's face lit up with a smile. 'I can't wait to see him. I could never have imagined that my little Jackdaw would do me so proud, and it's all thanks to Daisy's husband. I can never thank Marius enough for everything he's done for my son. Jack was born into poverty, but now he's a gentleman.'

'Yes, ma'am.' Judy had heard it all before, but she tried to look as if this was a revelation. 'May I be excused now, Mrs Tattersall?'

Mary raised herself to a more upright position. 'Not yet, Judy. I want a word with you before my son arrives. Sit down, please.'

Judy eyed her warily as she perched on the edge of a chair opposite the sofa. 'Have I done something wrong, ma'am?'

'No, of course not, my dear. It's just that things have changed since we first moved into Creek Manor. You were just a child then and we were all like one big family.'

'I'm sure we're very grateful for everything, ma'am.'

'I'm not asking for gratitude, Judy. But I'm neither blind nor insensitive. I know that you and Jack were always good companions, and I suspect that your friendship deepened into something more when he came home last summer.'

Judy felt the blood rush to her cheeks and she stared down at her clasped hands. 'Nothing untoward has ever occurred between us, madam.'

'I'm sure it hasn't, which is why I wanted to speak to you now. Jack will have to take over running the estate, because it's become too much for me, even with all the help I have had. Legally it all belongs to Jay, but I haven't heard from him since he left this house ten years ago, and I doubt if he'll ever return from Australia, which means that to all intents and purposes Jack will be Lord of the manor.'

'Yes, ma'am.'

'Do you understand what I'm saying, Judy?'

'Not exactly, ma'am.'

'This isn't easy because you're a sweet girl, and I'm fond of you, but Jack needs to marry a woman of good breeding, preferably someone with a decent dowry. The estate makes very little profit and the old house needs a good deal of renovation. Do I make myself clear?'

Judy bowed her head. Of course she knew all this, and she should have been prepared for Mary's blunt statement of the facts, but facing the truth had hit her like a physical blow. 'I understand, ma'am.'

'I knew you would. Don't think this makes any difference to your position here, Judy. I value you more than you can imagine.'

Judy rose to her feet. 'I have work to do, if you'll excuse me, Mrs Tattersall.'

'Of course. What am I thinking of?' Mary sighed happily. 'I'll just rest my eyes for a few minutes before I go upstairs and change for dinner. We have to keep up the traditions of Creek Manor, after all, and with luck Jack will arrive soon.'

Judy left the room quietly. She had known all along that her position was tenuous, and her relationship with Jack was doomed from the start, but hearing it put into words had been the final blow. She stood for a moment, and took a deep breath before making her way to the study. One thing was certain: no one would ever know how deeply she had been hurt, although it was her own fault. She had allowed herself to dream, and that was fatal for a girl born in the East End slums.

Look out for
the final book in
The Village Secrets trilogy

The

Country
Bride

Coming Summer 2020

And find out how it all began
in the first book in
The Village Secrets trilogy

The Christmas Wedding

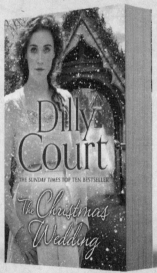

Available to buy now!